A DEAL WITH THE SHADOW KING

A DARK FANTASY ROMANCE

CURSE OF THE FAE
BOOK ONE

ANYA J COSGROVE

A Deal with the Shadow King

Cover designer: Bewitching book covers by Rebecca Frank

A Deal with the Shadow King/Anya J Cosgrove

ISBN 978-1-7381056-5-6

✸ Created with Vellum

FOREWORD

Lovely readers,

Some stories are not everyone's cup of tea. The hero and heroine in this novel wrestle with more than one type of monster.

Here's the trigger list for this dark fantasy romance, so you can decide for yourself. Be advised that, when in doubt, I chose to include a trigger rather than skip it.

- Blood and violence
- Profanity
- Detailed sexual content (where consent is freely given)
- Beauty and the Beast type of dubious consent situations (the heroine has to live in a castle against her will, she's forced to wear dresses and attend dinners, etc)
- Morally gray situations
- Death of a pet
- Age gap (the heroine is eighteen and the hero is an immortal Fae)
- Threats
- Cults and Religion

- Slut shaming (not by the hero)
- Misogyny (not by the hero)
- Mental illness
- Mention of physical abuse by a parental figure (no detailed descriptions)
- Mention of sexual assault (not by the hero, and no detailed descriptions)
- Emotional abuse by a parental figure (on the page)
- Voyeurism
- Masturbation
- Spiders
- Scars

PLAYLIST

Heart of Glass - Crabtree Remix (waltz scene)

Sweet Dreams - Cover by Emily Browning

Cosmic Love - Florence + The Machine

Scar Tissue - Red Hot Chili Peppers

A Martyr for My Love for You - The White Stripes

MAPS

Map of the Fae Continent

The Shadowlands Provinces

When dreams fizzle out and reality bleeds into shadows, how can you tell if you're awake?
- Alana (The Shadow Witch Trilogy)

To Em, who read my first 7 chapters ever and cheered me on for years to finish that first book. Without you, this 11th novel would never have been written.

A DESPERATE SUMMONS

Damian Morpheus Sombra, I pray to you. Shadow King, I implore you. Join me in flesh instead of in my dreams, and I will carve your name in my bones.

CHAPTER 1
A DARK MIRACLE

"Hold him steady," I tell Gerald.

The amount of swelling over Firenze's cannon bone indicates that it's fractured. A complete break like that is deadly for a horse.

The old farmer tightens his hold on the shiny bridle and strokes the white stallion's neck. "Easy, boy. The princess is here to help you."

Firenze settles down a bit, long enough for me to lay my hands over the shattered bone and let the magic flow, my powers easier to access by the day. The squishy, inflamed flesh slowly rearranges.

Gerald holds his breath, his grip wavering. He follows my movements closely, like he hopes to figure out the inner workings of my magic as if it was the motor of his mechanical plow.

Tingles heat my palms as the wound shrinks down to a gash. My core muscles cramp, but I soldier on to finish the job.

"Crops. The damage is too extensive." My arms shake. Ice prickles my fingertips, my companions oblivious to the sudden change in temperature.

It's a warning.

If I push past the discomfort, my lips will turn blue, and I might pass out. I let the magic fizzle out instead and eye the leftover swelling with a resentful pout. "It'll take a few days to heal properly, but he'll live."

Gerald's wife, Mathilda, clutches her goddess talisman. "Thank you, Your Highness. We're so grateful to you and your miracle."

I force a breath down my lungs to relax my jaw, annoyed by the mention of *my miracle*. The villagers always call it that, even though I know better.

"It's only right for me to help you. Besides, Firenze here is an old friend." I run my fingers over the stallion's pristine mane and pat his neck. Warmth radiates through his soft fur. "Now, you've got to be more careful, Firenze. I won't always be around."

The old horse neighs, a promise to keep out of trouble. To the villagers' eyes, it's only a coincidence, but I know he understood me. Horses have better instincts than people, and I've known Firenze for as long as I've been alive. When it comes to horses, there isn't one better in all the worlds.

I climb to my feet, my skirts peppered with blood. "I'll be back tomorrow to see if I can do more."

Mathilda hands me a bucket of water and a fresh rag. "You saved his life, Your Grace. It's enough."

"Still, I'll try to come before church." I scrub as much blood from my hands and clothes as I can, knowing Esme will throw a fit if I come home in a bloody dress.

The couple bows their heads in reverence, and Gerald escorts me outside. "I can take you home in the hay cart, princess. It's almost dark."

"No need. I love to walk."

Autumn leaves crunch under my boots. Maple trees tower on each side of the main road, almost completely barren. It's one of those perfect autumn evenings, when the crisp air of the night chases away the warm summer day and signals the switch in seasons.

Gerald rests an arm on the wooden fence separating his crops from the well-traveled path. "Your father wouldn't want you to wander alone at night."

I cough to stifle a nervous giggle. "Stay with your family."

He tips his hat. "Alright, princess. May the Mother protect you."

"By her grace."

The familiar goodbye is sour on my tongue.

Gerald spins around, and I hurry along the path. It's only a short walk to the royal summer house, but the orange sun slips under the horizon like it's scared to be caught hanging on.

The corn fields' golden shine dims in its absence, and shadows encumber the road. My brisk pace drowns out the ambient sounds, the carpet of fallen leaves loud in my wake.

The scent of pine needles, overturned earth, and wood smoke wafts through the air, the summer house fireplaces already lit for the night. I cover my white-blond hair with my hood and tuck my shoulders in to blend with the shadows. My affinity for darkness has blossomed in the last few weeks. My thoughts seem sharper in obscurity, my muscles feel stronger, and my movements are more fluid.

I'm terrified by what it means.

The iron gate creaks behind me as I slip inside the limits of the estate. The dull crunch of the leaves subsides, replaced by a buzzing cricket's choir. I run to the back door without alerting the guards—another clue that my magic has grown—and enter the house.

The servant's hall is empty but for Esme, my tutor, who sits at the kitchen table with her crochet hooks.

The warm glow of the fire prevents me from sneaking past her, and she jerks to her feet. "Penny. Thank the Mother!" The thick shawl wrapped around her slender silhouette moves along with her as she hurries over to me. "Where have you been? Your father is in a mood."

I untie my hooded cape and hand it to her. "I was at Gerald's farm."

The usually soft angles of her jaw stiffen, and she runs a hand down the slope of her narrow nose. "At this hour?"

The firelight brings her big, youthful hazelnut eyes to life. Esme could pass as my older sister, but she's actually much older. Her plain, brown dress finishes right below her chin with a collar of white lace—more fitting of an elderly governess than the twenty-something lady-in-waiting she pretends to be.

"Firenze broke his leg..." I trail off.

"By the Mother!" She bites her bottom lip, and her sharp gaze travels down the length of my body. "You didn't—"

Blood still taints my linen skirts, so there's no use in denying it. "I healed him."

Esme grips the end of her long black braid like she means to choke me with it. "Penny, how many times do I have to tell you not to use your powers in front of the villagers?"

"I don't know. Maybe one more time will do?" With a sheepish smile, I rush past her and climb the stairs two at a time.

She runs after me, one hand holding her crinoline. "You turn eighteen in *two days*."

My little sister Cecelia ambushes me at the top of the staircase, hands braced on each side of her, blocking my path. Dark brown strands stick out of her hairnet. "Cheater. You went out without me."

Esme catches up to my rear and swats my sister away. "Miss Cece, please leave us. I have to speak with your sister alone."

Cece sticks out her tongue before skipping to her bedroom at the end of the corridor, her long skirt flowing behind her. I grin and head the other way, eager to change out of my bloody clothes.

Esme shuts my bedroom door behind us with an exhausted sigh and leans her entire body against it, probably afraid that Cece will trample it down. After catching her breath, she focuses her attention back on me. "The Shadow seed grows within you," she hisses quietly, her voice thick with fear.

"Don't act so surprised, you told me it would!"

She's the only one who can tell that my magic is growing, and I resent her for it.

"Don't take that tone with me, young lady. You have to be more careful about using your powers in front of others, and especially so close to your birthday, or they will quickly realize the truth. You are about to discover the full flavor and extent of your magic. It could act up if you're not careful."

"Who knows...maybe the magic will die down after my birthday." I pull my dirty dress over my head and strip out of my skirts and long socks.

Esme rubs the shell of her pointy ear, a nervous tick she gets whenever she feels ambivalent about something. "It's one thing to *have* magic. It's another thing entirely to *use* it."

Esme is Fae, but she spent most of her life in Demeter, the biggest country in the old world. She's been hiding in my father's court ever since she was a child because she's a drought—a non-magic Fae. Being a drought is a big no-no in Faerie. Esme would have been slaughtered. The very existence of a drought is perceived as a threat to the land's magic, which is total horsecrap.

And just as she has no control over *not* having magic, I have no control over the way my powers grow.

She tightens my corset with a scold. "Have you had any unusual dreams lately?"

"No."

Yes. I've dreamt of a beautiful Hawthorn tree, thick with red fruits. Its branches were adorned with teal and silver moss. I should probably mention it to Esme, but every time I dream of the tree, I feel...happy. I'm sure it has nothing to do with the deal my father made with the Shadow King.

Esme fixes my hair, tucking a few loose strands back inside the hairnet. "Your father asked for you two to dine alone tonight."

My fingers twitch in response, and I hide my hands behind my back. "Alone?"

Pressing her lips together, she wrenches a formal dress over my head. "Yes."

The intricate buttons of the collar graze the hollow of my neck, and the navy chiffon skirt weighs me down after a wonderful day outside in my no-frills cotton dress and hooded cape. But the itchy fabric is the least of my worries.

"He wants to check in. He needs to know you're ready for what's coming," Esme says.

Ready? Ha!

Ever since I found out about my magic, I've been told it was evil. Sullied.

My powers originated in Faerie, a dark heritage from a forsaken land ruled by the most dangerous Fae of all, the Shadow King. My bedtime stories as a child were filled with elusive Fae creatures that slip through mirrors to feast on our nightmares and dreams, luring even the most valorous knights to their doom and coaxing beautiful maidens into their beds.

The Shadow King crafts living sins out of thin air and corrupts everything he touches, and I have to meet him in two days. All because my father made a deal to spare my mother from an incurable disease, back when she was pregnant with me.

"Here. Take this." Esme reaches into the inside pocket of her skirts and retrieves a tiny wooden box engraved with an ancient scripture.

Thy Mother's will is to be free of vanity.

"Is that—"

Esme nods. "A mirror, yes—but you can't open it now. Tonight, before bed, I want you to look at yourself."

A mirror... Sweat gathers on my neck as she hands me the precious, forbidden box, and I quickly slip it inside the hidden compartment of my bottom drawer.

"Now, hurry downstairs," Esme shoos me off.

I swallow hard.

If Father wants us to be alone, it means he's finally decided to speak to me about my...circumstances.

"Penelope. There you are," he calls from his seat at the dining table, looking as drunk and miserable as I'd expected.

"Father." I give him a quick curtsy before sitting at the chair to his right.

The dining room is all decked-out for the occasion. In his mind, a silver butter knife and a bigger chandelier can apparently make up for the twisted fate that awaits me, and I resist the urge to roll my eyes.

He lays down his cloth napkin over his knees, his gaze slippery and unfocused. "I figured we needed to have a chat. Your birthday is the day after tomorrow."

I keep my spine straight and stare down at my lap, knowing better than to argue with him, especially when he's been drinking. "I'm ready, Father. I will not disappoint you."

"You see...the Shadow Court uses tricks that might make it hard for you to keep a straight head. Don't drink their wine, and eat as little as you can. They will try to corrupt you with their manipulative ideology, delicious booze, and attractive bodies—" He screws his eyes shut and shakes his head forcefully. "I should never have agreed to that bet. That demon tricked me."

Father calls his deal with the Shadow King anything from "a dark bet between kings" to "a God-forsaken piece of horseshit." Depending on how drunk he is when he's talking about it.

"Esme has taught me well, Father." I press my lips together to mask my impertinent thoughts. I know all of this already. Father always throws a fit when I bring it up and leaves it to Esme to fill in the blanks and take care of me and Cece. Does he have to rob me of my last few precious days of peace?

If only Mother was still here...

He swipes his goblet up, and a few droplets spill over the rim, the air suddenly charged with guilt. "Don't forget. As long as you remain a maiden, he's not allowed to touch you without your consent. I made sure that part of the deal was crystal clear."

Heat gathers on my cheeks. He doesn't mean it exactly as he said it. Of course, the Shadow King can *touch* me, but he cannot *bed* me without my consent. Despite the special education I received under Esme's tutelage, my ears burn. Sexual pleasures are not discussed or encouraged in my world, but since I'm cursed to spend so much time in a land of debauchery, Esme has taught me words that my sister will probably never hear.

Lust. Orgasm. *Cock.*

I shake my head to banish the terms from my mind, trying not to think about the drawings she showed me.

"Can you tell me something else about the bet you made? About how I should act?" I look at him expectantly. Now that I'm almost an adult, he might be allowed to tell me the whole truth about it.

"Esmeralda has already told you all the details I could share." Father clears his throat a few times before he adds, "Your mother was right when she hired Esme to teach you the ways of the Fae. With her help, you're a bit more prepared. Fae can't lie, so be wary of their *exact* words, because they will twist them to fit their designs."

"Yes, Father."

He stares down at me like he longs for absolution. He wants me to say that everything will be fine, but how could it be? He passed down the burden of protecting Demeter from our most fearsome enemy to me, his *daughter*. And I have no idea what will be demanded of me.

He promised the devil Fae that healed my mother that I would cross to the Shadow realm and live in Faerie two weeks out of four, for an entire year. By the end of that year, I will either have earned my freedom or somehow condemned my people to live under his reign. Father sold me, and gambled his crown to boot, and a part of me hates him for it. Especially since a stupid accident claimed Mother's life too soon anyway.

Now that she's gone, Father clearly regrets ever making the deal in the first place.

The way I conduct myself during the next twelve months will determine my kingdom's fate for centuries to come, but I'm precluded to know the exact terms of their *contract*—or how my future actions might doom my people.

All will be revealed in due time, Esme promised.

Until then, I have to keep my wits about me and suffer the king's whims. If I refuse to go, he wins. If I don't play by his rules or try to flee, he wins. The odds are rigged in the devil's favor, but what is owed to the Shadow King is owed in full.

And it's my turn to pay up.

CHAPTER 2

FLINGS AND PROPOSALS

Church is packed the next morning, troves of villagers vying for a seat in the first few rows behind us.

The day of the equinox signals the end of summer and, with the change in seasons, our return to court. It's the villagers' last chance to thank Father for his visit, but most of them are here to catch one last glimpse of what they call "the blessed princess"—ergo, *me*. If they knew where my magic truly came from, they'd hunt me down with pitchforks and torches, but my talent for healing—the only power I've been allowed to share—is seen as a blessing from our beloved Mother.

I managed to visit Firenze early and finished healing his leg—I bet Mathilda already told half the villagers.

Excited whispers resonate in my wake on our way out of the holy building. I let my mind wander, trying to think about anything other than the sermon that highlighted the virtues of abnegation and unselfishness.

Father mounts his horse and waves goodbye to his subjects, probably rushing back to deal with one crisis or another. I'm tempted to ride the carriage home, but before I make a decision, the crowd disperses, revealing a tall, familiar silhouette beyond the church's white picket fence.

Isaac Longbottom leans against a tree in the church's orchard, his arms crossed over his torso. The handsome boy smiles as our gazes meet, his bright blue eyes shining in the midday sun.

Cece spreads her arms above her head and twirls. "Oh, what do I see? A fair knight waiting for his fairer maiden. Sir Isaac is simply taken by your radiant beauty, sister. How shall you repay his loyalty?" She chuckles, dropping the dramatic act. "Look at him, he can't stop staring because you guys ki—"

"Shush, Esme will hear you." I slap her arm to keep her quiet.

Doubling-down on her theatrics, she bats her eyelashes and purses her lips to make wet kissing noises.

I cringe, my jaw slightly askew. "Crops! You annoy me *so* much."

I should never have confided in her.

"You annoy me more." Cece peels her fashionable hat from her brown bun and holds it behind her back, the ribbons attached to it blowing in the autumn breeze. "Go to him. I'll convince the witch to stop by the bakery. It'll give you enough time to escape." With a wink, she prances over to Esme.

Dearest Cece... Esme's got her work cut out with her.

I press a hand over my mouth to cover up the huge, unladylike grin threatening to surface, and meet Isaac by the orchard, the skirt of my light yellow dress scraping against earth.

"You look like a real life girl, Penny," he teases me, his gaze riveted on the white ribbon tied above my hips. "Come now. I'll escort you home."

I link my arm in his and scold him for his forwardness. "Don't get any ideas. You're taking me straight home."

"Maybe a quick stop under the willow tree?" he breathes softly against my cheek.

My ears burn, and I bite back a giddy smile. "Alright."

Since *the witch* came into the picture, I'm allowed more freedom than most girls my age. Father's guilt can go a long way toward special privileges, and the rules at the summer house are even more flexible.

Isaac, my life-long friend, courted me this summer.

The other night, we kissed under the willow tree behind the stables. I wouldn't risk losing my virginity before marriage, knowing the Shadow King could use that against me. No, Esme knew I would never cross that line, so she allowed me this *fling*—but she still wants me to pretend she doesn't know.

Isaac and I had climbed trees and explored mud fields growing up, earning me my reputation as a tom boy, but he doesn't mind my lack of love for the piano forte and crochet. If anything, he likes me better for it.

Once we're far enough from the village, the distance between us melts, and Isaac wraps an arm around my shoulders. All of a sudden, my long-sleeved dress feels a bit stuffy.

I curl into his side, and we slowly make our way to the back of Father's estate, dragging our feet to make the moment last. Orange and yellow leaves pepper the countryside, and the tall corn and wheat fields are ripe for the upcoming harvest.

As we reach the cool shade of the willow tree, I unpin the hat from my hair and hang it up on a nearby branch.

Isaac gathers my hands in his. "I was surprised to hear that the king didn't plan anything for your birthday tomorrow."

Ohhhh, he planned something, Isaac. He's selling me out to a dark Fae.

I fake a small yawn to mask the growing unease in my belly. "I told him not to. Throwing a party in the city would have cut our time here short."

Isaac and I can't see each other much in Lundan, Demeter's capital. His studies take up most of his time, and there's too many unfriendly pairs of eyes in the city. We wouldn't get away with the same type of carefree behavior as we do here.

"I brought your birthday gift with me," he says softly. The

solemn tremble of his voice gives me pause, and I freeze when he bends to one knee. *Oh no, no, no—*

"Penelope Emanuelle Darcy, I've thought of nothing but you all summer. You were my friend for years, but the last few months, you became so much more. Will you marry me?"

The leaves above our heads bristle in the wind, casting shadows upon his face. The sweet proposal echoes deep in my soul, but alas... "Oh, Isaac."

Lines appear on his forehead, his hopeful, loving expression slowly melting into a guarded frown. "I'm the son of a duke, a perfectly acceptable match."

I've discouraged all marriage talk this summer, trying to buy some time, but clearly, I haven't done a good enough job. *Boys never do what they're told,* my mother always said.

"You know I would love nothing more than to accept, but Father..."

He climbs to his feet, his eyes vulnerable once more. "I will ask for his blessing, of course. I just—I got ahead of myself."

Tears threaten to spill over my cheeks, but I keep a straight face not to alert Isaac. He can't know why I need to decline his proposal.

A mix of sadness and anger bubbles up my throat. "Father needs me. Mother's death is still too fresh in his memory...if you ask him for my hand, he'll tell you the same thing. One more year, that's all I ask."

He combs his fingers in his brown hair, leaving it all disheveled. "A lot can happen in a year, Penny."

He can't know that I'm cursed to spend half the year in Faerie. No one can know. After the year is over, if I manage to win the bet, I'll be free to marry—but not before.

He squeezes my hands, his palms hot and sweaty. "Say yes now. Let's leave the countryside as fiancés, and we can wait for spring to be married. That's almost a year."

My eyes dart to the ground, his compromise reasonable enough, making it harder for me to keep my head. "I really wish I could," I whisper.

The wind blows dried leaves past our feet as we stand stock-still in front of one another for a few breaths, our chests rising and falling.

Isaac tilts my chin up with his index finger. "Are you in earnest? Do you really just need more time?" His bottomless blue gaze searches mine. "Don't be cruel with me, Penny, and tell me now."

"I would never lie to you about this," I answer, my voice cracking in spite of my efforts. "I want to marry you."

He inches closer, his voice melting down to a whisper. "Then I'll wait for you."

A small smile breaks through my despair, and I nod emphatically at his offer. "Thank you."

"I'm leaving for Lundan tonight." He bends down, our lips a hair apart. "I'll miss you, Penny."

"Me too."

He presses his lips to mine for a second, and my heart booms at the sweet, forbidden caress. The scent of his skin—a mix of cologne and soap—sparks a searing heat below my ribs.

"One year..." he says, dragging his thumb across my cheek.

"One year."

The fleeting joy dissipates, and a stone sinks in my stomach at my deceit. Even though a formal promise isn't spoken, this conversation counts as one, and I don't know if I'll be able to honor it.

Obvious disappointment darkens Isaac's features, but one corner of his mouth curls up. "I'll see you soon in the city. May the Mother smile upon your travels."

"By her grace."

The hunch of his retreating back is a direct dart to the heart, and blood rushes to my ears. I bite the inside of my cheeks not to call after him and blab away all my secrets, wishing I could tell him the truth, but how could I even start? No matter how delicately I phrased it, he'd never look at me the same way again.

Shaken, I stay in the gardens for most of the afternoon, reading quietly under the canopy of the willow tree. Esme is too busy with her preparations for the move to bother me with any last-minute advice, and Cece isn't back from her riding lesson, yet.

Around five, the wind dies down, and the sun falls quickly in the sky.

"What are you reading?" Cece asks, her chin suddenly on my shoulder.

The way she sneaks up on me, you'd think that girl was magic, too.

I snap the book shut, the purple and gold leather cover shining in the sunset. "Nothing, really."

The thick layer of mud at the bottom of her dress tells me she played with the horses in the pasture after her riding lesson. She shuffles to her knees, her eyes wide, and dried flakes of dirt fall to the tartan blanket between us. "Wait a minute...I recognize this book. It's from Esme's forbidden collection, on the very top glass shelf." She wrenches the volume from my hands and leafs through it. "A Fae book. I can't believe Father agreed for you to read a Fae book." She narrows her eyes. "Unless you managed to steal Esme's key? Crops, Nell, I'm not a kid anymore. I could've helped."

Everyone else calls me Penny, but Cece prefers Nell, even though it drives Father crazy—as does her foul language.

"Watch your mouth, *young lady*," I say with a nasal edge to my voice, imitating Esme. "It's a history book is all. Esme said I could read it, and I'm sure she'll let you have it too when you're older."

I hold out my hand for her to return it, and she complies with a huff. "Still, I'm here if you ever want to steal her key...or her broom."

Our gazes meet, and we erupt into a fit of giggles, only sobering up when Cece peels herself off the ground. "I'll change before dinner. See you in an hour."

I wave goodbye and return to my reading. I wasn't lying about it being a history book—sort of. The writer crafted a fascinating picture of his Faerie travels, but now I'm distracted.

I chickened out last night. I couldn't bring myself to look at

Esme's gift and kept it in my pocket all day instead, exhilarated by the prospect of seeing my reflection for the first time.

The weight of the small wooden box becomes too heavy to ignore, and I scour the empty garden to make sure I'm alone before prying it out. The intricate carvings over the lid separate in two flaps when I click it open. Inside, a folded piece of black cloth covers the small mirror. The two-inch wide piece of glass falls into my open palm, and the sharp glint of light reflecting off its surface feels eerie and exciting.

Heart-pounding, I gaze down at it with wonder. It's wild to see myself so clearly, and not only in portrait or at the surface of a muddy pond. The painters didn't quite do justice to my clear green eyes, and a thrill shoots up my spine.

A woman isn't supposed to think of herself as beautiful, but I can't understand why. Beauty is a gift from our goddess.

A raven lands on one of the lowest branches of the willow tree in the last gleam of twilight, and the ruffle of its feathers is louder than it ought to be. I tilt my head back to look at the bird.

Just as I'm about to shrug off the unease at the pit of my stomach, the waning breeze picks up. Gooseflesh blooms at the base of my neck. I quickly cover up the mirror, bury it in my skirts, and jerk to my feet. In the blink of an eye, the shadows casted by the branches of the willow tree swell to cage me in.

A furious wind blows at my back, and the fallen leaves littering the garden tumble in the opposite direction they did all day, rushing toward the summer house.

Above my head, the raven takes flight, and its cold cackle numbs my ears. My corset is suddenly too tight to breathe. Someone's here. I can feel it.

Magic tingles in my palms, and the distinct pressure of a gaze roams my body. A cluster of dried leaves stops abruptly in front of me, bumping into a solid, invisible wall.

Fear drums in my veins as I squint at the night. "Show yourself."

CHAPTER 3
I SHALL NOT FLEE

A nightmare shimmers into view. Shadows hover around the apparition, snuffing out the dim garden lights. A black jacket, pants, and boots cover the tall, masculine silhouette, topped with a matching hood.

The veil of darkness hiding him from view thins as he inches closer. He's tall enough that I have to tilt my chin to gaze up at his face, and I bite back a scream.

White streaks—no, claw marks—scar the solid obsidian mask that prevents me from seeing his face and his eyes. The terrible accessory finishes right above his mouth, revealing human lips and a chin dimple. His skin is slightly darker than mine, and his jacket is stretched over his large shoulders. Peculiar drawings cover his knuckles—no doubt some Fae alphabet.

"I—I still have a few hours left before my birthday," I whisper.

Did I summon the Shadow King just by looking at my reflection? *Stupid girl. You should have left the damn mirror up in your room.*

The monster cocks his head to the side, and the certainty that he can actually see through his solid mask fills me with dread.

I sink my nails into my wrist to get a grip on my nerves. "Have you no tongue, Shadow King?"

"I wanted to spare you long, tearful goodbyes. The ticking of fate's clock can drive a mortal mad," a low, ethereal voice answers.

I roll my shoulders back with as much confidence as I can muster. "And why would our goodbyes be tearful? I'm not leaving them forever. I shall see them again in two weeks."

A wicked chuckle falls off his lips. "A lot can happen in two weeks."

The sentiment echoes Isaac's earlier claim, and shivers crawl up my spine. "You will not corrupt me."

"Me? Probably not," the faceless king snickers.

The husky response resonates deep in my soul, a dark lullaby composed especially for me. I tremble as he inches closer, but I will not cower at my destiny, so I dig my heels deeper in the autumn leaves not to flee. His mesmerizing shadows sting in a way I've never felt before—a mix between the buzzing I get in my fingers when they're numb, and the snap of a fire burn. Esme called it the *bite of power*, a calling card for Fae to proclaim their level of skill. She said experienced magic users could play with the strength of their *bite*, dampening or deepening it to appear more or less powerful as a ruse.

My demon is all shadows over shade, his power so formidable that it drums in my head like a living pulse.

"Have you ever glimpsed at the worlds beyond the sceaware?" he asks.

"Sceaware?" Does he plan to humiliate me for my lack of knowledge of Faerie?

"It's the gateway between worlds. The proper name for what you call 'mirror.'"

I grip the piece of reflective glass in my pocket and wrench it out. "You mean this?"

His top lip curls in disgust. "No."

Darkness swarms around him, startling me. The small mirror

slips between my fingers, but I catch it before it reaches the ground and flatten it to my chest.

"That scrap of metal isn't worthy of the name. Come." He spins on his heels and heads for the corner of the gardens.

Shadows gather on our path, the guards oblivious to our presence as we cross the hallway to the king's quarters.

"Are you taking me to my father?" I ask.

The Shadow King remains silent as he veers toward a section of the summer house I've never visited. We head down a round stairwell to the basement, and I skitter in his wake.

The acrid scent of mildew spices the air of the uninhabited... dungeon? Metallic bars run vertically at the front of a few rusted cells, and moss fills the cracks of what looks to be an ancient, dilapidated prison. Judging by the thick layer of dust and grime on the paved stones, no one has stepped foot in here for decades. The only footprints visible are ours—mine and the ones I can only assume my captor made when he came in to collect me.

At the back of the cold, humid room, a worn-out mirror stands a few inches shorter than the monster at my side. Murky glass reflects our silhouettes, and I hold my breath. I've never seen a mirror besides the tiny one in my pocket, but seeing one this big...it's more than forbidden. It's impossible.

"Since you're not trained in the ways of the sceawere, you have to wear this." The masked king pries a long piece of black silk from his pocket.

"But mortals can't travel through mirrors," I whisper, suddenly terrified. Only monsters can travel through glass, at least according to the books I've read.

"You bear the dark seed, do you not," he purrs, the end of the sentence not rising in question, like the answer is both obvious and laughable. "You are Penelope Emanuelle Darcy, eldest daughter of Phillip Fredric Darcy, the current king of Demeter."

"Yes," I say with regret.

I really, really wish I wasn't.

Still, the ceremonial way he whispers my whole name casts a nefarious spell over me, and I step closer without meaning to. I'm sure I've heard his voice before, calling out to me in the dead of night. In sweaty dreams that haunt me long after they're gone.

He ties the scrap of fabric around my head, blinding me, and I can't resist the urge to hike it up my brow. My instincts scream at me not to let that demon out of my sight. Not for a second.

Pulling on the knot in a chastising manner, he clicks his tongue. "Never remove the blindfold, or the nightmares that prowl the in-between will claim you."

I press the fabric to my forehead to keep it from sliding down. "How do you expect me to travel if I can't see?"

"Just hold on to me," he says, his arms now spread in invitation.

A nervous hiccup shakes my body. I do not want to walk into his sinister embrace, and my pulse flutters at my neck. The deep, paralyzing thuds of my heart urge me to turn on my heels and run.

The first test.

I shall not flee.

I shall not give in.

I shall endure.

I approach him, and the heat of his body is as dizzying as the bite of his magic. Darkness eddies my vision, and my bottom lip quakes, but he guides my hands patiently to his shoulders.

Musician calluses bump along my knuckles, and the fleeting skin-to-skin contact softens my knees. The sleek fabric of his jacket is fresh and closely knit, different from the crumbly caress of wool or the simple and rough touch of cotton. A long metallic line runs down the front of the strange garment, and a thick hood covers his hair—and ears.

He picks me up without a hitch, one arm braced lazily under my knees. My breasts strain against my corset, my breaths shallow and uneven, and the world beyond my monstrous captor blurs into an ocean of black.

"Now, pull the blindfold down and hold on tight," he says. His hot breath scatters goosebumps on my neck, and he strolls forward, unencumbered by the added weight.

Liquid ice spreads over my skin, the pain as sudden and unexpected as a snake bite. In a flash, I'm both torn apart and glued back together. Frost stings my cheeks, and I grip the king hard, desperate for him not to drop me in this hellish place. My arms instinctively wrap around his neck, and my nails dig into the fabric of his collar.

"Easy, kitten, you're alright." A tinge of humor warms his husky voice as he lets go of my legs. "You'll get used to it."

I hold on for dear life. "I don't want to get used to it."

"No need for claws. Not just yet. Unless you want to hang on to me some more..."

If I could have crawled over his shoulders, I would have. *I certainly tried.*

A furious blush heats my cheeks, but I finally let go of him, surprised to find solid ground beneath my feet.

The dark king dusts off my arms like he's making sure no part of me went missing during the voyage, and I tear the blindfold off, now standing in a bedroom riddled with paved stones. A wardrobe towers next to the neatly swept hearth, and a dark brown chest lays at the foot of a large bed.

A two-person bed...

"Where are we?" I try to hide my nerves, try to mask the fear and curiosity on my breath, thinking about the drawings Esme showed me.

"Your bedroom."

Remember, he can't touch you without your consent.

A chamber pot and a tub are visible behind a semi-opaque screen that splits the space in two, and the large free standing mirror that occupies an entire corner of the room shocks me to say the least.

A creature flies in from the glass as easily as I put one foot in front of the other. "A lean summer brings a leaner winter," it mumbles. "Only three seeds this year, half as much as last year..."

Eyes wide, I stare at the three feet tall, floppy-eared apparition.

Deep wrinkles crack its dark blue skin. "By Morpheus, ye look as though ye've just had yer wings cut off, woman. I'm a sprite. Hevny ever seen one?"

"No. Never," I admit.

The sprite isn't wearing clothes, but it's not that jarring considering her body is shaped like a tree trunk. Long fingernails polish off her look, the claws sharp enough to scratch my eyes out if she so desired. Still, seeing her whole face is a relief, her pink eyes truly beautiful.

The king walks over to the only door and spins around to face me, hands hidden behind his back. "I leave her in your capable hands, Baka."

Baka bows to the Shadow King. "Ye know I'm not one to complain, Samhain...but with only three seedlings to tend to, I might as well find a new hobby." She smiles at that, though it doesn't quite meet her big eyes. Her gnarly hand wraps around my arm, tugging me toward the copper bathtub. "Come on, now. We have to get ye ready to meet the king."

I almost topple over, my gaze darting to the masked man. "The king? But—"

"See you later, *kitten*." With a sly smile, the dark man saunters off, clearly pleased with himself. I gape at his hasty retreat, and the door closes behind him without a sound.

"That wasn't the king?"

Baka giggles like I've just said something incredibly funny. "You'll see the king at dinner. He's throwing a banquet for the new seedlings."

My brows pull together, my mind reeling. "Seedlings?"

"Why are ye here if not to be trained in the ancient ways of our house?" She bows her head respectfully. "I'm Baka, your handmaid," she adds like she just remembered her manners.

Trained? "I'm Nell."

If I'm to survive in this realm, I need to be smarter and quicker on my feet than Penelope Darcy. Why did I assume the king would fetch me personally? I shouldn't have presumed anything, and I need to be more careful going forward. Their polite manners must be a ruse, a way to ease me in.

"Let's get you in the tub, Nell. You smell like a horse," Baka says.

My nose wrinkles, and I take a discrete sniff. It's not *so* bad...

The sprite flaps her wings and rises into the air once more. A touch of hesitation comes when she starts unfastening my corset. "I hevny seen this model in ages...are ye from Demeter, Nell?"

"Yes." I watch our reflections in the mirror.

She unlaces the tight knots and makes quick work of it despite her small size, her mouth twisted in a pout. "By the spindle...they will eat ye alive, deary."

I draw in a slow, controlled breath to keep the fear at bay and strip from my clothes, ignoring all the alarm bells going off in my mind. I'm bathing—naked—in Faerie in front of a creature I didn't even know existed five minutes ago... so much for Esme's tutelage.

I shall not flee.

I shall not give in.

I shall endure.

CHAPTER 4
LITTLE BLACK DRESS

"I can't wear this. *Any* of this." Hands clenched around the fluffy robe Baka gave me after my bath, I eye the dresses she laid out for me. Just looking at them heats my cheeks.

Baka's face creases. She empties the tub the same way she filled it —with a single snap of her fingers. "You're young, seedling. Enjoy it."

What the crops does this have to do with my age? "It's...obscene."

"It's pretty."

I press my lips together, hands on my hips, no closer to winning this argument than I was five minutes ago. "Is there another option? Can I keep my own clothes?"

She shakes her wrinkled blue head with a grimace. "Ye'd stick out like a sore thumb, and this banquet is expected to hold up the decorum of the court."

A crude, vulgar decorum—but this is another test. I straighten my spine and consider the four dresses again, feeling like I'm playing an impish version of eenie, meenie, miney, moe.

The yellow one has no sleeves whatsoever, but its long silk train makes it the most conservative choice. The skirt of the empire-waist, green dress is so short that it would leave my thighs bare, and I fail to mask a cringe at the thought. The black one has too much cleavage. The white one is all holes and lace, and the bridal color unnerves me. *No. Definitely not white.*

"Let's try the yellow one," I finally say.

"A classic."

I put it on, and the prickly crinoline scratches my thighs. "Where are the socks?" I'm not used to the friction of fabric on my bare legs.

Baka raises her brows, both of them thick as branches. "Socks? You mean the ones you were wearing? They couldn't have been comfortable."

Tears sting my eyes. I look exactly like one of the courtesans in Esme's book. Is the whole night planned around my public humiliation? Will I be mocked? Bullied? Assaulted?

I almost tear the dress off, feeling hideous and cheap. "Bring the black one, please."

"Brave choice," Baka cheers.

I'm not sure who I resent more, the Shadow King for forcing me into these clothes, or Father, for selling me out in the first place. It's certainly not Baka's fault. If I have to stand in front of the Shadow Court in nothing but a scrap of fabric that counts as a dress in this evil land, I will not let them revel in the certainty that they rattled me.

I work the dark dress over my head. Layers upon layers of black and gray chiffon lick the floor, the skirt not as scandalous as the neckline... Two strips of fabric run over my shoulders down my front, leaving the path between my breasts completely bare, almost to my navel.

Depending on how the light catches it, the one layer of chiffon covering my breasts becomes almost see-through and reveals the roundness of them. Heat pools in my gut, but I find solace in the fact that the color compliments my skin. I no longer want to punch the mirror, and a heavy sense of acceptance settles in my chest.

I shall endure.

"The satin pumps are right here." Baka deposits a feminine pair of black shoes near my feet. "I gave you the shortest heel I could find."

I slip my feet inside them, happy to find a comfortable fit despite their eerie appearance.

"And we should leave your hair down." Baka releases my white blonde hair from the net, removing the clips and ribbons until it flows down to my waist. She uses a golden brush to comb through the knotted, frizzy strands, and they quickly become smooth and perfectly shaped.

My jaw drops. "That's sorcery."

"Welcome to Faerie." On a mischievous chortle, Baka hangs the discarded yellow dress back in the wardrobe. She should burn it, really, but I bite my tongue not to say so and look at myself in the mirror again. I run my fingers through my hair with a sense of wonder. I haven't been permitted to wear it down outside the confines of my bedroom since I turned fourteen, and the absence of the clips and net is...freeing. I wish I could run outside with the wind in my hair like I did when I was a child.

Baka fluffs it one last time, the small lift of her hands somehow giving it more volume. "Lovely," she says, pleased with herself, before she glances at the small clock on the dresser. "It's almost time. I have to go. May the eyes of the Seven shine upon you, seedling."

She flies back the way she came, as though it's the most natural thing to do. The mirror ripples in her wake like a pond under a clear summer sky. My nails click over solid glass as I test the feel of the reflective surface, but I sense no path or magic to speak of.

How does it work, exactly?

Curious, I trace the bronze trim with my fingers. The glass dims, taken over by a human-shaped shadow, and I jolt away from the apparition. The budding elation fluttering in my belly condenses into stone.

Nightmares prowl from the other side of the mirror.

This is supposed to be my bedroom, but if monsters can stalk my every move and come in and out of the glass at will, I don't see how I'll get a whiff of sleep.

A soft knock draws my attention away from whatever evil lurks inside the *sceawere*, and I bring my loose waves to my front to cover my breasts before inching open the bedroom door.

The dark man from before stands in front of me, his mask still firmly planted over his face.

"You lied to me." I cross my arms, shielding myself further from his blank, metallic gaze.

Surely, he can see me, can't he?

One corner of his mouth curls up, the motion small and yet perfectly rehearsed. "You assumed I was the Shadow King. Was it so wrong of me not to disabuse you of that notion?" The dark man turns on his heels, and I follow him down the hallway.

Fae can't outright lie, but they certainly can lie by omission.

The warm light of the torches hanging from the ceiling reflects off the man's black and white mask as he leads me through the labyrinth of the Shadow Court. Each tight corner reveals a new stretch of expansive, dark tunnels, the carpeted hallways seemingly carved through solid stone, most of them slanting upward. In Demeter, it would be unthinkable for a maiden to be escorted through darkened passageways by a man that isn't part of her immediate family, and I play nervously with my fingers, keeping a good five feet of empty space between us.

A couple of blue, wingless sprites carrying linens and burlap sacks cross our path. They pause as we draw near and bow respectfully to my guide—a lord or knight of some kind, I presume—before resuming their journey. I peek over my shoulder to check for a scar or a welt left by their cut wings, but their backs are too bumpy for me to be sure.

"What are you doing?" the dark man asks softly, his head tilted to the side. "The sprites are loyal, trustworthy creatures, I assure you. You do not need to fear them. Ever."

"I was looking for their wings," I admit, leaving out my fear that they might have been cut off, like Baka briefly mentioned.

"Some sprites are born without them," the man explains in a soothing tone, making me think he understood exactly what I was asking.

My spine relaxes a bit, and we resume our ascension until we reach a thick gold-plated door at the end of the next corridor. The Fae holds it open for me. "If I may...you look beautiful, kitten."

I feel his gaze roam over my naked back as I walk past him, and my cheeks flush. "Thank you."

The wide room on the other side possesses all the bells and whistles of a lavish banquet hall and is situated a few stories above ground. Large checkered panels allow for a hot and heavy summer night breeze to flow in, the air thick with humidity. The sweet aromas of ginger spices, lavender, and incense fill my nostrils.

"Is it still summer here?" I ask, the pleasant atmosphere soothing my nerves.

"Late spring, actually, and I'm already sick of the heat. The palace is much more comfortable in autumn. Seasons pass quicker here than in your world, so you'll see for yourself soon enough."

Garlands of lanterns flicker above our heads, and lush gardens spread beyond the edge of the open-air balcony adjacent to the banquet hall, the details of them hidden in darkness.

Men and women wearing masquerade masks sip on crystal flutes and chat in small groups around the hall and balcony, the setup similar to a Demeter banquet if not for the outrageous apparel. I thought the Shadow King meant to set me apart, but my dress is on par with what the other women are wearing. The excited chatter doubles at our arrival, and quite a few courtiers crane their neck around to steal glances at us.

Four tables are set in the dimly lit reception hall. The biggest one forms a half-circle that sits about a dozen patrons and faces what I assume to be the king's spot, a table furnished with a padded black and gold throne. The two remaining tables are set at the ends of the half circle and are perpendicular to the king's, with three seats each. A humongous frameless mirror looms behind the throne, stretching the entire length of the wall.

My dark chaperone picks two crystal flutes off a floating tray and hands me one, but I shake my head. Father said no wine. "None for me, thank you."

"Your loss." He gulps down the extra flute at my refusal and sets it back on the tray. The floating drinks fly from group to group under my awestruck stare, and I'm about to ask how it works when a short man rushes over to us.

A forest-green jacket stretches over his round belly, the buttons threatening to burst. A silver mask covers his eyes but reveals a plump, red nose and sun-battered skin. "One, it's been too long."

One? One what?

The dark man nods in greeting. "Good evening, Effias."

"By the spindle, the seedlings are certainly gorgeous this year—if not numerous." Effias grins a happy, effable smile. "Best wishes, my dear. We're all counting on you." He presses his pink, swollen hands together before facing the dark knight again. "Give your brothers my best wishes. And remind Three that he still owes me a horse."

Wait... Who the crops is named One?

One—if that's in fact his name—pulls out a chair for me at one of the three-seater tables in a perfect picture of gallantry, but I hesitate. The copper tableware shines under the glow of the lanterns, the ominous greeting from Effias still stuck in my brain. *What is a seedling? And why would this Fae count on* me?

One abandons me to my fate and strolls to the balcony, spreading his arms. "Welcome, High Fae of Sinistra, Umbra, Sombra, Fantasmagorie, and Nocturna. Please take your seats. The feast is about to begin."

I sit on the edge of the chair, and a red-haired woman slumps into the seat next to mine. "Hey, I'm Mara. I'm a seedling, too." She's not wearing a mask, and freckles pepper her young, open face.

A man with dark black skin peers over her shoulder. "And I'm James. Is it true you're from the old world?"

"Yes, are you from the new?" I examine the two newcomers with interest, their excitement contagious. They're wearing similar fashions as me, seemingly unaffected by Mara's bare thighs and strapless dress—or my own see-through cleavage.

"Yep. Fresh out of Denver, and James is Canadian," Mara says.

James nods and sits next to her, our table now full.

It must be the name of her kingdom. "I'm from Demeter. I'm Nell."

"Nice to meet you, Nell. I didn't think people from the old world bleached their hair. It's really pretty. God, I'm famished." Mara snaps her fingers, and a floating tray dashes over to our table. The crystal flutes clank together, and she slides two of them next to her empty wine glass.

"What do you mean?" I ask, confused about her comment on my hair. Even though she used the word *pretty*, it didn't sound like a compliment.

She raises one of the crystal flutes to her red-painted lips, her attention fixed on something else. "Who's the hunk?"

My brows furrow. "Excuse me?" Some of the words blurting out of her mouth make no sense.

"The tall Fae with the black and white mask?" She waves in the dark man's general direction. "Who is he?"

"His name is One—I think."

Her gaze roams over his body, and she licks her lips. "Get me some of that...a swimmer's body and a chin dimple? I'm hooked."

My jaw drops. I'm shocked to hear a woman speak so plainly about a man.

James' shoulders wiggle underneath his white jacket. "I don't know...the claw marks on his mask set me on edge."

I nod in agreement and spread the cloth napkin over my knees out of habit. Most of the guests are seated by now, and food magically appears on our plates. Greasy, fragrant aromas rise from a steaming piece of meat—a bird of some kind—and an array of root vegetables.

Saliva fills my mouth, but I resist the urge to taste the food. I've eaten a large breakfast today, so I can skip this meal like Father advised. Mara and James dig in without a second thought, and I observe the cheery High Fae instead, each of their masks unique and mesmerizing.

Men and women laugh in earnest along the half-crescent table, patting each other's backs and leaning into their neighbors without a shred of self-consciousness.

After a few minutes, Mara ties her red hair back in a bun at the nape of her neck with a tiny, round piece of fabric, and elbows my side. "Why aren't you eating?"

I shrug. Her table manners rub me the wrong way. "Mortals shouldn't eat Faerie food."

"What are you going to do? Starve yourself to death? We live in Faerie now," Mara says with her mouth full, unapologetically stuffing herself with the second serving that appeared on her empty plate.

Has she moved to Faerie for good? Of her own accord? What the crops is going on here?

"I'd rather ease into it."

Mara pouts at my answer, and James gazes nervously into his wine.

Glasses and cutlery clink in a rhythmic melody throughout dinner, but One doesn't touch his food, either.

As dessert is served, the dark Fae is still sitting alone at the identical table on the other side of the room, and the two empty seats next to him tickle my curiosity.

He's wearing a mask, so it doesn't make much sense, but I could swear he's playing hide and seek with me. Every time I glance over to him, his impassive, covered face is angled to the High Fae, but whenever I look away, I feel the pressure of his gaze on me.

I test my theory a couple more times, certain it can't be a coincidence, and clutch the cloth napkin in my lap in frustration. I'm unable to catch him with his mask angled in my direction, but I'm almost sure...

Finally, I raise my wine glass between us to stare at him through the amber-tinted liquid on the guise of rating its color, hue, and transparency. The subterfuge allows for a long, unabashed look, and this time, his lips quirk up in the shadow of a smile.

Before I can decide whether to smile back, a sprite flies to the king's table and clears his throat. With slender arms, thick brows, and pink eyes, he's very similar to Baka, and his brown skin is textured like the bark of an ancient tree.

He reads from the parchment in his hands with an air of ceremony, "All rise for His Majesty the King."

CHAPTER 5
IN HIS NAME

Compared to Baka's accented rasp, this sprite's voice is smooth and clear as a church bell. The Fae patrons stand, along with One, and we imitate them, the tables in front of us suddenly empty but for our wine glasses.

Mara leans closer to my ear. "God, this is so exciting."

James laces his fingers at his front, not sharing her enthusiasm, the weight of the moment dragging down his shoulders.

"Lords and ladies of the Shadow Court, please welcome your one true king. Damian Morpheus Sombra, keeper of dreams, weaver of fantasies, and master of nightmares," the sprite announces.

The Fae lords and ladies raise their wine glasses in cheer. "In his name."

Dark clouds roll in and obscure the large wall behind the throne, and I hold my breath. The now black-as-ink surface of the mirror ripples in the king's wake as he steps out of the glass. At first, his silhouette is blurry and incomplete, but the shadows cradling the dark specter slither out of view one by one like feathers being preened and smoothed over his back.

A black jacket with bronze accents shows off his broad shoulders.

The fabric is embroidered with writing in the Fae alphabet, and a sleek, golden mask covers his entire face. The close-fitting collar of his shirt rests immediately below it, and thick gloves conceal his hands. Not one inch of skin is visible.

I thought only seeing the lips and chin of the dark knight was bad, but this is much worse.

The Shadow King doesn't sit on his throne but marches over to our table instead. James quivers under his scrutiny, and Mara bites her bottom lip, her stomach clenching like she's about to burst into a fit of laughter.

The king breezes past them and immobilizes in front of me, tall and intimidating. He snatches my long-stemmed wine glass from the table and discards its contents to the floor with a flick of the wrist.

He raises the other hand in my direction, asking me to come closer. The wordless command echoes in every fiber of my soul even though no actual sound came from his mouth.

The pull of his magic compels me to walk around the table and stand by his side. His bite of power sinks into my pores like pure, voluptuous poison.

The king tugs on the end of his left glove and pries it off. Blood whooshes at my temples as I offer him my hand—though he didn't ask for it.

A gold ring snakes around his middle finger—the only part of his body that looks human—and inked Fae alphabet runs down his knuckles.

My heartbeats slow down, one sluggish thud at a time, my very pulse regulated by his proximity. He reaches out and sinks a pointy fingernail into the tip of my index finger. Blood rises in its wake, but the sharp pinch barely registers.

Time stops. The Fae lords freeze, some with their mouths half-open on a gasp, others clutching their necklaces or gulping down a mouthful of wine, each of them perfectly still. A drop of blood hangs from the tip of my nail, suspended in time, and perfect silence ices the scene.

The king walks in a circle around me. His fluid movements are in total contrast to the petrified banquet hall. A burst of heat brands my chest, his powerful aura softening my legs.

I feel his stare travel across my hips and breasts before it lands on my parted lips. He traces the v-shape of my dress with his ungloved hand, right above my navel. Our skin touches, and he draws back like he felt the flare of static electricity between us as vividly as I did.

Goosebumps scatter on my neck, and my gaze latches on to One, his obsidian mask darker than it was a minute ago. At first, I believe he's paralyzed too, but his shoulders roll underneath his black tunic.

The king grazes my waist, and One's nostrils flare, but his rigid stance melts back into a subservient bow—so quickly in fact that I wonder if I imagined it.

The king draws back a few inches, and the drop of blood hanging at the tip of my finger finally falls into the wine glass. In a blink, the spell ends, and life returns to the room.

Mara and James join us. The Shadow King pricks each of their fingers in turn, their blood joining mine at the bottom of the glass until the red liquid foams and expands.

The king raises the blood wine to the glow of the lanterns. *"Three of them will be trained, but only the strongest seeds will sprout,"* he says telepathically, his words heard and yet not spoken. His terribly beautiful inner voice is apparently projected to the entire room, because the other guests nod and smile in response.

What the crops?

With a snap of his fingers, the empty glasses in front of the Fae lords fill to the brim with the same shade of bloody wine.

One raises his glass to the patrons. "May the seeds grow strong."

"May the seeds grow strong," the High Fae respond in unison, the clinks of their toast resonating in cheer.

Men and women drink the blood greedily.

A metallic taste lingers at the back of my tongue, but Mara and

James smile, quite literally bewitched by the Shadow King. I anchor my gaze to One's black and white mask so as not to suffer the same fate until the king ushers his guests to the balcony, leaving us behind.

One slowly walks over to us and grazes the flesh of my upper arm. "Come on, kitten. I'll take you back to your room."

I play with my fingers, my pulse quick and irregular. "It's over?"

My two fellow seedlings jolt out of their hypnotic state. "What happened?" Mara asks with a dreamy edge to her voice.

James rubs his palms together to warm them up. "I feel pulverized."

I bite the inside of my cheeks. I expected...worse. Not merely offering me a meal, pricking my finger, and sending me to bed.

One sighs. "You two, stay here. I'll escort you back to your rooms one at a time."

I utter a quick "good night" before following One out of the banquet hall. We head deep inside the belly of the castle, away from the fragrant Faerie night.

"Is your name truly One?" I ask him.

He picks up the pace, his tone almost cheerful. "You have an issue with that name?"

"No." I take note of his non-answer.

Magic and names are entwined. They made a big show of presenting the king's name and accolades, and One recited mine in full when he fetched me from my home.

The dark Fae opens my bedroom door, but he doesn't come inside, merely waiting for me to enter. "Sweet slumber, kitten. I'll fetch you in the morning for your first lesson."

The lock clicks behind me, and I test the knob. I'm trapped. The Shadow King doesn't want me to roam his halls at my leisure, and a claustrophobic ache squeezes my ribs. I'm his prisoner. Baka had laid out a silk nightgown on the bed, so I change out of the dress.

Red embers shine in the fireplace. *No windows...* I hadn't noticed that before. This section of the palace must be entrenched deep underground for the air to feel so cool and stale despite the warm night I witnessed upstairs.

Before I crawl under the covers, I yank the duvet off the bed and drape it over the reflective glass, convinced it was the king's silhouette I saw in it, earlier.

I'm certainly going to sleep with one eye open.

CHAPTER 6
IN PIECES

The first rule of the curse is: never take off your mask.

Even scraps of a puzzle end up making sense when you stare at them for long enough. Even a shredded soul can go on living. When you're patient.

And I've been patient for my new pets to arrive more than anything else in this life.

The sceawere's murky undercurrent clears long enough for me to spy on each of the seedlings in their new rooms.

James Robert Collier is a quiet, responsible young man. Being one of twelve boys, I'm sure he's spooked by the silence. He stares at the ceiling with the covers up to his neck, homesick though he'd never admit it. He's probably too meek to become a true hunter, but with enough studies and force of will, he could make a decent weaver.

Mara Daniels is an aimless high school student with mediocre grades and dubious taste in men. She's still up, busy prying the thick makeup off her face. I'll be surprised if she lasts a month.

The both of them will draw attention away from the real treasure. Their combined, tepid powers confirm the not-so-discrete looks and whispers the High Fae exchanged this evening. This year might be the worst one yet...if it wasn't for the third.

Penelope Emanuelle Darcy.

Eighteen years I've waited for her. The delicate and refined taste of her magic—clover sprouts and cinnamon—is still thick in my mouth. And like any devil finally presented with something he craves, I'm tempted to swallow her whole. To let her glimpse at my true nature and see a piece of the old me reflected in her lime-green gaze. But that'd be stupid. Mindless.

A seed can be crushed in one bite. It can also be planted, watered, and cared for. That way, you get a tree. Then, you can pluck its fruits or chop it down for firewood.

But a tree takes time, and I don't have a lot of time left. A tree needs sunshine, and that's the one thing I'm not good at.

Given the current state of the Shadow Court, my decision to train Penelope with the others might prove difficult to justify, but I can't let her—or anyone—know how special she truly is. I almost scrapped the idea of training her a dozen times, but if she sprouts, her magic might be strong enough to buy me a chance.

One *last* chance.

The childish old-world legends about Faerie are probably to blame for the fact that she didn't touch her plate, and she'd covered the mirror in her room with her duvet to block my line of sight. I'd only have to reach my hand out to slide it off. I almost pay her a visit to lay the duvet back upon her sleeping form. That would send a clear message, but I don't want to show my cards just yet.

A part of me is tempted to make her life hell while another yearns to see her smile.

Doubts and regrets burn my chest, and I bite the inside of my cheeks to keep my mind from wandering a dark and dangerous path. Exhausted from all the schmoozing, I remove my hooded jacket and discard my mask on the bedside table. To my surprise, it feels lighter than it has in a long time.

The black fabric shines in the night, dark and deep as the bottom of a well, and I avoid my reflection in the golden-trimmed mirror.

I don't remember what it's like to feel whole. To get up without pain twisting at the seams of my sanity. To smile without an agenda and laugh in earnest. A terrible sickness has taken root in me—and my kingdom—because I trusted the wrong woman.

That won't happen again.

I will reverse the dreadful fate she inflicted upon me and save the Shadow Court. I will not let her take my dreams—be they nightmares or fantasies—away.

Nothing will get in the way of my duty. Not even a witty, flawless beauty like Penelope Darcy.

I've got new rules.

All work, no play. No distractions. And most of all, no exceptions.

Making an exception is what got me cursed in the first place. I can't let anyone discover my secret. I've got to win that stupidly wretched bet and tear Darcy's kingdom apart, even if I have to chop her into little pieces and feast on what's left of her soul to achieve it.

CHAPTER 7

LESSON ONE

Quietness often brings a sense of peace, but it's also unnerving. I stir awake after my first night in Faerie with the absolute, definitive certainty that I did not dream. That I *could* not. The monsters that inhabit these lands do not prey on their own.

Cool silk hugs my body, the nightgown so different from the ones I'm used to. I pass my fingers through my messy waves and stifle a yawn. *Happy birthday to me.*

The duvet I placed on the mirror suddenly flies about the room, a throng of curses emanating from it, and I jolt to my feet on the bed.

"What in the name of Morpheus—" a familiar voice utters.

"Baka?" I climb down the mattress and help her wrestle free of the fabric.

She blinks up at me. "Why was yer duvet covering the mirror?"

"I was afraid," I admit.

"Bah! Ye think a duvet would stop the Shadow King if he meant to visit ye in the dead of night?"

I wince at how ridiculous it sounds. "I didn't want him to *see* me."

"Child, the Shadow King sees all."

I half-expect her to present me with more salacious dresses, but she lays down black undergarments, a tunic, and pants on my bed.

The set is similar to the hooded ensemble One wears, and I run my fingers over the clothes. "How do they sew the threads so closely together? The fabric is like nothing I've ever seen."

"It comes from the new world."

Faerie connects my world—the old world—to the new, but I know very little about this realm.

"The new world's seamstresses are very talented," I say.

Baka grins, showing her crooked blue teeth. "You could say that."

I slip into the clothes, following Baka's instructions, shocked by the sight of myself in the mirror wearing pants. The stretchy fabric molds my legs and feels way smoother than the socks we wear underneath our dresses. I run my palms over my hips and backside, the fit surprisingly snug and comfortable, and test the tunic's hood.

Baka adjusts the belt on my left hip. "Let me help with the boots." She reaches down and teaches me how to lace them up, and I quickly get the hang of it.

The knee-high boots are doubled with a thin metallic layer, and the threads holding them in place shimmer with silver accents. They cover my legs and feel comfortable, so I don't mind these new clothes as much as yesterday's dress. If unconventional, they show almost no skin.

Baka works my hair into a thick braid, the long strands tied away from my face, and passes me an over-the-shoulder bag. "I packed a breakfast for you."

My stomach grumbles. I haven't eaten Fae food yet because of Father's advice, but I'm famished. I rummage through the bag, find a perfectly benign apple, and sink my teeth into its soft flesh. The juicy piece of fruit melts on my tongue, and I swallow the fruit down in six or seven bites.

A shadow appears in the mirror, but this time, it thickens into solid form before One steps out of the glass. "Good. You're ready."

I wet my lips, trying to adjust to the fact that he can walk in and out of my bedroom at will and discard the apple core discreetly into the trash. "What are we going to do?"

"You'll see."

The mischievous edge of his voice riddles me with adrenaline.

One leads me through the door and into the tunnels. *He wouldn't look so calm if he planned to torture me, would he?*

I can't keep all the anxiety inside and blurt out, "Are you going to hurt me?"

He stops cold at that, but he doesn't meet my gaze, merely staring at the path ahead. "Why would I want to hurt you, kitten?"

There he goes again, answering my question with a question. "Because you're Fae."

Both fists balled at his sides, he starts walking again. "Is that all?"

I pick up the pace to keep up with his long strides. "If the question makes you so mad, why don't you just say *no?*"

"I've been nothing but *polite*—" The word is heavy with meaning, full of fire and disappointment. A hot line of shame tickles along my spine before he finally spins around to face me. "Look. I won't pretend my world is always pleasant. It's dangerous and unforgiving, but I plan to train you, not hurt you. Okay?"

The answer soothes the ache between my ribs. "Okay."

He's holding his answers close and his secrets closer. A small voice in my head urges patience. If I'm being tricked, I'll know soon enough. No need to kick and scream just yet.

We reach the last bend in the tunnel and cross through the door to the outside. The humidity is still jarring, the air not as heavy as it was last night, but probably building toward a scorching afternoon given the early hours. A small winding path along the walls of the castle offers glimpses of the interior courtyard, but tall green hedges obstruct the view.

Star-shaped blooms run along the covered porch. The series of umbrella-like clusters sag away from thin, leafless stems, hanging a few inches above our heads. Absolutely gorgeous. At the end of the small path, we emerge inside an open-air war room.

Mesh walls with diamond patterns open to a towering row of bushes on each side of the square-shaped training ground, their branches laden with lush foliage. The set-up offers seclusion and privacy from the outside world—and no doubt a respite from the hot, humid day. The sun sneaks past the vegetation in a few golden spots, casting shadows upon the sleek gray floors.

Weapons of different shapes and sizes hang on the wall closest to us, and a door-shaped mirror with round edges on its upper end is set in the stones next to it. So far, almost every room in the castle has direct access to the sceawere.

A blue, cylinder-shaped bag half my size hangs from the ceiling on the opposite side of the room. Various mannequins and targets pepper the space. The wooden back wall is painted with red and blue concentric circles, at least fifty yards away from where we're standing.

One picks a crossbow from the bunch. "The Shadow Court is in charge of nightmares, dreams, and fantasies." He aims at one of the targets on the opposite wall, and the metallic bolt lands straight in the center of the bullseye. "Nightmares sometimes take on a life of their own, and it's my job—along with the other hunters—to keep them in line."

I peruse the assorted weapons. "You hunt...nightmares?"

"Yes. I'm in charge of the rogue nightmares, and Two keeps the Dreaming's magic from fading."

"And Three?" I ask quickly. "The red-faced Lord mentioned him at dinner."

One rolls his shoulders back, the crossbow falling to his side. "Three weaves fantasies. They're more...volatile."

"Why are fantasies more *volatile*?" I ask, imitating his ominous tone. Not waiting for his answer, I lift a jeweled sword and wince at the weight, quickly returning it to its holder.

Knights always make it seem so easy during tournaments...

"Fantasies are the dreams that overcome you when you're awake. They lurk at the edge of the mortals' subconscious and influence both dreams and nightmares."

A chill tightens the skin at the nape of my neck. "If you guys are in charge of it all, what does the king do?"

A dark cloud pulses around him, his lips pressing together for a fleeting moment. "The king rules over the entire kingdom."

Sounds like the king doesn't lift a finger around here.

Hands linked behind my back, I skip closer to One. "And why do you wear a mask?"

The stiffness in his spine eases, and a touch of warmth returns to his voice. "You want to see my face, kitten?"

Yes. If I could see his eyes, I'd know whether I could trust him or not.

He rubs the narrow path between the obsidian mask and the edge of his hood, allowing me a glimpse of his ear. "The mask protects our magic. It needs to be worn at all times in the sceawere."

I arch a playful brow, the answer more of a diversion than a true explanation. "We're in Faerie, now."

The corners of his mouth curl up. "Even if I wanted to remove my mask in your presence, I wouldn't. As long as you don't have the Faerie sight, it would be too dangerous."

"How does a mortal get the Faerie sight?" I dead-pan.

"You'll be tested, and if we both do our jobs correctly, you'll pass. The king will grant you the Faerie sight, then."

I think back to his earlier phrasing. "So you plan to train me, not hurt me, but you can't promise I won't get hurt."

"This is real life, kitten. Anyone who promises you'd never get hurt is lying—or plans to lock you in a tower." He leans closer, and my confidence waivers. "The king agreed to work your training around your schedule, but every seedling has to put in the effort."

I hate how the bite of his magic already feels familiar. But the shape of him—tall and muscular, cut from a block of moving shadows—I'll never get used to.

"And if I don't?"

His lips press together in a grim line. "I think you already know the answer to that. Anyone can be broken, but the Shadow King would break you quickest of all. If you made trouble."

Anyone can be broken... A bitter-sweet edge glazes the words, and I get the feeling he's talking from experience.

Eyes cast down, I play with the end of my thick braid. "What do you know of the bet my father made with the king?"

"Only the king and your father know the exact terms of the deal. I'm supposed to train you so that you can be initiated in our way of life."

"Train me how, exactly?"

He tips his chin to the crossbow and hooks a metal lever to the front. "Since you've never trained with weapons before, a crossbow is a good place to start. You use the lever to push the string back." He acts out his instructions. "With the nut in the open position, you only have to use a bit of force to span it."

My curiosity is dampened by the reminder that I'm not here of my own free will, but still...my fingers itch to touch the sleek, silvery bolt.

I sink my nails into my palms not to reach for it. "In Demeter, women aren't allowed to train with bows."

One smiles and hands over the loaded weapon. "As you so graciously pointed out, we're in Faerie, now."

I pick it up slowly, like I'm reluctant to touch it at all. I can't let my excitement show. "Teaching me how to use deadly weapons is a stupid strategy on your king's part."

"Are you planning to shoot me, kitten?" he asks, apparently delighted by the threat.

"Mm. Not for now." It's heavier than expected, almost as heavy as the sword, and I swallow hard. "These bolts are different from the ones my father uses."

"They're made to hunt nightmares, not venison. Now, aim at the target."

A thrill shoots up my spine as I rise the crossbow toward the closest blue and red circles. I've seen men do this many times. Seems simple enough.

I squeeze the trigger, and the power of the shot amazes me. The bolt buries inside a hay dummy 25 yards to our left, eons away from where I intended it to go.

Lips curled down, I expect One to make fun of me, but he hands me another bolt and the lever and waits for me to reload it myself. Like a real teacher would. And he's patient, too.

I struggle for a second, my muscles screaming in protest, but quickly raise the loaded crossbow at the target again.

"Good. Now, use your powers," One says. "Feel the weapon in your hands. Concentrate on the string. Feel the tension there, ready to be released upon your command." He grazes the string with his middle and index fingers.

Goosebumps scatter on my neck, his breath hot on the shell of my ear, and I shake out the urge to look at him, concentrating on his instructions instead.

"The bolt is power. The string is a way for you to control that power. Humans practice this art for years, but we get to cheat our way to a perfect aim. Harness the energy in the string and concentrate on where you want the bolt to go."

Distracted by his proximity, I press the trigger again. The bolt shoots to the edge of the intended target, and magic buzzes at my fingertips.

A masculine chuckle chimes in the space between us. "You've used your powers before."

I bite the inside of my cheeks to mask my giddiness. I should *not* be enjoying myself. "Why am I here? Really. Why does the Shadow King want me?" I ask, reloading the weapon.

One straightens my aim, his arm flush against mine. "The king needs you here because the magic running in your veins means power for the kingdom."

Maybe a quick chat about personal space would do us both good. The heat of his body is dizzying, the scent of campfire and ripe pears raising all the hairs on my neck to attention.

A tiny half-moon scar is visible under his chin, and I stare at it for a moment. "If all he wants is my magic, why doesn't he just take it?"

My dark teacher pauses for a long, long time. "Maybe he will, but he'd prefer for it to grow as you serve the realm." His quiet tone brims with something sweeter than foreboding. More like...hope.

A chill tightens the skin at the base of my neck as I let the bolt fly. It lands slightly closer to the center, but my arms are simply too sore to fire another.

One retrieves the crossbow and hangs it back on the wall. "You can practice in this gym anytime you want. Hand-to-hand combat will be the real challenge, but you're not ready—you need weeks of physical training to prepare for that. I'll also teach you how to blend in with the shadows—"

"I've been avoiding the guards back home for months. Blending with the shadows isn't *that* hard." My mind catches up with my boastful claim, and my cheeks flush.

Where the crops did that come from?

One tucks his tongue beneath his canine, his jaw slightly askew. "You're a surprising student, Miss Darcy." He looks as if he's about to add something, but he just spins around and waves for me to follow.

You don't have to impress him, remember? He's a man, but he's not a diplomat, a guest, or a suitor. He's still your captor.

We leave the *gym* through the sliding door in the target wall and march under a set of latticed archways past another green hedge until we reach a wide trail. A series of balconies similar to the one I saw last night run along the stone building. Some of them encompass a single room, while others run along the curves of the castle.

A tall Hawthorn tree towers in the middle of the gigantic interior courtyard, and my heart booms in my chest. "Wait. Where are we?"

"The king's sacred gardens. The castle's interior courtyard is completely isolated from the rest of the Shadowlands. You'd have to run for fifteen minutes in that direction before you'd reach its limits. The trails circle back after that."

That's...big.

"I've been here before. In a dream." My voice shakes with a mix of anguish and joy.

He shakes his head. "Mortals do not dream of Faerie. The threads of the Dreaming don't allow it. You must be thinking of a different tree."

He's not lying, but he's wrong. Another loophole to the "Fae can't lie" rule. If a Fae believes he's saying the truth, he can spread false information. This Hawthorn tree is an exact replica of the one I saw in my dreams, and while it's similar to the scriptures' sacred tree, it's different enough for me to be sure.

"In Demeter, we have a sacred tree too," I explain. "It's in Gaia's temple, but it's not half as big or beautiful as this one—" I force my mouth shut.

I'd love to let him know exactly how wrong he is, given how many times I've dreamt of this lovely tree, but it's smarter to keep a few secrets to myself. If I'm not supposed to dream of Faerie, maybe it means something.

One motions to the smooth rock path. "You will run in the gardens for half an hour, four times a day—morning, midday, evening and night—until you can do so without fatigue."

His strange command pulls me out of my fascination for the Hawthorn. "Why?"

"To get in shape. I will teach you how to use the punching bag and lift weights. The bibliotheca will be open from noon till midnight, if you want to check out some books. Since you're meant to accompany me to the new world to hunt nightmares, you not only need some muscle, but some inkling of what awaits you there, sheltered as you were in Demeter," he says matter-of-factly, his contempt for my country plain as day.

"I don't appreciate your tone, and I'll have you know that I'm in *excellent* shape," I clip.

"Bah! Maybe by your standards, but you have no idea what the real world is like."

His wry smile irks my temper, and I cross my arms. "I know quite enough, thank you."

"Don't lie to me, kitten. Even from behind this mask, I see your rosy cheeks and hear your quickened heartbeats. The uniform fits you like a glove, and you stand an inch taller in it than you did yesterday in your old-fashioned dress. You're curious." He buries his hands in the pockets of his jacket. "If you have to stay here, you might as well learn something useful."

To my horror, he's right. If I need to play by his rules, then I might as well learn as much as I can. It's not like getting in better shape will make me lose the bet.

If only I knew the exact terms...

Mara runs in our direction, wearing only a camisole and *lycra shorts*—as Baka called the strange undergarments. She slows down as she draws near and eyes me over. "It's hot as hell. Aren't you sweaty in that?"

My gaze flicks to the ground between us. "I'm alright."

I am a little hot, but the way Mara stands there without an ounce of shame floors me.

One gestures to the second-floor balcony towering behind us. "This is a common area for all trainees. You can grab a bite to eat up there at any hour, and the bibliotheca is right through these doors." He points to the gold-plated double doors under the balcony.

A man stalks out of the shade of the common area and curls his hands around the railing. "Mara," he calls out.

The redhead waves goodbye. "I'm late. I'll see you later."

The newcomer's mask is made of shattered glass, and my heart hammers.

"That's..." I trail off, shocked.

"Two."

Blood races at my temples. "He's—"

"Identical? Not precisely." One offers his brother a curt nod, his bottom lip tucked between his teeth.

As *precisely* as I can tell, the newcomer is an exact copy of the man by my side, though I have only his body type, mouth, and chin to compare. *A swimmer's body*, Mara called it, though I'm not sure how that expression equates to *appealing*.

But it does. No question about it.

The shattered glass on his mask reflects the bright sun and blinds me for a second. My entire being quakes under his scrutiny, his predatory stance curdling my blood, but he quickly slips back inside the building.

CHAPTER 8
ALL THE WAY

The next day, I awaken from a slumber so deep, I might as well have flirted with death. It pains me to admit, but One was right. I'm not *in shape*. I ran my heart out yesterday morning, midday, and evening, and crashed in bed early, the stress and exhaustion of my first day in Faerie catching up to my body. Nothing bad had happened, and yet I tremble at the thought of doing it all over again today, my calves and hamstrings riddled with pain.

"Good morning, Nell," Baka greets me from the foot of the bed.

I stretch out my sore arms and crack my neck. "Good morning."

A fresh uniform lies on the duvet, but Baka points to the back of the room. "I took the liberty of drawing you a fresh, hot bath."

My heart sings at the prospect. "I love you."

She giggles at my outburst. "Come on now, princess. Let's soothe yer sore muscles. Stretch first, then the bathtub. I added a few of my special herbs to the water to get ye ready for the day." She teaches me a few stretching exercises that turn my cramped muscles into a slightly more supple mass.

After we're done, I sink inside the tub with a low hum. The water is smooth and velvety, like I'm sinking into a tub of heated honey—but without the stickiness.

Baka starts brushing my long mane. "It's so long. Doesn't it get in the way? Do you want me to cut it?"

I purse my lips, considering her question. No other woman here wears her hair quite as long as me, but I'm torn. "A princess is expected to never cut her hair."

"In Demeter, maybe. But not here."

"I like it as it is, but thank you."

The discussion does bring me back to my first night, and Mara's ambiguous comment. Water sloshes around me as I shift to look at Baka. "Why did Mara say that I had *bleached* hair? What does it mean?"

The sprite snorts. "She's ignorant is all. Ye have what they call platinum blonde hair, and in the new world, women use a product called *bleach* to achieve that look."

"Oh." I frown at her answer, unsure why anyone would want to change the color of their hair. I relax in the water, pondering the differences between the old world and the new.

After the bath, Baka sends me on my way. The layout of the tunnels and stairs that lead to the palace's ground floor is starting to make sense, and I quickly reach the long trail that weaves in and out of the gardens. Still too sore to run, I keep a brisk pace and walk a full loop.

Near the end of the path, a low buzzing sound captures my attention. Small black birds whistle and cackle in the small fountain near the arched trellis, and I inch closer to take a better look. The wings of the creatures are thin and papery, with matching ears. Oblivious to my presence, they frolic in the water.

Not birds... They've got long, pointy noses, and a few of them hold small flowers to their mouth like big jugs of nectar. And they're all naked.

A storm of joyous gargles, round buttocks, and tiny, hairy armpits splash around in the water, and I crack a smile. Suddenly, one of them squeaks in warning, and the flock of creatures scatters in the wind—all but one.

The black imp flies right in front of my face, and I draw back, spooked. Before I can escape, he tilts his chin up with haughty glare and slaps my nose.

The brief contact stings, and my cheeks burn at the evident reproach. "Whoa, sorry."

An indignant *hmph* echoes through the trees as the creature flies off in a blur of smoke.

What the...

I take cover under the balcony to regroup. I can't forget where I am, not for a minute. Faerie is full of dangers—and little bats that take their privacy seriously. Guilt for ogling the imps' bath routine mixes with an unfathomable sense of wonder in my blood.

Feeling a little foolish, I rub down my sore nose and climb the steep staircase to the second floor.

Where is everybody?

Long metal railings open to the glory of the royal gardens, and the unobstructed view of the Hawthorn steals my breath. Its thick green canopy filters the rays of the Fae sun, and teal moss cascades down its white branches. A few strands tumble close enough to the banister for me to reach for it.

Faerie can't be as bad as Father wants me to believe if it houses something so beautiful.

My dark teacher and fellow seedlings are nowhere to be found, so I grab a quick bite to eat. The table in the middle of the balcony offers a wide array of choices like fruits, pastries, water, juices, and coffee. Seamless mirrors line the exterior walls, reflecting the gardens back to me, the scenery endless and ethereal.

I sample a few known breakfast items and nibble on a pulpous, sweet and sour yellow piece of fruit. The peace and quiet, along with the beauty of the gardens, ease my homesickness.

The sun is at its zenith in the sky when I finally decide to check out the bibliotheca One talked about. Behind the golden-plated doors, stacks and stacks of books stretch three stories high above my head. A dozen working tables and chairs are set in regular intervals on the ground floor, and light filters through the stained glass windows.

A beautiful round medallion window shines above the others. The multi-faceted masterpiece depicts the Hawthorn's branches and roots and bathes the room in yellow, red, and teal hues.

"Hi, welcome." The tall woman behind the librarian desk waves me over.

I tiptoe closer to her, my jaw slack at the bounty of books in this impressive library. "Hello."

Unlike Mara, this woman wears a loose black shirt and faded-blue pants, a very masculine look that hides her curves. Her raven-black hair is tied in a plain ponytail at the back of her head and contrasts nicely with her light brown skin.

The clear shade of her gray eyes reminds me of a pleasant, rainy summer day. "You're the seedling from the old world, aren't you? Mara told me about you," she says.

"Yes. I'm from Demeter."

Her jaw hangs open at the news, and she eyes me up and down. "Aren't you like...super religious?"

I stare at her until she blushes.

"I'm *so* sorry. That was rude. I'm Lori. I'm a sprout." She extends her hand, but I'm not quite sure what she wants me to do with it.

Only the strongest seeds will sprout.

"So you were..."

She lets her hand fall to her side. "A seed, yes. There are four stages of training. Seeds, Sprouts, Sepals, and Stigmas. Seedlings are seeds that haven't taken their vows yet."

"Botany for the morally challenged," I mumble.

"Sorry?" Lori asks, her hand flying to the criss-cross ear cuffs covering the roundness of her ear.

"Demeter citizens worship Gaia, the Mother of all life. Botanical terms are usually reserved for the study of her sacred plants," I explain.

Esme gave me lessons about different religions and different gods, but it's still jarring to meet people who have no idea who our Mother is and what she stands for. Despite Lori's assumptions, I'm not half as religious as I should be. If Gaia was really as just and benevolent as my father implies, I wouldn't be stuck here.

"So seeds, sprouts..."

"Sepals and stigmas," she repeats patiently before pointing to my face. "Did you get slapped by a Nyx?"

I reach out to graze the tip of my nose. "Oh, yeah."

"Pesky little devils. Don't worry, the red mark will fade in about a day."

"Good to know." I lean on the desk, trying to contain the storm brewing in my chest. "Are there other...creatures I should be wary of?"

"Nope. The castle is pretty much empty. The other hunters are all away on assignments, and the weavers live in the new world. There are sixteen of us in total. Long before my time, I heard there were *dozens*, but—" Her gaze falls to the ground.

"Go on."

"I shouldn't. Not until you've taken your vows."

My heart beats faster in my chest. This woman isn't new to this world, and yet she's not Fae, and so far I get nothing but good vibes from her. Maybe she's my only chance to get real answers about what the king plans to do with me.

"Vows? What do they entail?" I ask wistfully.

Vows of chastity are spoken by Gaia's priests and priestesses. Vows of obedience must be sworn in marriage. But I don't think Lori means either of those types of vows.

"I can't speak about the specifics. It's an initiation thing. You can never know what's coming. Only... Don't expect to make it all the way through the ranks. There's only been one new Sepal in the last few years, and there hasn't been a Stigma in *decades*."

Don't expect to make it all the way...

My breath stutters. "What happens to the people who don't make it all the way?"

"Sorry. I don't know the details, and even if I did..." she trails off with a wince.

"You couldn't say. Got it." I rub my nails along a crack in the wood of her desk, searching for a more innocuous question. "Where is One?"

The stiffness in her spine eases. "I haven't seen him since lunch yesterday, so he's probably off-world, leading the great hunt."

"Huh?"

A grin spreads across her face. "Great hunts increase the magic of the realm, but they are incredibly dangerous. You'll be lucky to catch a glimpse of One before your first trial. Sucks for you that you got nightmares first. I got dreams, and Two *craves* his pupils' attention."

I blink away my surprise—and disappointment. I should be relieved, really, but I'm just confused. "What the crops am I doing here if the king and my mentor are nowhere to be found?"

Am I really expected to train, or is it just a ruse? So far, all my preconceptions about Faerie or my place here were misconstrued... I don't know what to think anymore.

Lori's face creases in either confusion or commiseration, or a mix of both. "Things get quite busy for Faerie folks before St-John's Eve. One should be more available after the solstice."

"St-John's Eve is a Fae holiday, right?" I ask.

She gives me a sharp nod. "The Fae Summer celebration. Each Fae *holiday*"—she mimes air quotes with her hands—"brings the monarchs together for a ritual that ensures the survival of the realm. You should read about the Faerie seasons and rejuvenation of its magic. Foghar comes after summer and brings in the best food. And you'll want to learn as much as you can about Morheim, the Shadow Court's hunt. The hunters who do well there get to prove their worth, so to speak."

She peruses the cart behind her. "And you won't get into runes before you've completed the first trial, but it can't hurt to learn the basics. Some of those suckers are so damn similar." Her dislike for the "runes" is obvious despite the few odd words she used to describe them.

"How long have you lived here, in Faerie?" I ask.

I watch her open face for tells, but she exudes nothing but joy and confidence as she answers, "Fiona, Mitch, and I were all seeds last year." Her eyes dim. "The other three girls that arrived along with us didn't sprout."

I want to ask more, want to know what happened to the seeds that didn't sprout and get to the bottom of it all, but relationships need time, and confidences are earned. Lori has already told me a ton, and judging by her bubbly personality, probably more than she should have.

"Thanks for the insight." I scout the rows and rows of books with a pang of longing, my mind struggling to keep the Faerie seasons straight. "Since I'm here...do you have specific books to recommend?"

CHAPTER 9
SEVEN SEASONS

Later that night, I find James eating alone on the balcony. He motions for me to join him, and I scoot over to his table with a meat and cheese plate in one hand and a loaf of bread in the other. "Hi."

He lays down his utensils beside his half-eaten meal. "Hi."

I scout the rest of the balcony, but we're alone. It's a bit unnerving still to be eating, unchaperoned, with any man, but James' energy puts me at ease. "Where is Mara?"

"I don't know."

Mara sets me on edge. For all I know, they're both working for the king. I watch James' calm face for a moment, and the silence stretches into awkwardness.

"How did you end up here, Nell? I thought that people from the old world despised the Fae," he finally asks, his gaze fixed on the tablecloth, not meeting mine. "Are you here...you know...of your own free will?

The word *despised* sparks an itch between my eyes. "Why? Are *you* here against your will?" I keep my voice low not to let my cards show quite yet.

"Not exactly. I'm scared, to be honest, but I chose to come. Magic in my world is considered by most not to exist, so I didn't quite fit in. I've been pegged as a freak my whole life, and I wanted to learn…"

He looks sincere enough for me to relax. "Magic is very important in my realm, but it usually comes from our goddess' grace, reserved for her most devoted servants. Not from…sin."

A flicker of understanding shines on his somber face. "I'm religious, too, though I suspect not as much as you are. In the new world, spirituality sort of took a backseat to everyday life. For most people, anyway."

A current of energy ripples through the air, and goosebumps rise the skin at the back of my neck. Like a moth to a flame, my mortal gaze flicks to the dark and familiar silhouette heading straight for us.

Three…

My hunch that he was identical to his brothers is confirmed, and I swallow hard. Twins were creepy enough…but *three* identical men? That's a first.

One looks deadly, and Two seems cruel, but Three… Three moves like the villains in fairy tales—elegant and charismatic, yet dangerous. An iridescent mask covers everything but his mouth. Bewitching colors and patterns move with him, swirling into different shapes with every step.

He doesn't breathe a word as he immobilizes next to me, about five inches too close for comfort. A hot flush blooms on my cheeks, and I feel like he can not only see *through* his mask, but past my very skin into my most private desires.

He kisses the back of my offered hand with a secret smile that tells me all my hopes and dreams are his for the taking. *By the Mother… When did I even raise my hand towards him?*

After a few too many breaths, he draws back and turns his attention back on James, angling his chin to the side. *Come,* he seems to say.

"See you later, Nell." James waves goodbye and follows his alluring tutor down the stairs.

"Goodbye." I rub a sudden chill off my arms, wishing I could go with them.

Three's treacherous bite of power tingles along the sensitive skin of my neck for hours after he's gone, and I'm left all flustered, daydreaming about when I will see him next.

A FEW DAYS PASS WITHOUT ME CATCHING A GLIMPSE OF ONE, SO I FIGURE the dark Fae must not be very invested in my training. I feel slighted at first, then relieved—then slighted again.

Reading for hours on end, running, lifting weights, and shooting random targets with a crossbow, isn't what I pictured when Mother told me I would have to suffer the whims of the Shadow King and live in Faerie.

In the mornings, Mara, James, Lori, and I mostly train in the gardens. When the weather gets too hot, we grab breakfast—which is more like a lunch in Faerie—and take our studies inside, to the library or the gym.

Every day, Mara and James disappear with their mentors for a couple of hours, and Lori tends to the library from noon to midnight. Since I spend so much time among the stacks, we quickly develop a comfortable camaraderie, but she remains tight-lipped about the trials and the details of her past—so tight-lipped that I suspect someone chastised her after our first meeting.

The afternoon is well-advanced on the fifth day when I snap "America, A Quick Overview" shut and mark it as finished in my notebook. Feeling restless, I bite my lips, eager to learn more about Faerie, and peruse the catalogs again, but my choices are limited.

I only have access to a small part of the library since most stacks on the first floor are reserved for seeds that have spoken their vows.

The entire second floor is meant for sprouts, and the third is separated into two sections between sepals and stigmas.

Jealousy and longing pulse in my chest. The forbidden books remind me of the restricted section in my father's library—most of it reserved only for men.

An intriguing history volume titled "Damian the Dauntless: The Rise of Our Dark Sovereign" is marked in the ledger as the go-to book for information about the Shadow King.

Lori is helping a High Fae find a specific poem for a woman he's courting at the very back of the room, and I tip-toe closer to them to make sure they're still in the thick of it.

By the desperate look on the sprout's face, their search is a long way from finished. *Perfect.*

I grip the oak banister and crouch to sneak upstairs. About halfway to the second floor, a treacherous step creaks under my weight, and I hurry to the second floor landing. The filing system is easy to follow, but sweat beads on my forehead when I find the thin, black spine of the book I plan to poach.

I hook my index finger over the trim and pull, but the book remains resolutely stuck in place, like a spell prevents me from sliding it out of the stack.

With a frown, I tug on it harder and zap it with a flare of shadow magic, but it stays put. *Of course. No wonder Lori was so serene when she explained the rules.*

While she tends to the needs of the occasional High Fae customer, her presence is not *needed* to guard the books—nor would it be sufficient.

Crestfallen, I hurry back downstairs and turn to my second-best choice, "Seven Seasons, Eight Eternities," and start to read. By the time my new friend returns to our shared reading nook, I'm the perfect picture of good behavior.

As dangerous as it is to lose myself for hours in Fae literature...it's also wonderful.

The Faerie seasons last for one to eight weeks each and include different rituals that rejuvenate the land's magic. Each court and kingdom are responsible for one of those seasonal ceremonies, and the courts themselves are divided into light and dark.

Alaveen, the festival of the Sun Court, is held at the beginning of the Fae year. Lanterns are released to the sky as a way to honor the Fae's deceased loved ones—a lovely tradition.

The Spring Court celebrates the thaw of winter. Love is in the air, married couples renew their unions, and the entire season sees an increase in fertility for Fae women.

St-John's Eve takes place in the Summerlands during the solstice, but I can't find any details about it.

The harvest season is called Foghar, and big parties are thrown with all matters of excess.

Morheim signals the triumph of shadows over light, and the days grow shorter in autumn until the sun doesn't rise in the Fae sky for seven to ten days.

Yule celebrates the winter solstice. It comes with a pageant during which the Winter King chooses a wife. He marries a new bride every year. *Yikes!*

The year ends with Scebaan, a mysterious ball hosted by the Storm Court.

So many exotic customs and intriguing details keep me awake until the wee hours of the night, my curiosity only growing as I uncover more details about these magical, eerie lands.

CHAPTER 10

ONE, TWO, THREE...

Another week passes, but the upper floors remain dark and untouched. A few demanding customers keep Lori busy for most of the evening of my eleventh day in Faerie.

A few minutes before midnight, she yawns on her way over to my table and slumps onto the chair across from mine. "God, I swear, most of the High Fae are more interested in you than the books."

I arch a brow and peer at her over my latest read. "Hm?"

"Someone apparently shared with them that you're from the old world, and now you're officially an object of curiosity."

"Now that you mention it, a few ladies did stop by my table today to exchange pleasantries—"

Lori rolls her eyes. "Oof, they're relentless. Don't give them anything, or we'll be *swarmed* before too long. Sure, they're always eager to spy on the new seeds, but an old world seedling is a *big* novelty."

My voice rises a few octaves. "Don't they have, I don't know... better things to do?"

The thought that they should be curious enough about me to alter their schedules feels laughable.

Lori stands and switches off the lights with a wave of her hand, only leaving on the glowing orange sphere over the librarian desk. "Don't worry, Nell. Between the two of us, we can unravel their little scheme. We'll play dumb and give nothing away, and within a month, it'll blow over. You'll see."

After she locks the main entrance, she heads directly for the tunnels. "Good night."

"Good night."

Lori doesn't raise an eyebrow or ask questions when I leave in the opposite direction, and the scope of my newfound autonomy washes through me once more. I thought I was coming to Faerie to be a prisoner, and yet I've never felt so free.

I can eat what I want and go to bed whenever I please.

Moonlight bathes the gardens, and the teal moss covering the Hawthorn is fluorescent under its silvery rays. The air is warm and still, filled with sweet hints of dew and honeysuckle.

Breathing in the beauty of the night, I climb the stairs to the balcony to grab an apple from the evergreen buffet. I'm a little hungry after my evening in the library, and I love to gaze down at the empty gardens at this hour.

It's the middle of the night, and I'm wandering the halls of a Fae castle with no escort...

My heart skips a beat when I spot One sitting alone at a table. The moon reflects off the white claw marks scarring his mask. His back is hunched as he eats, the slouch so different from his usual posture that I pause.

Is it really him? He looks so...beaten down.

I clear my throat loudly to make my presence known, and his fists clench for a moment, but he quickly melts back to his earlier posture.

I rush over to him with a verve that surprises me. "You're back."

He doesn't answer or glance up from his food, but his shadowy aura thickens around him like a thundercloud.

A torrent of questions threatens to pour out of me as I slide into the seat in front of him and suppress the anger in my voice. "Why am I the only one left to her own devices? The others have lessons with your brothers almost every day, but you just left without so much as an explanation."

He leans back in his chair. "I figured I'd leave you a bit of space to acclimate. And you needed to put on a bit of muscle first. I didn't want you to faint at the first sight of a nightmare."

"Oh." To be honest, he's the one who looks about to faint right now, not me. "You look like you're carrying the weight of the world on your shoulders..."

He reaches for his wine glass and takes a careful sip. "Is it that obvious?"

I offer him a compassionate smile and wait for him to elaborate.

"There's so much to do. So little time to do it." He gulps down another mouthful of wine. "Nightmares need hunting, hunters need guidance, and seedlings come last, I'm afraid."

It's not exactly an apology, but I appreciate the sentiment.

"Is it because of the summer celebration? Lori told me that it gets quite busy for you around holidays."

"*Holiday* is certainly a misleading word for it." A dark chuckle escapes him before his voice rises a little. "I'm not decking the halls or carving pumpkins, I'm trying to save *lives*. Trying to keep the world as we know it from fucking *ending*."

"Can I do anything to help?"

He opens his mouth to speak but ends up biting his bottom lip instead, and the silence stretches on.

The slight hitch in his breath brings goosebumps to my neck. "Have I said the wrong thing?" I ask.

"Not at all. You're the first person to ask me if I need help since... forever, really. I don't usually share the weight of my workload with anyone." He rubs the top of his mask. "There's just something about you..."

The pressure of his unseen gaze is almost too intense for me to bear at this point, and I try to think of something to defuse the tension, but he beats me to it with an awkward cough.

"You spent a lot of time with Lori while I was away?" he says.

I blink one too many times, still wrecked by his blunt admission. "Lori's great."

He leans forward, the strange energy dissipating. "I agree. Don't tell her, because it'll go straight to her head, but she's my favorite hunter." With an elusive grin, he lifts a thick piece of meat from his plate and brings it to his mouth.

"Really? How did she manage that?" I ask in jest, my eyes never leaving his mask, yearning to see what lies underneath.

For whatever reason, I crave his attention. Maybe denying me a mentor was meant to spark this weird, misplaced feeling inside of me, and if so, well played. Reverse psychology works.

One chews slowly at my obvious flirtation, his fork suddenly hesitant to grab the next bite, and a faint, high-pitched chime tinkles through the gardens.

We both turn toward the source of the eerie noise, the air now several degrees colder. An unnatural breeze blows through the thick vegetation, the leaves of the Hawthorn in a twist, revealing their silvery underside.

One's fork bumps the rim of his plate with a loud *clink,* and he stands abruptly, tossing his napkin over his unfinished meal.

My brows pull together. *Something's not right.*

I jump to my feet and search the gardens. "What's happening?"

Two marches out of the building and grips the railing, staring out at the Hawthorn. The broken glass shards on his mask gleam in the moonlight. Three runs out of the gym one story below and looks up at his brothers, his iridescent mask all black.

It's the first time I've seen the three of them together in one place, and the pulse of their combined power is palpable. It ripples through the air, and goosebumps brand my flesh from the top of my head to the very tip of my toes.

The delicate chime thickens still, and clouds drape the entire balcony in shadows. A slender white silhouette moves in the dark, quick and tall, and a quiet but unmistakable laugh pierces the night. Not the kind of laugh you share with friends, but a laugh that ices the soul.

Two's gaze darts in One's direction. "He got out."

Darkness pulses around One's body at the news, my companion now seemingly inches taller than he was before. Both men look intently at each other like they're having a silent conversation, and without another word, Two jumps over the railing.

One grips my wrist and hauls me toward the wall of mirrors at the back of the balcony. "Come. I'm taking you home."

My body obeys of its own volition, quite literally bewitched by his command. Once we reach the glass, One yanks my hood over my eyes and whisks me up in his arms, his strong grip not giving me an inch to spare. "Hang on tight, kitten."

The hard planes of his torso are even more unnerving than they were the first time he spirited me out of Demeter, but it's the obvious fear in his voice that terrifies me.

The sting of the frosty glass chafes my skin, and sweat gathers on my palms as we pierce the veil between worlds.

When One had fetched me from the royal summer house, he'd guided me through a rusty dungeon, so I'm surprised to find a polished, golden-trimmed mirror in the middle of a well-kept room on the other side of the sceaware today.

He sets me down, and my own will drips back into place.

I shake out the leftover tingles in my arms and legs. "Where are we? What just happened?" I ask.

The force of his magic is a huge wake-up call. *Every inch of me could be under his command at any time, if he so desired...*

One straightens his sleeves and jacket. "We're in Lundan. Beneath your father's castle." He thoroughly ignores the other half of my question, and I squint at him, torn between the urge to ask again and the certainty that he won't answer.

"Father would never keep a mirror here," I say instead.

A sarcastic snort pops out of his mouth. "Believe me, he would."

"But it's only been twelve days. Isn't it supposed to be two weeks out of four?"

"This arrangement is fluid, kitten. The king is the ultimate judge of the schedule."

I cross my arms over my chest and dig the balls of my feet into the ground. "I thought you didn't know the specifics of the bet."

"I know the basics," he snaps back.

Our chests rise and fall as we stare at each other, and I wish I had a mask to cover my emotions, too. "Who's out? What do *you* fear so much? Is it a nightmare?"

He growls in response and escorts me to the small interior courtyard with his lips curled down.

The gloom of midnight rain hangs in the air, the secluded garden morose in autumn compared to the luscious, colorful vegetation of the countryside—and downright ridiculous compared to the beauty of Faerie.

The summer house is much more cozy and fun. The Lundan castle is just not the same. I glance down at my black pants, knowing no one, especially Father, should see me in them. It's the middle of the night, and everyone but the guards are asleep. I should be able to slip past them no problem, my magic more powerful than it was before I left.

"Be safe, kitten." One angles his chin to my bedroom window, and I follow his gaze.

"Wait... How do you know which room is mine? Have you been here before?"

"Yes," he declares confidently.

I cross my arms over my chest. "When?"

"A few months ago. I was curious to see what you looked like," he admits softly.

My stomach flip flops, and even though I ought to be spooked or angry, the heat in my gut tells a different story. "You're creepy. You know that, right?" I say in jest.

A small smile tugs at his lips. "Don't lie. Given the chance, you would have done the same." His masked stare bears into me for a second before he shimmers in a shadow so deep, I lose sight of him.

"Goodbye, then... Be safe, too," I mumble to the empty space beside me, crestfallen to see him leave so quickly.

He's out... Who were they talking about? What could have made that inhuman sound?

Tiny shadow needles prickle my spine as I make my way inside the castle, past the unsuspecting guards, and reach my bedroom door. The rattling sound of the locked doorknob sends a burst of adrenaline through my body.

Esme locked my bedroom. She probably expects me to report to her as soon as I return, but I inch open the hallway window instead. The narrow ledge that runs around the entire building is wide enough to hold my weight, so I boost myself up and climb outside. If I was wearing my usual corset and dress, I'd never manage to balance myself on the ledge all the way to my bedroom window, but the slick Faerie uniform and boots do not get entangled in the vines or weigh me down.

I glide quietly along the wall, inch open my bedroom window— I'd broken the lock last year and kept it a secret—and jump inside. I've always wondered what would happen if I slipped out at night, unnoticed, but I've never had the right clothes—or the confidence— to do it before.

Exhilaration washes through me, and my cheeks heat with pride. I can't wait to see Cece's and Esme's expressions tomorrow when I surprise them at breakfast.

I ruffle through my dresser for a suitable nightgown and wipe the sweat from my armpits before pulling on my sleeping socks. The snug pieces of cotton are stretched tight over the new muscles in my legs.

The last two weeks, I'd tolerated the tight, long-sleeved tunic and washed myself with a hand towel after each run. Each night, I'd gone to bed with sore muscles but a newfound sense of freedom, and my slumber had remained undisturbed.

So different from my life here...

I expected to come back home full of shame and secrets, and while I've seen wild and unspeakable things, I'm not that...glad to be back.

Before I can dwell too much on why, I hide the book I brought with me inside the black clothes and cram them to the bottom of my hidden drawer. I slip under the covers, trying to recall the exact shape of the phantom I caught a glimpse of, earlier.

Whatever it was, One was desperate for me not to see it.

CHAPTER II

NO PLACE LIKE HOME

The next day, I meet Cece and Father for lunch in the dining room. "Good morning," I say with a cheerful wave. I had slept right through breakfast, coming home at such a late hour, and no one noticed I had returned, not even Esme. I guess they didn't expect me just yet.

Father's gaze snaps up from his plate and hovers at the edges of my body, not meeting mine. My heart sinks.

He's afraid to look straight at me and find me changed.

Cece jumps out of her chair and runs to my arms. "Finally!"

"Cecelia," Father scolds.

My little sister's cheeks are flushed as she looks me over, oblivious to Father's angry pout. "I was afraid you would never be healthy enough to travel to Lundan. It's been *weeks*, I was worried!" Hands on her hips, she squints dangerously. "Why didn't you write me? Were you really so sick that you couldn't pick up a quill?"

"I'm sorry?" I search the room for help, but Father still avoids my inquisitive stare. Did they really pretend that I was sick and stuck at the summer house? How do they hope to get away with it when I disappear again?

Cece's brows pull together, and she squeezes my upper arm through the puffy sleeves of my yellow dress. I shake my head, silently begging her to shut up.

She pinches my side, and I can tell from her angry pout that she knows she's been lied to. "Meet me in my room after my riding lesson," she whispers. "You better tell me where the crops you were, or else..." With that, she skips back to her seat and innocently butters up a piece of bread. "At least you can come to the ball with me."

Father clears his throat, half choking on a mouthful of ale. "I'm not sure your sister feels up to a ball, Cecelia."

I grip the skirts of my dress and squeeze onto my seat. "But I do, Father."

In this familiar room, the memories of the Shadow Court fade a little. The elegant masks, the gigantic gym, the stretchy, snug fabrics... Did I really spend twelve days training in Faerie? My hands tremble as I pick up a small silver fork, but the rough callus on my index finger where the bow string chafed the skin assures me that it wasn't all a dream.

THE DOOR TO MY BEDROOM CLOSES BEHIND ESME. THE FAE'S GAZE SHINES like she's excited to see me. That's a first.

"I can't believe you came back early! And here I was in the market shopping like any other day..." she wipes a hand across her forehead. "Let's see if you have a suitable gown ready for the ball. I can still alter one if needed."

My nose wrinkles in half-hearted denial. "I promised Cece to meet her in her room after her riding lesson."

Esme gives the chaise lounge a vigorous pat. "Don't be ridiculous. We have a lot to discuss."

She starts unpacking my dresses from the deep trunk at the foot of the bed, shuffles through a few old gowns, and finally settles on a burgundy empire-waisted dress. "Here. We can make this work in time for the ball."

I stand up at her instruction and slip on my usual corset.

The dark-haired Fae pulls on the laces and clicks her tongue. "It doesn't fit as it should. You've gained weight."

"I barely ate, like you said." A fierce blush creeps to my cheeks at the falsehood. I ate more than I intended to. Running four times a day simply made me famished, and as far as I could tell, the food in Faerie wasn't any different than the food here—a little tastier, perhaps, but not dangerous.

"Muscles, then."

I can't deny that, so I press my lips together. A few minutes later, a loud pounding on the door startles us both, and Cece's voice booms into the small bedroom. "Let me in, Nell, or I swear—"

Esme wrenches open the door, cutting her off. "Your sister barely made it home in time for the ball. I have many alterations to make on her dress, so shoo. You can berate her all you like later."

Cece's *you owe me* stare chills my blood. That girl will pry every single detail from me before the night is over. She'll peel my skin off, if she has to.

I shoot Esme a dirty look after Cece leaves. "You told her I was sick?"

The slender Fae rubs her face down with one hand, her voice muffled. "Your father insisted. It was foolish of him, but you shouldn't pout." She flicks my forehead gently with her bony middle finger. "We have to tell your sister the truth. Not the whole truth, mind you, but enough for it to make sense when you disappear again. I leave that to you."

I nod in agreement, relieved. Esme is often stuck in the middle, navigating the muddy waters of honoring my father's wishes while raising two young teenage girls, a task she was by no means prepared to take on when my mother hired her to tutor us.

She sticks a few pins and needles close to my breasts. "I'll work the bodice loose and lengthen the skirt. Don't move." She peels the gown off me. "So..." Her gaze briefly darts up to mine. "What happened with the Shadow King?"

"I'm...not sure."

Deep lines appear on her forehead, and she holds the pin she'd just tucked between her teeth away from her mouth. "Didn't he try to seduce you?"

My top lip curls in a *thank-the-mother-he-didn't* pout. "Not at all."

She crouches to work on the skirt, her movements a little more impatient than usual. "Start at the beginning. What happened?"

"There's not much to tell."

I try to recall the Shadow King, but all of the sudden, my memory of him is foggy, and the instinct to keep his court's secrets is almost undeniable. *Esme taught me so much. I should tell her about the banquet.*

Yet, my recollection of the events becomes fragmented like I'm trying to recall a dream I had a few nights ago. I know what happened in Faerie wasn't what we both expected to happen, and it unnerves me.

Esme observes me for a moment, her bottom lip tucked between her teeth. "I won't hold the truth against you, Penny. I swear it. Despite his faults, the Shadow King is handsome and charming..."

I want to say that he didn't really have any interest in me, but her quiet tone gives me pause. "You taught me to fear him."

"As you should." She climbs to her feet to pin the back of the dress, her rehearsed movements slower and softer than before. "Your father insists for you to remain steadfast to Demeter's customs... He doesn't understand how different Faerie truly is. By now, you must have seen and heard things that would be unthinkable here. I'm just saying that it's okay if you're not appalled by everything you saw. If you thought the king was...desirable. It would be our secret."

Esme seldom speaks so openly, and I twist around to face her. "You told me he was a vicious monster."

"I know my place, Miss Penny. Your father wouldn't have allowed me to raise you any other way, and I'm sorry that I had to keep you in the dark about some aspects of Faerie. Damian is a monster, but a charismatic one."

My pulse flutters at the mention of the king's name. Esme pulls the dress back over my head and starts working on the alterations. Esme is the best seamstress I've ever known. From the way she works the needle and thread, you'd think she had magic after all.

I sit on my hands at the edge of the chaise lounge and mull over everything she said.

After a while, she whispers. "Your mother... She kissed him, you know."

My eyes open wide, and I shift uncomfortably on my seat. "The Shadow King?"

Black curls bounce around Esme's face as she adjusts the last few inches of the hem. "Yes. When he healed her. She told me it was the most sinful moment of her life."

"He didn't touch me, I swear." A big grimace overpowers my face at the thought of my mother kissing the gold-plated mask of the Shadow King. "I only learned how to run and shoot a crossbow."

"He means to train you then. As a seed. Interesting." She hands me back my dress. "Let's see if it fits you better."

I wrangle the fabric over my head and smooth down the skirt over my crinoline. Esme fastens the tiny buttons covering the hollow of my neck, the red collar snug around my throat. The absence of cleavage is in stark contrast to the plunging neckline of the dress I wore in Faerie.

I roll my gloves past my elbows and check that they're in pristine condition for the ball. "What does it entail? To be trained? Is it a good or a bad sign?"

Esme fastens my pearl earrings, the hint of a smile playing with her lips.

Before she can answer, Cece barrels inside the bedroom, holding her ballgown to her chest. "I need to get ready too, you know. The carriage is already here."

Esme motions for her to sit on the bed and secures my hair up with a taupe hair snood with golden threads and pearl beads. "Let's hurry, then. We can chat later."

Once we're all ready to go, the carriage takes Cece, Esme, and me to the ball, and Cece struggles to hide her leg jitters. As per tradition, autumn balls start at sundown and offer a variety of apple ciders and wines. Women wear warm colors, their gowns decorated with orange, yellow, and red sashes.

The guests stop chatting and dancing to curtsy as the butler announces our arrival, and Esme quickly skedaddles. "I will meet you by the entrance after the cotillion."

Esme spends these soirées in the adjoining room. Ladies-in-waiting aren't invited to partake in the festivities, and Esme is regarded as particularly ill-suited because of her lower rank—and suspiciously pointy ears.

Cece links her arm in mine and ushers me deeper inside the ballroom. Stairs run down on both sides of the mezzanine to the ground floor where tables and chairs are set in the corners for the guests. Young, unmarried men and women do not sit, however, and gather in small groups around the dance floor instead.

My heart skips a beat when I see Isaac standing with his schoolmates by the delicacy buffet.

Cece tugs on my arm. "Let's dance."

"In a minute."

Eyes fixed on Isaac, I weave through the crowd and pick off a few grapes from the bushel in the center of the buffet table. Normally, he'd take the opportunity to join me, but he doesn't meet my gaze and remains safely tucked in the huddle of gentlemen.

Abigail Strauss walks over to me, blocking my view of Isaac. "Good evening, Princess. I'm happy to see you in good health."

I offer her a quick smile. "Good evening, Miss Strauss."

Abigail Strauss isn't what I'd call a friend, but she's the closest thing to it that I've got. Since Esme started tutoring me, I haven't opened up to anyone about my destiny, my magic, or anything that could betray my secrets. It's caused a rift between me and the other girls my age. It's hard to gossip about marriage proposals and the latest fashions when your entire life hangs in the balance.

Abigail plops a tiny piece of camembert inside her mouth. "You look different."

"I've been sick."

"You certainly don't look it. Your skin is glowing." A knowing grin ghosts over her lips.

She doesn't buy the scripted story.

Being a princess means being able to control the emotions on your face when you're out in society, so I force my eyes to widen and my brows to lift slightly, offering her the perfect picture of innocence. "Must be the medicinal herbs."

I might not wear a physical mask like the Fae do, but I'm wearing one all the same. I've chiseled it out of necessity.

While Abigail and I chat, Steven Finch approaches us from the side, creating a dent in the boy's huddle.

"Good evening, Mr. Finch," Abigail says.

Isaac steals a glance at me, all but forced to angle himself in our direction if he doesn't want to raise eyebrows. *What the crops? Why is he so stiff?*

"Good evening, Princess. Miss Strauss." Steven bows his head to each of us in turn, the bend slightly more pronounced in my direction.

Isaac finally unroots himself from his spot and greets us both. "Good evening, Princess. Good evening, Miss Strauss."

Abigail waves her fan dramatically and extends the crook of her elbow toward Steven. "It's very hot inside. Shall we all take a stroll through the gardens?"

Isaac reluctantly offers me his arm, and we fall into step behind the other couple. Thankfully, the gardens are not too crowded at this hour.

"Are you alright?" I ask under my breath.

"Your father denied my proposal." His ashen face and stark tone betray the depth of his anguish, and a lump forms in my throat.

"But—You said you'd wait."

He slows down until Abigail and Steven are out of earshot. "Why would the king allow us so much freedom this summer if he was not ready to accept my proposal? Doesn't he know how badly this could affect you if I changed my mind?"

Changed his mind?

I eye him sideways, the downward curl of his mouth spelling trouble. "We only kissed twice." Two modest ones at that. Peck. Peck.

"I know, but rumors can ruin lives."

The statement stops me cold, and I dig my heels into the stone pathway. "What rumors?"

Isaac's shifty gaze drops to the ground and causes my stomach to twinge. Reputation is everything in my world, and if a nasty rumor is somehow circulating about me, if there's even one word spoken in society about my shadow magic or my trip to Faerie...it would destroy my future. No exaggeration.

"Come along, you two." Abigail waves us forward with a gloved hand.

My heart beats heavy in my throat for the rest of the silent, awkward walk, and by the time we rejoin the festivities, I feel like throwing up the handful of grapes I swallowed earlier.

Isaac excuses himself quickly, and I'm stuck dancing the quadrille with Steven's brother to keep up appearances. The other girls whisper in my wake, their avid stares prickling my skin.

After the dance ends, Cece slumps on a seat at the edge of the dance floor, in view of the whole gallery, and I walk over to her.

"Oh, what rotten luck I have. And so early in the night, too. I just might cry!" Her face wrinkles in a desperate, fake-as-hell pout as she waves me over. "Penelope, there you are! I'm afraid I twisted my ankle, sister. Will you take me home?"

Cece always puts a little too much *actress* in her *princess*.

Eyes wide, I meet her determined gaze. "Of course."

Cece squeezes my hand and leans on me in the guise of

protecting her ankle. "Let's get out of here before these bats get the better of us."

"What did you hear?" I ask quietly.

"The official story is that you refused Isaac after leading him on all summer."

A low curse escapes me. "Crops!"

Esme joins us in a hurry with a polite smile plastered on her lips. "What's the matter, Your Highnesses?"

"My ankle twisted the wrong way, dear Esmeralda. How unfortunate! I need to lie down," Cece says.

Brows raised, Esme acquiesces to her dramatic request, and the butler calls for the carriage.

"How bad is it?" I ask my tutor on the ride home.

The ladies-in-waiting have a penchant for gossip, so she probably got a complete account of the rumors Cece overheard.

Esme's mouth curls down in a worried grimace. "I will try to smooth things over with the king before someone else tells him. He's put you in an impossible position..."

"Why did Father say no to Isaac?" Cece asks willfully, not-so-patiently waiting for me to fess up.

Esme shakes her head, denying my sister the answers she craves. "Not now, girls. You can discuss this at home." The pointed look she gives me tells me to be careful with my revelations, but I know the time has finally come.

The rest of the carriage ride is spent in stunned silence. After we've retired to our rooms, Esme quickly helps us out of our gowns and hustles out immediately after.

As soon as we're alone, Cece sits on the twin bed with a pillow in her lap. "What happened with Isaac? Why did you refuse him at all?"

I pry my hairbrush out of the dresser and sit beside her. "Nothing happened."

She shuffles to her knees on the mattress and spins around to face me. "You've got to stop protecting me. I'm old enough, Nell. What's really happening? Where were you the last two weeks?"

I open my mouth to speak, but can't quite form a complete sentence.

"You were in Faerie, weren't you?"

Way to go, Cece. That girl is magic, indeed. "Wh— "

"You all think I'm deaf or dumb or something, but I hear things, sis. I see you and Esme whisper with your Fae books. I've known for a while. It makes sense that you would have to go there because of your magic. I just don't understand why you didn't tell me before now."

My jaw hangs open at her breezy tone. *You went to Faerie... no big deal.* "How does it make sense? Gaia's children are supposed to enroll in the temple—"

A sarcastic chortle pops out of her mouth. "Like Father would ever go for that. He needs us both for grandsons. Many people's magic dies down, and they don't have to join the temple. I figured Esme hooked you up with a Fae shaman to cleanse you from your powers or something of the sort."

By the Mother! For two years I've kept this *huge* secret from Cece, and she just went ahead and figured it all out herself.

"It's more complicated than that, but yes. Esme and Father insisted for me not to say anything—at least not before I actually had to go," I say sheepishly.

Cece beams, proud of herself. "So... How was it?"

"Faerie?"

"No, church—Yes, Faerie! Is it as dark and debased as the legends say?" She asks, way too excited for my taste.

I relax on the mattress with my knees propped beneath me. "I don't know. The dresses reveal everything—and I do mean *every-thing*. People act and speak differently. Women wear pants, use crossbows, and eat whatever they want—"

Cece inches closer, her eyes full of stars. "What else?"

"There's a dark Fae...his name is One. He wears a frightening mask, but he's supposed to teach me how to use my magic," I say in the most neutral tone I can muster.

"*One?*" Cece's voice thickens with disbelief. "Who the crops is named 'One?'"

I grin from ear to ear. "My thoughts exactly."

Her eyes narrow, and the inquisitive gaze slaps the smile off my face more efficiently than all the kissing noises in the worlds. "Is he handsome?"

Busted.

"I have no idea. I've never seen his face. I don't even know what his hair looks like," I blurt out, trying to defuse the situation and failing miserably at it.

"What about the rest of him?"

My eyes bulge. "Cece!"

The look she gives me then...all fierce and serious. I shiver all over. *Crops... it's like I can't quite picture One in my mind anymore.*

The harder I try to remember what he looks like, the blurrier my memories of him become.

"What about the rest of him, Nell?" she repeats.

"He's very tall." My measured tone isn't fooling anyone, and my cheeks heat up.

My memories of One might be hazy, but my thoughts on his appearance are not blurry at all. Every time he gets a little too close, I feel lightheaded and warm and a little gauche.

The highest of all girly squeals rips out of Cece's mouth. "By the Mother! You like him! When *exactly* did you meet him? Is he the reason you refused Isaac?"

"I didn't refuse Isaac, exactly. We agreed to wait a year before finalizing our plans, so I don't know what possessed him to ask Father for my hand right away. No one can know about my trips to Faerie, so it didn't seem fair to accept his proposal until I'm back for good."

Her jaw slacks. "Wait. You have to go *back*?"

"Yes. I have to spend half the coming year in Faerie."

"Wow." Her brows pull together. "Why?"

"One said it would take about a year for me to snuff my powers out," I lie.

"Did you see the Shadow King?"

I avert my gaze, the threads sticking out from the pillow in her lap suddenly absorbing my attention. "Don't be ridiculous."

"Did you?"

"Um—only for a moment."

She slaps my arm with more strength than expected. "Horseshit! You did?"

My lips purse out of habit at her foul language. "Stop cussing!"

"Oh, you have to tell me *everything*." She covers her wide grin with her hands, and the elation in her voice makes me a little nauseous... but mostly relieved. Maybe 40% nauseous at the thought that my little sister knows too much, and 60% relieved that I don't have to keep so many secrets from her. I want to tell her everything, but my mind draws a huge blank when I try to think of the Shadow King.

Despite the obvious magic at work here, I recount my days in Faerie to the best of my ability. Some details are easier to recall, like the layout of the castle and Lori. Cece listens intently until the moon stretches high in the sky and the fire dies in the chimney.

Around two in the morning, sleep finally claims her, allowing me a moment to digest the events of the day. Being back home is... strange.

An itch blooms between my shoulder blades as I stare out my bedroom window. Without giving myself the time to chicken out, I cover Cece with my duvet, change into my tunic and pants, and sneak into the night. The warm, happy sensation I get whenever I run dulls the part of me that urges for caution.

It's not like I've lost my bearings. It doesn't mean I've been corrupted. Yet.

CHAPTER 12

IN SUMMER

St-John's Eve, the summer solstice celebration, is finally over. The sacrifice was successful enough for my enemies to overlook the dark circles under my eyes and the occasional twitch in my fingers. Elio isn't so easily fooled, though, and he peels himself off his frozen throne to join me in my dark corner.

The Hall of Eternity is an octagonal stone room with eight thrones, and the carpets that radiate out from the centerpiece of the room—the chalice—match the thrones they lead to. The black obsidian rock I'm sitting on frosts as my old friend nears it. "You look like death," he says.

The skin at the base of his neck is freckled with snowflakes, and exhaustion dims his ice-blue gaze.

"Right back at you," I crack.

Elio is the reaper king, after all. He knows a thing or two about death. We watch from the corner of our eyes as the monarchs filter out of the sacred hall and enter the Summer Court's ballroom through the large door behind the Queen of Summer's throne.

The guests are now free to enjoy the pleasures of the night, however forbidden they may be, but it's the one Fae holiday I've always abhorred, even before the curse. Light Fae love to play games, drink wine, and sex, sex, sex. It leaves all the hard work for us dark-lings, but it's not like I could find a lover here, anyway. The curse destroyed the part of me that could love, or even feel true attraction or desire.

Until Nell, my pesky inner voice chants.

"I wish you'd tell me what's going on," Elio says quietly enough for no one else to hear.

"I'm fine. How have *you* been?"

Nothing shuts up Elio Hades Lightbringer better than the prospect of talking about himself. The Winter King is drowning in secrets of his own, and neither of us have been in a sharing mood in decades.

The arch of his brow softens, and he shakes my question away like snowflakes on an ice dragon's back. "I saw you earlier. You could barely handle the sacrifice, and if I noticed, so did the others. If you're not in better shape for Morheim—"

During Morheim, all Fae citizens follow the Shadow Court's custom of wearing masks to ward themselves against the night-mares that roam the realm more freely. At the end of the season, each kingdom offers a tribute so that we liberate the sun and continue to protect them. Every Shadow hunter needs to bring their "A" game this year, or the magic I have left will dwindle, and we won't make it through winter.

"I'll be ready for Morheim."

Elio blinks a few times. "I hope so."

His gloomy words of encouragement unnerve me more than his earlier condescension.

I serve him a casual shrug, force my jaw loose, and add a trace of arrogance to my lips. "I have new seeds, and one of them is excep-tional. It won't be long until she sprouts and when she does, I'll be good for ten seasons, at least."

"Your seeds take *months* to sprout."

With a dismissive wave, I laugh off his concerns. "Not this one."

My situation is even more critical than he believes, especially after the clusterfuck yesterday. If Nell had caught a clear view of our unexpected guest in the gardens last night... I might have had to give up on her altogether. Just the thought turns my stomach.

Elio rakes his nails across the frozen patch at his neck, his eyes fixed on the chalice. "Every single one of us is doomed."

Seth Devine condenses into solid form behind his mother's throne, clearly eavesdropping. "Elio...ever the optimist." He was born to two kingdoms and yet none, his powerful magic split between light and dark, two opposing forces. His ability to turn into mist or wind is not even his most annoying quality.

Elio stiffens from head to toe, and his nose wrinkles in disgust. "Get lost, dandelion fuzz."

A thundercloud sticks to Seth's shoulders as he closes the distance between us. "I'm looking forward to this year's pageant, Elio. Your discarded wanna-be brides are always so...receptive to my soothing words."

Being three of the most hated and misunderstood Fae in existence, you'd think we'd find common ground, but alas... Seth's misery only loves the company of naked women.

"Why are you here, Seth? Don't you have wine and women to tend to?" I drawl in a dispassionate tone.

The prince of nowhere at all strolls around the sacred hall, appraising the thrones like he's browsing for new furniture. He drags a finger over the top of Elio's seat and rubs his fingers together, checking for dust. "Morrigan's presence was felt in the sceawere. The others were whispering about it before you two arrived."

The wretched name scrapes my insides and makes little bows of my gut. "Certainly nowhere near the Shadowlands."

Seth gives me a wide smile that says, *oh, you're such an idiot.* "She wouldn't lurk too close to home, would she? The question you should really ask yourself is: why would she be on the move *now.* I'd love to discuss that with you." He offers Elio a wide, impish smile. "Privately."

Elio meets my gaze for the first time since his wife died, and the unblinking stare chills me to the bone. "If Morrigan is left unchecked, the others will demand more from you. You need all the magic you can get."

"Don't worry about Rye. If she's in Faerie, I'll find her." I grit my teeth, her pet name sour on my tongue.

"You better. I've got enough to deal with at the moment. I'd rather not pay you one final visit." Elio bares his teeth to Seth in lieu of goodbye and hustles to the reception with his hands tucked inside the pockets of his silver jacket.

I turn back to the annoyingly well-informed prince and offer him a fake, bemused smile. He's more powerful than me right now, but I can't let it show. If he knew, he'd probably kill me right here.

He licks his lips, clearly excited to spell out my troubles. "Morrigan crossed the sceaware from Demeter to the fringe of Storm's End and vanished through the frozen hills of Wintermere..."

I've always known Morrigan was hiding in the old world. It's the only realm where people don't allow mirrors into their homes, so I can't hunt for her there without some serious investment of time and power—more than I can spare. But Wintermere is a different story.

"Elio would have told me if Morrigan had been through Wintermere."

My gaze latches on to Elio's back, the Winter King now sipping on a flute of Feyfire wine. From his scowl, you'd think it was tepid water—and not the most potent aphrodisiac in existence.

Seth leans closer to my ear. "Are you so sure about that? I know you two used to be friends, but look again. Elio has become one of his lost souls, and you know as well as I do what mistakes a desperate king can make when he's backed against a wall. What better prey than a hopeless king for a woman that longs for a throne?"

I examine Elio again and find the blueish tint of his skin a little worrying indeed. "You think Morrigan turned her sights to Elio?"

"I'm saying you don't know who your friends are anymore. And that's a dangerous position to be in, cousin."

Cousin is a way for royal Fae to address their equals by power—not blood, and a wolfish smile quirks my mouth. "I bet you'd be my friend...for a price."

"Perhaps," he says with a matching grin.

But I'm not that stupid—or desperate. If Seth Devine is searching for trouble, he'll find it, and I won't be caught in the crossfire.

I can't afford to be patient anymore. I have to move Nell's training along.

Demeter's castle pales in comparison to the wonders of the new world. Its long hallways and textured tapestries lull me into a dream-like state, and the scents encrusted in the carpets remind me of a past long gone, when wine and laughter—and the occasional blood splatter—still governed the Shadow Court.

The princess' room beckons, tucked at the end of a long hallway past the guards and staircase. Just as I'm about to walk down the length of the corridor to meet her, a high-pitched greeting stops me.

"Hello," the girl proclaims from her slender teenage body.

Her limbs are still stuck in the midst of puberty, a few pimples partly hidden in her freckles.

A powdery blue aura pulses around her, half the strength of her sister's, but I smile. Both of Emmaline Darcy's daughters bear the Shadow seed. How interesting.

"You're him, aren't you?" Nell's sister stares at my mask with guile, and I'm almost sure she can see the broken face behind it.

"Him?"

The teenager fluffs the bow at the front of her green dress like it constitutes a line of defense between us. "The Shadow King."

Isn't she clever?

I give her a shrug that's half denial, half acknowledgement. "Nice to meet you."

"Why do you wear a mask?" she asks.

"To hide my face."

Her suspicious frown deepens. "And why do you need to hide your face?"

I lower my voice, amused by her confidence. "Why do you think?"

"You won't change her, you know. She will change *you*."

"I think you're right." I bet her sister told her all she could remember about her time in Faerie, which is a problem. "How old are you, Cecelia?"

"Fifteen."

Only three years before she comes of age... I lick my lip. "I'll make you a deal."

The girl turns white as a sheet.

"If you promise to pretend not to know anything about me, the Shadow King, or Faerie, I will not erase your memories of me."

With a solemn nod, she clenches her knuckles around her flimsy green bow.

"But you have to promise not to berate your sister with questions and accept that she cannot share everything with you anymore."

She lifts her chin, the movement so like her sister that it loosens something deep inside me. "Why not?"

"Nice to meet you, Cecelia. See you again soon." I melt with the shadows, knowing better than to argue with a fifteen-year-old. If Cecelia Darcy is half as headstrong as her sister, she will not let me have the last word.

Their mother gave life to two seeds... One magic baby is a chance, but two is a pattern. Someone up their bloodline must have had Fae blood—though I can't fathom who.

The two princesses, along with all of Demeter's seeds, will strengthen my kingdom, which makes winning the bet even more vital. Once all the citizens of Demeter are connected to the sceawere, the magic in this realm will be ours for the taking.

Nell's bedroom holds no artifice, her religion preventing royal women from flaunting their riches. Hot embers crackle in the chimney, and I sit at the foot of her narrow bed. She's a means to an end, and yet...

The old me would have fallen hard for her. She's fierce and opinionated—not at all like I expected her to be. Despite my better judgment, her fresh, cinnamon-y scent fills places inside me I thought were dead forever.

In another life, I would have woken her with an impish kiss, eager to test the limits of her mortal body and hear her cries of pleasure. I would have taken her to see the wonders of my realm and watched her reaction to their beauty. Weaved her a perfect life and made all her dreams come true just to see her smile.

Oblivious to my presence, she sleeps. Her chest rises and falls, and just looking at her calms the storm in my heart. *So beautiful.* I would sell my blood, body, and soul to sleep soundly again, and even more to do so with her nestled in my arms.

I brush a white-blond strand of hair away from her eyes and wonder what she dreams about, but that's for her to know, and for Two to find out. The only thing I can do for her as I am now is spare her the nightmares.

CHAPTER 13
FIRST TRIAL

"Wake up, kitten," a hungry voice murmurs in my ear.

I jolt awake and open my mouth to scream, but One smothers the high-pitched shriek with his palm. The heat of his body radiates through his thick black clothes, and my fear melts.

The dark Fae is sprawled over me on the bed, so our faces are inches apart. His black uniform swallows the dim light piercing through the curtains. It's been twelve days since I last saw him, and my faulty memory didn't do him justice. The details of our conversations and all the facts I couldn't recall about Faerie stumble back into place now that he's here.

"How did you get in?" I ask, regretting the question as soon as I hear it.

He does me the courtesy of overlooking my fumble, the answer as plain as can be. He walked in. Because he could.

"Did you enjoy your *vacation*?" he asks instead.

"Yes and no." I press my lips together, searching for the right way to bring this up. "I couldn't recall the details of what had happened in Faerie. Like you'd put a spell on me..."

I watch for his reaction, and he slides even closer. "You haven't taken your vows, yet, so I might have put a small enchantment on you. For the safety of the realm."

I tuck a loose strand of hair behind my ear and hug the covers to my chest, wondering how I feel about that, but my brain is stuck on more pressing matters. One's breaths are uneven, and he doesn't look in a hurry to give me space.

It's so scandalous to have a man here, in my bedroom. It's completely forbidden, and yet One just strolled in with no regards for the rules. If rumors of a failed engagement with Isaac damaged my reputation, I can't imagine what would happen if the servants caught a glimpse of him in here.

A dark Fae in my bed... The images that come to mind dispense a healthy dose of adrenaline in my veins.

"Well... Leave so I can change." I shoo him away with a coarse whisper.

"You can change in Faerie." He grips the covers and yanks them off the bed with his tongue tucked between his teeth, daring me to follow him.

Startled, I jump to my feet and hold an arm across my breasts. "I'm not going downstairs dressed like this."

He opens the bedroom door wide, unfazed. "Just use your magic."

I catch up with him near the grand staircase. The windows above the mezzanine bathe the halls with light.

"See? There's no shadow."

He points to the thin shadow of the banister. "Shadows are everywhere, and eventually, you'll be able to create your own. Until then, you just have to crawl inside of the ones that are already there."

I check the corridor, but Esme's and Cece's bedroom doors are still shut. Concentrating on the small patches of darkness, I glide across the marble tiles until the skin of my arms prickles the way it does when I sneak around the guards at night.

One skips ahead. He jumps from shadow to shadow and avoids

the light like we're children playing a game of "the floor is lava." How many stories have I read in which a trickster Fae played, teased, and sauntered, leading a young maiden to her doom...

It pains me to admit there was some truth to them.

One runs past the guards at the bottom of the stairs and digs his toes in the ground. "Come on, kitten. You told me yourself *it's not that hard*. Show me what you've got."

I'm breathless and scared to be left behind and discovered, so I put my game face on and follow. One grins when I join him on the landing, and my heart hammers, quick as a wild bird. His proximity must boost my magic because I was never able to sneak past the guards during the day before.

Outside in the gardens, heavy rain beats the paving stones, and the guards cowering under the breezeway to stay dry pay us no mind. The thrill almost balances out my dismay at being jostled out of bed in my flimsy cotton nightgown. Almost.

Rain glistens down my face, and I wipe the fresh water from my eyes, feeling more alive than I've felt in a long time. Maybe ever.

As we reach the cover of the breezeway leading to the basement, I slow down. "This is fun."

One turns around to look at me, and the wide smile on his face disappears. He comes to an abrupt stop, and his entire body goes rigid, like he suddenly remembered something important that displeases him greatly. Something vital, even.

"Is everything alright?" I ask, searching for the source of his anger.

He's not half as wet as I am, the fabric of his tunic and hood water-resistant. My wet nightgown does very little to hide the roundness of my breasts, and I cross my arms over my chest as we continue on to the tall mirror beneath my father's castle.

"Hurry up, will you?" One says.

"Why are you suddenly so angry with me?"

The shadows around him thicken, and he picks the lock to the mirror room open with his magic. "I'm not angry."

"You look angry."

He flexes and extends his fists a few times before forcing them open. "I'm not. Let's go." The dark Fae doesn't spare me another glance, his mask angled to the corner of the room.

With a grim pout, he hands me the blindfold, and I tie it above my brows. "Is it about what I saw the other night in the gardens?"

One freezes in a perfect statue of a predator caught in a snare. "And what exactly did you see?"

The subtle shift in his stance sends my pulse flying. "Was it a nightmare?"

His spine relaxes at that, but his voice remains quiet and dangerous. "Not a nightmare."

"What, then?"

"Something else. Something broken." A dark hint of tenderness laces the words like he's talking about a long-lost lover. He spreads his arms to pick me up for our journey through the sceawere, but I take a quick step back.

"Something? Or *someone*? Two said that *he* had gotten out—"

"You're stalling. Do I have to remind you of what will happen if you refuse to come?" he says without a trace of humanity left.

"Are you serious?"

Magic electrifies the air, his tone cold and withdrawn. "Last chance, Miss Darcy."

What in the Mother's name—

The knot in my stomach swells to the size of a small sun, but I lower the blindfold over my eyes. I thought we were having fun. I can't understand what upset him to begin with, but he's clearly not willing to share his secrets—or his feelings.

The voyage isn't as painful as it was the last two times, but my pride aches when One dumps me in the middle of my Fae bedroom. He hustles out without a word.

"It was nice to see you too," I grumble after he's gone.

Baka flies in from the mirror. "Welcome back, Nell. Was yer trip home pleasant?"

"Of course," I bark.

Baka grimaces at the impolite greeting and lands on the bed, her light weight barely making a dent in the mattress. "I was just tryin' to make conversation. Dinnae bite my head off for nothin'."

"I'm sorry, I just—I got an abrupt wake up call." Shame licks my ribs. I peel the wet nightgown off and pat myself dry with a towel.

Baka's eyes soften. "Did ye swim here?"

"Haha. No." The dresser creaks when I pry out what Lori called a sports bra—the new world's equivalent to a corset, but lighter and flexible. "It was raining, and One was in a foul mood."

Baka nods in understanding. "He's not lord of darkness for nothin'."

Indeed.

"Do ye need anything else?" Baka asks.

"No, thank you. I'll grab breakfast and get to work."

It's strange to trade in my traditional clothes for a long-sleeved shirt, jacket, and pants, but to my horror, I think I prefer it.

My heart beats harder with each step on my way down the corridor. Cece berated me for details on the castle all week, and I could barely remember the layout of my Faerie bedroom—let alone the wonders of the gardens or the library. But now that I'm back, it's like I never left.

The maze of corridors that leads to the balcony next to the library feels familiar, and I quickly make my way to the breakfast buffet.

"Hey, girl. Good to see you back." Mara waves me over to her table, her fork deep into a thick omelet.

"Good morning."

She's wearing black tights—leggings, as she calls them—and a matching triangular scarf in lieu of a bra. Once again, I'm taken aback by the contrast between my life in Demeter and my new Fae reality.

"What's that about?" She wiggles her fingers in the general direction of my head. "Is that how you wear your hair in the old world?"

I grip the tight hairnet. I totally forgot to take it off. "Y—yeah."

Mara fluffs her flamboyant mane and gives me one of her ambiguous grins. "Wow. It looks super uncomfortable."

James sits next to us with a full plate. "Welcome back, Nell."

I offer him a small smile.

"Well, I'm off. Two's waiting for me." Mara packs the apple left on the table inside her bag, and I catch a metallic glint on top.

My brows pull together, my mouth suddenly pasty and dry. "You got a mask?"

"White quartz." Mara shows off her new mask proudly, the solid piece of metal fitting perfectly over her face—with no string.

"How does it stay on your face?"

My fellow seedlings exchange a glance, and Mara huffs. "Magic, silly."

"We passed the first trial a week ago. Baka told us you had some kind of arrangement to pace your training?" James says.

"Yes, well..." I lick my lips, unsure how to finish that sentence.

Before I can babble a falsehood, Two sticks his head out of the mirror. "Mara," he summons her.

The redhead jerks to her feet. "I'm off living the dream guys. Wish me luck." She hurries after her mentor, and her polished mask shines in the sun. An inked butterfly decorates her lower back, and the little knot holding the black scarf in place over her breasts is absolutely scandalous.

A hard stone sinks in my belly when she jumps inside the sceawere to meet Two.

I missed out by being gone, and that's true for both worlds. This half-and-half arrangement is a nightmare, my focus neither here nor there. I don't belong in Demeter as long as I still need to come here, and yet I don't truly belong here, either.

What a mess.

James excuses himself, too, and I wait about an hour for One to show up, but he doesn't. Whatever happened earlier, his enthusiasm for teaching me sizzled out. I join Lori in the library instead, eager to

hear her take on the last two weeks and apologize for leaving
without saying goodbye.

THE NEXT DAY, I WAKE UP WITH A STRANGE FEELING IN MY HEART. A SENSE
of impending doom. After my morning run, I head to breakfast, but
Lori, Mara, and James are impossible to find. So, I grab a bite to eat—
alone—and wonder for a moment if I'm truly awake.

A low *thump, thump, thump* pulls me out of my reverie, and I
search for the source of the pounding. Faint footsteps echo in my
ears, and I follow them to the other end of the balcony, away from
the buffet and library. A tight corner around the castle stone walls
opens to a round staircase that descends into a small, secluded
section of the interior courtyard.

The little nook is almost completely hidden in the vegetation.
Morning glories weave around the banister, the bell-shaped yellow
flowers drooping toward the earth, and I climb down the steps carefully not to disturb them.

A door screeches on its hinges at the foot of the stairs, leading
inside the castle.

"Nell..."

A warm breeze blows past my legs. Whoever is calling out for me
—whether it's One or the Shadow King himself—I wouldn't know.
Contrary to the other night, this sudden wind isn't cold, and the
rustle in the vegetation isn't alarming.

Is this the first trial Mara and James spoke about?

I wrench the hood of my tunic over my head and follow the pulse
of magic. Instead of a neat expanse of tunnels, the narrow passage is
uneven and entirely made of rock.

The door seals itself shut behind me, and my heartbeat spikes.
I'm trapped.

"Nell! Nell, it's me! I need help." The faint voice now sounds like Cece...but how can that be?

My blood turns to ice, and I cry out. "Cece?"

"Nell!"

I hurry along the pitch-black hallways, terrified and disoriented. Shadows nip at my heels as the passage slants downwards.

Condensation glistens down the walls, the tepid *ploc, ploc, ploc* of water becoming louder and louder. A small lake ripples to an unfelt wind at the bottom of the natural cave. The algae that grows in neat patches over an array of water-covered rocks lights the cavern with a teal glow, and a series of rusted pipes are encrusted in a rock wall.

Cece stands drenched to the bones in the middle of the lake, the water up to her hips.

The sight of her blue lips and pale skin turns my stomach. "Cece? Is it really you?"

"Please hurry, Nell. I'm stuck." A painful grimace twists her features, and she tugs on her right leg, her foot apparently stuck under a heavy rock. The wet gown weighs her down, the thick dress heavy with water.

"Stay calm. I'm coming." I reach the end of the path and climb over a slippery rock, my knees bent for better balance. A steep pile of hard rocks and rubble leads down to the lake.

"Hurry. There's something in the pipes," Cece whispers.

Halfway down the hill, I lose my footing, and pebbles careen down to the surface of the water. I grip the nearest rock with shaky hands to keep myself from toppling over and force myself to slow down. This cavern is at the heart of the infamous Shadow realm, where dreams, nightmares, and fantasies flourish. I've got to keep a clear head.

A low hissing sound echoes from the depths of the cave, and my muscles tense. A golden snake slithers into view on the opposite side of the underground lake, crawling out of a large pipe. Its scales gleam, its long body three times as thick as my upper arm.

Its general appearance is similar to that of a living reptile, and yet radically different. A spark of magic burns in its red eyes, and its body is almost see-through, like it's made of dark clouds instead of flesh.

A nightmare.

A burst of nefarious magic booms through the air, and I feel strangely drawn to the monster. The serpent pauses at my approach and tastes the air with its bicuspid tongue, the length of it partly hidden in the water.

"Nell!" Cece cries out, straining to break free.

I look around for a weapon, a sword, a bow—anything I could use to kill it, but even the biggest rock at my disposal wouldn't make a dent in the creature's scales.

The snake doesn't look twice at my sister but weaves to the edge of the lake instead. When it reaches the rocky bank, it stops with a sharp tail lash, waiting.

One more step forward, and it'll bite me. I feel it in my bones.

"Please, please, Nell. Don't leave me here," Cece whines.

Leave you here? I squint at my sister. I'd never leave her here, and she should know that.

"What's your middle name, Cece?" I ask quickly.

"What?"

My eyes narrow. "Your middle name."

Cece is supposed to be safe at home, in Demeter. There's no reason why she'd be here. No reason why she wouldn't answer my question.

The snake darts out, and I flatten myself to the stones at my back. A familiar tingle of power prickles my fingers, and the shadows around me thicken. Instead of merely hiding within them, the darkness takes tangible form, and I reach for it like a knight would brandish a shield.

I'm no longer a girl or a princess. I'm more than Nell in this moment, quick and untouchable as smoke.

Someone without magic can't begin to grasp the feeling of it being unleashed. Not molded into a tool or called upon for a specific task, but truly unleashed.

It's not like blood or water. It doesn't pulse or drizzle. My magic feels hot and heavy, like a dark stone under the desert sun. It's cold and uncontrollable, like an icy stream tumbling down the mountains.

Magic *drums*. Magic *soars*. Magic *lives*.

You think you're using it, but it's really using you.

Shadows move under my command and shield me from the monster. They are thick as fabric, but swift and pliable as water. A moment later, the beast gives a low hiss and angrily returns to its lair, allowing me passage.

I stare at the spot where the fake-Cece was, but there's nothing left of her, and I sigh in relief. I've hidden from Esme or the guards a dozen times, but never in such a formidable—and deliberate—fashion. The magic dims after a few seconds, and a hint of longing ties up my tongue. The power I just used wasn't all mine. I drew it from the stone, the underground lake—even the beast itself.

I drew it from them and had to release it, but a tiny fleck of it, barely a spark, blended with mine. It warms my hands and tickles my breast bone, and though it's as delicate and frail as a butterfly, it's also certain as the night sky.

The magic inside me burns brighter.

Joy expands my chest, and a smile tugs at the corners of my mouth until a larger, thicker shadow looms over me.

CHAPTER 14
BARE

I spin around and spread my arms, spooked by the apparition, but the darkness condenses into a familiar silhouette.

"Congratulations, you've passed the first neophyte trial," One says without smiling.

"That's all? I passed?" I bring a hand to my chest. "I felt the magic, it was incredible—"

His eyes narrow. "Don't kid yourself, seedling. You've barely got enough magic to breathe the same air as the Shadow King. Passing the first trial just means that you can *survive* in this world—nothing to boast about."

Grumpy, much? I try not to grumble and square my shoulders. "Was it necessary to use my sister as bait?"

"Kaat is a most clever creature. It uses what you love most to lure you inside its lair."

The loving way he speaks of the snake annoys me. "And what if it had succeeded?"

"Its bite is not lethal, but you would have proven yourself too weak-minded to hunt nightmares." He spins on his heels and threads deeper inside the cavern.

I glower at his retreating back and follow him past the underground lake and into a man-sized tunnel. The air grows colder as we descend into the earth, and we squeeze into a crevice at the end of the path. Solid rocks graze my body from both sides until the crack widens to create a square-shaped vault. Mirrors cover the walls of the chamber from floor to ceiling, interrupted only by the crack we just walked through. A shallow natural pool ripples in the middle of the vault, leaving only a few feet of paving stones on each side.

One lights the candles on an altar set up next to it with a snap of his fingers, the tiny lights reflected to infinity by the four mirrored walls.

The warm glow of the candles flickers over the oily surface of the natural pool like fireflies blinking in and out of view in a dark forest, and the slow ripples of the liquid clue me in to the fact it's probably not water.

I squint at my lonely reflection on the right.

One is only visible in the mirror to my left, and I jerk away from him. "What's going on?"

He seems unbothered by the phenomenon. "Penelope Emanuelle Darcy, you've passed the master of nightmare's first trial. Will you take the oath?"

The sizzle of his unseen gaze is both warm and suffocating. I open my mouth to ask questions, so many questions, but a thunderstorm clouds the mirror at the back of the room.

I wrangle my hands, my fingers cold and numb, and gasp when the Shadow King himself steps out of the darkened glass. The bite of his power tickles all over.

One slides backward in an awkward bow, creating a bit more space between us. "Your Highness." The word irks his tongue, and I catch a hint of defiance in his voice.

The king's golden mask shines under the light of the candles, his reflection only visible in the mirror to my right. Fae must absorb more light than mortals, but it's creepy to say the least.

One passes me a piece of parchment. "You must recite this vow to advance to the next phase."

"I—" I skim the elegant script. "It won't make me lose the bet, right?" I sneak a glance at the quiet king.

"No."

His cold response burrows in every crevice of my being, and I shudder under his scrutiny.

He can talk...

One inclines his head. "But from now on, the details of your visits to Faerie will be strictly confidential. The magic will bind you to your word. No enchantment needed."

Sweat gathers on my palms and sticks to the parchment as I read and recite the vow. "I, Penelope Emanuelle Darcy, promise your secrets will wither on my tongue and dry on my quill. I shall never betray the customs of your court to outsiders or try to bring an end to your reign. My word binds me for life, Shadow King, for if I break my promise, all that I am—flesh, blood, and bones—will be surrendered to you. Damian Morpheus Sombra, I ask you to open my eyes."

One's lips tremble as I reach the end, and he takes another step backward.

The king extends his gloved hand. "Your eyes shall be open." The hooded monarch leads me to the edge of the pool where five rock steps sink inside the water.

One walks to the opposite side. "These liquid shadows will crystallize your commitment to our court. Your mask will allow you to walk through glass. As long as you wear it, the nightmares that prowl the in-between won't be able to track you through the sceawere."

I crouch down and skim the surface with my fingers, not sure I want to go in there, but the shadows are warm and inviting. The thought of having a mask and being on equal terms with everyone else...

"Strip," the king says, the harsh command reeking of privilege and cruelty.

I stand up stiff. "Excuse me?"

"Maybe—" One starts.

The rest of the sentence dies on his lips as the king angles his face to him, and the scene freezes like it did the night of the feast. I can't move, only watch, as the king leans into my ear. "I won't ask again."

After a few endless seconds, One angles his face to the ground.

Hot saliva burns my throat, but the imperious desire to obey the king is undeniable. Unable to resist, I slide my pants down my legs and wrangle the long-sleeved shirt past my head. My long braid gets entangled in the fabric, and I slide it out of the way, my hands shaking.

The sheer stretchy black lace that counts as underwear in Faerie feathers to the ground without a sound, thickening the silence.

Tears sting my eyes. *I knew it was coming. I just let myself forget where I was and why.* Dread simmers in my mouth as I stand stock-still in front of the two men with nothing but my pain to shield me from their metallic gazes.

The king pries off one glove and grazes the length of my spine with the back of his hand. I hold my breath when he reaches my backside and follows its curve all the way to my thigh.

I shall not give in.

I shall not flee.

I shall endure.

"You're a real beauty." The fiend doubles back to my front and climbs my ribs one at a time with spider fingers, all the way up to my right breast. My nipples are hard as stone from the cold and the drugging fear in my blood.

Bile rises to my mouth. "I will *never* bed you."

The Shadow King laughs like my humiliation is a never-ending source of entertainment. "*Never* is such a big word. So final."

Despite it all, a sweet pressure builds in my belly at the fierce sight in front of me. One looks ready to lunge at the king, his back hunched, and the balls of his feet grounded. Even though he's standing on the opposite side of the pool, I have no doubt he'd make it in one jump.

The king lowers his voice. "I told him not to get attached to strays, but he doesn't listen. Look at him, so insolent. Pretending he's not dying to touch you himself. What a joke." Just as the Shadow King is about to squeeze the full and sensitive flesh of my breast and feel me up in front of his underling, he stops and kisses the back of my ear instead. "When we fuck, I'll make him watch, and believe me...he'll enjoy it."

Holy horses.

"Now, walk into the pool," the king adds, a hint of amusement at the tip of his wicked tongue.

The magic hold recedes, and I cross my arms over my breasts, each of my hands gripping the opposite shoulder. In three steps, I descend into the warm, silky black liquid, the pool deep enough for it to reach my belly button.

One gives me an encouraging nod. "Hold your breath for at least ten seconds before you come out, and try not to move. It won't hurt, but it's a bit unpleasant."

The calm instructions keep me from crumbling. I inhale deep and sink inch by inch inside the shadow pool, grateful for the intimacy it procures. My heart pounds recklessly in my chest. The shadows embrace me like a mother cradles her child, the long braid at my back tossed over my shoulder by a soft ripple.

Thank the Mother he's not allowed to force himself on me, but nothing prevents him from finding other ways to torture me.

The skin of my face prickles and burns, the sting not exactly painful but uncomfortable enough for me to wince as I count down from ten.

Ten. Nine. Eight. Seven. Six.

Five... A weight gathers at my brow, and I graze the edge of the thick mask.

Four... A sharp texture appears on it, the part covering my eyes no longer smooth, but spiky as though a few jeweled pieces are now sticking out of the stone.

Three. Two. One... The shadows pull me to the surface, quite literally spitting me back out, and I draw a sharp, delirious breath.

I can see through my newly crafted mask perfectly, as though I'm not wearing one at all, and my pupils adjust to the sudden intensity of the candlelight. Reaching inside the depths of my soul, I summon enough confidence to walk out of the pool with my head held high.

The thick substance sticks to my breasts and bottom half in strategic places like the shadows recognized my need for modesty and were happy to provide it. It's not clothes, but it's better than nothing.

I glare at the Shadow King, unwilling to show how much his disgusting stunt affected me. He shoves One hard with his shoulder on his way out of the vault, exiting through the mirror behind the dark Fae.

I let out a small whimper, surprised to see him leave so abruptly, and the tight knot in my stomach eases.

"Ugh. He's an asshole." One holds out a fluffy towel in front of him. "Here."

I dig my heels in the ground. "And you think that's enough of an explanation? That makes it all okay?"

"Everyone has to strip for the ritual, but it's usually not so crowded..."

I wet my lips. "Lucky me."

I'm not stupid. I can feel the pressure of his gaze on me. On my hips. My thighs. In the hollow of my neck, slipping dangerously close to my breasts...

"My eyes are up here, *asshole*," I say, trying his slang on for size.

He barely holds in a laugh as he wiggles the white cloth from side to side. "The towel is right here. You chose not to take advantage of it."

Ugh. I finally tip-toe over to him and let him wrap the piece of fabric around my frame. I'm still rattled by the whole ordeal, but One doesn't curdle my blood like the Shadow King does. Quite the contrary.

I wonder if he's really dying to touch me?

The tar-like residue from the pool now feels and smells like water, quickly absorbed by the towel, leaving my skin clean and smooth as a polished pearl.

One spins around to allow me some privacy, the stiffness in his spine gone, his long fingers rapping his thigh in a repetitive motion.

I slip my clothes back on and paw at my belly, still mortified by what happened, but with a little more countenance. "I don't feel any different." Curious, I peel the mask off my face and flip it in my hands.

A wave of emeralds travels from the corner of one eye and over the bridge of the mask's nose only to spiral over its right cheek. The otherwise smooth gold mask is almost weightless despite the size of the stones.

Beautiful.

"Now, can you tell me what happened the other night in the gardens? I just swore fealty to your monstrous king," I croak.

One gives a negative slice of the head, and I want to shake him until he changes his mind.

"Do I have the Faerie sight?" I negotiate, trying to find another silver lining to this wretched, indoor swimming session.

"Not yet."

I draw back as he leans closer. "What are you doing?"

"Do you want the Faerie sight or not?" A leftover from his earlier snark rises to the surface.

"Yes." I'm rooted in place, wondering what's about to happen.

One cups the side of my face and whispers so softly that the wild beats of my heart almost drown out the words, "Close your eyes."

A nervous hiccup quakes my throat, but I obey. *Why does he have the power to do this, and not the king? It's odd.*

He presses his lips on my right lid, and wicked tremors rock up and down my spine as he switches to the other side. The heat of his kiss is dizzying, and my chest heaves.

Magic spices up the air, but it's not at all like the king's paralyzing power. It's warm and comforting and strangely familiar.

When I open my eyes again, the colors are vivid and slightly askew, and I blink to dissipate the warmth in my belly.

One pulls down his hood. Loose strands of raven-black hair fall over his mask, and I almost raise a hand to brush them back behind his pointy ears.

Almost, but not quite.

"Congratulations, kitten. You're a real seed, now. Tomorrow, I will teach you how to travel through the sceawere."

CHAPTER 15
BEHIND THE GLASS

The glossy surface of the mirror at the back of the balcony reflects my ambivalence. I'm about to face my biggest fear —and probable doom.

"Are you ready?" One asks me with his arms crossed.

No.

"Yes," I answer instead.

We stand shoulder to shoulder in front of the glass, our slightly distorted reflections touching at the hips. The mix of humiliation and exhilaration from last night's trial still clouds my brain as I observe him from the corner of my eye. I went straight to bed after the trial, exhausted from the intense use of magic, and spent the entire day biting my nails, wondering when he would fetch me for my lesson.

He wears a long bow on his back, the majestic weapon held in place by a leather strap, with no quiver in sight. A neatly trimmed sideburn runs parallel to his ear, licking the edge of his mask and a string of discrete Fae drawings disappear under his hairline.

When you've only seen the bottom third of someone's face, and suddenly you get to see more, it's hard not to obsess over every little detail. Or at the very least, it's the excuse I use to stare at his tattoos and pointy ears a little longer.

"The sceawere is an endless labyrinth. It can take you anywhere you want, but it can also swallow you whole. Once we're inside, just stay close to me." He links our fingers and steps toward the glass like it's ordinary.

His hand is warm in mine, and I squeeze it without thinking. My whole body stiffens at the prospect of visiting the in-between world that lurks beyond the mirror.

I flatten my mask to my face with my free hand, drawing in a sharp breath and holding it in. A pinch of frost tightens my cheeks, the wave of silver in front of me quickly vanishing in favor of a kaleidoscope of colors.

One's silhouette is slightly askew, everything beyond him blurry and incomplete. I catch glimpses of every room in the castle like I'm seeing through a series of tiny peepholes. As soon as I focus on one image in particular, it hides from me, replaced by another. On this side of the mirror, the glass moves, wild gusts of intangible wind plying it back and forth.

Thousands of silvery strings ripple between the different reflections. Multiple networks of semi-translucent threads have been crafted into different shapes and patterns like an eclectic, woven macrame. Some strings are thick as wool while others are as slim as a hair. Their strange shimmer makes it hard for me to focus, and shadows lurk at the edge of my vision.

One caresses the back of my knuckles. "Breathe, kitten."

The fresh air clears the dark spots that were dancing in front of my eyes.

He lets go of my hand and rolls up his left sleeve to his elbow, showcasing the inked drawings on his lower arm. "I've seen you dawdle about with *Introduction to Runes*. Can you tell me the meaning of one of these?"

I press my lips together, slighted by the jab. I'm the most studious of the three seeds, and while Mara thinks that makes me a *dork*, I bet she's never even tried to paint the most basic rune. Forcing down a flare of anger, I concentrate on the familiar symbols.

The runes are laid out in three squares, the nine closest to his wrist bigger than the five by five ones in the middle of his lower arm, a set of a hundred written in such small calligraphy near his elbow that I shudder.

I hold out one finger and recite the first nine near his wrist from memory. "That's Fae, Faerie, male, light, flame, wind, stone, water, heart, and the one in the corner here is the mark for 'the lack of.'"

The last one is most clever. If I were to combine it with the rune "light," the combination of the two spells "darkness."

His mouth opens slightly.

I search the five by five square, my bottom lip tucked between my teeth. With more certainty than I possess, I trace the first three, the skin of his underarm soft and smooth under my fingertips. "And those are tree, flower, and apple."

"You switched the last two." He smacks his lips. "But impressive."

The corners of my mouth curl up, and I let a hint of arrogance show on my face.

That'll teach him to underestimate me.

"To travel through the sceawere, you need an iron-clad will." One raises his left hand to the network of strings closest to him and glides his fingers along the flexible threads the way a musician caresses his lyre. "The in-between is a sort of unending harmony. The strings are all part of a gigantic instrument, in a way, and traveling to the right place only demands the right melody. Runes act as a sheet of music and mark the desired notes."

He tangles his left hand in a hanging piece of woven threads. The ink on his knuckles darkens as he moves the strings between his expert fingers, and his right hand comes as a sort of violin bow, his fingertips pricking a few of the runes on his lower arm.

As he moves, peeks of the familiar rooms in the castle are replaced by foreign places. One handles the glass strings like they're part of the most fragile musical instrument in existence, and his loving, careful movements bring a shiver to my core. His black nails are cut short, his long fingers more nimble than I expected. Men who fight often trade their agility for strength, but not One, obviously. A big part of me wishes he would touch me instead.

"Traveling within a world can be as easy as cutting through butter, but a novice can tap the strings a little too hard—a false note, if you will—and end up in the wrong realm." He slows down, moving languorously, as though he's serenading a long-lost lover.

"The runes on your hand, they're...different."

He motions to his left arm. "Those are tattoos, inked permanently into the skin but these—" he flips his right hand to show me his knuckles. "They're the equivalent of musician calluses, branded on my skin by all my travels, some of the destinations so ingrained in my memory that they have become part of my flesh."

Woah.

"Play the wrong sort of song" —he flicks the threads roughly, touching the runes near the kink of his elbow, and a shadow condenses across several pieces of glass. A demonic pair of reptilian eyes stares back at us from the other side— "and you will attract the entirely wrong kind of attention."

The monster juts an arm forward, and I tug One away from its long claws, but the creature only manages to streak the glass between us.

A small, gentle laugh trickles off One's lips before he bends the strings again, now threading the runes closer to his wrist. "Familiar places come easily."

The foot of my Faerie bed appears through the fray, and I squint, but it's there one moment and gone the next.

"But if your mind isn't clear and focussed, if you let your fears get the better of you or muddle your runes, you will get stuck and wander the in-between until nightmares find you."

He twists the strings more rapidly, and I'm disoriented to the point of helplessness until he grabs my hand again and pulls me forward. Colors and shapes blur together, and the cold goodbye kiss of the sceawere peppers flecks of ice on my skin.

"Welcome to New York, a staple of the new world," he says, releasing me.

Tall, sharp-angled towers run up and up around us, ten times the length of the tallest castle in Demeter, stretching almost as far as the eye can see. Lights flicker in the large windows of the humongous buildings, all the way up to the empty night sky, and the road in front of us is black and crusty. A few cracks run deep into the unknown material and reveal a few lonely weeds.

The narrow alleys the coachman rushes through in Lundan come to mind, full of dirt, grime, and the occasional criminal.

Behind us, a rectangular container full of garbage reeks of rotten cabbage, the acrid smell clogging up my nostrils. The mirror we just walked through has a smashed corner and a white trim, the thin, flimsy-looking piece of glass leaning on the garbage bin, tilted to the side as though it's part of the trash.

I wonder at a world where a mirror so big could be left lying around, unattended. Do these people know anything about magic?

"Why are we here?" I ask, not understanding the point of the lesson, our surroundings dirty and drab.

"A hunt. What else?" One points to a dark blotch at the end of the alley and crouches, lowering his voice.

I squint, my eyes slowly adjusting to the darkness. A griffin pecks at something on the ground, its beak cutting through it with ease.

The half-eagle, half-lion creature tilts its head backward to swallow a mangled piece of meat, blood spraying its white feathers.

An oily, black sheen licks the underside of its wings, the griffin flapping them cheerfully every few seconds, its enthusiasm for its meal—a dog, I think—raising all the hairs at the back of my neck.

"Nightmares are fashioned out of the Shadow Court's magic. They're supposed to prey on the dreamers, but when they spill out of the sceawere to reach the awake, they threaten the proper flow of our magic. It's the hunters' job to kill them to release their power and bring it back to Faerie," One explains before approaching the creature.

He bows slightly in front of the griffin, a show of respect but not submission. The nightmare grazes the black, volcanic-looking road with its talon.

"Most of them are akin to animals, with the same urges and behavior. Others...are worse."

A burst of shadow stretches from One's hands and condenses into an arrow. A sleek, metallic glint reflects off its sharp head. Quiet as a ghost, he nocks it onto the string and draws his weapon. The creature cocks its head to the side, more out of curiosity than anything.

My pulse flutters, and I bite my bottom lip.

The bow gives a low *creeek*, but the phantom arrow is deadly quiet as it flies to the heart of its prey. Startled, the griffin cries out before it explodes in a cloud of smoke. Dark tendrils wisp out of its abdomen, snaking along the road in our direction until its body dissolves into nothingness. The serpentine remnants of the nightmare stretch toward us, and I dig the balls of my feet into the ground, ready to run.

"Don't move," my teacher orders, and I uncoil my muscles, watching with bated breath as the shadows blend into his skin.

"When we kill a rogue nightmare, we become a vessel for its power. The magic remains inside us until we return it to the Hawthorn, and when we do, both king and kingdom are strengthened by its return." A flush of heat colors his neck as he snaps the bow back over his shoulder.

"You killed it so quickly..."

One shakes his head. "I've been doing this for a long time. Believe me, it's not as easy as it looks." He digs a sleek rectangular-shaped metal device from his pocket and touches the center. Light blares from the previously dark contraption, and I recognize what Mara called a cellphone.

"We have to check out my place nearby. Something apparently

tripped up the alarm."

"Your place?"

He gives a sharp nod. "Traveling between worlds is more tiring than it looks, kitten. The king keeps dwellings in both the old world and the new. A ton of them, in fact." He grips my hand and tugs me back inside the crooked mirror, the depths of the sceawere as confusing as they were before.

When we emerge, we're no longer outside, but surrounded by tall walls that run up to a vaulted ceiling. The place must have been very close to the alley because it took barely a second to travel, and I recognize some of the fixtures of the new world that I read about.

A large bed—larger still than the one in my Faerie bedroom—occupies the opposite side of the living space. The large mirror we stepped through is glued to the wall, and a nearby sink is flanked by a string of white cupboards.

"Where are we?" I ask.

"A condo on the Upper East Side," One says as he discards his bow on the dresser.

Tall glass windows offer a jaw-dropping view of the lighted towers from before. Hundreds of them shine in the night, and I hold my breath as I take in how far up we actually are, the slim street below minuscule and downright scary.

I hold my arms out on both sides of me and backtrack toward the mirror. "We're so high up..."

"Don't worry, windows in the new world are thicker than bricks and harder to break than stones." He punches the glass forcefully with his palm, and I jump at the sudden move.

"See? Safe as houses."

He checks the lighted screen again and mutters under his breath before pushing the large double door open. We enter an immense closet, and he turns on the lights with a press of a button. I jump at the intense burst of light. Only the most modern houses have electricity in Lundan.

A golden amulet hanging from a hook reflects the warm glow of the electric chandeliers. Coffered spaces hold a wide array of clothes and weapons as well as a collection of trinkets, jewels, and figurines.

"There you are," One says.

In the far corner of the closet, a black and red spider the size of a small pig laps blood from the ground with its hairy pedipalps—the crooked appendage next to the fangs.

The body of a woman lays in a straight line next to it, deep lacerations running down her skin, and I shudder. "It's another nightmare."

"Yes." His voice remains calm and level, but I detect a hint of unease. One holds the creature's gaze until it stops eating. "You killed my maid. That's not very nice."

The arachnid's front legs twitch a few times before it turns its back on us and starts drinking the blood again.

One snatches a crossbow similar to the one I'm used to from the wall and presses it to my chest. "Kill it."

The heavy weapon isn't as hard to hold as it used to be. "Me?"

"Yes."

A silver bolt is already in position, and I raise it to the nightmare. Seemed easy enough with the griffin, and I've spent weeks practicing my aim.

"Aim deep below the eyes. A spider's brain is located close to its stomach."

I blow air out of my lungs and concentrate on the head. I've done this a hundred times by now, but a wooden target always stood on the receiving end—not a living thing.

I rationalize that these nightmares aren't really alive, merely moving puppets of shadow magic. My fingers tingle with warmth as I let the bolt fly, and the silver tip buries deep inside the spider, right below its eyes.

My lips quirk up as I lower the crossbow.

"Not bad. Not bad at all," One says.

The spider melts into eight strands of black smoke that wave across the room, creeping closer to us. They probe the soles of my shoes and twist around my ankles.

I shake my legs furiously. "By the Mother—"

"Relax, kitten. Let it in."

I force myself to stay still and allow the shadows to merge with my flesh. A boost of energy washes through me, quickening my heartbeat and spreading across my muscles.

When I'd passed the trial, I'd felt a tiny speck of magic merge with me and fill a tiny hole in my heart. The power I'm feeling now could fill an entire canyon, but just as I knew the magic from the underground cave wasn't mine and only there for me to use, this is merely borrowed as well.

I press a hand to my sternum. "Wow. I feel like I could run ten miles."

One moves to cover the dead body with a white sheet. "Your first kill. Congratulations. I just need to figure out how the fuck this nightmare got in here and we—" He stops abruptly, his mask angled to the ceiling. "Get behind me. Quick."

CHAPTER 16
SHADOW KISSED

I spin around in time to see a gigantic spider crawl upside down through the opened door, its hairy legs topped with blueish claws. Globulous eyes shine under the electrical lights, its upside-down face at eye level with mine.

Venom drips from its fangs and splashes the carpet in front of us. Tiny flares of smoke rise from the floor as the spider's saliva burns through the fabric. I dart behind One as the dark knight draws his bow to the mother of all monsters.

The thing hisses and scurries closer. It uses one of its legs to cleave the bow in two and slashes the front side of One's shoulder and chest in one sweep.

"Get down," One commands.

The spider strikes again, and I feel a breeze near my face as I fall to my knees. If not for the power boost from the tiny spider, my head would have been split down the middle.

"Stay on the ground and play dead. It relies on movement to attack."

Blood pours out of the gash in his shoulder as he slowly inches his arms behind his back, so slowly in fact that I can barely see him move. My gaze darts from the lethal creature to him—back and forth.

The spider snaps its fangs and screeches, the noises all wet and disgusting, like a hunter's knife cutting through flesh. Each sound is followed by another spill of venom. A droplet splashes my knee, and I clench my jaw. The liquid quickly melts the fabric of my pants, sending a painful throb up my leg.

And that was merely a drop!

I hold my breath as the creature shifts to the right, expecting its next goop of drool to career directly for my hip.

A long, dark cloud condenses into a spear at One's back, and he squints at the nightmare. "By the spindle..." he cocks his head to the side, "I know you," he adds a little louder. "Asabikeshiinh!" That last word riles the spider up quite a bit, and it springs forward, its claws scratching along the ceiling.

One transfers the spear to his uninjured arm and throws it at the monster. It buries deep below its eyes, and the spider drops to the floor next to me with a thunderous *thump*. Its legs convulse for a moment before it bursts into smoke, but instead of heading toward One, it crumbles nefariously in the air.

Flakes of darkness float about the room as I croak, "What did you say to it?"

"I said its name." He kneels next to me and huddles close. The heat of his body dissipates the fear in my belly, but he doesn't look quite as relieved as I am. "Show me where the venom landed."

I sit up and hike up my pants past the kink of my knee, and One inspects the venom burn with his bottom lip tucked between his teeth. The tips of his fingers graze the sensitive skin under my knee as he wraps his hand around my lower thigh to pull the small burn under the glow of electric lights.

He examines it from all sides like it matters more than the gigantic cut running down his shoulder to his chest. "You're good. It didn't sink past the first layer of skin."

I raise a tentative hand to his shoulder. "What about you? You're covered in blood."

A warm chuckle pops out of his mouth. "I'm used to it. And there's no venom in mine." One stands and shrugs off his jacket, the fabric shredded to bits, his black undershirt sticky with clots. "That spider was a special breed of monster that shouldn't exist. It's a nightmare, but not one that grew naturally in the Dreaming. It was weaved by an enemy."

I swallow the throng of questions swirling in my brain. Blood trickles down his arm on our way back to the kitchen, peppering the floor, and One pulls open the lid of a vertical metallic casket.

Light shines into a variety of receptacles, and I catch a glimpse of a plump tomato, so it must be a food storage unit.

He grips the hilt of an amber-tinted bottle and uncorks the top, tilting his head back to gulp down its content. "Want a beer—ale, I mean?" he offers.

I shake my head. "Let me see your wound."

With a low grunt, he tears what's left of his shirt off and inspects the damage. A nasty cut runs from the side of his left arm to the middle of his torso, and he skims the mangled flesh with the tips of his fingers. "What a mess."

Sweat and blood stick to his skin, the grooves and ridges of his muscles new and fascinating. I've only glimpsed at these shapes in paintings, and a hot thrill suffocates me.

Biting my bottom lip, I inch closer. "I could try to heal you..."

His brows pull together. "Have you done that before?"

"Yes. Can I?" I gesture to the cut running diagonally across his pectoral muscle.

He gives me a small, almost imperceptible, nod. "Only if you want to."

Mustering a confidence I didn't know I had, I lay my palm flat over his wound. "Why wouldn't I want to?"

"You look terrified, kitten. Your heart's beating way too fast..."

Magic electrifies the air as the wound slowly heals, and warmth radiates in my chest. The boost of magic I'd received when I killed the small spider melts inside One's injury.

"I thought I had to return the magic to the Hawthorn?" I ask, sad to relinquish the euphoria and strength that came with the power boost, but happy to put it to good use.

One grips the counter at his back, holding his breath. "In theory."

Once the healing is complete, I caress the fresh patch of skin on the guise of inspecting it, and my gut twists up in knots.

"Nicely done. I haven't been able to heal myself since—I wasn't sure your powers would work on me," One says.

"Why not?"

"Our magic is powerful, but sometimes I feel like it has forsaken me."

Our magic...

Something about the way he breathes the words sets my teeth on edge, and a wild hypothesis forms in my brain. "Were you a seed once?"

With a dark chuckle, he peels my hand away from his chest, breaking the spell. "Would you be less scared of me if I said yes?"

"I'm not—" I swallow hard, not ready to admit my wild heart-beats have nothing to do with fear. "But you're Fae."

"Fae or not, shadow magic is merely the metal we use to forge our own tools. You get to decide what shape your magic takes, and whether to grind its edges into smooth blades or braid it into unbreakable strings. Healing abilities are usually synonymous to a keen mind and a compassionate heart. Those qualities could make you a great huntress. Seeds have to show a minor but well-rounded ability for the three paths, but sprouts can focus their studies on only one or two... With enough training, you could learn to craft bolts of shadows out of the very palm of your hands."

"Like you did earlier with the arrow," I cut in.

"Yes." He walks away and enters the third, unexplored room. "I'm going to take a quick shower. You can help yourself to anything in the fridge." With that eerily benign offer, he shuts the door in my face, entombing himself and his secrets on the other side.

Holy horses!

Butterflies wreck havoc in my stomach as I wash my hands in the sink, set my mask down on the counter, and use a wet rag to pat my face down, wiping off a splash of his blood—and way too much sweat.

Curious about this incredibly small kitchen, I tiptoe over to the *fridge* and open it again. The neat rows of bottles and metal cans have words written across them in both bold and tiny calligraphy, and the drawers of fresh-looking vegetables and fruits leave me in awe.

I've never even read about some of these.

A jar of cold water on the bottom shelf beckons, and I rummage through the neighboring cupboards for a glass, my hands still tingling with adrenaline from the kill, the healing, and the warmth of One's skin.

He comes out of the bathroom in minutes, rubbing a fluffy white towel to his ear. His hair is all in disarray, no longer slicked back over his head, and the wavy black locks soften his lethal, curated look. He's still half-naked, but wearing a different pair of pants, and his mask is clean... The thought that he removed it in there dries up my mouth.

An eerie-looking shadow across his chest catches my attention. The anomaly hovers above the hunter's heart like smoke, and yet gleams in the night like liquid silk. I couldn't see it earlier because of all the blood, but the black luster draws me in.

I rinse out my glass to keep myself from touching it. "Earlier. Were you saying I could become...like you?"

He grabs another *beer* in the fridge and hops onto the island, legs dangling below him, barely an inch of space between us. "Would you want to?"

I return the glass to the cupboard to try and break the tension. "You're talking in riddles."

"If you pass your neophyte training, you could become a huntress." His broad frame obscures the city lights as he leans in ever so slightly. "Is that...something you'd want?"

A thrill spirals in my bones at the proximity of his bare chest, and I blush a thousand shades of red. He looks perfectly at ease to be half-naked in front of me, like it's natural.

Crops, it's hot in here.

"I could never—"

"Hypothetically."

I squint at him, desperate to see his eyes underneath the mask, desperate to know if I can trust him. "Yesterday, before I took the oath, you said my full name. Why?"

He swallows a mouthful of ale before answering, "Names are at the root of our magic. You can know *of* something without knowing its name, but to truly master it, or have any sort of real power over it, you must learn its full name."

Him and his brothers are hiding their true names. It's so obvious after this conversation; it's not even a question. Even Lori. Mara. James. I don't know their full names, and I even had the instinct to only give them a part of mine.

"So when I asked if One was really your name... It wasn't very smart." Still, something gnaws at me. "If knowing someone's name gives you power over them, why does the king present his to everyone? Why doesn't he keep it secret, too?"

"The king is the most powerful being in the Shadowlands. To rule over people, you must prove you're strong enough for them to know your name."

My nose wrinkles at the flaws in his logic. "That sounds ridiculous."

He cracks a smile. "What about your kingdom? Do you feel you have the right to rule because you are your father's daughter? Shouldn't a reign be built on more than blood?"

"I'm not allowed to reign. I'm a woman."

"Isn't that flawed?" He scratches the edge of his mask back and forth.

"Are there queens in Faerie? Queens that truly reign?"

He holds up three fingers. "Autumn, Spring, and Summer."

"Wow." *Almost half.* "And what does 'by the spindle' mean?"

"According to Fae legends, the fabric of the universe is weaved in real time by the gods through a single, golden spindle. Everything we are—everything we feel—is immortalized in an endless tapestry. And the different threads used decide what course our lives will take." He angles his mask to the ground between us. "Penelope means weaver, did you know?"

The sweet, eerie way my name rolls off his tongue emboldens me to inch closer, but I shake my head.

"She was a Fae queen. Everyone thought her husband had been killed at war, but she didn't believe them. Countless suitors tried to steal her away, but she set out to weave a burial shroud for him and vowed not to take any man to bed before she'd finished weaving it— a task she never intended on completing."

My stomach flip-flops. "Clever."

"The perfect name for a pious, loyal wife." He licks his lips and discards his empty bottle in the sink, a shadow darkening his mask. "The spider was planted here to attack me. Poor Clara—the lovely woman who kept the fridge full and paid my bills—was just collateral damage. We should deal with her body before we go." He jumps off the counter, and the strange smog over his heart thickens.

This time, I can't resist the urge to touch it, and my hand darts out of its own volition. "What is that?"

One snatches my wrist and holds it close to his chest, effectively covering the anomaly. "A leftover scar...from a past mistake." His lips press together for a moment before he adds, "No one is supposed to be able to see it."

"It moves." I try and fail to peek at it again.

One's voice quiets down, and his slow drawl riddles me with goosebumps. "It was a very bad mistake."

I stare at the claw marks, where I figure his eyes are, and graze the edge of his mask with my other hand.

"Don't—"

Despite his warning, I peel the layer of obsidian stone away from his face. His nails dig into my pulse point, but he doesn't stop me, my captive hand still locked over his heart.

I spent hours imagining what he looked like, wondering if the claw marks in his mask were a clue as to what laid underneath.

A scar runs from One's forehead to his cheek in a straight line, but it's by no means his most striking or bewitching feature. Liquid gold burns within his irises, and he draws in a sharp intake of breath. Our gazes are locked as I trace the arch of his scarred brow. His strong cheekbones match the shape of his jaw, and I follow the aesthetic curve of his nose down to his mouth.

His grip tightens around my wrist. "Careful, kitten."

"Why do you keep the mask on? You're...perfect," I ramble, stunned by his appearance.

"You think I'm perfect?" He snickers in a derisive manner and prowls forward. My backside bumps the island as he releases my wrist to wrap a hand around my throat. "Do you have any idea how *imperfect* I can be?"

"No," but the tug in my belly tells me I want to find out.

The base of his thumb settles in the hollow of my throat, and if he means to scare me, he's doing a very poor job of it. My gaze drops to his lips.

"Fuck." He curls a hand around the back of my neck to hold me closer, and I push myself off the ground to kiss him.

He meets me halfway.

When he takes advantage of my small gasp to slide his tongue inside my mouth, I respond out of instinct. The taste of charred pears and fine wine invades my senses, and a low, approving growl grates his throat.

This kiss is *nothing* like the ones I shared with Isaac.

Our tongues crash into one another, over and over again, in a slow, delectable dance. I can't get enough. I want more.

I want it *all*.

He angles my face to the sky and dips his head to lick the slope of my neck. The touch of his lips *there* is so overwhelming that I cry out. My knees wobble, but he pins me to the counter at my back, his strong thigh sliding between my legs.

The need to retaliate grows beyond my control, and I forget myself. Without an ounce of hesitation, I rake my nails down his shoulder blades and test the contours of his body. The feel of his strong, naked back sets me ablaze as I study which spot plagues him with goosebumps and which causes him to shudder.

My dark Fae reaches behind me and tugs on the end of my braid, pulling the thread down. He unravels it with both hands like he's been dying to do so for *weeks*. The caress somehow carries the weight of all the other wasted opportunities combined, his touch not the same as the touch of a mortal. Lithe. Heavy. Simply *more*.

We breathe together for ten, twenty, maybe a hundred breaths, and kiss as though we were always meant to kiss.

I draw away from his lips to taste the constellation of Fae tattoos behind his ear, and he meets my gaze. Something shifts, and all of the sudden, I feel lighter than air.

One's liquid-gold irises are like the pages of an open book, more revealing than the most sensual of fairy tales. Clearer than poetry. Sweeter than music.

His eyes are full of unsung songs.

I start to undress in front of him, unzipping my jacket and shrugging it off, eager for him to touch me. I wait for some measure of warning to spark a storm in my chest, but my dark Fae isn't offering the same sins I read about in books. The poor women in the stories Esme passed along were all left ruined and alone. They spent their whole lives regretting their moment of weakness and erred until their last breath, trying to repair the damage done.

I'd never regret his touch. If he were to break me with his hands, he'd make sure to glue me back together. I read all that in his eyes and more, along with the shape of his true name.

Spellbound, I scratch deep lines in his back, and he bites my bottom lip in response. The metallic tang of blood smears my tongue, and the eerie lightheadedness recedes.

One tears himself away. All the clarity I'd gained in his arms fades, and I bring a hand to my bloody lip, the name that had been on the tip of my tongue retreating back to the darkness.

Heartbeats echo in my throat, my chest, and the intimate, forbidden place between my legs.

"I shouldn't have done that," he croaks, his chin angled to the ground.

"I—Why?"

Wait...is he talking about the kiss, the removal of his mask, or the bite?

Blood stains my index finger when I pat the cut. "It's barely a nick—"

"Near the end. I didn't mean to enchant you." The swirl of shadow over his heart wriggles and writhes like a nightmare threatening to crawl out.

A fierce blush brands my cheeks. All the songs I'd thought I could read in his eyes...that really should have been my cue that something was wrong. *Crops.*

"It's my mistake. Let's pretend it never happened." He escapes to the darkness, suddenly invisible, his discarded mask vanishing along with him.

A chill envelops me, his heat gone, and the aftershocks of his kiss shiver through my body. "One?" I search the empty room, but the only sound audible is the loud pulse at my temples.

CHAPTER 17

A THOUSAND CUTS

"One abandoned you again, I see," Mara declares. She invades the nook at the back of the balcony I claimed as my own and slumps down in the chair facing mine.

The fragrant smells steaming from her full plate of eggs, cheese, and meat turn my queasy stomach.

"Good morning, Mara." I unfold my leg from below me and sit straight in the chair, resenting the accuracy in her statement.

One *did* abandon me last night and sent Lori to bring me home *in the morning*. The raven-haired girl offered a few encouraging words, thinking my lesson had gone badly, oblivious to the real reason her *boss* would leave me stranded in a world I don't belong in, in a bedroom adjacent to a dead body.

The half-eaten apple on my plate is peppered with brown streaks, and I stare at it for a moment, trying to summon enough strength for this conversation.

"When I saw him earlier, I thought he was about to murder somebody," Mara says.

I snap my book shut. "You saw him?"

Her fork digs into the pile of food, a big chunk already halfway to her lips. "Yes. I was just studying in the bibliotheca with Two, but One strode in like a horseman of the apocalypse and dismissed me with one look. Lori said you'd spent the night in New York…" her voice remains the same, but her eyes flick up to me for a second, the fork hanging in mid-air. "Did something happen?"

"I'm sorry. I have to go." I leave everything as is and hurry off to the stairs.

"Catch you later, alligator."

I shake my head, wondering what the crops is wrong with that girl, and sneak to the secluded, second-floor entrance of the library.

The stacks on the mezzanine run perpendicular to the railing, and my breath catches in my throat. A hooded figure crouches in the dark, in a perfect position to spy on the floor below. It's one of the triplets, but with his back to me, I can't tell which one.

Sweat gathers on my palms at the prospect of seeing One again, until his deep voice echoes from the floor below. "—to not overthink this."

"What are you hiding?" A snarkier voice answers. *Two.*

"Nothing."

Three looks over his shoulder and offers me an enigmatic smile. The third brother is the one skulking in the dark. The way he moves is so telling—so incredibly specific and bewitching—I feel as though he's weaving words with his body.

He puts one finger over his mouth and motions me closer. *Come. Quietly.*

"You can't speak, can you?" I murmur.

He shakes his head without shame or regret. *No.* With his book tucked under his left arm, he peers cautiously around the end of the stack.

Lori has deserted the front desk, probably busy with a customer on the floor above. I risk a glance to the ground floor and catch a glimpse of Two. The cocky brother steps closer to his twin until their masked faces are inches apart.

The differences between them are glaring, the second knight's movements jerky and less fluid. One possesses more of a deadly, feline grace, while Three is so stealthy, he might as well be made of smoke.

The cynical curve of Two's mouth deepens. "If nothing happened, why would you alter the schedule? Did she see something she shouldn't have? Is that why—"

"No! The kingdom needs magic, and she's got it in spades. The sooner she passes the first three trials, the better. I can teach her how to hunt later," One answers.

Wait... They're talking about me.

Three represses a full bodied laugh, quaking soundlessly beside me. He leans on the shelf behind him and removes his hood, shaking his head. He's got slightly longer hair than his brothers, but I spot a familiar cluster of tattoos behind his ear, and my cheeks flush.

Oblivious to our presence, Two walks over to a table layered with parchments and returns one of them to a scroll holder. "We can't agree to disagree on this. We've got to be on the same page, and that page has got Darcy's name on it. If she saw too much in the gardens or if she can't handle nightmares—"

One angles his chin to the sky, clearly annoyed. "She saw nothing, and she passed the first trial without a hitch."

Two picks up a book from the table and waves it in the space between them. "Then why are you getting rid of her?"

"I'm not arguing with you about this. You will do as I say."

Two freezes mid-step. "Excuse me?" He slides the volume he was holding in its rightful place with a chilling accuracy. "Need I remind you...the princess belongs to the *king*."

"I know."

A hard ball of nerves sinks in my stomach, and I glance sideways at the third triplet, but his face is shrouded in darkness.

On the floor below, Two whips his head around to face his brother. "She's meant to serve the king's needs. If it's better *for the king* for you to train her first, then that's what you shall do."

"The king's needs come first. Always," One says in one breath, the way you repeat a prayer—or rather a mantra.

The two men measure each other. One looks about to punch his brother out cold, but before he makes up his mind, Two turns on his heels and storms out, curses echoing in his wake.

Three brings two fingers to his forehead in lieu of goodbye and sneaks out the exit.

As soon as he's gone, I dart out of the stacks to ambush One before he leaves, too. "You're getting rid of me?" I shout without preamble, my knuckles white over the railing.

Not waiting for an answer, I scurry to the narrow stairs and take them two at a time.

If One is surprised by my arrival, he doesn't show it. He sits on the table he was using like everything is going according to plan and brings a large parchment up between us, his tone withdrawn and dismissive. "It's time for you to train with Two. Considering the strength of your powers, I'm confident you can pass the first three trials and sprout quickly, which will bring in more magic."

I clench my fists to keep from trembling. "Horseshit."

He doesn't glance up from the page he so clearly only picked up to avoid looking at me.

"You're switching me with Mara because of the kiss—"

"Don't flatter yourself, kitten," he cuts in, the usually endearing pet name dry and brittle. "I'm immortal. I've kissed a thousand women before you, and there'll be a thousand more."

My jaw opens and closes, my belly clenched tight as though I've swallowed a mouthful of ash. A thousand women... It puts things into much-needed perspective, and my anger for this unholy world returns full-force.

"A thousand women and no wife, you're a real...pussy monger." Heat sears my cheeks at my language, but I force a deep breath in.

That's what I overheard Esme call a duke who had many mistresses and no wife, but I don't know what possessed me to say such a thing. It's incredibly crude.

One clearly didn't expect me to talk back to him, probably hoping to shock me into silence, but him and his *thousand women* can piss off. Instead of fleeing, I walk over to him and stare until he stands.

He stretches to his full height, the oh-so-important parchment discarded in a flash. "Don't push me."

A piece of my soul rises to the occasion, craving more, and it frightens me. I'm so hot, I can hardly breathe. My mind is caught inside the countless stories I've read growing up, my imagination on fire. "Push you? What are you going to do? Enchant me again? Make me undress for you? Dance for you?"

The brazen questions echo across the stacks, and my heart beats in my throat.

One pinches on a loose, white-blond wave between his index finger and thumb and follows it down to the valley between my breasts. "If I'd wished it so, you would have danced for me until your paws were bloody, kitten. But that's not what happened, is it?" he says quietly.

We're hanging by a thread. I only wish I could see his eyes in this moment. I'm sure they would reveal all his secrets.

Lori's booming voice shatters the moment. "Yes, it's the only original copy we have. The very last one," she enunciates loudly. "You couldn't hope for a better reference on the subject."

My gaze darts to the third floor where a wide-eyed Lori glares at us over a row of books. She makes a frenzied horizontal gesture under her chin behind the customer's back, the motion clearly begging for us to *cut it out.*

One grips a fist of his hair as he retreats several feet toward the front door. A moment later, Lori climbs down the staircase with her customer in tow. She ushers the Fae lady to the librarian desk, and I recognize her from the banquet.

One forces an unnatural cheer to his demeanor and hurries off to greet his peer. "Isobel, how nice to run into you here."

Isobel offers him her hand to kiss. "We've missed you in Umbra, One. You promised to visit more."

He presses his lips to her knuckles, and the fake warmth in his answer is seamless enough to appear real. "Alas, the king needs me here."

Isobel Umbra is a tall and beautiful High Fae. A crown of braids holds her dark hair up, a feminine golden mask with jade specks resting on her small nose. My studies have taught me that she's the first lady of Umbra, one of the five provinces in the Shadowlands.

One chats her up with an easy smile. "Are you in the mood for a stroll through the gardens?"

"With you? Always," she answers longingly.

My teeth grit together as the two of them leave the library arm in arm, and Lori grimaces apologetically. "I interrupted something, didn't I?"

I blink a few times too many, the anger from before still running hot in my veins. "You could say that."

"Isobel is about the worst gossip of the Shadow Court. I couldn't let her see you two like this. One looked about ready to tackle you down and tear your clothes off."

I swallow hard, appalled by her analysis, and yet I can't quite deny it.

My friend scurries to the main entrance and quietly retrieves the triangular piece of wood holding the door open. She slips it inside the big front pocket of her hooded sweater before spinning around to face me.

"Spill. What's going on with your training?" She plays with the two cords of fabric sticking out of her hood. "I've never seen One so worked up before."

"He's infuriating."

She winces at that, and I can tell by her reaction that I've just said the wrong thing.

"You shouldn't get involved with him." She crosses her arms and looks to the ceiling. "Listen...the seeds who've gotten too close to one of the triplets, they've all—" she stops abruptly.

A line of fear crawls along my spine. "Tell me. Please."

Her clear eyes pulse under the glow of the chandeliers. "They've all vanished overnight, Nell."

CHAPTER 18
A FALLEN QUEEN

The oval-shaped mirror of the antique shop whines on its hinges as I step out of the sceawere and hurry out into the gray streets of Inverness.

A rainy breeze curls around the corner of the building in front of me and sends shivers down my spine. Earthy notes of moss, wet grass, and the dry fumes of a whisky distillery bring back memories of my youth, when I could remain out of Faerie for weeks at a time.

The paved street is empty but for a thirty-something mortal hurrying alongside the old brick walls. A black raincoat is wrapped around her frame, and the free ends of her knotted sash flap in the wind. She draws a sharp intake of breath. Even though she can't see me, she's got enough instinct to cross the street, but I'm not here for her.

I'm here for someone I haven't seen in decades. Someone I cared about, once upon a time. Before everything went to shit.

The woman I'm looking for knows better than to own a mirror, but her magical signature isn't exactly discrete, so I follow it to a small shop tucked deep in the back alley. A wooden sign above the solid black door reads: Pat's Pottery, Pots, and Potions.

A chime tinkles above my head when I enter the small shop. The rowan threshold steals the air out of my lungs, but I soldier through and pierce the old wood's enchanted barrier.

I pry my dark hood off my head, and rain peppers the floor.

The pungent, smoky aromas of Panyang Congou and lemongrass fill my nose. Three small round tables with tall stools stand in a corner, the other side of the room occupied by a rowan bar counter with a sink and a portable stove. An eclectic array of vials and jars clutter the shelves behind it. A few handmade ceramic tea sets have been left to dry upside down on a rag, and a waterfall of reflective glass beads guards the entrance to the shopkeeper's backroom.

By the spindle... A little bit more on the nose, and there'd be a cauldron boiling in the hearth.

I hit the bell with my palm, and a loud *ding* resonates throughout the room.

Breaking into a Fae's shop is fair game, but skulking around is not. Shadows dance along the rowan panes nailed to the walls, allowing me a glimpse at the secrets behind the grain of the wood. The wicked pulse of power blasting off the bronze ceremonial lantern in the corner throws me for a loop, but I know better than to snoop around Devi's things.

A discrete creak calls my attention to the alpine weather house fastened to the wall behind the bar where a girl holding an umbrella just switched places with a sunny gentleman.

I squint at the bauble, sensing a familiar presence within it. "I know you're in there, Faeling." I wait for a moment with no answer before my hand shoots out toward the wavering weather house.

Shadows spill from my fingertips to imprison the small winged creature that had taken refuge in it, creating a cage of black smoke around it.

"Fetch your mistress for me, Percy," I command.

The Faeling buzzes around the cage, the friction of its wings creating a flurry of sparks in the poorly lit room.

After a few unfruitful escape attempts, it finally settles down long enough for me to see its shape. Dressed in purple from head to toe, it braces its leather cuffed hands on its tiny hips with a sigh. "She doesn't live here anymore, she—"

"Do you remember what the punishment is for lying to me, Percival Arthur Batten?" I say ominously.

The Faeling squeaks in terror. "I swear it on my life, My Lord. She's not here."

"It's okay, Percy. I'll deal with him." The river of glass beads twinkles in the night, and a slender, barefooted Fae slips inside the room. She purses her full lips, the pout adding a sense of intrigue to her demeanor. "It's good to see you, *cousin*."

I grin dryly at the false appellation. "Devi."

No warm-blooded creature ever gets used to Devi—not even me. Back when she was at the height of her power, her renowned beauty was enough to spark wars. Her eyes—considered by most to be her most striking feature—are large and expressive, framed by long, dark lashes. Painters have failed to capture the silver-flecks of her irises or the radiance of her smooth brown skin.

A thousand men and women have fallen to their knees in front of her, but few ever stood up again. Mortals who stare into Devi's eyes for too long will love her until their last breath.

I will resent her for much longer.

Her thick mane is red as flame—and every bit as wild and untamed as she is. Each of the tousled strands carries a vivid crimson hue as she brings a hand to the multi-colored scarf wrapped around her forehead, and the constellation of dark freckles on her face is the only mask she ever needed to conceal her cunning.

"Now... Let poor Percy go."

I wave the shadow cage away, and the Faeling flies off with a huff, both figurines of the weather house screeching back inside the alpine chalet.

"Of all the dwellings in all the worlds, you chose this..." I glance around her witch hut. "...shop."

She motions at the empty fireplace. "It's cozy."

"It's beneath you. What will you do next? Card readings? Dances under the dolmens?"

She sticks out her tongue in disgust like she just bit into a frost apple. "Exile isn't exactly *fun*." She examines me from head to toe, and wrinkles appear at the corners of her eyes. "Blimey. By the looks of you, you'll get a taste of it soon enough."

Only the devil of spring, Violet "Devi" Eros, ever held enough power to ruin me, and ruin me, she did, though it wasn't exactly her fault. Only she knows the truth about my demise, and I hate her for it.

"I know that look on your face." She fills one of her more modern teapots and clicks the portable stove on. "Morrigan's back."

"Her magic was felt in the sceawere, somewhere between Lightning Point and the Frozen Hills."

Devi grips the lid of her tea chest, the only clue that she's about as furious as I am. "We knew she'd be back."

"But why now?"

She laughs at that, her melodic voice tugging at every crumb of manhood I still possess. "Have you seen yourself, Samhain?" She saunters over to me, her bottom lip tucked between her teeth, and skims my jacket with her long, black nails. "If I was an evil bitch looking to steal your crown, I'd only need one look at you to know you're *ripe* for the picking." She pushes into me and retreats, quick as a cat. "Tea?"

The sizzle of her wanton gaze sucks the air out of the room, but I shake my head. "I don't have time for games."

With a shrug, she picks up one small cup from the shelf. "Your loss."

Devi's idea of *tea* means soul-shattering sex that would cost me more than I can afford.

Steam whistles out of the tea set before she speaks again. "Rye used me as much as she used you. The arrows she stole from my quiver cost me my crown, as you well know."

My jaw clenches at the reminder. "She weaved a dreamcatcher spider, and we both know she couldn't have done it alone."

A sudden flash of hatred burns in Devi's eyes and drains the crafted warmth from her lovely, destructive face. "If the phantom queen weaved a dreamcatcher spider, she did so without my help. I haven't spoken, seen, or written to her in eighty years."

My chest deflates, the scope of her admission not lost on me. If Rye doesn't have Devi as an ally, then maybe I have a shot. Now, I only have to verify Seth's claim that Elio might have become her new target.

"Have you spoken to E lately?" I ask with fake aloofness.

Devi lets out a small snort. "Are we all to be considered traitors until proven otherwise? Elio might be a shell of the man he used to be, but he's not about to turn on you."

A tinge of guilt touches my heart. "So, he's not better?"

Her hands cramp around the tea chest she's holding. "What do you think? He lost another queen. And it won't be long before winter hits and he needs to marry *again*."

I bow to the fallen Queen of Hearts. "Thank you for your honesty." I turn around to take my leave.

The rowan threshold creaks under my heavy boots, but I hesitate and glance back at Devi.

She plops a handful of leaves in her tea set and twirls them around. "Anything else?"

I scratch the space over my heart without meaning to. "You kept a few arrows, I'm sure."

She flashes me her teeth, the smile devoid of any warmth. "Would I admit to that? If the others learned of such a transgression, they would have my head."

My gaze drops to the ground. "I'm guessing your successor hasn't been able to carve them sharp enough to pierce a Fae's heart."

Her knuckles turn white over the ceramic lid. "Ugh. Like that usurper could ever measure up to me."

"I know I haven't laid eyes on you in decades, but how long has it been since you last saw *me,* Devi?"

These intruding thoughts I've been wrestling with the last few weeks...they're not natural. No Fae catches feelings for someone so quickly. *Especially not me.*

Devi rinses her hands in the sink, and droplets of water splash the counter as she swats my concerns away. "Hush. I know better than to meddle in your affairs. I've learned my lesson. No arrow of mine will ever touch you again. You have my word." She glances at me sideways, her artful brows pulled together. "But don't lie to yourself, Samhain. Whoever the poor girl is...you're going to destroy her."

I step over the rowan threshold, not looking back. "Don't I know it."

After pulling my hood over my head and ears, I walk briskly up the road. Bright street lights reflect off the rain puddles as my boots clomp along the pavement. *A thousand women...*

Who am I kidding? Rye is the only woman from my past worth mentioning, but one woman is enough to wreck *everything.*

CHAPTER 19
GOSSIP GIRL

After my fight with One, I sulk in the gym most of the afternoon. Lori's ominous warning is stuck in my brain, and Two doesn't seek me out, probably as pissed as I am. I bury several bolts in the hay mannequin, aiming right for the swirly black shadow I drew over its heart.

When my fingers are numb from reloading and shooting the heavy weapon, I run ten extra laps to cool off. The frustration and lack of sleep from my horrible night alone in New York drags me down, and I fail to mask a sigh when James joins me on the track.

The man falls into step with me with a kind smile. "I've heard about the switch."

"Ugh." I pick up the pace, afraid to let too many emotions show on my face.

James waits for a full minute before broaching the subject again. "Did something happen?"

"Why would you assume something happened?" I snap, immediately feeling guilty for my temper.

"Two and Mara are thick as thieves, so I figured the schedule change must have originated on your side."

He's not wrong, and I eye him sideways. His figure is more athletic than when we first met, and his gaze doesn't quite hug the ground as much as it used to. "What about you, are you still training with Three? You passed his first trial weeks ago."

"According to Lori, the triplets usually keep their pupils for three to four months, laying the groundwork for the more advanced lessons and allowing enough time for them to sprout."

We're no longer running but walking briskly instead, and I wrinkle my nose as I contemplate his answer. "I thought a seed became a sprout after he or she passed the first three trials? Wouldn't it be best to get them out of the way early?"

"Maybe that's what they decided to do with you, maybe they feel that you can take it. Three said that I had the right temperament for fantasies, but nightmares should prove most difficult for me. I'd be scared to wash out if I divided my attention like that."

"I'm no genius. One must have switched me for a different reason," I say quickly.

We circle back to the hub where five figures dressed in similar uniforms have gathered under the Hawthorn. The group is speaking loudly, and we come to an abrupt stop.

"Do you know them?" I whisper not to draw attention to us.

James shakes his head, looking timid and nervous again. "They're probably the hunters Lori talks so much about."

Soot streaks their arms, masks, and necks, and I glance around the courtyard. A few sprites lurk at the fringes of the gardens, their normal routine interrupted by the bustle, but none of them seem alarmed.

One steps out of the gym with his arms crossed over his chest and leans in the doorway. The bastard doesn't spare me a glance as I wave, so I tuck my arms firmly to my sides.

Mara and Two appear on the trainee's balcony and brace their elbows on the railing, listening in as the newcomers pass around a bottle of hard liquor and exchange loud quips.

A slender, blond man with a plain white mask raises the

uncorked bottle in cheer. "We made it, bruh. No more labyrinths for me, thank you. Not for a lifetime."

"No? Are you growing soft on me, Cary?" A second man with dark curly hair and a thick, foreign accent steals the amber-tinted glass bottle from his grasp. "Color me disappointed." His ruby-encrusted mask twinkles in the sun.

"I'm overdue for a feather bed and some mindless fun," a third man grunts.

The one named Cary snickers. "You and Fi certainly had plenty of *mindless fun* last night."

A woman with flaming red hair marches over to the bottle for her share. "I thought we were gonna die. It doesn't count."

"You heard that, Mitch? You only got laid as a last resort."

The casual sex discussion throws me for a loop, and my cheeks heat up.

The fifth figure, a tall man covered in blood from head to toe, motions for his companions to settle down, his voice sharper than the rest of them combined. "Shut up, all of you. The king is here."

The Shadow King himself appears on the mezzanine a moment later.

Sunshine sparks off his golden mask, preventing us from looking directly at him, and I tent my hand above my brows to see better. The excited chatter dies in one breath, and the hunters all put one knee to the ground.

Caught up in the moment, James and I imitate them. One bows his head, but he doesn't kneel, and I catch Two rolling his eyes.

The tall man covered in blood and grime raises a bovine skull to the king. "We've come back from our mission, my king. I present to you what's left of the minotaur."

A shadow detaches from the skull—*or the man's arm?*—and flies off to merge with the king. His gloved hands rap along the railing, and he stands a little taller, the darkness that licks his silhouette now effervescent.

He finally nods at the leader of the hunt and whistles back inside without a word. I squint at the third floor balcony, trying to figure out which flight of stairs leads up there.

Lori runs out of the library. "Finally! I was beginning to worry. All these weeks alone with the rookies, with no one else around to haze them—" Her bright smile falters. "Wait—where is Drake?"

The leader discards the empty skull to the ground, and dried mud crusts off his back at the movement. "Dead."

Lori gapes at him, clearly shocked. "But—how?"

"He was sloppy."

I walk over to Lori and put a gentle hand on her shoulder. The others squint like they're seeing me for the first time, and their gazes travel from me to James, then to Mara up on the balcony.

Cary tucks his mask under his arm and raises a brow. "Three new seeds?"

Lori nods quietly, tears glossing over her clear gray eyes as I hug her.

Two rubs his hands together, drawing the group's attention away from us. "Let's celebrate at dinner, shall we? After you take a quick bath, of course."

The hunters nod, and the crowd scatters in all directions. I turn around to steal a glance at One, but the knight is already gone.

A sense of dread settles in my chest, my muscles sore and my mind exhausted, but I don't want to be left out of the loop, so I follow everyone's lead and head to my room to change into a fresh tunic.

When I get to the banquet hall, the tables have been rearranged to form a big circle—except for the Shadow King's throne, of course.

Lori waves me over to her. "Thank you for earlier...they were acting like nothing bad had happened, and it *sucked*."

"Was Drake a good friend of yours?" I ask softly.

"Not really. I mean—he was a bit of a loner, but that doesn't mean I wanted him to *die*." She covers her face with her hands. "He was our healer, and a great one at that. If only I'd been part of the hunt..." her voice cracks.

"Do you usually go with them?"

"I was on stupid library duty because I broke the rules, but it was all for nothing—" She braces her arms over her thighs, shaking like a Hawthorn leaf in the wind. "And now Drake..."

I cover her hand with mine. "Is there anything I can do to help?"

She opens her heart-shaped mouth like she's ready to tell me the whole story when Mara slumps down on the empty seat next to me, startling us both.

"What's up, bitches?"

"Hey," Lori sighs regretfully.

There's no assigned seating, but I'd planned to save the seat for James. I glower at my fellow seed and search the room for her mentor. "Where is Two?"

"He's running late. He had to get the dead guy's body and bring it back to Faerie."

Lori turns green. "See you later."

Mara sniffs the fish on her plate suspiciously. "What's with her? She looked like she was going to be sick."

"Her friend just died—" I start, but I don't have it in me to explain common decency to a woman that keeps putting her foot in her mouth and doesn't seem to care.

Mara isn't even listening, pushing aside her plate in favor of her wine. From the inattentive way she holds her glass, I figure she's already drunk.

Her tongue darts out of her mouth, and she licks her lips. "I bet the Shadow King isn't as handsome as the legends say. His knights on the other hand..." Her gaze is glued to the triplet's table.

The three Fae are playing a card game with a couple of hunters on the opposite side of the room. They gamble for money and trinkets, and Two curses under his breath as Three pulls all the winnings towards him with a provocative grin.

"You cheated," Two growls.

Three's chest vibrates with laughter, and he angles his palms to the sky. *Prove it.*

One sits back in his chair, distancing himself from his brothers. The weight of his gaze tightens my skin, and I arch a brow that asks, *"Did he cheat or not?"*

One bites his bottom lip not to smile and gives me a small, almost imperceptible nod.

"How old do you think they are?" Mara slurs in my ear.

I'd be lying if I said I haven't thought about it. "Late twenties?" I answer, keeping the truth for myself. I've seen One's eyes. They were not the eyes of a twenty-something man.

The redhead raps her long, black-painted nails on the table. "Three never eats, did you notice? I heard it's because he does...other things to sustain himself."

The way One stares at me from the other side of the room sparks a fiery storm in my chest.

"*Other* things?" I ask absentmindedly.

"Fiona said he's cursed and can only eat when he fucks, otherwise food tastes like dirt to him."

What the—

Mara eyes me sideways. "You must be the no-sex-before-marriage type. Sucks for you."

I grit my teeth, uncomfortable with the way she leers at Three. "Sex before marriage is unthinkable in Demeter."

She raises both brows in disbelief. "For women, you mean."

"Well...yes," I concede.

"It used to be the same in my world, really, but we've gotten past that bullshit." She lowers her voice like she's about to confess something scandalous. "I also heard that the knights aren't even allowed to marry."

My heart skips a beat, and I consider Mara with renewed interest. Judging by One's reaction yesterday, I knew I'd struck a chord with my jab, but I didn't think he was *forced* to live as a bachelor.

"What do you mean?"

Her tongue rests at the tip of her canine as she pauses for effect.

"Rumor has it that, as long as the Shadow King remains single, the triplets can't take a wife of their own."

"The Shadow King never married?" I ask, surprised.

She raises a brow as though I just called her a liar. "Is that so hard to believe?"

"All my research points to the fact that Fae royals *love* to marry. It strengthens their magic, so most queens and kings have to marry to keep their crowns. They keep witnesses around for the consummation part, and the Winter King even turned his nuptials into some sort of competitive pageantry."

"Wow, you've really got your nose stuck in a book, Old World. No...Oh! I've got it!" Mara slaps my upper arm, her eyes wide from the liquor, stuck in the inebriated phase where all your ideas are gold and you love yourself more than ever. She slaps it three times. "I bet they're doing it."

"Doing what?"

"Sex."

I roll my shoulders back, concerned that Mara is taking advantage of my naiveté. "Who's having sex?"

She glares at me like I'm dense. "The king and his knights. If they can't marry, it means the king has them all to himself."

My brows furrow. "But that's not—That doesn't make any sense."

Men don't have sex with men. I'm almost sure.

Mara laughs, but it's louder and lasts longer than any laugh should, and the difference makes the sound rather unkind. "You're kidding, right? Just look at Cary and Misha."

The two men smile at each other, in the secret way lovers do, but I've never seen any of the triplets look at the Shadow King with adoration—or even admiration. If anything, they always seem a bit... put off by their monarch's presence.

People with secrets think of gossip as an enemy, but it's actually the opposite. Gossip dilutes the truth, rips it to shreds, and scatters it in the wind of a stranger's breath until it's lost for good.

That'll teach me to listen to the musings of a drunk tattler.

CHAPTER 20

THREE BLACK EYES

I sleep in the next day and cut my first run of the day short when I spot the newly returned hunters installing a thick mattress from the gym in the clearing between the balcony and the Hawthorn.

Lori and James wave me under the shade of the sacred tree, and I dash over to them, my long ponytail braid swinging at my back. "Hey, what's going on?"

"Combat training," James answers.

A mischievous smirk glazes Lori's lips, my friend wearing the hunters' uniform for the first time since we've met. "It's more than combat training. It's a contest."

I wipe off the beads of sweat pearling on my forehead with my sleeve. "What are the rules?"

"No weapons allowed, but other than that, anything goes. The goal is to throw your opponent off the mat. Two fighters go at a time, and the winner gets to choose the next two. Losers are eliminated, and the last man or woman standing gets to lead the next great hunt."

I swallow hard.

Lori nudges my shoulder playfully with her fist. "Don't worry, Old World. It's not open to seeds, only hunters."

"I'm so glad that nickname is catching on," I grumble, sarcasm thick in my voice.

The big guy, Jo, jumps over a tall rock and shows off two pieces of crumpled paper. "Lori and Cary go first."

"Here goes." With an elastic band tucked between her teeth, she brushes back her black waves. "Wish me luck." She ties them neatly at the back of her neck and pulls up a black scarf over her head, leaving only her eyes uncovered.

Her mood is much improved from last night, and I've never seen her looking so...alive. The arrival of the big group shifted the entire atmosphere in the castle. Such a big, inviting space should never be left so empty.

Her opponent, Cary, runs away from his friends with a big grin on his face before turning toward us. "Heyyo, Lori! I'm over here! Come meet my fists, comrade." He jumps dramatically and lands on the corner of the mattress, making a circular movement with his arms like he's struggling to keep his balance, and finally salutes his audience. "Who wants to bet on how many black eyes I can give Lori?"

"One," Mara says, using her hands to amplify her voice.

Jo holds three fingers above his head. The leader sits on a flat rock with his black shirt rolled up to his elbows, and an elusive smile appears on his lips. "I say Lori wins with three."

James leans closer to my ear. "How do you get *three* black eyes?"

I shake my head, at a total loss.

The two hunters on the mattress circle each other.

Mara and Two are huddled close together on the opposite side of the fight, clearly engrossed in their conversation, but I force my gaze back to the sparring session. Cary's loud insults blur together, his strategy clearly to distract Lori, his foul mouth blasting a whole lot of nonsense.

Lori seems unaffected by even the most vulgar jab as she glides out of his reach and avoids the first series of attacks, never letting him get close to her. The crowd reacts to her smooth escapes with loud *ooohs* and *ahhhs*, making it hard for Cary to concentrate. He finally loses patience and jumps to grab her.

Her elbow collides with his left eye, "One." She slams the other one with a right hook, "Two."

Cary tries to knock her off balance and immobilize her in a bear hug, but she slips under his arm, spins around, and finishes him off with a kick between the legs.

"That's three," she chimes happily.

Her lethal poise and impressive speed sparks a sense of pride in my chest.

Who knew she was so good...

She presses her thumb to the middle of Cary's forehead to knock him off balance, and the poor bloke topples over to the grass, holding his groin.

James hisses by my side, his hand flying to his crotch. "I have my answer."

Lori pulls down her scarf, and her huge grin is contagious while Misha goes to help his friend up. "Ouch. That must hurt."

Cary stumbles to his feet with his back hunched, holding on to the tall brown-haired man. He gives Joseph a nasty glance. "How did you know she'd gotten so good?"

"Don't blame me. You're the only one who didn't notice." Jo dusts off his pants and strolls over to shake the winner's hand. "Congrats, little ninja. You showed him."

Lori beams at him. "Thanks, boss."

As the leader and more advanced hunter, I can tell his praises mean something to her. Before stepping off the mat, my friend curtsies like a trouper after a show. "Jo and Mitch."

The hunters clap at that.

Mitchell, the tall boy with more limbs than muscles, makes a weird gesture with his hand, showing just his middle finger, and everyone laughs. "Go to hell, Lori."

Jo shrugs off his button-down shirt, leaving only a thin gray camisole to cover his chest. "Sorry, Mitch. This isn't your season."

The two men circle each other, but before the second revolution is done, Jo breaks the pattern and slides a foot forward. Mitch draws back, skittish, and widens his circle to avoid the attack, but his leader anticipated his move and pirouettes in front of him. Mitch digs his heels into the mattress and braces his hands in front of his face, but instead of throwing a punch, Jo waits for him to go on the offensive, his feet inches from the edge. Thinking he has a shot at winning, Mitch roars forward, but Jo uses his friend's ill-advised momentum to swing him off the mattress instead.

Our gazes cross, and Jo offers me a wink. He points to two new fighters, and so the contest goes. I quickly realize everyone picks him for the next fight, the entire band of hunters united against him.

"Why do you guys always pick Jo?" I whisper to Lori.

"Jo always wins. It's his tenth straight season leading the hunt, and last fall he even won on a bad knee."

Everyone groans loudly every time Jo eliminates a player, the predictable fights ending quickly and without any real tension. Even Lori's flexibility and speed can't manage to hold the slick hunter off, and my friend is quickly eliminated.

It's all over before long, and the victor wipes his face off with a towel. "Since I gave you all a good whipping, I get to go against Two. For fun."

The tired grimaces melt from the crowd.

"You know me, I'm always up for a fight." Two unzips his thick black jacket and tosses it to Mara under a throng of applause. He's not wearing anything underneath, and the sight of his bare chest melts my brain. My breath catches when I catch a glimpse of a wide-tipped shadow over his heart.

The same scar...and just like One's, it moves with its owner, blurring slightly like there's a few seconds delay between its movement and Two's.

Before the knight can step on the mattress, Jo motions for him to wait, his gaze glued on something behind me. Murmurs echo around the gardens, and I crane my neck around to see what stopped him cold.

One contemplates the crowd for a long minute until the whispers die down. His voice is low and devoid of humor as he finally says, "What about me? Would you fight *me*, Joseph?"

"Sorry Two." Jo shakes out his fists and cracks his neck. "I can't pass up on that."

Two grins a little too widely, his distaste for the interruption clear as day. "Of course."

He crosses his arms, the muscles all knots and bulges, and leans back on the castle wall. Many of us continue to ogle at his nakedness, a fact that doesn't please him enough to erase his sour pout.

The combat starts as many others have, with Jo and One circling each other, but Jo doesn't have the same air of ease to him as he did before, his sight riveted on the dark Fae, his nostrils flaring. He's got the face of a man who has something to prove.

One side steps easily around whatever attack Jo tries, never going on the offensive, never breaking a sweat like he's merely humoring a child.

Jo's breaths grow heavier. "This is getting boring. Fight me."

But the crowd isn't bored, not in the least. Even the hard planes of Two's chest aren't enough to keep a pair of eyes away from One. The hunter is effortlessly charismatic as he evades Jo's attacks.

One veers off Jo's path once more and snickers unkindly. I'd originally thought his plan was to tire out his opponent, but I know better now.

He wants to humiliate him.

My eyes narrow. One is clearly planning something, and when Jo moves to kick his stomach, the dark Fae's edges blur with shadows. He catches his opponent's foot mid-air, and a sickening crack raises all my hairs to attention.

The leaves of the Hawthorn bristle at the sound, and Jo cries out, his yelp quickly melting into a low, manly grunt as he falls to the ground, his broken leg twisted at his side.

One faces the frozen crowd. Lori holds a hand to her opened mouth, and anger licks my insides. I'm gripped by a knee-jerk need to defend the poor man on the ground, but before I can move, One's loud voice resonates through the branches.

"Joseph here might have slayed a legendary nightmare, but he lost one of us in the process." He spins around to face the wounded hunter. "Your orders were to wait for me."

"Death is part of the game! Sacrifices need to be made!" Jo shouts, his pain obvious. Sweat pearls on his forehead, and shivers rock his body as he manages to stand up, his face wrinkled in a bitter grimace.

The sight of him scrambling for balance on one leg draws gasps from the crowd.

One tilts his chin up, every inch he has over his opponent magnified. "Do not pretend to teach *me* about sacrifices. If you had waited like you were supposed to, Drake would be here with us. *I* will lead the next hunt."

Jo grits his teeth and motions to his broken leg. "That fracture will take *weeks* to mend."

"You should have considered that before you sent our best healer to his death."

"I'm no good to the king without a leg," Jo spits.

One angles his mask to me for a brief second. "Lucky for you, one of the new seeds is already a skilled healer, so you can get that fixed. *Tomorrow.*"

The Fae rushes past me, and I hold out an arm to stop him, still reeling from the violence of the blow. "I could do it now."

The tired hunch of his back unravels my anger, the dark knight clearly not enjoying himself—or the pain he caused to his underling.

He pauses at my side, and I think he's going to bite my head off for my offer, but the tension in his spine eases. He leans close enough for Lori's brows to lift in alarm, and his breath warms my ear. "Don't. He needs the lesson."

CHAPTER 21

A KNIGHT IN DISTRESS

The morning after Jo's catastrophic duel with One, I tip-toe inside the infirmary. A dozen single beds furnish the long rectangular room, but all of them are empty except for the one Jo is laying in. A few rays of sunlight filter through the diamond-shaped windows, and the smell of clean laundry and antiseptic tickles my nose.

"Good morning. Lori told me I'd find you here," I greet my patient.

"I'm glad to finally meet you properly, Nell." The tall brown-haired man puts his book aside and shifts awkwardly over the white duvet, his broken leg stabilized by an external brace. Dark circles drag down his eyes and spell out exactly how his night went. "I'm Joseph, but everyone calls me Jo."

My lips quirk. "I caught that."

"I assume you came to heal me?" The end of the sentence rises in question, more out of politeness than doubt.

"Yes." Guilt heats my cheeks for not healing him yesterday. Despite One's memorable speech, I don't think anyone should be made to suffer.

Jo sighs in relief. "You're a lifesaver. If it wasn't for you, I would be out of commission for the entire season."

"It must hurt like a horseshoe in the brow."

"Ha-ha—that it does. Is that what they say in the old world?" Not waiting for an actual answer, Jo sits up. His knuckles turn white on the mattress as he dangles his injured leg over the edge of the bed. "Cary did his best to get me through the night, but he's no true healer."

Upon closer inspection, the fracture does look a little less appalling than yesterday. I kneel next to the bed and unfasten the bandages holding the brace in place. "One wouldn't have snapped your leg in two if he hadn't known someone could heal it."

"Don't be so sure. He hates me."

I draw power from the clean air, the creaky bed, and the solid ground. Power numbs my fingertips as his leg starts to shrink down to its normal size, and I tilt my head slightly to the side, waiting for Jo to elaborate.

"The king commandeered a great hunt to make up for the lack of seedlings this year. He sent us after the minotaur, but per usual, One wanted to control everything. He treats me like I'm inferior to him even though he was a sepal once, too," he says.

Wait... What?

My gaze snaps up to meet his, and my magic waivers. A faint *pop* rises from the half-healed leg, the surprise distracting me from my goal.

Jo clears his throat to mask a wince, his face angled away from his injured leg.

"Sorry." I rub my palms together to soothe the uncomfortable tingles and give myself a second to recharge.

"It's alright. You're new to this. But yeah, it's a bit of an open secret around here that the triplets must have been the last stigmas before Morrigan. They've got pointy ears, but it's easy enough to fake that with the right glamor. And they never remove their masks... That's not normal."

I consider his words carefully. "Are you sure they're not Fae?"

"I mean—they claim to be Fae, but Fae don't act so paranoid all the time." He shrugs like it's not a big deal one way or the other, but if the triplets aren't Fae, it means they can lie. It would shift my world on its axis.

I return my attention to his leg and let the magic flow.

"It must have been lonely here the last few weeks. James doesn't seem like much of a talker, and the redhead fawns over Two like a heifer in heat..." he says.

He's not wrong, and I press my lips together not to laugh. "Who's Morrigan?"

"Oh, she's a legend. Morrigan was the last stigma to complete the training process, and they say she got so powerful, she rivaled the king himself. Normally, becoming a stigma means immortality, glory—it's the ultimate reward for someone like us, but Morrigan..." He pauses for a few seconds. "The sprites say that she fell in love with a hunter, and that, on the eve of her wedding, the king killed her in a fit of jealousy."

Goosebumps prickle my neck. "Which hunter?"

Jo lowers his voice and glances at the door behind me like he's about to tell me something he shouldn't. "That's where the story gets muddled. A High Lord said that the man fled to another court after she died, but another claimed it was one of the triplets..."

I hold my breath.

Jo continues, "Isobel Umbra told me there used to be tons of people living in and out of the castle. When she was younger, the king would throw grand soirées for the gentry, and visitors from the other courts would stay for weeks at a time. There'd be music in the halls. Laughter. Children." He licks his lips, the mystery of the Shadow Court clearly gnawing at him, too. "But one day, about eighty years ago, the Shadow King shut his doors to the world, and now, only the High Fae of the Shadowlands are allowed to visit. A few sprites take care of the grounds, but they've been working here for centuries, and then there's us... The entire realm is basically suspended in time."

"No wonder the castle is so empty." I dry my sweaty palms on my pants. "There. All done."

Jo's eyes widen as he tests out his new leg. "You're awesome, Nell! It's not even sore or anything. You're going to be one hell of a sprout if you can do this as a seed. Thank you so much!"

A mix of pride and embarrassment brands my cheeks at his effusive praise. Now that we're both standing, he's got a few inches on me, and yet everything about him sets me at ease like we're old friends whispering alone in the infirmary.

I take a small step back. "You're welcome."

The book on his bedside table shines in the sunlight, and I pick it up, looking for a swift change of subject. "History of the Shadowlands, a Tale of Love and Betrayal," I read out loud.

My heart beats faster. I've seen this book in the ledger. It's a third-floor book. Greed and longing squeeze my ribs as I run my fingers over the cover.

"It's romanticized a bit, but it details the fall of the last king, Ferdinand Morpheus Nocturna."

I leaf through the book, and the calligraphy is tiny but easy to read. "How long has it been since he passed?"

"Give or take a century. Damian rose to power right after his death."

I blink a few times at the revelation.. "So...the Shadow King is more than a hundred years old?"

"Yes."

I bite my bottom lip and shiver at the thought of what lays underneath his golden mask.

Jo doesn't seem put off by the idea of immortality, and a hint of longing pierces through his measured voice. "Coming from Demeter, you must be used to hereditary monarchies, but the Fae do things differently. It's a meritocracy—the strongest lion becomes king of the pride. You do have lions in the old world, right?"

I shake my head, still clutching the book.

"Damn, what a pity. It means that the strongest individual gets to rule. It's usually one of the High Fae from the Shadowlands, but it doesn't have to be." He grazes the trim. "You don't have to read it all here. You can borrow it, if you want."

"Isn't that forbidden? I mean—" I look down, and my hair cascades down the side of my face. "It's a third-floor book."

A chuckle warms his breath. "Third-floor book...I like it. I'll make you a deal, milady." He presses his hands over mine for a second, long enough to make me blush. "I'll let you borrow the book to thank you for healing me, and no one has to know."

I gape at his playfulness. "Won't you get in trouble if someone finds out?"

"I can get in a little trouble to repay you for your kindness." He offers me his arm the way a young gentleman in Demeter would. The way Isaac used to. "I'm going to hit the buffet before I change, you wanna join?"

A smile escapes me. "Lead the way, milord."

TWO INTERRUPTS MY EARLY BREAKFAST WITH JO ALMOST AS SOON AS IT begins. I made sure to hide the book deep in my bag, below the others, but I still check that the flap is safely clasped as the dark Fae comes to a full stop next to our table.

The sneer stuck on his face doesn't bode well for me, and my eyes narrow at the intrusion. "Good morning."

Two looks down his nose at us from behind his mask. "I guess I'm stuck with you now."

Sunshine reflects off the stony rings on each of his fingers as he cracks them one by one.

Jo makes a face somewhere between an eye-roll and a sheepish grin. "See you later, Nell."

Both hands braced on the table, I reluctantly stretch to my feet. "Thank you for this morning. It was fun."

"Thank *you*. You saved me."

Two tilts his head back and groans. "Stop flirting and come with me. I haven't got all day."

I hurry after him, choosing not to let his attitude affect me. "If you hated the idea of training me, why didn't you say no?"

If he likes Mara so much, maybe he can be persuaded to switch me back. After my discussion with Jo, I simply *need* to speak with One alone, and if I convince Two to send me straight back to him, it'll make things much easier.

"Is One that much more powerful that you *have* to obey him?" I ask with my best air of naiveté.

Two cranes his neck around to look at me. "Don't play with me. I won't switch you back. If One gave you to me, he must have had a reason."

"Hm. Maybe," I say wistfully.

That compels him to stop, and the pieces of broken glass covering his mask reflect a dozen fractured views of my mischievous grin. He opens his mouth to speak but thinks better of it and starts walking again.

If I can goad him into asking about the switch, I might tickle his curiosity. According to what I've witnessed so far, Two is in love with himself. Big male egos are usually best served with flattery, and I can be twice as charming as Mara if I put my mind to it.

I've got practice, the tournaments back home full of young men dying for praise. *What a powerful horse you have here, Sir. Did you break him in yourself?*

But I'm not sure what makes the second brother tick. I need to get him on my side first. Earn his respect.

One is clearly not inclined to share his secrets, but if Mara is to be believed, Two's a tattletale. With the right incentive, he might spill the beans about Morrigan. I might just be spinning fairy tales, but something about the story Jo told me simply rings true.

CHAPTER 22
PAS DE DEUX

For my first lesson, Two guides me deep inside the belly of the castle. The air is stale in this part of the tunnels, and a few widely-spread torches light our path.

He's not wearing his hood, his shorter hair all disheveled, and I can't help but stare at the intricate web of tattoos that lick the back of his right ear. They are identical to One's, down to the faintest swirl that disappears under his hairline.

My plan for today is simple. I'll be a good student, stroke his ego, and get him to like me before I ask about Morrigan.

"Nightmare hunts might sound dangerous and exciting, but it's the Dreaming that truly powers this realm and its magic. The Shadow Court couldn't survive without it, and we all swore a sacred oath to protect it," he says on our way down a round staircase similar to the one I found during my first trial.

"Dreams are clearly better than nightmares," I answer with a quick smile.

He pauses and observes me for a moment. "What's with you today?"

"Mm?"

"You're awfully...nice. I told you before, you're not going to sweet-talk me into switching you back."

I consider him for a moment. Two might be in love with himself, but he's no fool, and maybe sucking up to him isn't the right approach. "I have questions."

He squints, and the hard line of his mouth eases. "So do I."

We pass through a vaguely familiar corridor before we emerge into the same mirror-covered vault where I had to strip for the Shadow King. The memories from that night turn my legs to lead, the spring in my step gone, my mood careening over a sullen edge.

Oblivious to my current state of mind, Two snaps his fingers to light the candles and shakes out his wrists before he rummages through the paint brushes on the altar.

I inch toward the shadow pool and stare at its oily surface, goosebumps riddling my arms. The dim light of the candles plays tricks with my mind, the curl of my lips so off in my reflection that it makes me look wicked—even cruel.

"Are you up for a plunge?" Two whispers in my ear.

His sudden closeness spooks me, and I spin around to face him with my hands tucked behind my back. The sudden move almost causes me to topple over and fall into the liquid shadows, but his hand shoots out to grab my upper arm, steadying me.

His mask reflects back my surprised face, and I reel at how similar to One he looks in this moment. Under the soft glow of the candles, in this mystical room full of treacherous reflections, he's a faithful copy of the man I've come to obsess about.

"You okay, Old World? You look about to pass out," Two says, finally jolting me back to reality.

"Yes. Sorry."

He's not One. And yet...it's like my body can't quite grasp the concept.

Two walks back to the altar, dips a small brush in an ink pot, and twirls it around a few times. "The sceawere connect us to our most sacred realm, but only the Shadow King and his most trusted hunters can access it without leaving their bodies at the door. You can't bring someone along into the Dreaming. Visitors have to find their way there for themselves, or in your case, with a little help." With a brow raised high, he holds his brush in mid air between us. "Arm out."

I flip over my wrist to offer him better access to the underside of my lower arm. The wet tip of the brush sends a shiver to my core as Two paints a series of runes over the sensitive skin. It tickles a bit, but I study his confident strokes, recognizing "Faerie," "tree," and "soul" as well as a fourth one I've never seen before, the intricate lines no doubt incredibly difficult to reproduce. The ink glistens on my flesh, as dark and ominous as the shadow pool behind me.

I consider the mirror, cold sweat gathering at my brow at the prospect of entering it alone. "Wait. What happens if I get lost?"

Two considers me with more seriousness than I thought possible. "If you get lost..." he pats my shoulders as though we're old friends. "Then it was nice to know you, Old World. I'll miss yah."

His insincere, satisfied grin is enough to convince me that he's not worried enough to actually entertain the question, and I throw caution to the uneven winds of the sceawere. My heart whispers: *if you get lost, One will find you.*

I step forward, and the frosty sting of the sceawere is not as jarring as it used to be. A quiet, steady string of glass waits for me on the other side. The maze of colors and shapes is distracting, but I concentrate on the task at hand. My heart beating in my throat, I raise a tentative hand to the supple, translucent strings hanging between the glass panes.

Quickly, a path paved in glass eclipses all others. The runes on my arms fade to a light shade of gold, and a sense of peace engulfs me. I walk to the "address" Two drew on my arm without too much difficulty and find him waiting for me there.

"Welcome to the Dreaming, Old World."

The familiarity of the misty forest scenery is oddly comforting, and I fall into step with my new mentor.

"Everyone that falls asleep outside of Faerie visits the Dreaming once in a while. Some come every night, others more sparingly. When you dream, you leave behind your body, your magic—everything but your soul. It travels here alone and feeds our kingdom in exchange for the entertainment we procure," he explains.

Like I thought...the Fae do not pray on their own.

"And who decides what we dream about? You?"

He rolls his eyes at my perfectly reasonable question. "I can't possibly deal with the individual dreams of the worlds' population, but I make sure the Dreaming leaves the wandering souls energized for their day. If mortals didn't get something in return for their voyage, they wouldn't come back. I also make sure they can leave. We don't want them to get trapped here, either." Hands on his hips, he gazes out at the rainy, fog-riddled forest with the beaming pride of a new father. "A soul is safe here. It can explore all its fancies without repercussions. Anything from joy to processing past traumas."

I sidestep the issue of not being able to leave, stowing it for later. "What's the difference between dreams and fantasies?"

"Fantasies are more specific. They reveal what mortals crave, sometimes beyond reason. Dreams can be just fun and meaningless. It's wise to remember the difference between the two." He guides me through the trees with the unwavering confidence of a man who knows exactly where he's going.

"And nightmares?"

We reach a small clearing, and he stops, the weight of his breath disturbing the thick fog. "Nightmares are by-products of dreams. Every once in a while, a mortal will dream of something so powerful that it takes a life of its own. Now, if the nightmare accepts the king's collar, it remains inside the sceawere and continues to feed the realm —dreams cannot exist without nightmares—but if it escapes, it needs to be put down. That's where my expertise ends and One's begins." He glances at me over his shoulder. "You made it here quickly, so you're not...half bad. Why did One get rid of you if you don't suck?" he breathes, his voice so similar to his brother's low baritone that I shiver.

"Who's Morrigan?" I dead-pan.

His tongue tucked underneath his teeth, Two smiles the way you smile to your opponent while bluffing in a card game. "Dropping false pretenses. Alright. I'll answer your question if you tell me why One switched you with Mara."

I bite my bottom lip and consider his offer. "Three questions."

He rubs his palms together. "Let's make it interesting. It's still early enough for the old world gentry to wander the Dreaming. There must be someone you're curious about? A boy, perhaps?" Two stares down at me like he can hear my quickened pulse, and maybe he can. "Tell me his name."

"Isn't it an invasion of privacy?"

"Oh, come on. What's your boyfriend's name?" His tone is laced with a hint of magic, and I find myself blurting out the truth.

"Isaac Henry Longbottom."

He raises his hand to the thick fog wall in front of us and calls Isaac's name. A languid pulse of magic ripples through the air. "Let's see what this mortal's subconscious yearns for."

Magic coats me on all sides, and I hold my breath for a moment, my skin prickling like I've just plunged into a hot bath.

The world blurs, and all of the sudden, Two's fractured mask gleams in the bright sunshine of my father's royal gardens, the apple trees around us suddenly thick with white flowers. "You're all flushed, princess."

"What was that? I feel...different." I look down at myself, my tunic gone, replaced by a traditional wedding dress. A long ivory train flows behind me, the laced sleeves tight around my arms. My hand flies to my hair, the white blond locks now braided inside a hairnet.

"Your boy sensed your arrival, and you became part of his dream," Two explains.

"What about you?"

"I know better than to be sucked in by a mortal's dream." He rubs his hands together. "Let's make this fake wedding interesting. If you manage to pull yourself out of this fiasco without waking him, I'll answer one question of your choosing."

"If I win, I want you to answer three questions." I bite my bottom lip and think for a moment. "One if I lose."

"Alright, but if you fail, I get to ask three questions myself. And whatever happens, you'll have to answer truthfully."

My nose wrinkles. "How do I know you won't lie to me?"

"I'm Fae."

"Are you really?"

Jo is right. If the triplets aren't Fae lords, they have to be stigmas that learned to only pass as Fae, which means I can't trust a word coming out of Two's mouth.

He rubs the sharp angle of his jaw. "Is that your question?"

"No. Let's just vow we both will answer truthfully... and I get one question regardless. One if I lose, three if I win. Same goes for you."

"Alright, but you have to ask your question first," he negotiates.

"Done."

"Now, let's see who wins." He extends his hand with swagger, but I can't let his obvious confidence erode mine.

I shake his hand, and a tingle of magic buzzes in my fingertips. Whatever just happened, it was a formal Fae deal, and breaking it would no doubt prove to be worse than answering truthfully to a few personal questions.

Isaac appears under the stone arch leading to the stables. The tunic he's wearing marks him as the Duke of Axel, his father's title, and his cloak is adorned with a white fur trim, embroidered with the royal insignia.

Two snickers. "A June wedding. How proper."

Isaac grabs both my hands in his. "Penny! What are you doing in here? I'm not supposed to see you before church."

"Isaac, hi." I glance sideways at Two, the dark Fae apparently invisible to my...groom?

Two motions for me to deal with Isaac as I see fit and examines the apple trees like he wants to grow them in his garden.

I turn back to dream-Isaac. "I—I missed you," I say, and for a moment, I'm taken over by the illusion. The tight corset, the button-down collar of the dress...they barely allow me to move—or breathe.

"Oh Penny, it won't be long now, and you'll belong to me. Properly."

My brows pull together at the peculiar choice of words, but I put as much cheer in my voice as I can. "Yes. Finally!"

I'm playing along, wondering why Two brought me here and what I'm supposed to do. This is a test, and I need to figure out exactly how to get out of this dream without waking Isaac. If dreams feed the realm and leave the souls content, then maybe I just need to get to the end of the scenario.

Isaac pulls me along past the stone archway, and I struggle to walk, the long train of my dress hindering my movements. He runs ahead of me, and suddenly, we're in a church. A seemingly endless red carpet leads to the altar where Isaac is now waiting for me—so far away that I have to squint to see him properly.

Two offers me his arm like he's the one giving me away. "Are you really going to go through with the wedding?"

"Why did you bring me here?" I whisper quickly. Many of the faces in the audience belong to friends and family, and I smile awkwardly at them as I start walking down the aisle.

The flower girl skips ahead and scatters rose petals in her wake, a white ribbon sagging on top of her basket.

When we get to the front, I spot Cece in the crowd. My sister is wearing a dark tunic with pants and a hood as she claps half-heart-edly in the first row.

Wait... This can't be Isaac's dream. Can it?

Two leans closer, his heavy breath on my cheek. "What do *you* crave, Nell? Do you wish to be the dutiful wife this mortal yearns to possess?"

Unease grows in my chest, the train of my dress suddenly much heavier than it was, and the corset much tighter. I glance back behind me and stifle a gasp with the back of my hand. The ivory fabric now runs at least thirty feet behind me, and the friction of it on the velvet carpet makes me cringe.

Two stops walking, bringing the wedding cortege to a halt. "Is that really the kind of life you desire? Bearing children—boys for crowns, girls for cradles. Isn't that what your father says?"

I grit my teeth and walk forward. "There's more to my country than you know. It's my home."

Two took me here to hijack Isaac's dream so he could rattle me. I wrench the jeweled veil off and tear the skirt of the dress.

Dream-Isaac's smile is wiped from his face, and he inches forward. "Penny? Are you alright, dear?"

"Get me out of here," I growl to the dark Fae.

Two shakes his head. "You get out."

"Fine."

The real test is coming. Magic pulses around me from all sides, the fabric of the dream almost palpable. Two wants me to escape, but Isaac will be jolted awake with a sour taste in his mouth the second I do so. From the moment the threads of the Dreaming pulled me inside the scenario, I didn't have a chance.

I draw in a deep breath and try not to think about the damn corset. Magic tingles in my palms, and a wisp of black smoke condenses into flesh next to me, shaped like a shadow of myself—a ragged runaway bride.

Two fashions a delicate collar between his hands, the shadow magic taking tangible form as he weaves a necklace out of thin air. The apparition bows to him, and he ties the collar around her neck, working her hair gently over it before stepping back. "Hello, beautiful."

She offers him her hand to kiss with a timid smile, and, for a moment, I feel like I'm intruding. I push through the discomfort in my belly to dispel the magic that trapped me inside the dream, and the shredded wedding dress disappears, replaced by my uniform.

Isaac draws a sharp intake of breath at the sight of my new clothes. "What the crops is going on? You're not Penny, are you? Guards!" he shouts for imaginary guards to come to his rescue, and my heart sinks.

"Wake up, Isaac," I say regretfully, giving the shape of him a big push.

In a blink, Two and I are back to the foggy forest.

My dark teacher nods emphatically. "A bit dramatic with the dress tearing and all, but it was certainly a memorable finale. You weaved your first nightmare, bravo!" A satisfied grin glazes his lips. "I still won, though."

"There was no way not to wake him once I'd been sucked inside his dream besides staying in there forever. That was the most unfair—"

"Tut-tut. Everyone hates a sore loser. You still have one question, so use it wisely." He licks his lips.

I wrangle my hands, unsure how to phrase my question to get the most out of this bad deal. "I heard about a woman named Morrigan..."

"Mm?"

"Jo said she was engaged to a hunter," I add, testing the waters.

"Jo said that?" Two opens his mouth, his lips torn between a cringe and a smile. "I'm not an idiot. I won't be baited into answering more questions than necessary. If you have a question about Morrigan, let's hear it."

I should confirm if he's Fae, but I can't pass up the chance to know more about Morrigan. A hundred variations of the same question tumble inside my mind, but I know Two might take advantage of a poorly-phrased question, so I decide to be as direct and clear as possible. "Was One ever engaged to Morrigan?"

Two's eyes widen, and his chest heaves like I've just punched him in the gut. "Why would you ask that?"

I lift my chin and hold his avid stare. "We had a deal. You have to answer."

"Yes," he spits out begrudgingly. "He was engaged to her."

My hand flies to my mouth. *By the Mother and all she holds dear...*

Two doesn't waste any time, his revenge-question ringing loud and true. "What happened between you and One that you think could most likely explain his desire to switch you with Mara?"

I press my lips together. If he'd asked differently, I could have claimed that I didn't know, or that I wasn't sure, but the phrasing makes it impossible for me to weasel out of the question.

A fierce blush heats my cheeks as my gaze darts to the ground. "I think that he got upset after we kissed."

Two loses all semblance of humanity, the cruel curve of his mouth lost in shadows. "And if I wanted to know all the details of that kiss, what would you tell me about it?"

Words bubble out of my mouth as though they're being raked out from the depths of my chest by his magic, and I offer him a play-by-play of the kiss and the circumstances surrounding it. I talk about the lightheadedness, the enchantment, and how the taste of my own blood shook me out of it.

I ramble on and on about the way One's lips felt on mine, and Two doesn't make fun of me for calling it "the most sensual experience of my life."

In fact, the man looks like I've just sank a knife in his gut.

When I finally regain control over my tongue, I fight back the urge to scream, the humiliation hot and heavy in my ribcage. I feel... used. I haven't made good use of my question at all. No wonder the devil in front of me insisted for me to go first.

"I'll reserve my third question," he says quietly.

"That possibility wasn't mentioned in the deal."

A wolfish smile blooms on his lips, the kind of smile that makes me doubt he's related to One at all. "It was not precluded either."

And just like that, I know I've been utterly played.

CHAPTER 23

RULES OF THE CURSE

"The first rule of the curse: we never take off our masks." Two's scoff resonates in my ears, dripping with contempt.

"Second rule: we avoid unnecessary contact with the High Fae—and the hunters. We never allow any of them to see our eyes.

"Third rule: we don't keep secrets from each other." The fucker takes a dramatic pause. "You really fucked up, One."

Shame burns my insides, but I still wish I could claw off his stupid smirk. "I know."

Two rubs his face down. "Why did you enchant her, though? That part confuses me."

I can remember the exact, wretched moment when I figured out I'd enchanted Nell. I could see my secrets slowly coming into focus in her eyes, almost like she was taming a wild beast from the depths of my subconscious. Drawing it closer. And closer...

And my magic reacted instinctively, putting her under a spell so she wouldn't get to the truth.

"Seriously. Why did you enchant her?" he asks again, impatient.

I grimace, knowing the truth will alarm him more than the rest of my mistakes combined. "I didn't *mean* to enchant her, it was pure instinct. My body reacted on its own."

"Thank Morpheus that it did, or we would be out of options."

He's right, but I hate it. I hate it *so much.* "She's different. The realm's magic feels smoother when she's around, and she healed me from the Dreamcatcher's cut."

He paces the room back and forth, hands linked behind his back. "Let's say she's different... If she is, then it was a mistake to treat her like a normal seed. We should make her life miserable enough for her to flee so we can win the bet and claim her magic now. Win-win."

"No. With her magic being as powerful as it is, we have no reason to doubt she'll pass the other two trials, and when she does, her powers will grow. What if taking her magic beforehand strengthens the curse?"

Two shakes his head. "I say we bring the experiment to an end. When we have Demeter, we can easily find a few dried seedlings to compensate for the loss of one sprout."

"No," I repeat, desperately trying to keep my emotions in check.

"It's a tie. Three?" Two tosses Three a glance over his shoulder.

The weaver of fantasies bites his bottom lip. Being mute, he's not much of a talker, and though he *can* speak telepathically, he almost never does. Still...I see the hunger on his face. He wants his turn with Nell, so for now, he's on my side.

I envy him. Must be nice to have so much clarity as to what you are and what you want.

He whistles a soft tune as he leaves, leaving Two and me to squabble.

"Okay. If we keep her, then she's a seed. She might have *smooth magic*"—he snickers, making fun of my earlier claim—"and a different schedule, but that's all she is. A seed." His eyes narrow, his glare almost hateful. "And you will treat her as such."

I grit my teeth. "Alright."

"No distractions. No exceptions. The kingdom needs us now more than ever, and the stunt you pulled put us in jeopardy."

I hate being chastised, most of all by him, and my patience for his power trip is growing thin. "It won't happen again."

"Your pet doesn't have a magical vagina—"

"Careful."

"It's not as though you could fuck her, anyway."

I flatten the bastard to the wall.

His tongue darts out, a mix between a grimace and a wicked smile. "You need a clear gesture to make her understand that you're not her dark knight from some romantic fairytale... Unless you want her to be the sacrifice for the Foghar festival."

"Foghar is already figured out," I clip. "Don't play with me."

"Still... I bet Three would agree. Maybe I ought to convince him to take Nell, instead."

I ram his big head into the wall again. "Is that really what you want to focus on after Morrigan sent a dreamcatcher to New York? Not here, not into the Dreaming where it would have wreaked havoc. No, she sent it to the nice lady who waters my plants. Do you know why?"

He shrugs like he's above such things as riddles—and decency. "Because she's a cruel bitch?"

"She's sending a message. No one is safe. If she could spare a dreamcatcher for such a menial task, it means she has others. Plural. She's saying she can hit us at any moment, probably hoping to scare us into doing something stupid."

Blood drains from his face, and he finally sobers up long enough to really listen. "If she had an army of them, she'd just attack. An army of dreamcatchers crawling into the Dreaming...it would suck what's left of our magic dry."

"Exactly. She's fucking with our minds because she's not sure of her victory. She needs us to make the first move, and a bad one at that."

"What should we do, then?" Doubt washes away his vile grin, and he rubs his forehead in a nervous manner. I've managed to get through to him.

I relax my hold on his shoulders. "We wait. We stop spreading ourselves thin and concentrate on the seeds. We concentrate on Nell. If she sprouts, Morrigan will have to fall back."

His brows furrow. "How are you so sure of that?"

"I just am."

I'm not sure at all, but otherwise, we're doomed. I keep that part to myself.

"Morheim is weeks away. If we manage to hold Morrigan off until the ritual, we'll get the chalice's magic and enough strength to last until spring. That'll give us plenty of time. We just need to be smart about it," I add.

If I spell out exactly how fucked we are, with only three seeds and an army of dreamcatchers on the loose, he's going to lash out, and I can't afford for him to spiral out of control.

"And you will cut ties with Nell and let me train her as I see fit? For the King?" his voice cracks, and I nod in spite of the roil in my stomach.

"For the King."

THE AIR BLOWS OUT OF MY LUNGS AS THE LAST HINT OF DUSK DRAINS FROM the night sky. *A clear gesture to cut ties with Nell. Here goes.*

The gym is empty but for her, the bane of my existence. Ever since the bet was made, that woman has been haunting my heart. First as a mere symbol of better days to come, second as an impossible puzzle, and now as the ultimate forbidden fruit.

I never expected her to take my world in strides, and now that she has, I can't stop looking at her. I cross my arms out of habit and lean against the wall, catching a smile from surfacing on my face as I watch her sink bolt after bolt into the hay mannequin at the very back of the room.

The swirly black scar she drew over its heart makes it clear that she's in fact hunting me, and I'm both delighted and terrified by the implications.

A long braid hangs at her back, knotted in the same fashion as the night I unraveled it. I close my eyes to rid myself of the memory and clear my throat to get her attention. "If I didn't know any better, I'd think you *want* to become a huntress."

She doesn't stop, a hint of sweat shining on her forehead. "But I can't, not without losing the bet, right?"

I push off the wall and thread deeper into the room. "Would you want to, if things were different?"

"I'm training, aren't I?"

She is training, and seriously, too. But giving her pointers on how to reload faster is not why I'm here. "That's not an answer."

She cranks up the string with the lever without sparring me a glance. "You're one to talk. You've been avoiding me, and I've been struggling to get a complete sentence out of you. I figured, since you're too childish to acknowledge my existence, I should just do this."

I almost dismiss her claim and build upon her insecurities that she's nothing to me, but I can't lie, and I'm not sure she'd believe me if I tried. *She's so sexy in her huntress uniform, calling me out for being the fucked-up coward that I am.*

A huge part of me wants to hold her in my arms again, no matter the consequences, and the reasons for my visit scatter like ashes in the wind.

"I'm here now. I can handle a few complete sentences."

She finally lets the crossbow fall at her side. "How good of you." She hangs the weapon back on the wall and throws me a glance over her shoulder. "Why do you keep the mask on? It's only us here, and I've already seen your eyes."

"Eyes are mirrors of the soul. If I let you see them again, you could steal it away," I answer playfully.

"What about my soul? Have you stolen it away?" she dead-pans.

You're supposed to pick a fight with her, not flirt.

I clear my throat and force some ice back into my voice. "Don't fool yourself, kitten. This isn't some romantic fairytale. I'm the villain of your story."

"You've yet to do anything villainous."

She's got that treacherous look on her face, the one that makes me feel like I'm no longer dead inside.

That look is fucking dangerous. It does more damage than an army of dreamcatchers or the most gruesome nightmare ever could, because it's filled with false hope. But I can't let her—or myself—believe there's a chance to become whole again, because there isn't.

So I stretch the truth as far as it can be stretched. "I'd kill you if I had to, but that's not what the king wants."

She glowers at the threat. "You're lying."

"I can't lie."

A hiccup quakes her ribcage, and she looks down at her feet for a fleeting moment. "Unless you're not really Fae."

Not really Fae?

I loosen my hold on my powers and allow for a hint of the old me to pierce through. Shadows wisp over my skin, and the room darkens. Tendrils of darkness lick Nell's shoulders, reaching for her and hugging her curves in every way that I can't. *By the spindle...the girl looks good in black.*

"Look at me." I cup her face to angle her chin up. "I swear to you, kitten. I'm Fae through and through."

She shivers at the dark, uneven pulse of magic. "I believe you."

I have to remind myself of why she's here, where she comes from, and what she believes in. I have to remind myself every minute of every day not to give in.

I spin around, putting at least four feet of empty space between us. "I'm no good for you. Letting this attraction grow will only make us miserable."

"Attraction, eh?" She observes me from behind her long lashes. "Did she die? Your fiancée?"

The words worm their way inside my foggy brain, and my blood stops cold. "What?"

She scurries over to me and plays with the zipper of my jacket, sliding it up and down. "Did the king kill her? Is that why you're scared to feel something?"

"What did Two tell you?" I say, the words barely audible. The mask isn't enough to protect myself from her gaze anymore, and my fingers tremble.

"I know you were engaged to her. Morrigan."

I cover her mouth with my palm out of pure instinct. "Don't say her name."

No mortal should say her name out loud, or she might hear it... After New York, I wouldn't put it past her to try and kill my seeds. I can't bear the thought of her and Nell in the same realm, let alone the same room.

Nell thinks that Morrigan was my long lost love, and that I'm still grieving her, and that's just so...wrong. I can't let her think that, no matter how convenient it'd be to use it as an excuse.

"I didn't love her," I say as I remove my hand.

Her brows arch in question, her cheeks warm. "You got engaged to a woman you didn't love?"

"It's complicated."

She leans into me, her open gaze flicking up to mine like she can see through my mask. "Tell me."

The pull between us has grown beyond anything I can control. I can't explain it. It's annoying as fuck.

I grip her upper arms and hold her back, feeling like I'm standing on the edge of a dark, bottomless hole. "If you don't stop now, I'll do something we'll both regret."

"Like kiss me again?"

I clench my jaw, summoning the most wicked parts of me to the surface. "I could do a lot worse. I would gladly tie you to my bed and make you forget all about your home, your family, and your beliefs."

She blinks a few too many times, a deep red flush branding her chest and cheeks.

"You think I'm angry when I'm with you. I'm not angry. I'm *hungry* for you. I'm meant to lure mortals into the Shadow realm and feed on their dreams and fantasies...meant to seduce them into coming back every night, and yet not so much that they don't wake up."

The truth burns, finally unleashed. For weeks now, I've been thinking about Nell's white blonde hair, her perfectly smooth skin, and her bright smiles... But not in the way she envisions.

I've been daydreaming about wrapping her braid around my fist as I thrust into her, about kissing the valley between her breasts after I'm done, and drinking in the shape of her lips as she begs for more.

I stroke the back of her ear with my thumb. "But not you. You, I'd keep for myself. If things were different, I would steal you away from your puritan of a father and worship your body until you belonged to me forever. You'd *never* be allowed to leave." I pull her forward until our lips are a hair apart. "But I *can't*."

"Because I belong to the king," she breathes softly, and her nails scratch a tantalizing path down my chest. "Well... the king isn't here. And I promise not to tell if you don't."

My face falls at her certainty. *If only.*

At the last second, I take a giant leap back and turn my back to her. "You're not hearing me. We're *done*."

Morpheus be damned. I said all those things to scare her senseless, to make her understand exactly how dark my soul is. We could never be friends, not the way my body has been howling for her.

Why did she look like she was about to consent to whatever scenario my dirty mind came up with? She was raised in a world where the very mention of sex is frowned-upon. Where women who give in to any pleasure are vilified. How did this happen?

Truth be told, I'm ready to break all the rules for her. *Fuck the curse!* I'm tempted to throw away my mask and spill all my secrets.

If I haven't been struck by one of Devi's arrows, it means I have no excuse for my behavior. It means I'm dangerously close to betraying my promises—my very self—for a woman I vowed to destroy. For a stupid crush I never asked for. For pleasures I can no longer enjoy, broken as I am.

Luckily, I can still win the bet without Two finding out about this disaster. I can still save the realm, but not without breaking Nell— and what's left of my soul—beyond repair.

CHAPTER 24
HOMECOMING

"Focus your mind on the place you need to find," Two says on a heavy sigh, his tone so different from One's—impatient and dry.

The runes I've drawn on my wrist should allow me to return home. I ply the glass of the sceaware between my fingers and my lower arm but only manage to glimpse at the wrong bedroom, my queen-size bed undulating beyond the surface of the glass. "That's my room here in Faerie," I say, frustrated.

Two lets out a low chortle. "You used 'Fae' and 'Faerie,' are you really surprised?"

I shake out my shoulders and grip the handle of the inked paintbrush, quickly drawing "a lack of" next to the other runes and switching some things around.

Two clicks his tongue, his annoyance palpable. "That's sloppy at best. Dangerous. You'd probably end up anywhere in the old world or the new."

"What should it be, then?" I snap. "Teach me."

He shakes his head. "What it'd be for me is immensely different to what it'd be for you."

"How does that make sense?"

"If you sang a song longing to return home to the castle you grew up in, how could it be the same song I'd sing to visit a drab building in a strange land filled with superstitious fools?"

I punch his upper arm as hard as I can, but my obnoxious tutor only flashes me his teeth.

"Come on, now. Focus."

I stop trying to make a sentence and think of music. Music isn't brains, it's guts, and so I hit "heart" and "flame" and concentrate on Cece.

The mirror in front of us ripples into the basement of my father's castle. *Yes! Victory!*

Two blinks a few times, clearly surprised by my breakthrough. "Hmm. Not bad."

"That seems to be the only compliment you know."

The grumpy pout on his face is sweeter than chocolate, and I do a little happy dance. The new inked rune smudges my arms, the ink we use for runes clearly not as magic as the one used on paper. "I get why I don't have tattoos, but most of the others only have a few. It's clearly a pain to redraw the runes every time, I'm sure."

Especially since a wonky-looking rune could leave an imprudent traveler stranded in another world.

"Permanent runes are earned. One by one." He motions for me to *shoo.* "I trust you can find your way back in fourteen days?"

I offer him a wry grin. "As long as you don't enchant me to forget."

"No enchantments needed. You know the rules. If you fail to show up…"

"I know. You win. I lose…and I can't know more. Got it."

He cracks up, the smile more genuine than any previous smile adorned by his beautiful mouth. "This bet was really rigged in our favor, wasn't it?"

"Absolutely."

My heart stumbles. Two is worlds apart from One. He doesn't

have the same voice, the same temperament, or even the same facial expressions, but no matter how many times I remind myself of that, my body disagrees. After last night in the gym... I won't let One forsake me so easily.

"Anything else?" Two asks, his brows raised in question.

I shake off the nerves and turn my back to him, erasing him from my vision. "No, I'm good." I slip on my mask and step through the glass, leaving Two and his sarcastic quips behind.

It's early in the morning, so my father's castle is bustling with activity, but my powers have grown, so I stay easily out of sight, using the shadows in the foliage of the gardens and the dark corners of the castle to skip to my room to change. I open the door—I asked Esme to leave it unlocked this time around—to find Cece crying on my bed.

The surprise pulls me out of the shadows, and we both gasp in unison.

She clutches the letter she's holding. "I couldn't reach you in Faerie, Nell. I'm sorry."

My current thoughts vanish at the obvious anguish in her voice, her red eyes quickening my pulse. "What's going on? Is it Father? Esme?"

She shakes her head, her cheeks flushed, and wipes her tears off with the sleeve of her lavender dress. "No." She hands over the crumpled letter. "I opened your letter. I know you warned me never to open them, but Mathilda Haysting wrote to you while you were gone. Firenze cut his leg, and it got infected... I think they're going to put him down soon. They were holding out for you, but Father told them you were very sick."

"You did good, Cece." I kiss her forehead. "Come on, we have no time to waste."

"You mean—"

"Let's go!" I hurriedly trade my huntress uniform for a dress.

Esme enters the room, her nose wrinkled on a sad, hopeless grimace. "I was afraid you'd say that... I already asked the king if we could go, and he said no. Besides...the Haystings have probably already cut the poor horse's suffering short."

"Where is he?" I ask Cece.

"His office. But—"

Seeing red, I storm out of the room.

"Miss Penny, please take a moment to think," Esme shouts behind me.

Climbing down the stairs two at a time, I hurry past the main hall and the confused guards to reach the end of the southern corridor. Before they can come to their senses, I barrel through the closed doors of Father's office with a confidence that would have eluded me in the past, but I won't let Firenze die. Not on my watch.

My bravado fizzles out faster than a falling star as I take in the sight of the two diplomats sitting opposite my father. *Oh no...* I certainly interrupted an important meeting.

The men's deep frowns cause me to slow down, but I straighten up my skirt and walk to the king with my head held high. "Please excuse my ghastly interruption, Father, but I have an urgent matter to discuss with you."

Father clears his throat loudly, a fierce red tint sticking to his cheeks and nose. "Please give us a moment."

The men look a bit cross as they step out of the office the same way I came, and I wait for the thick doors to close behind them before saying, "I want to go to the Haysting's farm and heal Firenze."

Father's eyes narrow, and he slowly rises to his feet, his gaze angled to the side like he'd rather look at the empty wall than his own daughter. "*Urgent* would be you or your sister risking death or disgrace. *Urgent* would be news of a rebellion in the kingdom, or a declaration of war from our neighbors. A horse dying is not a good reason to barge in here as though you're some savage, uneducated child. Women are not allowed in here, as you well know. "

"You're right. I apologize," I say, mostly to appease him. "Be that as it may...I think Firenze's condition is worth my attention. And time is of the essence."

He waves my concerns away with a mean, dismissive gesture. "Silly girl. It's only a horse."

My teeth clench. "I want to go."

"Me too." Cece runs inside the room, a desperate Esme clutching her skirts to slow her down.

"Now, girls, you shouldn't talk to your father this way," Esme says in a chastising but hesitant manner. Our Fae governess sways from side to side like she doesn't quite know which leg to stand on.

Father looks at Cece and Esme in turn, but he still won't look directly at me, and his stubbornness is a direct dart to the heart. He gambled away my freedom—to a Fae king, no less—and condemned me to this half-and-half fate. I don't truly belong to either world while I live out his *contract*, and he should find the courage to look me in the eyes.

"If you don't arrange a carriage right now, I'll go alone," I say quickly, my chin held high.

Father chuckles unkindly. "And how do you propose to do that without my help? Do you have your own money, or your own horse?"

My jaw clenches in the angriest line it has ever known. "I don't need money. I can walk there. Through the mirror you keep downstairs." I'm not sure I could find the Summer house in the sceawere, but I could find my way back to Faerie and beg One or even Two to take me there.

Father's face becomes white as a sheet. "What did you just say?"

"You heard me."

His already red face turns almost purple. "If you can walk through mirrors, you're no daughter of mine!" he shouts before whipping his head around to look at Esme. "You told me she wouldn't become one of these crawling, disgusting creatures. You swore there was no way she could be transformed into a Fae."

I jerk away, terrified of what he might do.

Cece gawks at me, her pupils wide and deep, but I don't detect a hint of fear in them. In fact, if I had to describe the fire in her eyes with one word, it wouldn't be sadness or disgust or fright. More like unabashed curiosity. Even...excitement.

Esme clears her throat loudly after a moment of quiet reflection. "Do not worry, Your Grace. This is nothing but an empty teenage threat." She looks down her nose at me, her best haughty governess voice on full display. "Say it's not true, Miss Penny. Admit that you've made up this unspeakable lie to upset your father so he would cave in to your silly demand, and I will accompany you to visit the horse." She wets her lips, her keen intelligence shining in her eyes. "By the Mother, tell the truth, and I swear that I will get you there today."

I know what she's doing. It's clever. She gets to pacify Father by coaxing a false apology out of me, and if he decides we can't go regardless, she can cite her formal promise as a reason to find a different way to punish me.

A Demeter woman knows never to swear on our Mother's head, but Esme can pass it off as a foreigner faux-pas. Despite the fact that she's lived here for decades, she can claim she didn't know any better.

Thank you, I try to convey with my eyes.

She offers me a discrete nod.

Father will punish me. He'll think of something I would have found dreadful in the past to assert his authority, but no punishment could truly impact me anymore. If he takes away my books, I can get new ones from Faerie. If he grounds me, great! It doesn't matter because I'll be a social pariah for at least another season anyway. And if he decides to punish me physically, the way he did after mother died...I can always sneak out of the castle without being seen.

CHAPTER 25

A LESSON IN BIOLOGY

The sun is quickly dropping in the evening sky when the carriage rattles to a halt in front of Gerald and Mathilda's farm.

"We're not too late. Thank the Mother!" Cece shouts before she climbs out and runs toward the crooked farmhouse.

Firenze's white mane blows in the breeze, his bridle attached to the wooden fence next to the stable. The once proud horse is merely a shadow of his old self. His defined ribs are visible in the distance, and his head is hunched in capitulation.

The crisp autumn air makes me grateful for the thick wool over-coat Esme forced me into. I tighten the collar around my neck as we walk to the pasture, half-frozen mud crunching under my boots.

Gerald and Cece catch up to us a moment later.

"By our Mother's grace...I was just about to put him down. Mathilda couldn't stand the sight of it..." Gerald's gaze falls upon me, his hat crumpled in his tight grip. "Are you sure it's wise for ye to be here, princess? Yer father said you were too sick to travel—"

I pick up the pace, anger threatening to pierce my royal exterior. "Don't worry about me. I've never been better."

"Alright, then." He secures his hat back upon his head at my resolve, and we all hurry to the sick horse.

"Oh, poor Firenze..." Cece says, her voice strangled.

"Don't worry, Cece. He'll feel better in a minute." I climb over the fence, wishing I wasn't wearing such a big dress, the thick skirts slowing me down.

Firenze's ears turn toward me with interest, and I raise my hand to his muzzle. "Hey, you. Don't worry, I'm here now."

Willing myself not to notice the fetid smell coming from his front limb, I press my hand to it and jolt backwards, startled by the feel of it. It's colder than I expected, and stiff as stone. Firenze barely holds his weight upon it, his other leg trembling at the effort.

Closing my eyes, I draw magic from the mud, the earth, the fence and the prickly hay. I summon it from the wood of the barn and the warmth of the sun itself, from Gerald and Cece and Esme... I draw magic from everything in sight, and feel emptier still.

The wound remains as deadly as it was, so I try again, without success.

"What's going on?" Cece asks, but I shush her.

"Give me a minute."

I try again. And again.

My fingertips blacken, and ice runs thick in my veins, but I continue to try until I'm covered in sweat. To no avail.

Finally, I search the pasture and muddy fields as though I might summon One to my side by just thinking about him. The mirror in the basement of the summer house comes to mind.

"I could ask for help—" I whisper.

Esme squeezes my shoulder, and her sudden proximity sends my heart into a frenzy. "You can't heal what is already dead, darling. No one can. Not even the most powerful Fa—of our Mother's disciples."

No. I'm here. I made it in time. There must be something—

I give it my all in one last attempt. My belly cramps, my hands cold and clammy like I'm running a bad fever, and my whole body starts to shake. Dark lines creep up my hands like poison ivy slithering up my arms, the shadow magic taking more than it gives as I stretch it to its breaking point.

Esme clears her throat. "Enough, Miss Penny. You will exhaust yourself." The warning is thick in her voice.

I'll soon be engulfed in darkness and alert everyone to the true nature of my powers. I wouldn't mind it if I thought it could save Firenze, but I can feel the magic threatening to freeze me to the core without giving much in return.

Firenze nuzzles my side weakly, as though asking what's going on... The joy at making it here on time crashes and burns into a volcano of dread in my chest.

"Nell?" Cece squeaks.

The terrible truth falls like a blanket of snow over my well-crafted denial. "I can't heal him... It's too late."

Cece flattens her palm to her mouth and croaks, "No."

The white stallion neighs softly, and my heart breaks at the familiarity and gentleness of the sound.

"If only we'd come sooner," I add, full of regrets.

Gerald nods with his lips pursed in a sad, resigned frown. "It's not your fault, princess. I've been delaying the inevitable, hoping your miracle could save the poor boy again, but he's suffered enough." He pats down his horse's neck. "Here ye go. Good horse. Ye'll be alright now."

The old farmer is no doubt used to these kinds of things, but Firenze is his favorite horse, and so his voice is not quite as steady as I'm sure he wishes it to be.

Firenze lets out a heavy breath, and I bury my face in his mane, my arms wrapped around his neck. The smell of him is like summer and sunshine... Grass and the carefree joy of a child in a prairie, being taught to gallop for the first time.

Cece does the same on the other side, crying in earnest. We stay there in stunned despair for a minute, holding him tightly.

"Do you wish to leave, Your Highnesses?" Gerald asks, signaling that the moment has come. The disappointment written in the bend of his brows is so thick, I can't bear the thought that I gave this poor man false hope.

Cece clutches Firenze harder. "No, we want to stay until the end," she declares with a determination that will not be denied.

"Come and stand behind me then. The both of ye." The click of his pistol turns my stomach.

Esme looks at Firenze with her brows lifted and a weirdly upbeat smile. "Biology is a marvelous thing. In the face of infection, the body separates itself from the threat by cutting the blood flow to the limb."

I resent the obvious awe in her voice, but Gerald doesn't appear to be insulted by her macabre musings. "Yes, quite marvelous indeed. Too bad horses can't live with only three legs," he says.

Cece shakes her head in disbelief. "What a witch."

The old farmer tips his hat once more, saying goodnight to his horse for the last time, and I can't help but screw my lids shut at the squeeze of the trigger.

The death of the beloved animal is agony.

The wheeze of Firenze's last breath tramples my last defences, the gaping hole in his forehead oozing dark, burgundy blood. The light leaves his eyes, but his lids remain open.

Under the blue, cloud-streaked sky, Firenze's dead eyes are as big as the moon.

Staring at me. Staring at my incompetence.

Tears roll down my cheeks, hot and prickly. Few things make grown men cry, but this is one of them, and the strangled sob Gerald fails to swallow echoes deeper in my soul than if he'd screamed.

"I'm sorry for your loss, Gerald." I squeeze his hand, even though I shouldn't. Royals aren't supposed to touch commoners.

He clears his throat, taken aback by the gesture. "No need to worry, princess. An old man like me's been through worse."

The carriage ride home is filled with stories of the great horse, Cece eager to tell us about the time he lost a shoe in the river, while I recall the time I dyed his mane pink.

"Father was livid, of course. His proud stallion, full of pink braids right before church..." I explain between sobs, my eyes itchy from all the crying.

Cece cracks up, her laugh interrupted by an inopportune sneeze. "He was the best horse."

Esme wraps her up in a hug. "There will be other horses, kid."

"But none as good as him."

"None as good, of course." She kisses the top of Cece's head. "But maybe...half as good?"

Cece grins through a sob and nods. "Yes. Maybe half as good."

I stare out the carriage window with a slightly lighter heart, still feeling like I haven't done enough. I could have at least tried to contact One or Lori or Baka. If I was more powerful, I might have been able to heal him.

If I could communicate with Cece while I'm in Faerie, I might have learned of Firenze's illness sooner, and he'd still be with us.

Father is gone when we return. His minister tells us that pressing matters needed his attention at our borders with the neighboring country, Danu. While I'm sure he won't forget my insubordination, I have a little time to grieve in peace.

The next couple of weeks, I stay home while Cece enjoys her first autumn out in society. My reputation is still in shambles, and my morale is not high enough to endure the unrelenting gossip.

I find myself removed from the mere thought of climbing back into Lundan's elite good graces. Instead, I run at night, and spend the days reading through my empty schedule with an emptier heart.

Esme joins me late in the library one evening and reads out loud from my mother's diary. "Whenever an unmarried woman finds herself in the middle of a scandal, the only sensible thing for her to do is to remove herself from the situation entirely. Assuming the scandal is not big enough to destroy her reputation, merely hinder it, she can hope for a fresh start in late winter. By then, boredom has settled deep enough in her peers for her to be a novelty again—and her faults merely welcomed entertainment."

It's intended to be a pep talk, the clever Fae using my dead mother's wisdom to pacify me and encourage patience, but I feel numb.

"Did she write anything on the subject of being fed to the wolves for no good reason?" I crack.

Esme's lips quirk in the shadow of a smile as she ignores my cheeky comment and continues to read. "When that time comes, a woman must be very careful. While second chances are viewed as honorable, thirds would just be vulgar."

She fails to hide a snicker, and I raise my brows. "Do you really believe in all of this?" I ask.

"What do you mean?"

"Do you miss Faerie? I mean—people here treat you differently. I've read about droughts, and most of them choose to stay in the new world. Why choose Demeter?"

"I wasn't just condemned to exile, Miss Penny. I was to be slaughtered." She closes the diary and bites her bottom lip.

I stiffen in my chair, suddenly worried—and immensely curious. "Why?"

"Because I knew one too many secrets." She lowers her voice even more. "What if I told you there was a way we could stay in contact while you're over there? There's a basic Fae trick I could teach you..."

Eyes wide, I consider her serious face with a tinge of excitement. "I was thinking the same thing. I need a way to communicate with you and Cece in case something happens."

She gives me a sharp nod, a sense of understanding and urgency pulsing in the air between us. "Pull off your sock."

She pulls two sewing pins from her bag. "I'll sterilize them first, so there's no risk of infection." She holds the two pins to a nearby candle until the metal end glows red. After it's done, she blows on them to cool them down and pricks her finger with one. "First, we both sink the end of our pin into our fingers and coat it with blood."

I follow her instructions, and once the pins are coated in red, we exchange them.

Esme shows off her naked ankle and points to the slight concave depression below the bone. "We push it here, right to the bone." She presses her lips together to hide a wince as she sinks the pin inside her flesh, the small, pearly black head sticking out.

I grit my teeth together and do the same.

"It's not fancy magic by any means, but if I pull on mine, you'll feel it." She wiggles the head of the pin, and a somewhat unpleasant but tame sensation tickles my calf.

I nod, thrilled to have a way to stay connected to her and Cece, however small or primitive it is.

She opens her mouth to continue her explanation, but Cece enters the room. My sister's long nightgown licks the floor with a soft *swish* as she walks over to us. "Don't stop on my account."

Esme quickly pulls her sock up her leg and stands to put the diary back on the shelf. "I was heading to bed, actually."

"Why did Father go to Danu so suddenly?" Cece asks. "Isn't it already winter over there?"

Esme's cheek ticks in response. "I don't know." If she wasn't Fae, I'd call horseshit on that answer, but the weird look on her face quickly melts away, and she takes her leave. "Don't stay up too late, girls."

The fire casts mesmerizing shadows on the wall as Cece sits next to me on the chaise lounge. "Something's not right. I feel it here." She rests a hand over her heart, and her blue eyes glaze with sorrow the way they used to after our mother died.

"You're bleeding," I say.

The tip of her index finger shows a drop of blood, but she licks it off with a shrug. "Oh, it's nothing. I just pricked myself with something, earlier." Her hazelnut eyes bore into me. "When do you have to go back?"

I avert my gaze, afraid to face her disappointment. "Tomorrow."

"So every fourteen days..."

"Yes." I hesitate. "You haven't asked a lot of questions about Faerie." I expected her to harass me the last two weeks, and yet she didn't.

She shifts closer and reaches for my hand. "It's not that I'm not curious."

"Really? You're not afraid of me now, are you? Are you angry that I couldn't heal Firenze?" I ask.

"Oh Nell... I'd never! I just—I figured you're probably not allowed to share everything with me anymore." A bright red blush colors her cheeks. "Esme said something about your trips to Faerie being private, and that I should be discreet."

A small cry of relief escapes me. "Since when do *you* listen to Esme?"

Cece shrugs, and I reach down to pick up the book tucked under the cushion. "Here, I figured you should have it."

Her eyes widen. "What is it?"

I caress the golden cover before angling it to her. "*Delusions of Winter*. It's the first Fae book I ever read. Mother gave it to me."

"Mother gave you a Fae book?" Cece's eyes flood with tears.

"When I turned sixteen. It was the night she told me about my magic."

She picks it up like it's the goddess' sacred shroud and holds it close to her chest. "I'll guard it with my life."

"Nothing so dramatic as that. It's a poetry book. The Fae King of Winter wrote it."

Her gaze drops down to her lap. "I hate that you have to leave... But most of all, I hate that I can't go with you."

A quick, comforting smile glazes over my lips. "Don't worry. I'll see you soon, Cece."

"How does it work? Are you just going to *poof* into nothingness?" she asks, the discretion she promised Esme clearly forgotten.

I press my lips together for a moment, unsure if I should tell the truth or not, but her open gaze coaxes information out of me better than any court inquisitor. "I'm going to hide in the shadows and sneak past the guard to get to the mirror downstairs."

"There's a mirror downstairs?" she gasps.

"Yes, and it's *huge*."

"Can I see it?"

My smile falters. *What would Father do if he knew that I showed it to her?* "Maybe next time."

"I love you, Nell."

"Love you, too."

We hug and get to bed, and before I know it, it's time for me to leave.

There's something insidious about going back to Faerie by myself. Do I have to return exactly fourteen days later? On the hour? Can I just decide to go whenever I please as long as I'm not late? What if I'd gone early last night? Would that have made me lose the bet?

I pace the mirror room, looking at my pocket watch. Twenty minutes to go... Surely, leaving twenty minutes early would bear no consequence? What if I was a minute late?

Ugh, I hate not knowing.

The glass darkens suddenly. I tighten my grip around my quill and step closer to the mirror to see better as the silhouette slowly sharpens into focus.

On the other side of the glass, a woman holds a matching set of daggers on each side of her at my approach, but the familiar shape of her shoulders melts my fears. It's not the Shadow King or one of his dark knights, but Lori.

A thin, almost translucent sapphire mask is visible through the opening in her black scarf, and I offer her a small wave. She drops her fighting stance and steps in from the glass.

My pulse drums in my veins. "What are you doing here?"

My worlds are colliding—I can't deal.

Lori grins proudly, and her shadow daggers vanish, the magic-made weapons flaking off into dark ashes. "Two promised to relieve me from my library duties for a week if I was able to make my way to you without assistance. I've never been to the old world, so it took a bit of time." She looks around the room, and her excitement is contagious. "I'd love to ask you for a tour, but we have to hurry. The harvest celebration starts in an hour."

CHAPTER 26
HEART OF GLASS

A pleasant evening breeze ghosts along my neck as I soak in the beauty of the gardens from the empty balcony. The luscious rumples of my ball gown sag against the balustrade, and a full-bodied shiver takes hold of my body despite the warmth of the night.

My strapless dress leaves my shoulders bare, the golden-flecked ivory skirt made to match my mask. A layered fishtail braid tumbles down my left shoulder, and I pick nervously at the knotted end.

Instead of the usual banquet, the Foghar festival is a fancy standing picnic. The high tables peppered on the fringes of the dance floor and on the balcony fit four to five people each, but there's no seat to speak of. The set-up encourages—or rather forces—the guests to mingle. Tiny portions of mouth-watering meals are being passed around by magic trays, but I'm not hungry.

The triplets are a no show so far, as is the Shadow King.

"Emerald and gold—how pretty," Isobel Umbra chimes as she joins me in my secluded spot. "You look like a fine jewel, seed."

"Thank you," I answer politely before taking a sip of water.

Isabel's blood-red dress shimmers as though it was stitched in twilight. Most of the Fae ladies are wearing beautiful ball gowns showcasing earthy tones like dark orange, burgundy, and violet-red, and I stick out like a dove in a field of fallen leaves.

"I saw you the other day, in the blibliotheca," she says.

"Yes, I remember." I brush the sensitive patch of skin at my temples, grateful for my mask.

It can be a tremendous advantage to wear one. I only have to nod and smile as I endure her scrutiny. Not having to check my facial features or hers allows me to watch for other signs. Finger twitches and the incline of one's chin can tell you more about them than their brows, and it's easier to reign in my emotions without the pressure of constant eye contact.

"Between you and me, the court is curious about you. It's not often that we get an old world seed, let alone a princess."

I make sure not to move my head as she says the word. Aside from the dark triplets and the king himself, no one here knows I'm a princess. Mara hasn't found a way to belittle me about it, so I'm sure she doesn't know, and I even kept it from Lori.

"Which task did you get first?" Isobel asks, forcing my attention back to her.

"Nightmares."

"Oh...you must spend a lot of time with One." Her tone is now dangerously sweet, and I get the feeling that her patience with me is wearing thin. "Does he plan to show up for the Foghar festival tonight?"

"Actually, I'm studying dreams now. With Two."

Her top lip curls up in an ugly, disbelieving smile. "Is that so?"

I grip the railing, my long ivory gloves shining in the moonlight, and catch a glimpse of Lori near the buffet. Taking advantage of her arrival, I excuse myself from Isobel to greet her.

The skirt of Lori's blue dress undulates around her frame like liquid silk as she stumps over to the hors d'oeuvres, her sapphire mask complimenting the look. While her chosen fashion is not as formal as mine—with no gloves or necklace—and her usual earrings still in place, she's a vision. Her golden skin is simply glowing, making the rest of us look pale and sickly in comparison.

Lori grips a triangular glass and stuffs a spoonful of sweet potato mousse in her mouth. "I hate these things," she mumbles with the spoon tucked between her teeth. "They always force me into a damn dress."

"You look gorgeous."

"Hmpf. I don't care. I want my hoodie and pants." She eyes me up and down. "You don't look so appalled by the Fae fashions as I thought. Didn't you tell me you weren't used to showing skin?"

I blush deep red, her remark gnawing at my insecurities. When Baka had carried the dress into my bedroom, I almost clawed it out of her tiny, wrinkled hands. "It's the most beautiful gown I've ever seen. I just—it was so beautiful, I had to wear it."

"Hey, sorry." Lori grabs a champagne flute from an incoming magic tray and pinches the front of her dress with a disgusted pout for emphasis. "You look fabulous. I'm just crabby because of this wretched thing."

Misha—the curly-haired hunter with the sharp accent—joins us with a full plate in his hands. "The High Fae are quite interested in your progress. Everyone's asking about you."

My lips purse together. "Why?"

"They're here to spy on the king." Lori explains, always quick to jump to my rescue when I need information. "The seeds reflect the strength of his magic on a given year, and I bet Isobel Umbra caught more than she let on the other day."

"Agreed. She all but grilled me with questions earlier."

My friend half covers her eyes with her open palm, peering through her fanned fingers. "Oh, here we go. Two's here."

I crane my neck around in time to see Two stand on one of the tables.

"May I have your attention." He raises his wine glass in the air, his speech slightly slurred. "I'm happy to report that all three seedlings have made it through their first trial."

Applause resonates in the banquet hall, and Two offers them a quick bow, relishing the attention.

I stand on my tip-toes to glance over the crowd.

Three decided to show up, too. The silent triplet shakes his head with a humorous grimace like he finds his brother unredeemable. The red embroideries on his black jacket highlight his muscled frame, and he's got a gorgeous Fae lady hanging on his arm.

James chats with a group of Fae lords, the timid seed looking like a fish out of water in the middle of the huddle.

"Where's One?" I ask quietly.

Lori tilts her head back to gulp down the last sip of champagne, and a smudge of red lipstick taints the rim of her empty flute. "I guess he wasn't in the mood for schmoozing. It's not unusual for him to miss these events."

"I thought it was an official Faerie holiday, shouldn't he be made to bear through it like the rest of us?" I say, crestfallen.

She eyes me up and down. "You're grumpy tonight."

"Am not."

She grins from ear to ear. "Are too."

A sprite with a smooth, deep voice clears his throat. "All welcome his Majesty the King. Damian Morpheus Sombra, king of shadows, keeper of dreams, weaver of fantasies, and master of nightmares."

The crowd grows quiet, and Two hurries off the table with his lips curled down. The narrow root of the table he was standing on wobbles at his hasty retreat and knocks him off balance. He tumbles to the ground, and his ass hits the floor hard just as the Shadow King steps out of the glass.

The king's faceless stare latches onto him, and Two peels himself off the dance floor with a humiliated pout.

The Shadow King dressed up for the occasion. His tunic has been weaved from the shadows themselves, and a wispy cloak floats at his back. The darkness within it is so impenetrable that it dims the light in the entire room. A stitch of orange on the side of his pants matches the bright harvest decorations, but the tiny splash of color makes the rest of the ensemble darker still.

He sits on his throne with a perfect air of ease, his hood snug around the edges of his mask. Shiny leather gloves are pulled tight across his knuckles as he grips the armrests, and the High Fae return to their food and conversations.

A few lords and ladies come over to greet me and introduce themselves. I evade their questions as best as I can until they give up and leave me to my peers. Mara joins us, and Lori finally convinces me to try the bite-size food—it's actually pretty delicious. I drink a little wine, and the weight of my confusing visit to Demeter slowly lifts off my shoulders.

"The king seems even more taciturn than usual," Lori remarks.

The king doesn't mingle, the few High Fae courageous enough to engage in conversation quickly rebuffed by a sharp slice of the head. He's clearly not in the mood for schmoozing.

He watches the celebration from behind his mask, perched on his throne like a vulture atop a dead pine. Perfectly unattainable.

"I've never seen a monarch act like this," I admit. "It's not a proper way to rule."

Misha cranes his neck to glance at the king. "He always does this on holidays. Shows his face without truly engaging with anyone. It drives the High Fae mad, of course, but it reminds them who's in charge."

Mara takes a sip of her wine. "I heard he hasn't spoken a word out loud since he banished the other courts from the grounds."

I frown at that, remembering how cruelly he spoke to me the night of my first trial. *Does he only speak to me?*

Misha raises his brows in a secretive manner. "It makes sense. That's around the same time as when he started wearing his full-face mask. I heard that he got badly burned during a dragon hunt, and that his tongue melted off."

Lori clicks her tongue in a chiding fashion. "That's nonsense. I heard him speak with One once. Three is the only mute Fae around here."

I nod in agreement, relieved that I'm not the only person who's heard the king speak. The faceless monster who bargained for my life weighs heavily on my mind lately... and I can't say I've learned much about him in my time here. Damian the Dauntless.

Two drops a cherry stem inside his empty glass and pries Mara from our circle. "Let's dance."

He whisks her to the middle of the floor and motions for the string quartet to play a cheery, jig-like song, and I'm impressed to see them work through it with a shred of dignity considering their intoxicated state.

Mara's black dress leaves little to the imagination, the short skirt barely covering her ass.

Jo takes her place in our group at the small round table. His navy jacket flatters his masculine silhouette, the collar of his white shirt crisp and tidy.

"It's so unfair. They let the men wear anything they want," Lori whines.

Jo wiggles his shoulders under his jacket, his chin tucked in. "What are you talking about? It's a nice tuxedo."

"From the new world. The Fae lords wear scarves, tunics, and tails. We're encouraged to follow their customs, you know," Lori says.

Misha shrugs at the reproach. "Isn't it nice to mix the fashions? It shows open-mindedness."

"Open-mindedness would be *not* forcing me into a dress. Mara is wearing a *miniskirt* for crying out loud." Lori goes off into another tirade about her gown.

Jo inches closer with a sheepish smile. "If I'd known it would upset her so, I would have worn something more traditional," he whispers. "You're absolutely gorgeous tonight, Nell."

My lips twitch, my eyes instinctively dropping to the ground even though he can't see them. "Thank you."

Cary weaves his way through the crowd and wraps an arm around Misha's shoulders. "Hey, hot shot." The easy smiles on their faces give credit to Mara's claim that they are in fact a couple.

The fast-paced dance tapers down to a slower rhythm, and Jo extends his hand to me. "How about a dance, milady?"

"With pleasure."

I've danced my fair share of waltzes, and to my delight, Jo doesn't take advantage of my lack of corset to grope my body. He holds me at a gentlemanly distance and leads through the dance with a steady hand, not perfect, but with enough finesse to impress me.

"You're a good dancer," I praise him.

"My mother taught me. We don't have a lot of opportunities to waltz in the new world. The way you dance, you must do this every day."

"Such obvious flattery would be considered pretty forward in Demeter." I add a false air of decorum to my answer to tease him, and I'm taken aback by his charming smile.

We sway back and forth, and the heat of his hand is pleasant on my waist. The bronze mask covering his eyes complements his skin nicely, and I find myself grinning back at him before the song is over.

"Thank you for the book," I blurt out, suddenly wishing I could see his green eyes.

"Anytime, Old World." The music tapers down again.

Jo adds a fun, silly twirl at the end, and I collide with his chest with a gentle laugh. "I'm almost done with it. I'll give it back to you tomorrow."

Claps resonate across the sleek checkered floor to praise the musicians, and Jo and I join in. After a quick pause, the string quartet starts a languid, forlorn tune. It slowly picks up from a few timid notes, and my grip on Jo's arm tightens.

The music seeps inside my pores, and the soul-shattering whine of the violin prickles my heart. Most of the lords and ladies stop moving and exchange quick whispers between themselves.

The cellist plucks the cords of his instrument like he's hanging between life and death, and the bassline harmonizes with the violin in a powerful, intricate melody.

I glance over my shoulder to the Shadow King, surprised to find his throne abandoned, and my pulse quickens. A gloved hand taps on the shoulder of my partner, and Jo sidesteps, bowing to the king.

I curtsy at his arrival and drop my gaze to the ground. My whole body freezes as the king extends his hand in my direction. A sheen of cold sweat gathers at the back of my neck, and I swallow against the roil in my stomach, feeling faint.

For a moment, I think that the Shadow King's magic has stopped the flow of time, but Jo shifts his weight from one foot to the other, and the stares of the High Fae tickle my shoulders.

I search the masked faces in the crowd, but none of them can help me. Mara's lips are pressed in a grim line. Lori gapes. Three pushes himself off the wall at his back, graceful as a cat, and abandons his female companion, but I quickly lose sight of him.

A discrete creak of leather booms in my ears as the king flexes his little finger and raises his offered hand by a quarter inch, signaling that I should take it *now*. At last, I succumb to his demand.

Snubbing him in front of his court... I shiver at the possible consequences.

The king's blank golden mask shines in the darkness. He guides me away from my original partner to the center of the room, but my eyes are fixed on our joined hands.

Black and ivory gloves.

Leather and satin.

A firm yet gentle hand on my shoulder blade...

I cover his right arm with mine. He's stronger than I knew, his body broad and powerful as he tugs me close and whisks me into a dizzying waltz. We fly around the dance floor. Our movements are so fluid that I glance down to check if I'm still touching the ground.

The other lords and ladies quickly follow suit.

Dark gowns flow around us, and my ivory skirt is the only white flag in the middle of a bloody battlefield. The music thickens in my bones as the two of us move in perfect synchrony. I feel drugged—or rather enchanted. The king's bite of power sinks its claws inside me better than if he'd skewered me with a sword, and I jump at the chance to observe him more closely and fact-check a few tidbits of gossip. From this angle, I catch a glimpse of his neck and see no burns to speak of.

Nothing but smooth, tanned skin, interrupted only by the ghost of a crescent-shaped scar.

Leather brushes along my naked back, and the small caress packs a powerful punch. Two's angry words resonate in my ears. *She belongs to the king...*

No wonder One freaked out when we kissed. This is why he's avoiding me; why he's not here.

The entire world melts away. The dancers, the clink of glasses, the glow of the lanterns... Everything disappears but the king and me, the both of us bound together by this haunting, exquisite piece of music.

No cruel threats, no crude mention of sex or abuse. In fact, his bite of power is incredibly soothing, and I almost weep when the song stretches into its last decrescendo.

The king holds an arm to his chest and offers me a respectful bow. The skirt of my dress sweeps the floor as I offer him a full-blown court curtsy to atone for my earlier indecision.

The melody finally stops, and I press a hand to the hollow of my neck, feeling like a puppet liberated from its strings.

"What do you want from me?" I whisper.

He balls his fists, and I wait with baited breath, presuming he's about to turn on his heels and storm off without the simplest of explanation.

When he finally speaks, his voice is both swift as a breeze and hypnotic as a campfire. Strong as stone, but gentle as the ripples over a bottomless pond. It is no human sound.

"Nothing. Everything. Too little of what you owe, and more than you can spare." He tilts his head in goodbye and walks off with the poise of a man who owns the room—and everyone in it.

The crowd closes around me after he's gone, a school of sharks honing in on a discarded prey. Lori elbows her way through them without hesitation and grips my hand, her red-painted lips parted in horror.

CHAPTER 27

DANCE ONLY WITH ME

B efore tonight, the High Fae were merely curious about me. But the way they gawk after the Shadow King leaves the dance floor makes my skin crawl, all discretion forgotten.

"Is there something you haven't told me? You have a different schedule than the other seeds. Is there a reason why the king would stake his claim on you?" Lori asks.

"Claim? I—"

While everyone is still focussed on me, I catch a glimpse of Two and Mara leaving together, his hand at her waist.

"Don't play dumb." Lori frowns like she expected better of me. "He might as well have pissed in a circle around you." Lori's fingers tighten hard around my wrist as she pulls me closer to the other hunters. "We need to get her out, or the High Fae will eat her alive. Let's go to the library."

"I'll get sustenance," Misha answers seriously.

We all sneak inside the library, and Lori motions for me to sit on the librarian desk with her while the other hunters form a circle around us.

"So, what's your story, Old World?" she asks for the whole group.

James, Misha, Fiona, Jo, Mitchell, and Cary all hang on to my next words. I realize how close they truly are, and how they've started to include me in their group, hopefully out of instinct that I belong here.

Their expectant faces ignite a tinge of guilt in my stomach. Isobel Umbra already knows I'm a princess, so I might as well tell them myself before they hear it from somebody else.

"I'm a princess. Back home. That's why I have a different schedule," I lie. "I didn't want to be treated differently, but my father insisted on it. What happened tonight with the king...it took me by surprise, I assure you." I end with the truth and offer them a sheepish wince.

The severe curl of Lori's mouth tells me she doesn't quite believe me. I catch her gaze, trying to convey my remorse, and she finally nods. "A princess, hey? That's rich."

Everyone in the circle laughs.

"Did the king invite you to his bedroom?" Jo asks, his face a little paler than usual.

"No!"

"Let's all stay here for the night, then, and leave the Fae to their silly traditions," Lori adds quickly, and I can't shake the feeling that I'm missing something.

We spend the next two hours passing wine around and exchanging secrets, my new friends eager for some mindless fun as they teach me how to play "Never Have I Ever," a game where pretty much everyone gets to drink themselves silly but me.

When the party disbands, Jo hangs back to speak with me one-on-one. He rubs his face down, and his words slur together a bit as he says, "Jesus—I like you, Nell, but I won't antagonize the king on purpose. It's best if we keep our friendship on the DL...at least for a while."

I have no idea what "on the DL" means, but I get the general idea and refill my cup of wine, nodding like he's making sense.

"No hard feelings?" he asks.

I force a fake smile on my lips. "None." I raise my cup in cheer and gulp it down until there's nothing left.

He zig zags out of the main entrance, leaving Lori and me alone in the library.

"What traditions were you referring to, earlier?" I ask.

She shifts her weight from one foot to the other, her lips twisted in a pout. "Foghar is not just about food and wine. The Fae usually choose a partner to have sex with before the night ends... We all thought the king might summon you to his bedroom."

The memory of Two and Mara slipping out of the ballroom together comes to mind at the news, and I refill my cup again. "Thank the Mother he didn't, or I would have given him a piece of my mind."

"What are you going to do?" Lori's gaze falls to the bottle I'm holding. "Besides getting shit-faced, apparently."

"I don't know." I've replayed the dance inside my head a hundred times, and I don't see how I could have foreseen—or better yet, prevented—the situation.

Lori paces the length of her desk back and forth with her arms tucked behind her back. "The sovereigns of Faerie are ruthless and powerful, but it's a well-known fact that any mortal who catches their eyes will suffer."

"I believe you."

She pats my shoulders, staring straight into my eyes. "Then you should leave. The next time you go back to the old world, stay there."

There's real fear in her clear gray eyes, and a guilty sob bubbles out of my mouth. "I can't."

I give in and tell her about everything. The deal my father made, the reasons for my weird schedule, and the haunting kiss I shared with One... I tell Lori about the doubts plaguing my mind and the twinge at the pit of my stomach whenever I think of home.

A few minutes after we've gulped down the last of the wine, I feel dizzy but determined. "And that's everything."

"Wow," Lori blinks a few times, still digesting all the information. "I mean—Wow." She unfolds her legs and discards her empty cup on the desk. "Are you still in love with this Isaac guy?"

"Isaac?" I look down at the dark surface of the red wine, One's terribly beautiful face coming to the forefront of my mind as I answer. "No. I'm not."

I thought I loved Isaac, but after his unspeakable behavior at the ball and the way he behaved in the Dreaming... I'm not sure I truly knew him at all.

"And your father—I'm sorry, but he sounds like a douche."

My brows furrow. "Douche?" I'm pretty sure it means "shower," and I don't get it.

Lori shakes her head like I'm the most annoying person in the world. "He's a jerk. A jackass. A schmuck. A prick. An asshole."

"Pretty much." I should be mortified to speak so plainly about my father and the king of my country, but hey, it's the truth. "He's a total douche," I shout a little too loud.

Lori giggles at my drunken attempt to embrace her slang.

"Sorry, I thought it meant 'shower,'" I add with a sheepish grin.

A chortle pops out of her mouth, and she rolls over with laughter, giggling until she can't breathe. Tears streak her cheeks, and when she finally finds the strength to stop, she wipes them off slowly with her hands. "Oh. Oh. That's the funniest thing I've heard like—ever."

I chuckle along with her. "That's me. The funniest girl from the old world."

"Thank you for telling me, Nell. I won't betray your trust, I promise." She smiles from ear to ear, hesitating like she can't quite move without bursting into another fit of laughter. "But I do want to hear more about the songs you saw in One's eyes."

"That's it, I'm going to bed," I say quickly.

"Don't go! I was kidding." She reaches out for me and links our arms to keep me from fleeing, and my lips twitch at the spontaneous outburst.

"I know, I'm just exhausted."

"Wait. We have to be smart about this." She jumps to her feet, her usual grace blurred by the overindulgent intake of alcohol as she bends over her desk and reaches for something hidden underneath. "Here. Wear this." She presses her favorite hoodie—the one with a red bull silhouette on its front—to my chest. "This way, no one will look twice at you on your way back to your room."

"It's almost dawn."

"Still, we should take precautions."

Her instructions don't quite fit with my secret plan to find One and demand answers, but she's got a point. She helps me unzip the side of my dress and bunches it under the desk.

Now wearing only underwear, I throw Lori's large hoodie over my head, the hem coming down to my mid-thighs, and tuck my braid carefully out of sight. "How do I look?"

"Like me, honestly. If someone sees you from afar, they'll assume you're me and not think twice. You're not exactly known for lurking about the tunnels in your underwear. I'll stay here for ten minutes and follow. I need to sober up."

"Alright, goodnight." I peck Lori's cheek like I would Cece and leave her in the library, heading silently to a section of the underground tunnels I never visited.

Mara let it slip the other day that the triplets slept under the gym, in the northern section of the tunnels, so I tiptoe down the unfamiliar corridor, hoping I've got the right one.

The doors all look the same, and I become confused after a few intersections, unsure if I'm still heading in the right direction.

Just as I'm about to give up, a scream pierces the night. Alarmed, I hurry down the closest hallway, the rough carpet scratching my bare feet. I follow the sound around a tight corner and emerge in front of another series of identical doors. Forest-green paint chips off the wood panels in large clusters, a few areas sanded down to the grain.

"Please, please, please," a woman begs, and I slow down, inching closer to the sliver of light in the distance, wrapping myself in the deepest shadow I can summon given my intoxicated state.

The door of the bedroom is ajar, and I peek through the light and see a woman lying down on her back. Mara.

A high-pitched sound whizzes out of her, and I steal another glance, catching a glimpse of her arched back and hard nipples. Heart pounding, I stop playing chicken and hide deep inside the shadows of the doorway, the destructive urge to spy on her trampling all reason. I'm both fascinated and disgusted by what she's doing, and all the scandalous drawings in Demeter couldn't have prepared me for the reality of...*fucking.*

One of the triplets is standing between Mara's legs, his bare bottom perfectly visible in the night, the fireplace burning bright next to the bed. The angle prevents me from seeing too much of their private parts, but each crackle of fire highlights the man's corded muscles as he pounds in and out of my fellow seed, the woman who sat beside me at breakfast and dinner so many times.

I catch a glimpse of an iridescent mask as Three flips Mara to her stomach, and she crouches on all four, her breasts dangling. Both relief and surprise hit me at once.

Three?

"Fuck, yes." She raises her rump in the air. "Harder."

My breath stutters as she reaches her arm toward the corner of the room, and Two appears with a golden cup in his hands, half-naked and grinning at the scene in front of him. "See? I knew you'd like fantasies, too." He sips on his wine, watching his brother pleasure himself with Mara. "How is she?"

Three shrugs as he starts to move his hips again, his expression a bit too relaxed for what he's doing.

"Oh...yes." Her voice is brittle, as though she might break if Three stops, not minding their little chat one bit.

What the crops? Why is he here? Just watching?

She certainly does not look like the women in the drawings, happy for her body to be used instead of terrified, clearly taking pleasure from it.

Two reaches out to twist her breasts, and after a moment she

cries out, shaking, and falls to her stomach on the bed. The movement causes Three to slide out of her, and he steals the cup from his
brother's hand.

I stifle a gasp with my hand at the sight of his erect cock, feeling
like I might melt into the floor, and grip the end of the hoodie.

Three gulps down the rest of the wine and wraps a lazy hand in
Mara's red mane.

"Open your beautiful mouth, Mara," Two murmurs in a low baritone that sends tremors down my spine.

Three is huge, but the wanton seed obeys his command, and he
slides his manhood all the way inside her mouth. I grab my throat,
imagining how painful it must feel, but Mara moans in approval, and
my brows bend in question.

My heart fanfares—*boom, boom, boom*—and the heavy thuds
drown out her moans. Suddenly, a hand closes around my wrist,
hard enough to bruise me.

"You shouldn't be here," One hisses under his breath. He quietly
closes the bedroom door shut, his mouth pursed in anger.

He's not wearing his usual tunic, but a simple cotton shirt with
short sleeves.

"I'm sorry," I whisper quickly. "I got lost."

"You should be in bed, where you belong. The sun is about to
rise. It's dangerous to be out here—" He hauls me along the dark
corridor, his hand stiff around my upper arm.

"Don't tear my arm off for nothing. It's only your brothers and
Mara—"

He lets me go and rakes his hand through his dark hair like he
wants to tear it out of his skull. "You shouldn't have seen that."

The motion leaves his waves all disheveled, like the night of the
hunt, and I dry off my sweaty palms on the front of Lori's hoodie.
"Why? Would it get your brothers in trouble to bed the king's seeds?"

I wonder what he's doing here, dressed like this—Wait...

"Were you about to join them?" I ask out loud without really
meaning to, my heart racing, my inhibitions lowered by the wine.

He squints, clearly taken aback by my question. "What?"

"When you caught me. Were you about to join them?" I repeat quickly, my words slurring together.

If the Fae usually take a lover on Foghar... it makes sense.

The corners of his mouth curl down, telling me I've struck a chord. Before I can move, he grabs my jaw with his right hand, the move unexpected and bold. My stomach flip-flops, and the muscles in his arms tighten as he takes a good sniff. "You're drunk."

An itch between my shoulder blades prickles my skin, and tears threaten to leak into my eyes. "Why would you want to bed Mara of all people? You said you couldn't get involved with me."

He laughs—the sound dry and unkind. "She's *nothing* like you."

"Oh? Go ahead then!" I yell way too loud not to be heard inside the room, not caring if my bluff is blatantly apparent, my heart in smithereens.

One clasps my wrist and pulls me deeper into the tunnels and away from his fucking brothers. "Let's get you to bed, you're wasted —and acting like a child."

He manhandles me along the slanted corridors, and each turning corner calms the storm inside me. I glance at my escort sideways. If he was about to join them, he's not going to, now. I'm not sure how I can be so certain of it, but I am, and the weight pressing on my chest eases.

Shadows engulf us in darkness, the illusion powerful enough to fool the sprites, and the few servants we cross paths with are oblivious to our presence. When I brace myself on the wall for balance, the wine thick in my blood, One picks me up in his arms.

I hide my face in his chest and wipe a treacherous tear with the sleeve of Lori's hoodie. The scent of pears and smoke tickles the roof of my mouth, the hint of musk underneath making me quiver. No matter what logic dictates, my body craves the touch of the dark Fae. I long for it the way frenzied cows crave the safety of a burning barn, heading to disaster.

Once in my room, he lays me down on the bed, but I wrestle

against his hold to sit up. "I'm not tired." I grip a fist of his black t-shirt, and my other hand sneaks under the hem of fabric to touch his stomach.

Quick as lightning, he takes hold of my wrists and shackles them above my head. The back of my skull hits the pillow, and the hoodie rises up over the waistband of my underwear.

One's nostrils flare, and he presses me down to the mattress with his weight. "Bad, bad kitty."

I shudder from head to toe, wishing he'd kiss me already, his riding stance on my thighs absolutely scandalous. It'd be so easy for him to slide his long hands under the hem of the big sweatshirt and feel my waist, my stomach, my breasts... so easy...

"Kiss me," I breathe, half-mad.

"Hmph. Sleep the wine off, kitten, or by the spindle, I will enchant you to sleep." He presses my wrists harder into the duvet to emphasize his point, and I offer him a pout that would put any spoiled four-year-old to shame.

"You wear your threats like armor, but you don't mean them. Not when it comes to me."

He lowers his voice, his nails digging into the supple flesh of my arms. "Don't be so sure. A couple of my previous threats sound fucking good to me right now." Inhaling deep, he places a sweet kiss at the angle of my jaw, and my chest heaves in longing.

"Goodnight," he whispers before jumping from the bed. He dumps the bulk of the covers over my naked legs and spins around to leave.

"Wait!" I call after him. "Why did you miss the ball? You should have been there." My intoxicated gut tells me the king wouldn't have acted so brazenly in his presence.

One pauses and grips the doorknob. It's a long pause that tells me he's about to skirt around the truth. "You already know why you didn't see me there."

The door closes behind him with a loud *thud*, and I groan out loud. His scent fills my lungs, and my skin burns, craving more. The

sight of his naked brothers branded me, and the hold of the Shadow
King lingers on my shoulder blade.

My gaze darts to the mirror, and I wonder if the monarch could
have been watching my fight with One, just now. I hide under the
covers, smoothing them over the length of my body, but sleep
evades me.

I loathe Mara for the enraptured sounds she imprinted in my
ears, and my hand snakes down my abdomen of its own volition. I
bite my lips, infuriated by the wetness I find there, aware that I've
been thoroughly corrupted by the Shadow Court.

Two's salacious remarks haunt me, along with Three's naked
buttocks and One's deep, hypnotic voice. Envy cramps my guts as I
touch myself for the first time since I came to Faerie, the forbidden
caress seemingly innocuous compared to the temptations of this
world.

I finish hard, shivering and panting in my two-person bed,
feeling emptier still, and pray the shadow obscuring the glass is only
a figment of my drunken imagination.

CHAPTER 28

MORNING GLORY

The next day, a humongous headache keeps me in bed for the entire morning until Baka brings in water and a special Fae medicine for *hangovers*. After dark, I finally summon enough motivation for a brisk walk, my usual routine forgotten.

The night is warm enough for me not to need a jacket, so I leave the thick uniform on the bench near the gym and head straight for the path weaving closest to the Hawthorn. I'm about fifteen minutes into my walk when I hear powerful footsteps up ahead.

The main path crosses the smaller trail around these parts, and I walk around the bend in time to see One running with his back to me.

"One! Wait!"

Ignoring my plea, he dashes toward the northern section of the gardens at the same strenuous pace, and I break into a run.

Up ahead, an arched trellis encroaches on the path on both sides, the hedges thick with flowers and leaves. The vines are so tightly knit in this section of the trail that they hide the night sky, and darkness swarms around me.

One slows down because of the narrower path, and it allows me to catch up to him.

I graze the flesh of his upper arm. "One, stop!"

The Fae screeches to a halt with his arm balanced on each side, the little rocks covering the path scattering in all directions. Three's iridescent mask is dark in the night, and his long hair is slicked back over his head, making him look too much like his brother. He checks both sides of the trail like he expects a nightmare to jump from the bushes before I feel the weight of his gaze on me.

His usual magnetism turns my belly to lava, and after what I saw last night... I can't breathe.

He motions to my navel, my chest, my face with one hand before making a downward motion and opening his palm. *Are you okay?*

I nod, bottom lip tucked between my lips, and his spine eases.

He removes two small white contraptions from his ears. High-pitched music blares from them, the harsh rhythm pounding like a wild animal in my ears despite the low volume, and I realize he truly didn't hear me chase or call after him.

"I'm sorry I startled you. I was looking for your brother," I admit quietly.

His shoulders hike up, his neck angled to the side as he scratches his breast bone. *Am I that much of a disappointment?* he seems to ask.

"You look like him in the dark." I hate the weak tremble in my voice, but there's no use denying it.

He gives a soft smile and a gentle nod. *That makes sense.*

An elusive grin ghosts over his lips, and he snaps a white, bell-shaped flower off the vines that snake around the trellis and offers it to me.

Taken aback, I murmur a quick, "Thank you." My gaze zeroes-in on the wispy scar over his heart.

Holy horses! That scar... Three brothers with the exact same scar, it's not natural.

Three combs a rebellious lock behind my ear and tips his chin down to his chest. *You can see it, right?*

I nod at the unspoken question. One seemed spooked that I could see the black wisp of smoke, but all I get coming from Three is a sense of quiet acceptance.

He wraps my hands in his and presses them to his chest, the gesture tender, but bold.

My breath stutters when he bends down to kiss me, but I retreat swiftly, pulling away from his grasp. "Well... Goodnight."

He holds both palms in front of him in a calming motion and digs his heels in the ground. *Wait.* I sink my nails in my palms not to spin around and run as he pinches his lips in a gesture of apology and shame. *I'm sorry.* He places a hand over his heart. *Really.*

The silent conversation sparks unfamiliar shivers inside me, not one of them unpleasant. He's terrifyingly similar to One, and between Three's shirtless state, my sexual frustration, and the soft morning glories grazing my arm...it's a recipe for disaster.

A hiccup shakes my throat. "I—I need to get to bed."

His shoulders sag, and he angles his beautifully haunting mask to the ground. *Sorry to hear that.*

I return to my room in a haze, still clutching the damn flower. When I get there, a velvet box with a note waits for me on my bed. I pry out the handwritten message from the ribbon and let out a nervous giggle.

Penelope... I apologize for my unspeakable behavior the night of your first trial. I wasn't myself. I had this made for you. It'll please me if you wear it.

—Damian

The beautiful calligraphy seems to move by itself on the page, but it's only tears blurring my vision. I click open the velvet box and swallow hard at the sight of the crescent-shaped pendant.

How appropriate.

I rub down my face and shake out the nerves. For whatever reason, the king has decided to court me. A knot forms in my stomach, and I'm not sure this *gift* is better than forcing me to strip. I'm still obligated to wear it and play by his rules.

I clasp it around my neck and toss Three's flower in the fire. Looking at myself in the mirror, I clutch the emerald. For better or worse, I've caught the king's eye. The golden chain suddenly feels like a noose around my neck, more obvious than a hot-iron brand on a horse's rump.

THE STUFFY DAYS OF SUMMER ARE OFFICIALLY BEHIND US. FAERIE IS different from Demeter in that when the seasons change, they really change on the day—the weather doesn't go back and forth over the course of a few weeks.

After Foghar, the days shorten immediately, and the Hawthorn's ripe fruits and leaves adorn red, orange, and yellow colors overnight.

The next couple of weeks are spent in a cloud of sweat and tears as I dive deeper into the Dreaming with Two. The dark Fae is eager to take me through a hundred different, freakishly vivid dreams of all the people I know, making me despise most of my acquaintances.

Everyone's a beast, deep inside. When it comes down to it, all souls yearn for what they can't have.

"Two claims that I need the practice to become impervious to the enchantments that govern the Dreaming—but it feels like torture," I tell Lori over breakfast, the both of us sitting together on the balcony.

The day is particularly windy. The corner of the building protects us from most of the chilly draft as Lori nibbles on her croissant, huddled inside her hoodie with her legs propped beneath her.

"Don't worry, if he's got you running circles in the Dreaming at all hours of the day, it's because you're good," she says.

"I don't think so. He hates me."

The relentless schedule—pulling me out of bed at odd hours of the night, or keeping me awake for long stretches of time—might be enough for me to lose my mind if it goes on any longer.

Lori pats my hand in a reassuring way, peeking over the railing at Jo and James who are doing yoga together on the grass. "Two doesn't hate you. He just loves himself more." Her tongue darts out to touch her bottom lip, her cheeks rosy in the autumn chill as she adds absentmindedly, "I'm telling you. The triplets ride their best students the hardest."

I blush at the sexual connotation, and Lori's eyes bulge as she leans forward in her seat. "Shit! I didn't mean it like that, I just—"

"I know. Any sightings of One? Or Mara?"

The two of them haven't been seen since Foghar, and I can't quite quell my jealousy at the thought that One is giving her very *private* hunting lessons somewhere off-world.

"No, and the High Fae haven't visited since the harvest celebration, either. I swear...it's like they've been banned from the library altogether. I'm bored out of my mind." She rolls her neck back and forth against the headrest of her chair.

I miss One. I miss our quarrels and the way he gets under my skin. I keep thinking about Foghar, and the way he rushed me to bed. The look on his face when I begged him to kiss me lives in my soul, and I can't help but wonder how differently he might have acted if he'd believed I was in my right mind.

"Have you heard from the king? Since, you know..." Lori motions in the general direction of my chest, the emerald pendant still locked around my neck.

"Not at all."

Jo approaches us from the side. "Hey, Nell. Lori." He pats off his sweaty face with a towel, naked from the waist up like he's not at all bothered by the wind. "Here's the book you asked for. I'm sorry it took so long," he says with a wince as he hands it over, the real cover masked by a different dust jacket.

Ever since the king staked his claim at the ball, the men in the group have given me a wide berth, and I'm surprised to be back in Jo's good graces.

"Err—thanks."

I pretend to read the fake dust jacket, and Lori snorts. "Oh, come on. Do you think I'm too dumb not to notice that you've brought her a book she isn't supposed to have access to yet?" We both stare at her for a moment, and she rolls her eyes. "I'm not an idiot, guys."

"Sorry," I say quickly.

She stands up and gathers her things. "Hey, I don't want to know any more. There is no way I will spend the next quarter on library duty again. Uh-uh."

"How did you get stuck on library duty, anyway?" Jo asks, and I clench my teeth, remembering how torn up Lori looked the last time we broached the subject.

"Nope. Still not answering that question." She shakes her head forcefully and walks away from our contraband book club.

Jo doesn't seem in a hurry to leave, which I take as a good sign. "One is back." He shrugs on a black t-shirt before taking Lori's empty seat. "I saw him last night."

My eyes bulge, my spine suddenly straight as a bolt. "And Mara?"

The light in his eyes dims, and he inches closer. "When I saw One was back, alone, I asked Two about her. Mara is gone, Nell. She washed out of training two weeks ago." He pauses, hesitating. "Since there's only three seeds this year, the king decided not to broadcast it too publicly, so keep it to yourself, please. I wasn't supposed to tell anyone about it."

The quasi-continuous strain I've endured in my ribs the last two weeks eases at the knowledge that One and Mara are not together, after all.

Jo moves to stand up, but I grip his arm to stop his retreat. "Wait a minute. Could it explain why the king closed the library?"

"Probably. To have a seed wash out before Morheim...it's going to worry the High Fae."

"So it's not about me and the dance?"

He relaxes in his seat, beaming. "You're in the clear, milady."

All the tension I've been carrying around drains from my body, my breaths coming more freely than they have in days. The High Fae ban is not about me, and the king hasn't shown his face once in the last thirteen days, so maybe after my next trip to Demeter, everything can go back to normal.

I observe Jo from underneath my lashes, suddenly feeling much better. "You look...wary."

"Truth is; I'm worried about our future. The king's magic has grown weak, and Morheim is coming soon. Our tepid hunts won't be enough to keep his court happy. The Sombras' influence dwindles with every passing season, and the talk in Fanstamagorie is that a formal challenge could be issued to the king. If they find out that he can't even keep the few seeds he has, he might have to abdicate."

My heart fanfares. "Abdicate? But who would replace him?"

He thinks for a moment, his eyes half-mast. "Another High Fae, I guess."

"And what would happen to his knights? To us?"

What would it mean for me and the bet? If the Shadow King was overthrown, would it nullify our deal? Or would his successor inherit my fealty, along with his magic?

Worst thing is... I'm not sure which possibility scares me the most.

"One would die before he swore fealty to a new king. Two's a wildcard, and Three only cares about fucking beautiful girls—" Jo says.

A fiery blush sears my cheeks, and my gaze flies to the ground between us.

He offers me a sheepish grimace. "Christ—I offended you."

"It's okay." I shake off the hot line of embarrassment, but the slight shred of hope from earlier burns and dies in my chest. If

Damian is about to lose his throne, then it means that he's even more motivated to trick me into losing the bet. "Thank you for the book. I'm going to check on Lori."

I excuse myself and build a fort in the library, reading through Jo's book for the entire day, desperate to find a clue as to how courting me could help the king keep his crown.

Damian the Dauntless: the Rise of our Dark Sovereign is the second-floor book I coveted for weeks when I first arrived. It's a fluff piece about the king's exploits, detailing his rise to power through sheer force of will, incredible cleverness, and some ill-advised choices. It's written in a boisterous style, and I find it impossible to reconcile its depiction of the Shadow King with the stoic, elusive monarch I've met.

Historians always exaggerate the virtue of their current rulers while minimizing their faults, but this book is just...wrong.

"You look ready to pull your hair out," Lori says over my shoulder. "Wait a minute...is that the book Jo lent you? It's nonsense."

I unclench my fist and let it fall to the table, my heart in my throat. "I agree. The Damian in this book is ruthless and clever, yes, but he's also lively, arrogant, audacious—not at all like the Damian we know."

My best friend shrugs. "I guess even the Shadow King was young once."

"Or something so terrible happened that he became a totally different person." I lower my voice, barely able to admit my number one fear. "What if he *needs* to court me...to boost his magic?"

If Jo is right, then the Shadow King didn't send the necklace to mess with me. For whatever reason, he needs to win the bet *soon*, and courting me must be part of that.

"No, he could easily take our magic if he wanted... Oh!" Lori's face wrinkles in a deep cringe. "Would marrying you make him win that bet he made with your dad? He'd get your magic, then, too. And maybe even your kingdom?"

My blood runs cold at the thought. "Wait. That's insane." *Marriage? I can't even—*

"I'm probably wrong," she adds quickly, but the damage is done. Her dubious hypothesis struck a chord.

"If he truly wants to win my affections, why does he stay in the shadows, barely taking the time to get to know me at all?"

Lori ties her hair on top of her head in a messy bun, and the string of earrings decorating the shell of her ear gleam under the light of the chandeliers. "I'm sorry to say this, but if the Shadow King wants to marry you for your magic, I don't see how you could change his mind."

I shake my head, willing my brain—and my damn pulse—to slow down. "What is he going to do? Knock me over the head and drag me to the altar?"

"Don't joke about that," Lori says quickly. "Fae marry almost exclusively for power, and they have crazy wedding rituals. Most dark Fae believe that a union celebrated under the first Morheim moon is twice as potent. A marriage announcement could boost the king's magic enough to discourage a formal challenge."

"And then, he wouldn't have to abdicate," I say, slowly putting two and two together. "But Morheim is only a few weeks away. Since consummation is such an important part of Fae weddings, he'd need my consent!"

Lori paces the room back and forth, and I realize this is no longer a crazy brainstorm session. This could be *real*.

"You'd probably be all for it with the right enchantment," she adds.

I press my lips together in a hard line. *Does that count as consent, in this wicked world?*

"He can't," I say loudly, more for my own benefit than Lori's.

She covers my hand with hers, the graveness of the situation clouding her gray eyes. "Don't worry. I won't let him. If he plans on marrying you against your will, it'll be over my dead body, Old World."

A heavy sigh quakes my lungs. I know I've got a true friend in Lori, but I can't fool myself. We've all sworn an oath to the Shadow King, and if he does claim me as his bride, the others will let him have me. Even One.

That's why he's been so distant. No one can stop the Shadow King, and when he comes for my magic, One will step aside and let him have it.

"I bet he thinks I'll agree to marry him not to lose my magic. That gives him consent. *And* he wins the bet." My mind is ablaze, but something's not adding up. I feel it in my bones. "Crops! I need to research a way out, but I've got to go home."

Two weeks lost, when there's only so many days left before the Shadow King comes for his due. I need more time to train and figure this all out.

"When do you leave?" Lori asks.

"Tomorrow."

And for the first time, I really, really wish I didn't have to go, which scares me more than all the wild conjectures and conspiracy theories my brain is currently weaving about the Shadow King.

Given the choice between my old life—without magic—and marrying the king, I'd have to leave Faerie forever. But the answer is certainly not as clear-cut as it used to be.

CHAPTER 29
'IMPOSSIBLE

Dreams are intimate. Precious.

There are dreams that leave you energized, and others that leave you longing. Now that I know they're meant to fill a well of magic in the Shadow realm, I'm nervous to fall asleep.

Moonlight streams through the thick glass of the castle windows as I shift from one side to the other in my tiny bed. The hearth is quiet, and it's been hours since I finished the discarded book on the bedside table. Now that I've gotten used to sleeping in thin, silk gowns, the rough wool of my thigh-high socks is even more itchy than before, and I fight off the urge to scratch my legs.

I do not want my soul to leave my body and err to the Dreaming, but, as my training with Two taught me, the sleeping mind does whatever the hell it wants, and before I know it, I'm standing in the middle of a golden corn field in my yellow country dress.

A red and black checkered picnic blanket lays in the middle of the small clearing behind the summer house, the sun low on the horizon. A bushel of grapes and the neck of a champagne bottle stick out of a wicker basket at my feet.

What the crops?

One stands on the opposite side of the blanket, studying the scene.

"What are you doing here?" I ask. Ever since One carried me to bed during Foghar, I haven't caught a glance of him. I watch for his reaction, trying to discern if he's truly here or not.

"I came to visit you. Are you expecting somebody?" he makes a casual gesture toward the picnic, and I hold back a nervous laugh.

Am I expecting company in a dream? I glance down at the wine and fruits. "I don't know. You're the expert. Are you really here, or am I only dreaming of you?"

"Let's find out." He leans in, taking me completely by surprise, and kisses me softly on the lips.

The simple way he reaches out for me—like it's normal—makes my heart swell, and I stand on the tip of my toes.

He presses his forehead to mine, not deepening the kiss but giving me time to take it all in instead. "Did that feel real enough to you?"

"Yes," I answer without a trace of self-consciousness. He lies down on the blanket and pats the empty space next to him, but I hesitate. "What's happening? Where did you disappear to after Foghar?"

He shifts to his side, his elbow propped beneath him. "I had business to take care of in the new world."

"Did it have anything to do with Mara?"

He chuckles a little too warmly in response, and my eyes narrow. It feels too real to be a dream, and yet...

That's not One.

Without giving him time to react, I kneel down next to him and peel off his black and white mask.

His irises gleam in the sun—a twist of gold and silver—and I wonder if he's incapable of faking One's eyes, or if he's simply forgotten what they look like.

I offer the impostor a wry smile. "Hello, Two."

A wicked grin transforms his face, betraying his true identity.

"Well played." He glances around the gardens. "I was curious to see what you dreamed about, princess. I was right to believe you didn't crave holy matrimony with your vapid duke."

"This doesn't mean—"

"It means *everything*." With an evil wink, Two drapes himself over me and pins me down to the ground with his weight, holding my wrists above my head. "But you can't have One."

Eyes closed in a mix of confusion and shame, I squirm under his hold, trying to break free, but my treacherous body warms in response to his.

"I heard you the other day, and I don't care what you think. I don't belong to the king," I growl.

A maniacal laugh quakes his chest like this is all a big joke, and he drags his nose along the curve of my neck. "You crack me up, Old World."

I force a lump down my throat. In spite of it all, I'm still caught in the haze of the illusion, and my mind drifts back to the similar way One pinned me to my bed. Their bodies and mannerism are even more similar in the Dreaming, but I hate myself for the heat plaguing my belly and the desire coursing through my veins. "What did you do to Mara after Three slept with her?"

Two leans closer, his hot breath caressing my collarbone. "Mara played her part. Are you ready to play yours?"

In a blink, the blue sky darkens into night, the golden scenery suddenly bathed in moonlight like the colors were suddenly painted over by a shadow.

A raven crows overhead, and a chilly wind blows past my ankles as One ripples out of the darkness. His informal clothes—jeans and a black shirt—are the same as the ones he wore the last time I saw him, when he caught me snooping.

"Leave her alone," he snarls at his brother.

He's technically the nightmare, crashing a dream, yet he's everything but. He looks fierce, perched on the balls of his feet, ready to fight his brother off me. *And hopefully take his place.*

Two scatters to his feet, but he doesn't flee. "Don't act all territorial with me. Three will train her next. Do you expect me to believe she will pass his test as she is now?"

The shadows thicken around us as One pushes his brother away from the blanket. "Leave us, or by Morpheus—"

"Do you hear yourself? Have you forgotten what happened the last time a woman came between us?"

Smoke rises from One's body, the pulse of his anger palpable. "Leave! Now!"

A ripple of light and smoke glitches over Two's body, and he vanishes as though he was shoved out of the Dreaming by his brother's powers.

One finally angles his mask to me. "I'm sorry. Two shouldn't have intruded on your break to continue your training. But you passed his test, however cruel and unfortunately scheduled it was."

I hug my knees, willing my ragged breaths to slow down. "I passed?"

"Yes. You recognized the illusion. As soon as you wake up, you will be ready for the third and final part of your training."

"Fantasies."

He gives me a sharp nod. "As cruel as they can be."

I swallow down the lump in my throat and push aside the skirt of my dress, making space for him on the blanket. "Please stay for a little while."

"I really shouldn't," he says, but he sits beside me all the same, taking in our surroundings. The leaves of the willow tree bristle above us, the fields of corn stretching as far as the eye can see. One's fingers twitch over the tartan blanket. "Oh kitten...why would you dream of me?"

I nudge his side. "Admit it. You missed me, too."

"I—You missed me?" He fails to mask a smile, and a soft chuckle escapes me.

"I did." I shift to my knees beside him and keep my hands in my lap. "Why do you hide from me?"

"I had to hunt alone the last couple of weeks. For the one who weaved the Dreamcatcher spider." He angles his chin to the ground, and the small tilt makes him look nervous and almost...timid. "And honestly it's easier...not to see you every day," he finally adds.

I'd be crushed if it wasn't for the desire rumbling right beneath the surface of the words. Feeling bold, I peel off his scarred mask, and he lets me. My voice cracks, my feelings for him taking a life of their own. "Why can't you be my teacher? You're better than them. Stronger than the king himself."

He leans forward and tucks a strand of hair behind my ear. "How do you figure that?"

"When the king freezes us, you only pretend to be under his control."

A sinister shard twinkles in his golden eyes. "I'm weak. If I wasn't, I wouldn't be here with you."

The sentence quickens my breath and squeezes my belly with need. He might be infuriating and stubborn—and completely off-limits—but I want him. Most of all, I crave the kind and hard-working man that hides beneath the mask of the severe, unfeeling hunter. I've caught enough glimpses of him by now to know he's real.

"Your emotions don't make you weak, One," I say.

"They do if they make me want to break my promises." He stares into the distance. "An old friend of mine wrote a famous quote. True love transcends crowns, blood, and flesh. Love has—"

"No masters, only slaves," I cut in. "It stings too fast for you to see, and when you recognize its scorpion's tail, you're already dead."

"You've read *Delusions of Winter*?"

"Five times. It's the first Fae book I ever read. My mother gave it to me when I turned sixteen, about a month before she died."

His brows lift. "Your father let you keep Fae poetry in his library?"

I press my lips together, torn between the instinct to defend my father for his beliefs, and my own twisted emotions about them. "He knew I had to learn more about this realm. A lot of books were...

cautionary tales. *Delusions of Winter* was romantic." I glance down, unable to look at his beautiful face while we discuss this.

"You find depressing poetry romantic?" It's a rhetorical question, and when I don't answer, he adds, "It's Elio's most famous collection of poems. His queen died about fifty years ago and since then, he hasn't been the most joyful fella."

I swallow the hard lump in my throat, my gaze stuck on a red thread of wool sticking out of the blanket. "Grief is hard."

"How did your mother die?" he asks softly.

The question throws me off guard. "She went out riding one morning and didn't come back. They found her body the next day. At the bottom of the ravine."

He wraps an arm around me, and I hide my face in the crook of his neck. We stay like this for a few minutes, breathing together, and I wonder if I can actually smell him, or if the hints of pears and charcoal are just figments of my imagination.

"I get that you're not allowed to get too close to me, but we're not really here..." I trace the arch of his split brow, and he shudders at the touch.

He doesn't stop me when I close the distance between us and cover his mouth with mine. Warm and soft lips greet me, and with a small grunt of defeat, he dives in for a deeper kiss. The brush of his tongue slithers deep in my belly. He tastes of sweet wine and oak barrels, but with a hint of scorched earth.

A touch of agony.

Last time we kissed, it was unexpected. Now, there's no denying how hungry we both were for it to happen again.

I push him down on the blanket and straddle him, his shirt riding up to his navel. He holds me close, learning the curves of my waist, and I use a burst of magic to switch my heavy, bothersome dress with the black, stretchy undergarments of my hunter's uniform. "Isn't this better?"

One growls at the sudden change, his hands now flush on my

hips, and digs his fingers in the flesh of my ass without shame. "Better for crossing lines that shouldn't be crossed."

I burn for him, the feel of his muscular body driving me to insanity. His chest is a treasure trove, the ridge of his stomach hard and delicious beneath my fingers. The fullness between my thighs is unbearable, and I grind myself against him to add friction to the ache. *By the Mother, I wish...*

My lids flutter. "I need more. Please."

He flips us over so I'm pressed between the rough tartan blanket and his body, the weight of him almost divine. He slides two fingers up my ribs to the elastic of my bra, and the fabric flakes off into nothingness.

His tongue dips into my ear. "Just this once... Because you asked nicely."

He sounds like a wounded beast liberated from its cage. Not at all the voice of a man who's about to surrender.

Hunger simmers at the back of his throat, and his rough kiss steals my thoughts as he covers one breast with his hand and squeezes it. My nipple is so taut and sensitive that I cry out, my back arching off the ground.

The tip of his nose traces a fiery path down the slope of my neck, and a jolt of pleasure pulses between my legs when he sucks my other nipple inside his mouth, the first one now crushed between his index finger and thumb.

It's too much, and I squirm below him, trying to cover myself.

One spreads my thighs open with his legs and holds both arms above my head. "Don't you dare. I want to see all of you."

My dark Fae explores every inch of my chest, his caress rough and yet not careless or random. His lips and tongue are warm and wet, but never sloppy. Like he possesses a detailed map of my body and studied it long before tonight.

"I want to remember every groan of pleasure that passes your lips. Every little detail."

Somehow, him giving me *more* only makes me feel *less* satisfied, and a desperate moan parts my lips. "Please."

With a wicked laugh—the sort of sound I'd expect to hear from Two—he slides his hand to the apex of my thigh, inching lower, until he's right where I need him. I feel like a fish dangling off his hook, but still, he denies me.

A tortured breath rushes in. "You're cruel, my dark Fae." A long finger pushes inside me, and my head snaps back to the blanket. "So cruel..."

"Shh." His eyes burn as he drags across my heated flesh in lazy strokes. "Look at me, kitten, and relax your thighs."

I obey, and he wets his bottom lip, his eyes full of pride and mischief.

He has the map to those depths, too, hitting just the right spot with just the right pressure, back and forth. The sensations are like nothing I've ever experienced. Under One's touch, I'm not the same. I'm impatient and greedy and a little mad. A storm of fire rolls in, invading my belly, chest, skin, and soul.

He drinks in each and every single one of my sounds and praises me for them until my lips tremble, the pleasure sharp and heady. The storm spills out to the tip of my toes with a violent quake.

"Oh!" The pleasure radiates all over, and I draw in a sharp breath, the madness receding, replaced by a tentative sense of peace.

But still, I yearn...

The friction of One's clothes on my bare skin fills me with rage. My fingers reach for his belt, but he shackles my wrists to stop me.

I tug against his hold. "Let go of me. I'm getting my revenge." After what he did to me, he can't expect me to just sit there and let him get away with it. Best believe me, I'm going to make that Fae beg.

This is just a dream. If we crossed that line in the Dreaming, then it wouldn't count, would it?

"By the spindle, kitten. I want to take you right here." He squeezes my hands. "But I *can't*."

"Can't? Or won't?" Our noses bump. "Is it true that you can't marry as long as the king remains single?"

A touch of regret colors his eyes. "Yes."

Holy horses! His gaze falls on something behind me, but when I crane my neck around, I only catch a glimpse of smoke billowing through the strands of wheat. He lets go of my hands and retreats by a few inches.

Cold air washes over me, and I cover my bare breasts with one arm, exposed and vulnerable. "And does the king want to marry *me*?" I ask, my voice barely recognizable.

He observes me with dark eyes and a darker frown. I almost think he's going to answer, but he moves to disentangle himself from my embrace instead. "I have to leave."

I grip his shirt to delay his escape. "What happened to the king? Why does he need to court me? Is he really going to lose his crown?"

"Lose his crown?" his face hardens. Thick shadows hover around him, agitated and dangerous. The tendrils of smoke cradle my skin. "Who's putting these ideas in your head? Is it Joseph?"

"Don't be like that." I cup the side of his face. I need him to focus on *me*. "I don't want Jo. Or the king." A blazing heat creeps up my chest. "I want *you*."

A dry chuckle rocks his throat, and he shakes his head like I'm losing my mind. "Oh, kitten... What you want is impossible."

CHAPTER 30

CONFESSIONS

Aloud knock on my bedroom door startles me awake. The first hints of dawn are barely visible in the night sky, and I pat down my chest, my heart hammering.

I'm in Demeter, wearing my usual nightgown—not having a midnight *picnic* with One in endless corn fields. *What a dream...* Yet, I know he was really there. If I could only get him to share his secrets, I'm sure there'd be a way for us to move forward together.

The loud knocking sounds again, and this time, I'm conscious enough to react. "Who's there?"

"The king has asked to see you, princess. Please get dressed and come with us."

"Now?" I inquire at the closed door, wondering what in the Mother's name could be going on for Father to fetch me at this hour. Nothing good, I'm sure.

"Yes. Now," the guard says plainly, clearly used to people following orders without question.

The middle of the night would be the perfect time to punish me to his heart's content without an audience.

I shudder in the dark as I put on a heavy robe and greet the two men waiting by the door with a serious nod. "Take me to him."

Father is waiting for me in his sitting room, and I offer him a small curtsy as I wait for our audience to leave. Gloomy fog sticks to the stained glass of the large checkered windows, and the wax of the candles has run over the rim of the chandeliers. He's been in here all night, and judging by the number of empty bottles on the table, he's drunk.

"Here I was, catching up on my duties, when I found this." He waves a letter at me. The thick wax seal is already broken.

"What is it?" I ask calmly.

The dark tremble of his voice makes me quake. "It's a letter from the Duke, inviting me to his son Isaac's engagement party."

My breath catches, and I bite down on my bottom lip not to grimace. "Engagement? To whom?"

"Abigail Strauss." His bushy brows pull together in a line that spells ultimate trouble, his grip loose on the brass cup. "What did you do?"

Tears prickle my eyes. *Isaac is engaged? How? When?* But no matter how slighted I feel by the revelation, it's the least of my problems.

"What did you do?" he repeats, venomous.

Doesn't he remember that he refused Isaac's proposal, too? I couldn't possibly have said yes, and yet he's acting like it's all my fault.

"I had to refuse Isaac's offer of marriage." I keep an even, congenial tone, my gaze not rising past his chest to create the perfect picture of a meek and dutiful daughter. "But I never—"

"You're *soiled*, aren't you?" he spits out, the word bitter and all-consuming.

I blink, desperately holding on to my princess mask to hide all the rage simmering just beneath the surface. I know better than to argue with him when he's in this state, and I keep my gaze glued to the ground. *If only I was anywhere but here.*

"You let that disgusting Fae bed you."

My gaze snaps up, my thoughts of corn fields and soft lips erased by the disgust in his voice. He's my father and king, but right now, he's nothing more than a drunk who let his guilt and fear take over his rational mind.

"No!" I declare with as much indignation as I can muster.

He considers me for a moment, his glassy eyes distant and cold. "From now on, you shall remain in your room, and your sister will not visit you. Esme will bring you food, and you can bathe at night, when your sister is sleeping."

Oh no... When I imagined all the ways he could punish me for my bravado, I thought of everything but this, and I fail to mask the biggest wince.

"It was a mistake to let you influence her. I should have separated you two the moment you left."

The ball of saliva in my throat burns with grievances, but I hold on tight. "It's not what mother would have wanted—"

"Don't argue with me. You're lucky I don't send you away altogether. I should have never agreed to that bet."

It's not the first time he says it, but I'm finally brave enough to answer, "Don't you realize how I feel when you say that? If you hadn't made the deal, I would never have been born."

His eyes flash with something worse than hatred. "Yes, and it would have spared me a lot of grief." He waves me off to my room, refilling his cup, and I put one foot in front of the other on my way out of the room.

Now that my worst nightmare has become reality, what am I supposed to do? Count down the minutes until I break the rules and sneak into her room? Even if he locks the door from the outside, I still have the window...

Or I could go back to Faerie and visit Cece's dreams?

A dangerous thought crosses my mind.

Why wait?

If I'm supposed to remain locked inside my room for the next four days, what's stopping me from going back to Faerie early?

Instead of threading back upstairs, I wrap myself in a cloak of shadows and run for the basement with my mask safely tucked in my skirts.

Once there, I press it to my face and grab the quill and ink I left down here. Sweat gathers above my brow as I draw the runes for "Fae" and "Faerie" on my lower arm, but in my haste, I fudge the "Faerie" rune slightly at the edge.

The icy depths of the sceawere swallow me whole, and I take a minute to find my footing in the maze of glass. The distortion of a hundred peephole views of the castles, both here and in Faerie, blur together.

I feel colder than I've ever felt, the tips of my fingers numb as I tear through the moonlit reflection of the trainee's balcony and fall to my hands on the paved stones.

The Hawthorn's leaves are still as a corpse, the fall evening crisp and silent.

"Nell! Nell, are you alright?" Lori's voice pierces the night. She jumps to her feet and runs up to me, wearing her huntress uniform and stretchy gloves. She kneels beside me, and her eyes buzz around the quiet balcony like she expects to find nightmares on my tail.

Trembling like I've been blown in by a storm, I shift to my knees. "Oh, Lori..."

A few pieces of rock dig into my palm, and I bring them closer to my chest as Lori wraps both arms around me. "What happened?"

I hide my face in her lap, and a few strangled cries rock my body. "Isaac decided to marry someone else, and somehow my father blames *me*. He thinks that I'm ruined. Soiled. That's what he called it. That's how he thinks of me now."

The panic I barely held in back home quakes through me, one bitter wave at a time, and Lori tightens her hold around me. "Oh, Nell... I'm so sorry. It's not true. It's horseshit, like you'd say. Look at me."

I force the sniffles to taper off and meet her gaze.

"Am I worth any less because I've had sex with a man?"

I'm not surprised by the admission. I've realized by now that her world holds almost no shame in sex. "Of course not."

She nods at my answer. "Of course not. And the same goes for you, Old World. No matter if you've had sex or not, you're still you. It doesn't change a thing. You are kind and smart and a total badass with a crossbow, and you better believe that has got nothing to do with any man's penis."

Her tirade coaxes a teary laugh out of me. "If only that was true in my world, but my father doesn't want me to come near my sister anymore. He thinks I'm going to corrupt her." My voice breaks. "She's everything to me, Lori. After my mother died... I can't lose her, too."

"You won't." Lori threads her fingers through my hair in a soothing manner. "I understand. Siblings hold a part of our soul..." Her teary gaze wanders off to the gardens, to the silvery silhouette of the Hawthorn, and reflects the pink hues of sunrise. "I never told you why I got stuck on library duty. I was supposed to help out with a hunt, but instead, I snuck out to visit my brother."

Deep lines wrinkle my forehead. "Your brother? You went to visit him in the new world?"

She shakes her head. "No. I'm mortal, but my grandmother was Fae. As such, my brother and I both have magic. I displayed all the qualities of a Shadow seed, but his magic was different. Lighter. And so he chose to train in the Spring Court." She starts to braid my hair, her soft movements lulling me into a dream-like state. "Spring is all about making babies..." a wince twists her lips. "And a big part of their duty is to make mortals fall in love. My brother used to carve arrows for Freya, the Spring Queen herself."

"Arrows? Like Cupid's arrows?"

"Cupids are actually not at all cute and cuddly, believe me. But I found out Ayaan had been accused of treason and sentenced to life in prison. They said that he was selling his arrows on the black market, but I don't believe it. They won't even let me talk to him—" she pauses abruptly.

"I'm so sorry. Can I do anything to help? Did you ask the others?"

Eyes wide, she shakes her head. "You're the first one I've told. Freya is dangerous as hell, and she *despises* the Shadow King." Her lips pull together in a hard, determined line. "But I'll get Ayaan out. I just have to keep faith and continue my training until I'm powerful enough to help him. So don't despair. You'll find a way to be with your sister. I'm sure of it."

I rest my hand over hers and give it a small squeeze. "And I'll help you find a way to clear your brother's name."

We smile, both sad and relieved to have each other.

Muffled voices rise from the gardens. "Thank you for this. I'm going to head in. I don't want anyone else to see me like this." I motion in the general direction of my puffy face.

She chews on her bottom lip. "Do you want me to come with you? I can get one of the others to cover for me."

"I'm better now, thanks." I give her a big hug and wipe down the last batch of tears, ready to shake it off and fight forward. "I'll get some rest."

I weave through the covered porch toward the entrance to the tunnels and come face to face with One.

The dark Fae freezes on the path, and I stop, too, stunned. An hour ago, I was pinned beneath him in a make-believe cornfield. *What a difference an hour can make...*

Our chests heave as we stare at each other, my salt-freckled cheeks and red eyes impossible to conceal.

"You're not supposed to be back, yet," he finally grounds out.

I catch a sniffle from surfacing and clench my fists at my sides. How does he manage to sound so detached when I'm simply dying inside. "You said this arrangement was fluid. Now, I need it to be fluid *for me*."

He cocks his head to the side, his silence suffocating.

"It won't make me lose the bet, right? I mean—it's just a few days early."

I need time to figure this out. Just a little more time.

"No...it's fine." One rubs the angle of his jaw, and a heavy sigh whistles out of me, my entire chest deflating. "You should go and meet with Three. As long as you're here, you might as well get started on fantasies right away. At this hour, he must still be in his bedroom. I'm sure you remember where it is."

A fierce blush heats my cheeks at the brazen reminder of my voyeurism session, but I stare at him until his throat bobs. "I thought I'd come to a sinful land when I first came to Faerie. I never imagined I'd be more scared to be *home* than to stay here. With *you*." I walk closer and graze the collar of his jacket.

I can't help how I feel, and I'm tired of hiding it. I know he feels it, too.

He takes a deliberate step backwards, his hands firmly tucked behind him. "Sin is a man-made concept, kitten. What's sinful for a civilization is the basis of the next. So the mortal wheel turns."

I arch a brow and press my luck, taking a giant leap forward. "Is there no sin in Faerie?"

He digs his soles in the ground, the game of cat-and-mouse over before it even started. "The only sin known to my kind is lacking the strength to do your duty. What's the happiness of one soul worth compared to the good of the many?"

A deep curve furrows my brow. Is he really going to pretend that nothing happened between us? "Is that what Mara was? A sacrifice for the good of the many?"

"The king didn't want Mara. She didn't mean anything."

I step forward until we're inches apart. "But he wants me?"

"Yes." His eyes flick to my lips. "And you mean more to him than you know."

How could I mean anything to the king? My magic might be important to him, but not me. "Is that all you have to say?"

All the masks in the worlds couldn't hide the fact that One is shaking—holding himself from reaching for me.

He pinches my moon-shaped pendant between his index finger and thumb, and his knuckles brush the hollow of my neck. "What happens in the Dreaming stays there for a reason... I could admit how much you mean to me. Tell you how different my life has been since you've arrived, and how you've filled me with a blinding, dangerous sense of hope. But it wouldn't change anything."

"You could also ask me why I'm crying. Hold me in your arms."

"I can't."

The dejected words are quickly becoming an impregnable wall between us, and tears sting my eyes. "You're just a coward then." I spin on my heels and walk away, leaving him and his damn *duty* behind.

In the tunnels, Two peels himself off the deepest shadow, slick as an eel, and falls into step with me.

I jolt away from him and pick up the pace. "Whatever it is—I'm not in the mood. I passed your little test, didn't I? I'm supposed to meet Three now."

"Suit yourself. I came to tell you One's secret"—he licks his lips expectantly—"but if you'd rather not know..."

I dig my heels in the carpet, frozen in place. Some traps are both obvious and unavoidable. I know Two doesn't have my best interest at heart, and yet I have to hear him out.

I have to know, once and for all.

Two leans into my ear, the coveted shape of him twisting my insides. "One can't bed you because of us. That's why he's so cranky all the time."

A burst of indignation bubbles up my spine. "What?"

Two slithers even closer, and the heat of his body dizzies me. The discussion we're having is about as unexpected as a horseshoe to the stomach. "The three of us are cursed, and the ramifications of that curse prevent One from indulging his feelings for you—or taking any woman to bed for that matter. That's why he rebuffed your advances in the Dreaming. That's why he's holding himself away now."

"But Three—"

I've heard enough gossip to know Three's not celibate.

"Three's the exception."

I shake my head, rejecting Two's claim, and pick up a brisk pace, heading to my new mentor's bedroom. "No. One keeps his distance because of the king—"

"One *hates* Damian. He'd steal you away from any king, but he *can't*. At least not alone." Two slows down as we near the door to Three's bedroom. "The three of us... We're a package deal. I told you before. You can't have *one*, that is—not *just* one. If you want One, you must take all three of us."

I shoot him a glance over my shoulder. "How convenient for you."

"I'm ready for my third question." He licks his lips and slides in front of me to block my escape, forcing me to stop or walk right into his embrace.

I swallow hard as he peels his shattered mask from his face. The silver and gold irises behind it are conniving and beautiful—a thousand times more powerful than they were in my dream.

The blackest parts of my soul are laid bare under his scrutiny. There's no wicked or unkind thought I could hide from him, and I know that—given the chance—he'd lap them all up to make me clean again.

He licks his lips, relishing his victory. "Do you feel something for just One, truly, or are you drawn to all of us?"

The bend of his brow speaks volumes, and I grit my teeth together. "You and your brothers are physically identical, so yes, I am attracted to all three of you."

He taps my nose in a condescending manner. "That's my girl." He leans in like he's about to whisper a dirty secret into my ear. "If I kissed you right now, you wouldn't back away."

"Don't be so sure—"

He steals my breath with a kiss that's both vicious and undeniable, his hands hard at the back of my head. I gasp, and his tongue takes advantage of my surprise to slip inside my mouth, as sharp and cruel as its owner.

The rough caress goes straight to my belly. Contrary to the one we shared when he was pretending to be One, Two's kiss is a promise to cradle and love every dark desire I ever nurtured. It's insidious, and I almost feel wretched enough to kiss him back, but I tear myself away instead.

"I don't want you." I rub off the forbidden taste of him with the back of my hand, the pulsing heat between my thighs catching me in a lie.

"Yeah, you do. However ugly you think it is, it's the truth. Remember, pet. Three for the price of one..." His satisfied smile is heavy with promise, like he knows I'm bound to give in at some point. "Think about it. I know I will."

CHAPTER 31

ON THREE

The green paint of Three's bedroom door is weathered and worn, with patches of bare wood showing underneath. It brings back vivid memories. Whatever happened to Mara on Foghar, he was the instigator. He took her as a lover, and she disappeared. What if he's planning to do the same to me?

After One's rejection, and Two's salacious proposal, I'm almost tempted to let him try.

I knock on the worn and peeling wood, feeling a bit run-down, too.

I should be in bed right now.

Three comes to the door wearing his full uniform and his iridescent mask. He cocks his head to the side and peers behind me like he's wondering what's going on.

"Hi. One said I should train with you today?" I say, suddenly feeling faint.

He opens the door wide with a loose grin on his face. *Come in.*

I dip my head under his outstretched arm and walk inside. But instead of a regular bedroom, I find an art studio on the other side.

The bed I saw the other day is now tucked in a corner, and an easel towers in the center of the room.

A series of half-finished portraits are stacked against the wall on one side, and an array of painting supplies are scattered over the desk next to the easel. Three kicks off his boots and motions for me to sit on the green velvet chaise lounge in the middle of the room.

I obey and tap a mindless beat on my thighs to chase off the nerves.

The third brother's silence has never been quite so unnerving as this. Our previous encounters have always been short—if memorable. He doesn't look at all in a hurry to explain his intentions.

Instead, he shrugs off his black jacket and dumps it on the back of his desk chair. The white button-down shirt he's wearing underneath softens his somber look. He peruses the brushes and tubes on his desk as he cuffs up his sleeves above his elbows.

"How am I supposed to learn if you can't speak? According to everyone, fantasies are the hardest."

He peels off his mask, and I hold my breath. I've kissed both of his twin brothers, but Three's...different. He's got iridescent irises, long lashes, and shadows flicker over his skin like a dark fire burns inside of him—barely contained.

While I gawk, speechless, he installs a fresh canvas on the easel between us and glances up at me.

I sink my nails into the velvety cushions. "Wait a minute. Do you want to paint *me*?"

Three bites his bottom lip in a sheepish manner. *Yes.*

He mixes the paint on his palette, his white shirt barely hiding the planes of his chest. He looks...younger, somehow, though I don't know how that could be. Long strands of jet black hair fall haphazardly around his face.

"Is it really necessary?"

The corners of his mouth curl up, and warmth radiates through his colorful, shimmering gaze. *Humor me.*

"Don't you need more light to paint? I mean, it's awfully dark in here..."

Asking a shadow knight if he needs more light is probably in my top five dumbest questions, but I can't help myself. I feel...defenseless in front of Three. How can I argue with someone who doesn't speak? How can I hang on to my pride when words can't come between us?

After a minute, he motions me forward. *Come and see for yourself.*

I've only been posing for a few minutes, and he skipped the sketching part and went right to painting, so I don't know what I expect.

Three painted textures and shadows, but somehow, I can see myself within them. My eyes glaze over, and suddenly, the blotch of paint isn't so abstract anymore. Lines rise out of the canvas and draw a couple locked in a passionate embrace.

I look back at the couch, where a version of myself and One are now kissing, our bodies far too exposed for me not to blush.

I bite back a mix between a growl and a moan. "Alright, alright. I get it. I dream about One. I fantasize about him. You guys don't have to act so smug—"

Three's light chuckle rumbles down my neck. He waves his hand at the fleshed-out fantasy, and the couple melts into human-sized shadows. The couch shifts into a hay mannequin, and the shadows reshape themselves into lifelike copies of Cece and me. The fantasy version of me draws the crossbow at the target. The bolt flies directly for its center before fantasy-Nell hands the crossbow to my little sister.

With a hand pressed to my chest, I watch my shadow self give Cece an archery lesson, and my heart gives a long, forlorn thud.

Cece. My fearless little sister.

Three squints at the daydream, and my chest rises and falls with ragged breaths. This snippet of fantasy was stolen from a foreign place in my subconscious. I haven't let myself speak the words aloud

—or even thought about it in a structured way—but I desire it beyond reason.

To have Cece by my side, learning with me and sharing stories about our day... It's selfish and unattainable, but I think she'd *love* it here. She wouldn't have to water down her spark to fit in, or worry about what people think.

Tears mist my vision, and Three presses his nose to mine softly. He takes my hands in his and entwines our fingers. The touch is unexpected. Intimate.

We look at my fantasy together, and Three embraces me the way a dancer embraces his partner, our fingers still entwined. He's so tall that the top of my head grazes the underside of his chin, and I can't help but sigh at his closeness. *If only One was so brazen in his affections.*

But again, in the shadows of Three's art studio, the differences between them aren't quite as clear. These cats certainly look identical in the dark, and I have to concentrate not to spin around in his embrace and touch the angle of his jaw.

He slips a hand under my shirt, his palm flat against my belly as he presses me to him. *I want you.*

My entire body tingles with warmth, and I spin in his arms. His hands settle on my waist, and he flicks his gaze to my lips, patiently awaiting my answer.

My heart pounds harder for each breath, the temptation to accept his offer as drugging as Fae wine. He inches closer, and a searing heat radiates between my thighs.

I raise a hand to his full, sensuous lips, the shape of them identical to One's. "What happened to Mara?" I ask. "What did you do to her? Did you *feed* from her, too?"

His eyes dance. *Maybe.*

My mind flashes back to the shape of his ass as he moved in and out of her, and envy cramps my gut. "Is that what you intend to do to me?"

He kisses each of my fingers slowly before pressing his lips to my pulse point. *You're different. Precious.*

"I don't understand," I say.

Three crushes me to him without an ounce of shame, his hardness pressing into me. "I'm hard for you, kitten. I want to worship your body until you scream my name. I want to feel your walls pulse around my cock and defile you in ways you've never even dreamed of."

I shiver at the secret, raspy quality of his voice. "I—" The familiar pet name throws me for a loop, and my brows pull together. "Kitten?"

His eyes reflect only one color in the darkness. Solid gold.

"One?" I whisper, tracing the shape of his mouth.

His lips twitch.

Three might just be using his magic to feed into my fantasy, but I don't know... It feels real. And the third brother has never spoken out loud before. According to everyone, Three is mute.

I link my hands behind his neck and sneak my fingertips below the collar of his button-down shirt. "Kiss me again."

CHAPTER 32

ONE'S SECRET

My eyes snap open, and I jump to my feet. I'm on the third floor of the library. A few pieces of parchment are scattered around me, but I could swear I was about to cross a line with Nell that would bring the kingdom to ruin. I rub the tantalizingly familiar haze off my face, my dick throbbing in the confines of my pants. Nell's spicy cinnamon taste is still sweet in my mouth.

I was researching the next great hunt, when I...fell asleep?

What the actual fuck? I dreamed that I was kissing Nell—only I haven't dreamed in decades, and the threads of the Dreaming don't allow sleepers in from Faerie. The fog lifts, and a second, life-altering hypothesis forms in my brain.

I race to the hallway leading to Three's chamber through the closest mirror, blood pulsing at my temples...and in my cock. *Is this really happening? Because if this is really happening...*

Two's got his ear to the door, listening to Three's room like a horny teenager. He smirks at my arrival. "Well, look who's here. Your precious seed is in there with Three. I wonder what they're doing—"

I grip his collar. "Shut your big mouth and listen. I merged with Three."

"That's impossible," he huffs.

"Just for a minute, but I did."

The quasi-continuous, sarcastic line of his mouth falls. "How?"

"He was with Nell, and suddenly I was with Nell, too, and I spoke to her, but it was really his body."

"That hasn't happened since—"

"The curse, I know," I seethe.

"Wow...sounds like your little pet's got a magical vagina after all."

I shove his chest hard, but he just laughs.

"Cheer up, comrade. A glitch in the curse is exactly what we need. Let's see what's going on in there." He raises a hand to the door, but I stop him with an iron-clad grip.

"Don't be stupid."

"She's about to fuck Three, isn't she? I bet she's more *ready* than you think. What if it's a sign? What if all we have to do is drain her magic to break the curse?" he says with enough confidence to shake me.

"You're dreaming."

He paces the length of the corridor back and forth. "We should at least try. What's the worst that could happen?"

I glower in response, not in the mood for thick and completely unnecessary allusions. "We could destroy our only viable lead to a cure."

His face wrinkles in a pout. "I hate how you think."

"Ditto."

He plays with his hands in a series of nervous movements that signals exactly how indecisive he's feeling. "If Nell fails the next trial, we'll *have* to take her magic. Merge or not, if she doesn't sprout, we can't keep her."

"Agreed."

He finally stops jittering long enough to look me up and down. "Aren't you angry that she's cheating on you in there?"

"Are we really going to argue about the semantics of the curse again?" I bark, my patience for his cruel musings growing thinner and thinner with each passing second.

His previous hesitation is blown away by an asinine smile. "I know all about your little note. *And* the necklace. Did you really think you could get away with it?"

"You're the one who said I had to make it clear to her that she was here *for the king*."

He tilts his head back in a snort. "Well, he's not about to get on one knee, is he?" The words reek of cynicism, but I disagree.

"It's not the craziest idea," I say.

"Are you—"

We exchange a glance, and I can almost see the gears turning in his head. He's starting to understand my meaning, and I'm not sure if I'm thrilled or downright terrified that he's considering it.

Why the fuck did I say that? It's insane.

The door slams open, and we both shimmer to the deepest shadow as Nell barrels out of Three's room like the hounds of Cimmeria are after her.

Three looks shell-shocked, his white tunic hanging open and his pants undone, his unsatisfied cock visible through his boxers.

Two winces and motions to his crotch. "That's got to hurt, man."

We roll our eyes in sync.

"Did you feel the merge?" I ask.

He waves us inside and slumps down on the green couch at the center of the room, his head tilted back on a gruff sigh. *Yes.*

"What happened?" I ask.

A wry grin touches his lips. *I seduced her.*

Two flashes his teeth. "Not thoroughly."

Three makes a swift back and forth motion with his hand like he's erasing a blackboard and weaves the rest of the story. First, with his gesture for Nell, he points two fingers at his eyes, and then motions to himself and to me, and finally to his heart. *But then, she looked at me, and I felt different. I felt like...*

He tilts his hand from side to side in hesitation and holds up one finger for us to wait. Then, he crouches to the ground and makes a series of sweeping gestures like he's gathering dirt scattered across the floor with his hands. He cups his other palm over the metaphorical debris like he's holding a treasure and brings the sum to his heart, eyes cast down.

My fingertips go numb. I know *exactly* what he means.

A sad smile glazes my lips as I draw in a shaky breath. "I felt it too. Exactly like that."

Two presses his lips together. "You felt whole again? How can that be?"

Three moves his clasped hands in a blooming motion. *And she sprouted right then.*

The sliver of hope in my chest burns big and bright as I breathe, "Nell sprouted? Without a formal trial?"

Three confirms it with a grave nod and touches his breastbone, curling his fingers to mime a digging motion over his chest. *She coaxed the magic right out of me.* He shakes the emotions off his face and winces at his still stiff erection. *It was hot as hell.*

Behind him, a fantasy version of Nell steps out of the mirror, and Two licks his lips. "Now, it's a party."

My mouth dries up. "Could you not do this *now*, I mean—"

Three throws me a nasty look and relaxes in his seat, the woman already bending over him.

Two and I both watch the fantasy suck his cock, green with envy. If only we could have a full life without each other, but alas...he's the only one who can have sex. Even though Three can't speak, can't taste food, and is basically forced to fuck an endless string of fantasies to sustain himself, I still feel like I got the raw end of the deal.

"Imagine Nell's pink tongue running over the tip of your cock, arousal dripping between her legs," Two teases cruelly.

"Stop!"

"Like I said: magical vagina. We should see it through."

I flip him off, my face hidden in my palms. "The other day, you wanted me to cut ties with her, and now you want me to seduce or marry her?"

"I want *us* to seduce her. We need magic, and we needed it yesterday. If a white dress is what you need to convince yourself to take her magic, it's not the worst idea."

I brought it up, but now I'm freaked out beyond belief. "We can't —I was rambling. We vowed to never get married—"

"You missed the Foghar ritual because of her, did you not? And invited her to dance in front of the whole court. You clearly have feelings for her."

I pinch his shoulder as hard as I can. "If we marry her, we might as well paint a red "x" on her forehead. She'll never be safe again."

Two opens his mouth in outrage. "And what about us? We can't go on as we are. Morrigan will not be content to lurk in the shadows for much longer, so whatever happens next, your pet might not survive the fight that's coming."

Three groans in approval as the perfect replica of Nell finishes him off, swallowing every gulp of his seed before vanishing into thin air, leaving Two and I horny, unsatisfied, and dangerously close to blows.

This is what happens when a soul gets cleaved into four, not-so-equal parts. If you think getting along with your family is hard, try arguing with broken pieces of yourself every day for *decades*—it would drive any man mad.

And trust me when I say he's even worse off for it when he's king.

CHAPTER 33
WEBS

The lingering taste of Three's kiss burns my guilty lips as I run out of the tunnels to the gardens. A few tiny snowflakes blow in the wind, the red leaves of the Hawthorn blanketing the earth. The cold air soothes my shameful heart, but it does nothing to erase the touch of ecstasy running through my veins.

For a moment there I thought...

Goosebumps brand my flesh, and I wrap my arms around my frame, suddenly chilled to the bone. I had abandoned my jacket in Three's bedroom, and the thin black t-shirt I'm wearing does little to shield me from the elements. I'm scared to double-back to my room and cross paths with the third triplet, his magnetic pull almost impossible to resist.

No matter how much I try, my body really can't tell them apart, and the magic at work in Three's studio even befuddled my brain.

For a moment, I really thought One was in the room with me. I recognized the familiar shape of his lips and the gruff inflections of his voice.

I push open the library's golden doors and cower inside the

heated sanctuary. My best friend's gaze zeroes-in on me from behind the desk, and I smooth down my hair with one hand. The strands are so disheveled that Lori is bound to notice, but she doesn't look twice at my head.

Her cheeks are rosy, and a sense of urgency shines in her gray eyes as she hurries over to me. "I found her, Nell. I found Mara."

My brain takes a moment to catch up, still tangled in Three's embrace. "You found Mara? Where?"

I search the room for an explanation, as though Mara might actually be hiding amongst the stacks.

Lori squeezes my hands and pulls my attention back to her. "I've been practicing my tracking all week in the new world, running errands for Two. I figured I could afford a quick stop in Denver. I failed at first, trying to find Mara's magic in the sceawere, so I went to her brother's restaurant instead. She was always going on and on about taking us there one day, and I remembered the name. She was waiting tables there like nothing happened, and when I greeted her, it was like she'd never seen me before."

Air blows out of my lungs. "She doesn't remember us?"

"She doesn't remember *anything*. All her memories from Faerie— gone." Lori lowers her voice, sneaking a glance behind us to make sure we're alone. "Remember when I said that I couldn't track her by her magic?"

I give her a quick nod.

"She's got no magic left. No bite of power at all. The king must have taken it on Foghar. That's what happens to the seeds who wash out," she explains, a thick sense of relief overpowering her voice.

We both feared that Mara had been killed, so the truth seems benign in comparison, but my heart hammers. Returning home without any memories isn't as dire as what I'd imagined, but the thought fills me with dread and rage.

I always figured that, if I got through the end of the deal and won the bet, I'd fulfill my duty to my kingdom and still...have options?

I didn't know exactly what kind of options, but I hadn't imagined my time here would simply...disappear. My magic, my memories.

"I don't want to forget," I say quickly.

Lori frowns at my sudden outburst and looks me up and down like she's seeing me for the first time. "What happened to you? You look different."

I ignore her question, the swirl of anxiety thickening in my blood. "I know I was forced to come here, but now... I don't want to forget. I don't want to go back home without a shred of understanding of how my life went up in flames. Even if I come back as a blank slate, my father will never treat me the same again. Never."

"You won't wash out, Nell. I'm sure—"

The tinted glass above our heads smashes to a million pieces, and daylight blares through the library, a thick shadow perched above the hole.

A spider the size of a deer crawls inside the library. The nightmare's edge wavers like a mirage in the sunlight, the dark blaze at its core thickening as it scurries across the ceiling.

Lori spreads her arms on each side of her and summons her shadow daggers to life. The weapons emit a tiny hissing sound at the direct contact with the sun rays, struggling to take shape. They blink in and out of existence as Lori presses her lips together in a grim line.

A second and a third spider creep inside the building, and her arms fall limply at her sides. "Run, Nell!"

Acting purely on instinct, we dash out of the library and bolt the golden-plated doors shut behind us, sealing the monsters in—at least for a moment.

"What are they? I've never seen nightmares like these before, and for them to attack in broad daylight—" Lori starts.

"They're dreamcatcher spiders. One killed one back in New York," I explain quickly.

We're near the entrance of the tunnels, but before we take cover under the breezeway, a man's voice blares through the vegetation. "Help!"

I can't identify the voice because the cry is too distorted and faint. Lori and I search the gardens for the source of the scream and follow the sound toward the gym. I snatch a crossbow from the wall and load it with a silver bolt before strapping the quiver to my belt.

The sliding door at the back of the humongous room hangs open, and we hurry over to it, but I slow down near the start of the running trail.

Blood peppers the path I've passed through about four times a day since I first came to Faerie. Way too much blood.

"What are you doing? Leave them alone! Help! Help!"

Lori's daggers burn like black fire on each side of her, and she dashes forward.

James sits in a giant pool of red in the middle of the path, surrounded by death. A hint of frost ices the blood, and I catch a glimpse of a white specter fleeing the scene.

The sight of my fellow seed drenches me in cold sweat, and I run toward him. "James! Are you alright?"

"The spiders came from nowhere. I couldn't help them," he says in a state of absolute shock. A pulse of blood oozes from his mangled neck. "I couldn't fight, so I played dead, and this—this thing came for them."

"A reaper..." Lori trails off, white as a sheet.

Next to James, Fiona's and Mitchell's bodies sag over the earth, their limbs crooked at unnatural angles. Nasty burns riddle what's left of their skin. Lori bends over them to check their pulses in turn, but there's no question that they're already dead. Both were half-eaten by the same type of spider One killed that dreadful night in New York, and my frazzled heartbeats pound at my temples.

No nononono.

"We were heading towards the tunnels. Jo was supposed to go to the bibliotheca to warn you guys," James croaks.

Lori and I exchange a terrified glance. "Can you stand? We have to find Jo."

James wraps an arm around both our shoulders, but he can't hold his own weight, and he's way too heavy for Lori and I to carry.

"Give me a second. I'll heal him." I press both my hands to his wound and push my magic forward. The healing comes quick, with an ease I've never known, and my brows furrow.

James squeezes my upper arm, his breath still ragged but coming in easier than before. "Thanks, Nell."

"Let's go!" Lori pushes us forward, and the Shadow huntress watches our rear until we turn the corner.

I clench my hand tight around the stock of the crossbow as we make our way around the hedges to the clearing in front of the trainee's balcony.

"Jo! We're here!" Lori shouts as loudly as she can, and James and I follow suit.

Jo erupts from the library, a long black scimitar in his hand. "You're alright?"

"Yes. Let's get inside the tunnels."

A dark blotch of movement darts out of the bushes, and Jo lets out a guttural scream. The spider runs past him and crawls across the Hawthorn's trunk. Its claws carve deep white scars in the bark of the Shadow Court's sacred tree, and my stomach cramps.

Jo holds pressure to the lash in his injured arm. The spider must have sampled him for dinner as it ran by.

Another spider tiptoes out of the same bushes, and Jo goes on the offensive as Lori dashes forward to kill the one desecrating the Hawthorn. I sit James down on a flat rock. The man is still fighting for breath. He must have lost a ton of blood.

A blur of movement in the branches above catches my eye, and I raise my loaded weapon. "Lori, watch out!"

The silver bolt flies toward a third spider careening directly for my best friend's head. The bolt buries deep in the creature's brain, and the eight-legged abomination topples over to the ground. Venom splashes the earth, an acrid smoke rising from the spill.

The three dead spiders flake off to nothingness, but they are quickly replaced by five others. A fresh batch crawls in from the different paths leading up to where we're standing.

We slowly tighten the ranks around James until we're all facing a different direction, our backs almost touching. I take a couple of the arachnids out from a distance, but come up empty on the third reload. There's no bolts left in my quiver, and I still haven't managed to craft one out of thin air.

Another wave of monsters stalks out of the bushes, and I count at least a dozen.

Jo twirls the long scimitar in his grip and shoots me a regretful glance. "Nice knowing you, Old World."

Lori presses her lips together. "Shut up! It's not over, yet."

We're about to find out exactly how many spiders it takes to kill a duo of hunters and a couple of ill-fated Shadow seeds.

CHAPTER 34

DREAMCATCHER

The spiders click closer and closer. The sharp claws at the end of each of their legs tap the stones in a series of sickening *tinks*, and bile rises to my mouth. Lori dashes forward with her arms spread out on each side of her, keeping a humongous one from approaching the huddle, but another one takes advantage of her movement to scurry over to my side.

I smash its head with the crossbow, but the weapon is not pointy enough to pierce its thick exterior shell. James throws a heavy rock, but it just ricochets off the eight-legged monster.

The razor-edge of the spider's front legs slashes my left thigh, and blood pours out of the wound. The pain lashes through me, as bright and intense as a bolt of lightning, and a long scream slips up my throat. I fall to my ass next to James, cradling my leg.

Adrenaline rushes through my body, and I condense all the frenzied currents of shadow magic I possess into my palms. A long blade shimmers into view, and I grip it in my hand, the spider now inching on top of me. My jaw clenches in disgust as its dark body obscures the entire gardens from view, and my lips part in desperation. The proximity of the nightmare snuffs out my magic better than a monsoon smothers a spark of fire, and the shadow weapon in my hand withers into nothingness.

The hollow shard in my soul where all my fears and insecurities live throbs at the monster's approach. All my dreams and hopes crumble to ashes. In mere seconds, the spider gobbles out all the fight left in me, its terrible magic more paralyzing than a snare.

Right as it's about to strike again, the monster cocks its globulous head to the side and merely extends its fangs forward to taste my blood. A drop of venom leaks from the tip of the crooked appendages next to its mouth and burns through my thick jacket, right to my upper arm.

"Oww!" I cry out.

The poison melts my skin like a needle heading straight for the bone. I can almost feel the foul, oily liquid as it penetrates my bloodstream, and the oppressive warmth that comes with the contamination quickly spreads down my shoulder. The spider emits an excited, high-pitched squeak, and all its eyes zero-in on me.

Somehow, it recognizes my blood. *By the Mother!*

Before it can decide whether it wants to eat me or not, an arrow hits it square in the head. The pointy end sticks out of its chin, inches from my heaving chest.

A series of high-pitched noises whistle out of the nightmare before its legs give out underneath it. It poofs in a cloud of dark ashes, leaving me in tatters, but alive. A dark shadow jumps over the rails of the balcony and lands almost on top of me, crouching to face the next member of the swarm with a snarl. One.

Tears streak down my cheeks as I sag against the ground in relief.

He stands tall and draws his bow once more, the nightmare hunter sinking arrow after arrow into the arachnids. Lori rests her hands on her thighs, and a few deep cuts run along her arms. Jo falls to his knees next to James, the hunter holding his guts in with both hands. "About time he showed up," he murmurs, white as a sheet.

Sweat pearls above my brows, but I force the shock out of my stiff muscles and crawl over to him. "Don't move."

The magic comes quickly as I heal him, and I take care of the wound on my thigh, too. It vanishes quickly, but the venom-laced cut on my arm is unresponsive to my magic, which puts a damper on the hot sense of relief coursing through me.

Jo stands up without a hitch and helps me to my feet. "Thank you, Old World."

The healing hasn't returned all the colors to his cheeks, but he's alright. He shakes out his fists, looking ready to jump back into the fray, but One holds out an arm to stop him. "Wait. Everybody behind me. Now."

Lori slices into one last spider and rushes over to us as Two and Three erupt from the tunnels. The two Fae dash over to flank their brother and raise their arms toward the spiders. In a flash, the monsters stop moving. A couple of them hang in mid-air with their claws out—suspended in time.

A crescent wave of pure shadows spreads out in front of the triplets. The ground shakes. The black void takes tangible form, pulling wispy smog from its center to create a long, deadly weapon. Its sharp edge glistens, devouring the sunlight and burning darker still. The air is heavy with the force of a power I didn't know existed, and I bite my bottom lip as the shadow blade suddenly snaps and springs toward the spiders, killing what's left of them in one sweep.

One finally lowers his bow, his whole body wrapped in darkness, and the onyx-and-gold weapon vanishes into thin air. "That's all of them."

He looks shaken after what he just did, and we all gawk at him in shock and awe.

Lori stares into the empty gardens, her eyes wide, and her breaths quick and uneven. "Are you sure?"

One marches over to me and grazes the blood tainting my clothes with his fingertips, his lips curled down in a sullen pout. "How did they get inside the castle?" he asks Jo, his eyes never leaving me as he takes stock of my injuries.

"We don't know, yet. Mitchell and Fiona were dead before I got here." Jo reports quickly, content to obey the chain of command he so often resents—at least for the time being. "Cary and the sprites are guarding the entrance to the tunnels, so the others are all safe and accounted for except Misha."

"Misha is off-world on assignment," Two adds with a sigh.

"Jo and Lori, barricade the secret entrances and make sure all the sprites are safe," One orders. "Two will check the barrier while Three tends to the dead. I'll take care of Nell's wounds." He squeezes my good shoulder, standing closer than absolutely necessary. "Come on, kitten. I'm taking you to your room."

My eyes narrow. I was ready to let him off the hook because of his heroic rescue, but not if he's about to treat me like a spineless, fragile thing. Everyone else is hurt and exhausted and in shock, too. Why would I be the only one to leave?

"I want to help—"

He leans closer, his stark tone daring me to argue with his orders. "*Now*."

I hurry in front of him and blaze toward the tunnels. "You said that we were done and that you had to keep your distance. Well… keep it. I can find my own way."

He presses a hand to the small of my back for a fleeting moment. "We need to deal with the poison in your body, or you'll spend the entire night dry-heaving in a pool of sweat."

"I feel fine."

I know he's right, but for all we know, we might all die before the afternoon is over. If a new wave of spiders comes, or if the king decides he needs to steal my magic and my memories in one breath in order to defeat them, I'm done for.

I'm simply boiling inside, and Cary frowns as we rush past him. "What are my orders, boss? Is the king safe?"

One wraps an arm around my shoulders. "The king is fine. Stay here and guard the tunnels." he croaks, out of breath. He discreetly uses me for support as he chats Cary up about the details of his assignment. That fight must have taken a lot of him, but he clearly doesn't want anyone to notice.

"Wow, Nell. I can feel your magic from here," Cary says with a small smile. "Congratulations."

"Err—Thanks." Now that I have a second to think about it, he's right. *The way I healed James and Jo earlier. It was so easy.*

"Nell is hurt. She needs rest," One says a little too casually, and I squint at him.

Cary nods and returns his attention to the entrance. I wrap an arm around One in the guise of using him as a crutch, but he's the one who truly needs it. After a good minute, One pulls away, apparently strong enough to walk without my aid.

Why doesn't he want his underlings to know he's in bad shape?

The tunnels are dark and claustrophobic. The stale air and waning light spark a fresh wave of panic inside my heart.

One's fingertips brush the sensitive skin of my hairline as he whispers, "You sprouted faster than any seed ever has. That's a formidable achievement, kitten."

The soft tremble in his voice makes him sound awed and almost...humbled. He doesn't know how my sudden leap in training came to happen, and a fresh wave of guilt brings a sickly sheen of sweat to my forehead. "I kissed Three," I blurt out, red-faced. "For a moment, I thought he was you, and things got out of hand—" I say without looking back, afraid to face his disappointment.

One waves away my tortured admission. "It doesn't matter."

I come to an abrupt stop near my room, my mouth opened in outrage. Whatever negative reaction I expected, this is worse. "It matters to me."

The violence of the fight is still thick in my blood, and I'm not sure if I'd rather kiss him or slap him for acting in such a business-like fashion. The end result doesn't justify what I've done, and I can't stand to see him act so cold and collected about it.

"You're a sprout, now," he insists, dismissing my feelings—and most likely his own—once more. "Nothing else matters."

I move to punch his chest before I can form a conscious thought, but he grips my hand in mid-air.

"Careful now, kitten."

We're just outside my bedroom, and his unforgiving hold forces me to back up until I'm leaning on the door.

One presses our joined hands to my heart, and we both stare at each other for a moment. "Your magic has grown beyond anything I'd imagined. Don't you feel it?" His voice is low and almost...hungry.

The pressure of his hand on my chest mollifies my legs. "I do..."

"You have more magic than me right now." Wicked tremors quake him, but his gaze flicks to my lips.

"What you did out there took a lot out of you."

"It cost me *everything*." He leans in and rests his forehead on mine, but he doesn't kiss me. Instead, he reaches for the doorknob with his free hand and pushes me inside. The lock clicks behind us, and the sound brands my neck with gooseflesh.

The contrast between the death and terror we just witnessed outside and this oasis of safety is maddening.

"Remove your shirt so I can take a better look at this." He motions to my injured shoulder, and I bite the insides of my cheeks.

Did he truly only come in here with me to deal with the venom?

The adrenaline from the attack fizzles out, and a heavy ache blossoms in my arms and legs. I take stock of the bite and realize it's much worse than I'd thought. "Can you heal it?"

His breath stirs the hair that escaped my loose braid. "Not without supplies."

"Why not? I healed you from a dreamcatcher cut before," I tease, trying to lighten the mood.

"And that was no small feat in itself, but my wound wasn't full of venom. Lie down so I can get to work." He removes his jacket, discards it at the foot of the bed, and motions for me to lie over the duvet.

I sit and peel off my shirt, but the sports bra underneath shields me from his gaze. The nasty shape of the venom burn coaxes a wince out of me. Black veins snake from the wound, the poison slowly creeping under my skin, and my stomach clenches.

"By the Mother!" I reach out to touch the sensitive flesh only to grimace at the pain. The slight pressure is torture, and my eyes dart over to One, full of fear. "It's already spreading."

"Don't worry, kitten. It'll be better in a few minutes," he whispers. "I can't believe you fought with me all the way over here. It must hurt like the seven hells."

Now that I'm not half as panicked as before, it does burn and itch like fire fleas. "I was too mad at you to notice."

His lips twitch. "I got that."

He lights the candles on the dresser with a flick of the wrist and knocks on the mirror. A few seconds later, Baka flies in with a mortar and pestle in one hand and a few other supplies bunched under her arm.

The sprite's gaze bounces from me to the dark Fae, and she bows in reverence. "I just heard about the attack. Do you want me to tend to her, Samhain?"

One dismisses her offer with a kind smile. "No need. I'll stay. Take care of the others, Baka."

The sprite draws in a breath, her pink eyes full of velvet and sunshine. "Consider it done." The tenderness in her tone sends warm shivers through my body.

One removes his mask and sets it on the nightstand. The soft glow of the waning fire fills the silence, and Two's earlier claim echoes in my ears. *One hates Damian. He'd be willing to steal you away from any king, but he can't. At least not alone...*

"Is Samhain your real name?" I ask.

One doesn't miss a beat as he mixes the herbs with an oily elixir. "No. In ancient Fae, Samhain means *darker half.*" He warms the contents of the mortar over the embers. The rescue might have drained his magic, but he's still mesmerizing.

The light of the fire caresses his proud jaw, and a hint of sweat beads over his split brow.

"Why did you not want them to know how exhausted you were out there? Why hide it?" I ask.

"I can't afford to be weak right now." He stirs the mixture again and returns it to the fire. "The king needs you safe now more than ever. He can't afford to lose the bet if you die. You have to go home, Nell. Until Morheim starts."

My eyes widen. "I thought the king wanted me here for the first Morheim moon?"

From my perspective, the chances that this attack will change the king's designs toward me are null. If anything, he's going to need my magic even more.

Shadows flicker over One's pensive face, playing hide and seek with his cheekbones. "Who knows what the king wants anymore..."

I sit up and prop a few pillows at my back. "I can't leave you, Lori, and the others to face the nightmares alone."

One sits close to me on the bed and wipes off the venom burns with a wet cloth. He moves with confidence, and yet his touch is gentle enough to mollify my bones. "Don't move. It might sting a little."

He spreads the salve over my throbbing skin with his fingers, and I grit my teeth at the heat. The mixture of herbs quickly coats the venom-infected burn, and in an instant, I feel a thousand times lighter.

A sigh of relief escapes me as I relax into the pillows. "Thank you." The ointment quickly hardens over my skin as it cools.

One lays down the salve and cloth on the bedside table. "Morheim might be depicted in your books as this terribly anxious time, but for us, it's sacred. Beautiful. The moon's always full on Morheim, and when she reaches that apex in the sky on the first night—it's the most beautiful moment of the year."

The raw emotions dancing in his eyes rake through me, and I wish we could stand under that moon together.

"A full moon sounds lovely, and not very dark," I breathe.

"Shadows do not exist in absolute darkness. Like most things, they need light to grow. Morheim is more than an opportunity to scare young Faen into obedience. It's the foundation of all life. Without it, the sun would never surrender his place in the sky. He's awfully arrogant, you know." He chuckles—mostly to himself. "But Morheim forces him to reflect on his flaws. Without it, he'd burn too bright, scorch our crops, and heat our seas..."

The tip of his index finger curls around the edge of the hardened salve, and he peels it off in one fluid motion. I'm relieved to see nothing but smooth skin underneath.

"There. Good as new." He traces a circle over the new flesh with his thumb, and my belly tightens at the caress.

I rest my hand over his. "Why is Three allowed to touch me, and you aren't?"

A dark shroud clouds his golden gaze, and he retreats by a few inches. "It's complicated."

"I'm in love with you." The admission is guarded despite the sweetness of the words, but I almost died today. I can't afford to keep it to myself anymore.

One stands and extends a hand toward his discarded mask. "You're infatuated with me. There's a difference."

I steal the scarred piece of onyx from his reach and hold it behind my back. "Don't pretend to know how I feel. You're infuriating, hard-working, kind—I know my own heart. I *love* you."

"You can't love *me*. I'm *nothing*." Self-loathing drips from every word as he prowls closer to reclaim his most-prized possession. "I'm barely alive."

I rise to my knees on the bed and grab a fist of his shirt with one hand, right over his heart. "You feel alive to me."

His hand freezes over his mask, his resolve wavering. "I have nothing to offer. I'm a ghost of who I used to be. I—"

I stand on the mattress. The bed gives me a few inches on him, and I wrap my arms around his neck. There are no songs hidden in his beautiful eyes today, no enchantments waiting to hold me captive. Just fear.

I sink a hand inside his dark hair. "The king needs magic. What if he decides to take mine? Would you let him?" Shivers brand my body as I chuck out the words. "Am I going to forget ever coming here? Will I remember Lori and the others? Will I remember *you*, or will the king take everything from me?"

One strokes my hips before coaxing me off the bed. My body glides against his as he sets me down, and he presses his forehead to mine. "What if he doesn't have a choice? He can't let the kingdom burn because of Morrigan's army."

My blood races in my veins. "Morrigan? I don't understand. If she's alive—what does she want?"

"Me. But since she can't have me, she'll destroy me." One cups the side of my face and traces the shape of my lips with his thumb. "She can't ever know about you."

"Why not?"

"Because you're the first thing since that damned curse that makes me feel whole," he growls.

"And that's bad?"

"Very bad." He nips my bottom lip. "The worst." His voice is low and fragmented, like I'm about to wrench a secret from the depths of his soul.

"Why?"

He finally presses his lips to mine. "Because I'd die to have you."

The sweet pressure of his tongue blows all thoughts of Morrigan out of my mind.

All thoughts of my old life, my old self, and then some.

I melt into the kiss as One falls forward on top of me, his weight pinning me down on the mattress. His leg sneaks between my thighs as he pulls me up and aligns my head with the pillows. I'm hanging on for his next breath, his next moan, his next kiss. If lust does that to mortals, I'm not at all against it. It's a clarity I've never known. My body roars for what it craves, even beyond reason. It was good in the Dreaming, but it wasn't real.

This is real.

I peel his shirt off and spread my legs to make space for him. The feel of his hardness against my inner thigh fills my blood with fire, and I scratch two parallel lines in his shoulder blades. "Stay for the night."

He shakes his head, and the hungry, unsatisfied gleam in his eyes melts me from the inside out. "You don't know what you're asking."

I trace the scar splitting his brow. "Before coming here, I thought Fae were dangerous and wicked. I thought I was coming here to suffer in some evil land that would try and destroy me."

"Evil is a point of view."

"No it's not. There's not a shred of evil in you." I struggle to keep a semblance of composure, and the tremble in my voice grows three times too loud for me to sound confident as I say, "Two said we could be together if—if I agreed to take all three."

One grips my wrists and holds my hands above my head. "He shouldn't have said that."

"Is it true?"

He buries my knuckles even deeper in the pillows, and the dark curve of his mouth sends my pulse flying.

"What would you do with the three of us?" he chokes.

His attempts at deflection only harden my resolve. "Humor me. Is it true?"

The last of the embers twinkle in red and orange hues in the hearth, our fingers still entwined above my head.

"Yes and no..." he trails off regretfully. "Morrigan's curse ensured that I couldn't so easily replace her. I can't feel true compassion, can't love—can't even fuck you properly." He grinds his hip forward, making me doubt his assessment, and my lips part at the friction.

Our noses bump, and I stretch out my neck to kiss him. "Just try. I think it might work."

Two stalks out of the shadows. "Tell her the whole truth—or by the spindle, take a moment to look at yourself."

A third silhouette slowly comes into focus on the other side of the bed, and I hold my breath.

They're all *here*. And they're not wearing their masks.

Two plops over to the empty space beside us on the bed. "You can't deny it... The four of us together is a tempting idea. With a little luck, it could even break the curse."

My cheek digs into the pillow as I angle my face to him. "Break the curse? Is that possible?"

One lets go of my hands and sits up over me on the bed, his chest rising and falling. My gaze follows the defined muscles of his bare chest down his stomach to the v-cut shapes of his hips, and I lick my lips.

Two shifts to his side next to me and tucks his arm under his head, so close that I could count his eyelashes. "Curses are more like songs than spells. Morrigan wrote the lyrics, but the melody was left to the spindle of the gods. Curses have a loophole—a loose thread that can be unraveled. Clearly, it has something to do with you." His tongue darts out to touch his bottom lip as he leans closer to my ear. "One might be a pessimistic ass, but he has feelings for you. He's hard for you—even though that should be impossible. You're a game changer, pet, but it terrifies him."

One jumps to his feet and covers the obvious bulge in his pants with one hand. "It can't be as easy as that."

"You don't know. Her magic is growing beyond what any of us had dared to hope. She is drawn to us, and we *all* yearn for her..." Two rolls the end of my braid between his index finger and thumb. "If we manage to break the curse, the king won't have to steal her magic and make her forget she ever set foot in Faerie."

The shimmer of silver and gold that frames his pupils softens. Two is difficult and rude and a tiny bit evil, but in this moment, I can almost believe he cares for me.

Three feeds a few pieces of wood to the fire and moves to sit on the opposite side of the bed. His hand curls around my shoulder like a promise.

One looks as if he's about to tear his brothers off my bed, but I extend my arm in his direction. Flames flicker over his handsome face as he considers my offered hand, but the most stubborn of the bunch still holds out.

Two loses patience first. "Alright, let's vote. All those in favor of getting naked together to see if it'll break the curse, say *aye*."

Three flips his brother off with a warm chuckle, and the tender touch of his fingers along the ridges of my spine clears up any doubt I could've had on where his vote lies.

"No," One growls.

I make my way to my infuriatingly stubborn *darker half*. "Aye." I entwine our fingers to show him I mean it and tug him closer.

Sometimes, the only thing left to do is take a leap.

CHAPTER 35

TROIS POUR UN

The weight of my decision steals my breath, but doubts creep inside my foggy brain, so I clasp One's hands even harder. "Wait a minute...will the king be able to force himself on me if I'm no longer a maiden?"

Two breaks out in a fit of giggles. "Don't worry, pet. Losing your virginity has nothing to do with your father's bet with the king. And we wouldn't let *anyone* touch you against your will."

One glowers at his brother. Something dark and foreign pulses in his eyes, and I anchor my gaze to his. "Not even the king?" I ask.

Two unbuttons his shirt as though it's a done deal. "Not even him."

Three caresses my lower back and presses his nose to the side of my face. *You belong to us, now.*

"What about an unplanned pregnancy?"

"No chance of that happening with all the contraceptive tea we're drinking," Two says.

One lets go of me and balls his fists at his sides. "You can't agree to this."

I shake from head to toe, overwhelmed by the grim curve of his mouth. "Why not?"

"You're dying to say yes. Why are you fighting it?" Two asks his brother. He looks giddy, which should alert me that this is the worst decision of my life.

Three of them. Three Fae lovers, when it's sinful to take just one... Three identical men that couldn't be more different.

I run a hand down One's arm and trace the shape of his muscles to the runes tattooed near the crook of his elbow. The caress coaxes a heavy groan from his lips, and my fingers glide along his smooth skin until his liquid gaze meets mine. The other two fade to the background.

"I love you," I whisper.

"I love you, too. At first I thought I couldn't...and then tried so hard not to—" A cloud passes over his features, and his throat bobs, "Are you sure you want this, kitten?"

My chest heaves with longing. "I want *you*. I need you to stop thinking about tomorrow and concentrate on tonight. On *us*."

If there's a chance for us to be together, and maybe even break the curse, we have to take it. The old beliefs I used to cling to are brittle and dry, so I might as well bury them. I want to know what it's like to be his. I crave his kisses and his smiles, and if he would only give in to our love for *one night*, I just know it would be enough to carry me through anything.

"I feel safe with you." I glance at the three of them in turn. "All of you."

They look even more similar now, standing in a circle around me, and I do not feel like a prey, but a treasure to be cherished and protected.

The intimacy of the moment is almost overwhelming despite the crowded bedroom, like it's perfectly natural for us to gather here together. The powerful magic that pulses whenever the three of them are in the same place seems at peace. Now that their desires are aligned, their combined energy is smooth and comforting.

Two's tongue darts out to touch his bottom lip as he pries a long scarf from his pocket. "You need to wear this."

It's the exact same piece of silk One used when he first took me through the sceawere, and I shiver at the memory. "Why?"

Two moves to stand behind me, and his soft breath stirs the hairs at the back of my neck. "It's a secret, but it won't keep you from enjoying this, I promise." He ties the fabric around my head, and darkness blinds me completely.

"Wait." I hike the silk up my brow, just like I did on the first night, unable to leap just yet. "Do *you* want this?"

One presses his forehead to mine. "Two's not wrong. I've been *dying* to touch you," he murmurs against my lips. "All of you."

The possessive way he squeezes my hips drives me mad with lust, and a low growl quakes his throat, his last defenses shattered by the admission. He plants a fiery series of butterfly kisses down my stomach and kneels at my feet. A searing heat liquifies my gut when he dips his tongue inside my belly button, and I bury my hands in his black hair, holding him close.

Two moves to my side and angles my face to him, his thumb hard against the curve of my jaw. "I knew you'd give in... Kiss me, pet. Show me how much you want me."

His wide, satisfied smirk brings out my mischievous side, and I press a finger to his lips instead. "After the hell you put me through in training, I should just make you watch until the very end."

He's always playing games, but he looks downright terrified by the threat. "Please, don't." He grips a fist of his hair, leaving it all disheveled. "I beg you."

Three's chuckle rumbles on my shoulder as he kisses a fiery trail down my hairline to my shoulder blade and wraps me up from behind.

Two holds himself away, his eyes dark and desperate. "Don't cast me aside." He reaches for my hand and places a quick, tender kiss on my wrist. "I'm sorry." His nose wrinkles, and the next words come out gruff, like the very thought of an apology is heresy. "I should have treated you better, and I promise to do so in the future."

My brows lift in surprise. "I accept your apology."

I smile, and he bends down, angling my face to him once more. His lips are hard and yet soft on mine, and I reciprocate the kiss tenfold. All that was left of my inhibitions and fear-laced thoughts vanish along with the feel of his mouth. Two swallows the darkness inside me drop for drop, ravenous for more.

Three unhooks the little clasp in the middle of my bra, and the fabric feathers to the ground. My mouth hangs open on a gasp as Two pulls back and drinks in the sight of my bare chest. Three covers my breasts with his hands and tests the feel of them, still standing directly behind me.

I lean into his touch. "Oh, please."

One licks the sensitive spot below my navel and hooks his fingers under the hem of my pants, pulling them down and peeling them off my legs one side at a time. He kisses my inner thighs, both hands holding on to my waist, and his mouth slowly inches closer to my heat. "Fuck, you're so wet."

Two sneaks a hand down to my folds to test his brother's claim and growls, "*Soaked,* in fact." He sinks one finger inside me without preamble and quickly brings it to his mouth for a taste. The devious way he licks off my arousal from his finger destroys my brain.

One takes advantage of the moment to kiss the space between my thighs. *Holy hells!* My hips buck, and my legs threaten to give out under me, but Three holds me upright. He bites down on my earlobe, the flash of pain delicious and new. It keeps me grounded as Two plays with my breasts, treating them as though they were made to be used and abused by him. Three finally lowers the piece of silk back over my eyes with a playful slap on my ass.

In the dark, each of their touches is multiplied tenfold. It's easy to feel the difference between Three's sensual lips, Two's impatient hands, and One's fierce grip.

"I can still tell you apart."

"For now, maybe. But when you're high with pleasure, you won't be able to remember your own name, let alone discern which one of us is inside you," Two says.

My heart somersaults.

"I've got you, kitten." One hooks my leg over his shoulder. I grip a fist of his hair and close my eyes, my head falling back on Three's shoulder.

I shudder, more vulnerable than ever, and yet feeling more powerful than a king as One's tongue pushes me to the brink of a sweet, sweet death.

Two claims my mouth again with a rough kiss, and the spicy, salty scent of my arousal invades my senses. Three holds my back to his chest and sucks on my earlobe, one hand wrapped around my midriff.

Somehow, the thought that they're both here, watching One pleasure me, makes it even better, and the shame of it never comes.

The pressure of their tongues both hurts and liberates me, and I writhe for more friction. One stretches me open, sinking two fingers inside me. Without mercy, he rubs a secret spot near my pubic bone that sends electric zaps of pleasure across my belly until I'm panting. "Yes!"

But he stops right there—at the edge of the precipice.

I choke on a sob. "Please, One. I want you inside me." The clench between my thighs *aches*, wild and dangerous.

A hard hand curls around my throat. "Just him?"

"All of you."

Two strong pairs of arms guide me to the bed, and the mattress hits the back of my knees, forcing me to perch on the edge. They keep me right there, legs dangling. The sound of a zipper and the soft *thump* of discarded fabric fills me with anticipation. The hollowness in my belly throbs for One to make me his, and I spread my legs wider as an invitation. "Please."

"Fuck, kitten," One gasps, and the tip of his hardness teases my forbidden, sensitive flesh.

Cold air blows across my breasts, and my brows furrow. "I can only feel one of you. Where did the others go?"

"We're all here," One whispers in the crook of my neck, and just like Two promised, their touch blurs together.

"I don't—"

He kisses me hard and slow and steady.

A lazy hand slides along my thigh, holding me open, and a thick cock pushes inside me slowly. "We're all here, kitten."

I draw in a sharp breath, waiting for the pain I'm sure should follow, but there's nothing but sweet, tortured bliss. One buries himself to the hilt, the feel of him pressing inside me absolutely glorious.

"Are you alright?"

"Yes!"

He thrusts harder, not quite so patient anymore.

A hot mouth sucks on my nipple as One stretches me and fills me, over and over again, and I feel like I'm going to die. "It's too much!"

A gentle hand cups my cheeks. "You want me to stop?"

"No! I just—I need to—"

A chuckle echoes in my ear. "You want to come."

"Yes!"

My lover guides my legs over his shoulders and pushes even deeper. The feel of him—thick and snug—steals my breath.

A hand snakes to my sex and draws sharp circles over the sweet bundle of nerves between my legs. My skin burns like I'm about to be torn apart, and I arch off the bed, holding on to the duvet, searching for my other two lovers in vain.

"Come for me, Nell. *Now.*"

I scream, my body, my soul—even my magic—dying to obey his command. My walls pulse around his cock like a snare meant to keep him there forever, and my heart hammers in my throat. The pleasure spreads to my toes and blazes across my entire body.

"Fuck, kitten, it feels too good. I never want to stop."

He doesn't stop, and the feel of him is so perfect and raw that another wave of pleasure pulls me under.

After a few seconds, the others return to my side. Hot, violent tremors threaten to overwhelm me, but Two and Three hold me steady. Their heat wraps me up in an inferno of love. One reaches his release in a series of curses, and my cheeks burn at the dirty praises rolling off his tongue as he fills me with his seed.

His weight vanishes, and a hungry mouth swallows my last whimper with a kiss.

I tear the blindfold off. "Did it work? Do you feel different at all?"

One struggles to catch his breath, standing at the foot of the bed, and I sit up to reach for him.

"We're nowhere near done with you, pet." Two traces the length of my spine and slaps my ass. "Get on your knees. It's my turn now."

I should be alarmed at how little they all seem to care for the curse at the moment, but I understand how lust can fudge your priorities, so I play along.

I throw Two a sizzling gaze over my shoulder. "Say, *please*."

Tongue tucked between his teeth, Two raises his brows. The v-shape of his hips leads my sight down to his aching cock, and I swallow hard.

He's not going to say please again. If anything, he's going to make *me* beg. I crouch to all fours, and Two caresses my buttocks like it's a prize.

The tip of his erection brushes my swollen sex. "Will you let me have you? Just me, while the others watch and envy me?" he asks on a low growl, and it scares me how much I want to please him.

His warm hand closes around my throat, and my chest heaves. "Yes."

He pushes inside me slowly, dragging out the process for as long as he can. When he's all the way inside, he pulls out and starts all over again.

The angle is much more primal, the kind of sex a princess is never supposed to enjoy. Rough, but slow.

One isn't put out by my eagerness to be used by his brother in this way. He stares at me with beastly pride as Two tugs on my braid and bends my body for his pleasure.

Soon enough, the other two Fae are not content to just watch anymore. One pulls me in for a kiss and drags the silk back down over my eyes.

The three of them take turns inside me, spinning me in their arms to slide in and out of me until I'm not sure which one of them is thrusting deep inside, and which one of them is buried in my mouth.

I expect to feel dirty or ashamed, but to the contrary, I feel free and powerful. Happy. I don't care what my father or the Shadow King planned for me. I know I'm made for them and them alone.

Curse or no curse, they belong to me now. Forever.

CHAPTER 36
THE LONGEST NIGHT

"K itten, wake up." One's lips brush my ear as I stir awake. "I need to go."

I blink, not exactly sure when I dozed off. Adrenaline dispenses a healthy dose of fear in my veins as I search the room. "Where did the others go?"

"They got up at the crack of dawn." One traces my shoulder blade in a soothing manner. "Something's not right with the barrier that keeps nightmares and outsiders away. Something is weakening it from within."

The way his lips curl down at the end of the sentence sends my pulse flying despite the sweet caress. "You think someone inside the castle might be helping Morrigan? A hunter?"

"Or a weaver. One of them might be hiding in the castle. Stay here. I'll find the mole." He dives down for a slow kiss, and a line of goosebumps across my back chases the touch of his warm hand as he withdraws.

My heart pounds in my throat. *It could be like this every day. Every morning and night.*

"I can't stay in here like a coward. Let me help. Please."

He hesitates, pressing his mask in place. "I asked Lori to secure the bibliotheca. She's the only one I trust given how she didn't partake in the last disastrous hunt. But don't let anyone else come too close to you, okay? Like your pal, Joseph."

Jo? I think back on our conversations, trying to discern an ulterior motive to our friendship.

I slip my bra and t-shirt on. "I'll steer clear of him. Be careful out there."

One blinks a few times like he can't quite believe what I've just said. "It's so easy with you. I never thought I could feel like this."

A playful grin twists my lips. "If you hadn't fought me every step of the way, it could have been easy much sooner."

"Come here." He grips a fist of my shirt and draws me in for one last kiss before heading out through the free-standing mirror.

Baka flies into the room about ten seconds after he leaves and smiles from ear to ear. "That boy finally realized the truth, then?"

I secure my belt around my hips and raise a brow. "The truth?"

"He loves ye, thank the Seven. He might finally learn to love himself. From the moment he learned to walk, that boy never felt like he was enough."

"You knew him? When he was young?"

With a warm chuckle, Baka starts to change the sheets. "Aye. I was in charge of his father's estate and came to court with him. He had ambition, that's for sure. More than was good for him. He wanted to be the best at everything, but it led him on a path of self-destruction... Morrigan took advantage of that, and ever since she cursed him, he's believed himself incapable of love. Not only unworthy of it, but incapable. Hopeless. I'm glad ye came along to show him how wrong he was."

"You're really fond of him."

She nods, her smile showing a full row of crooked teeth. "His mother died when he was only a wee thing. I take credit for his manners."

"What about the other two?" I smile, picturing how the triplets were growing up. "With all the rumors I've heard about Three, it's hard to imagine him as a kid."

Baka pauses for a second before the corners of her pink eyes wrinkle, making her already creased face even more joyful. "Hard to imagine, indeed."

I FEEL LIGHTER THAN AIR AS I MAKE MY WAY TO THE LIBRARY.
The hole in the stained glass has been magically mended, and rain beats hard on the windows, a bolt of lightning streaking through the sky. The strong winds clearly managed to send half the books flying from the shelves before the sprites could fix the window, and puddles of water shine across the glossy floors.

Lori is sifting through a series of wet books on the third floor, sitting with her legs crossed in the middle of the puddle closest to the previously broken window.

She sighs as I draw near, pinching a spine between her index finger and thumb. Water drips to the ground as she lifts it up. "The damn spiders derailed the spell that protects the stacks. Some of these books have no known copies. They're invaluable."

She lays her palm flat against the cover of the leather-bound volume to dry it, but I can tell by the tired frown on her face that she's exhausted.

"Here. Let me help." I kneel beside her and pick up another damaged book. "Talk me through the process."

She slides the book she just dried into its rightful spot. "It's easier than healing flesh. You'll be fine."

I flatten my palm to the cover of a leather-bound volume about Demeter and push a hint of magic forward. The moisture dries up in an instant, the water sucked right from the pages, and my skin itches with heat. While drying books is easy, it does take quite a bit of energy to do it.

"How many of these have you done?" I ask.

"I don't know." She shrugs, her gray gaze empty as she prepares to fix yet another book. "A couple hundred so far?"

I rest both of my hands on her shoulders. "Alright. Time for a break." I lead her down the stairs to the librarian's desk, and the docile way she follows my instruction tells me exactly how tired she is.

"You're all wet and cold. You need a hot shower and some food. I'll take over for a while."

Shivers rock her slender body. "Thank you. I'll be quick, I promise."

I know better than to scold her for being so hard on herself. Two of her friends just died, and even if I didn't know Mitch or Fiona for a long time, I grieve their loss, too. "I'm so sorry about Mitchell and Fiona."

She screws her lids shut and shakes her head. "We trained together—I just... Sometimes, I feel like we're all going to die." She cries in my arms for about a minute before drying her tears with her hoodie's sleeve. "I'll take a quick shower and come straight back. If you hear anything—and I mean *anything*—hurry inside the tunnels, okay?"

"I will," I promise.

After she's gone, I take stock of the damage. If magic didn't exist, most of these incredible tomes would be ruined. I dry and inventory the books that fell from the top floors and line them neatly on the desk after I'm done.

I work in silence for about fifteen minutes until a freakishly warm breeze caresses my cheeks, and I turn back toward the main entrance. A minute ago, a wooden beam held the thick double doors shut, so the low *creak* of the hinges quickens my pulse.

"Who's there?" I call out, spooked.

An uneven wind blows forward, fanning the pages of the books laying on the table. Instead of a spider, a beautiful man appears, his bare feet not touching the ground. He looks lighter than air and ready to step off a cloud, but he finally lands and finds his footing on the checkered floors.

"Hey there." He buries his hands in his elegant jacket's pockets and stares up at the chandelier above Lori's desk. "Nice digs."

I hold my breath.

Heavy rain seeps through the cracks left over by the intruder. He's got short dark hair, and his light brown skin is perfectly smooth. A clear purple gaze meets mine and turns my brain to mush. An array of silver earrings shines along the curve of his pointy ears, and his embroidered black and gray ensemble makes him look fresh out of a fairytale.

I've never seen a high-born Fae without a mask—besides One. The way this man flaunts his hauntingly beautiful eyes for everyone to see feels scandalous.

"Who are you, darling?" He leers at my long blonde mane the way a wealthy lord examines the show horses at an auction, and my spine stiffens.

"I—I'm Nell." I want to walk away, but I offer him my hand to kiss instead, and I have to chew on my bottom lip hard not to blurt out my whole name.

"I'm looking for Damian, Nell. Can you help me?" He tilts his head to the side and ghosts his full, sensual lips over my knuckles, and a zap of electricity travels from my hand to my belly.

This creepily handsome Fae is lurking around the castle, looking for *Damian* like the Shadow King is as accessible as any man. *What the crops?*

"Hey!" Lori dashes over to us, no longer wearing her uniform, but her hoodie and jeans. "You're not allowed here." She shoots me an alarmed glance over her shoulder, keeping most of her focus on the stranger. "Put on your mask, Nell. Quickly."

She pries her own mask out of the big pouch at the front of her hoodie. I retrieve mine from my bag, and we both secure the accessory over our awestruck faces in unison. With the mask on, the stranger doesn't look quite as enticing as before. He's still gorgeous, but I no longer want to give away all my secrets and obey his every whim.

Lori stands tall, a set of shadow daggers flickering to life in her hands.

"You're trespassing on the Shadow King's lands. Identify yourself."

"I'm Seth. Who are *you?*" Even though he's asking her the same question he asked me, he no longer looks like a horse connoisseur looking for his next ride.

"Lori."

Purple thunderclouds thicken Seth's irises, and I grip Lori's arm out of instinct. Now that he's seen her, the Fae doesn't even spare me a full glance, looking her up and down like he's just won a terrible prize.

He licks his bottom lip, the sight of his tongue almost indecent. "Now that we've all been properly introduced... Where are you from, Lori?"

Lori grunts at the personal question, but before she can answer —or tell him off—One slithers in from the shadows. He comes running in like some magic warned him of the newcomer's arrival, and his presence causes the glow of the moon over the gardens to vanish.

"Seth. You know better than to come here unannounced." His body creates a barrier between Lori and me and the unexpected visitor.

Seth barely acknowledges the arrival of the Fae, his gaze still fixed on Lori. "I have urgent news to share."

"Leave us. *Now.*" One dismisses us, and we obey at once, the urgency in his tone making my heart thud in my ribcage.

Seth buries his hands inside his pockets and flashes us a dashing smile. "Goodbye, ladies. I'll see you again soon, I hope."

We climb the stairs to the third floor and spy through the stacks.

The wide gaps in the mezzanine's railings allow for a glimpse at the two men as they chat.

"Who is that?" I ask, the man's smile still imprinted in my retinas, my hand still pulsing where he touched it.

"Judging by the look on One's face and the man we saw... I'd say the prince of nowhere at all."

"Prince of what?"

"Oh, he's infamous. There's an entire chapter about him in *A Taste for Crowns*. He was born out of wedlock, and his birth created quite the stir, given that his royal parents were both married to other people at the time."

I rub down the warmth leftover by his lips on my knuckles. "That explains why I let him kiss my hand."

"Believe me, we both would have done worse without our masks on to protect us. He's a man whore, that one. A rake," she adds for my benefit, but I understood her meaning perfectly.

A sudden burning sensation pierces my leg. "Ow."

"Are you alright?"

"Just a cramp. Sorry."

My heart hammers, and I excuse myself to my room with a hint of sweat at my brow. The pain is almost numbing. Esme is tugging on the head of her matching pin in Demeter, and she's tugging *hard*.

One did mention that the king wanted me to hide in Demeter until Morheim, so I can probably afford a quick trip back home.

CHAPTER 37
LITTLE BY LITTLE

S eth grins at the women's retreating backs. "Lori's gorgeous. She reminds me of someone—"

"Lori's off limits." I cut him off, knowing exactly where this conversation is going. I'm not in the mood to entertain Seth's crazy conspiracy theories. Not today.

"Don't you see? If Elio's harboring Morrigan, you've got the perfect Trojan horse for the Yule pageant—"

"Everything's fair game for a son of love and war, isn't it? Why do you care so much about Morrigan, anyway?"

On St-John's Eve, I thought Seth was just trying to stir trouble and sow dissension and paranoia in my heart, but he's motivated by something else. Still, he doesn't answer my question, and impatience thickens in my blood.

I watch his demeanor carefully and bare my teeth, ready to bite. "If you don't share your secrets, I'll start thinking that Morrigan sent you to mess with me."

A deep shadow moves across his face. "The bitch stole something from me. Something I'd rather keep quiet."

Progress. Finally. "What is it? What do *you* love enough to miss?"

We measure each other with a chilling gaze, and he lets out a small chuckle. "What it is is not important. Just know I'd give anything to get it back. Give me Lori, and I'll bring you Morrigan's head before the year's end."

If he thinks I can wait until the Yule ball to act, he can't help me. Either way, I deny his offer on the guise of protecting my favorite hunter. "I told you. Lori's off limits.

He pouts like a five year old at my refusal. "You say that now, but don't come crying to me when the bitch steals your throne."

I dig my heels into the ground and let my powers build in the air, the darkness thickening around us like a noose. "Fuck off, Seth. Or I'll make you regret ever setting foot in my kingdom, uninvited."

The prince's purple gaze burns in the night before he obeys, like a promise to get back at me for turning him away. Still, my magic is steadier than it has been in a long time, and I breathe easier after he's gone.

Once his magical signature disappears completely, Two sneaks out of the shadows. "The alarms were set off by the dandelion fluff, not Morrigan. The fucker's gone, so we might as well find Nell." Two grins from ear to ear. "I'm ready for round two, and don't pretend for a moment that you're not dying to taste her again."

A heavy sigh rocks my body. "You bug me."

"Let's go over it in detail. When you spread her thighs and positioned yourself at her entrance, I was so fucking jealous. That's when I felt the merge."

"She noticed it, too," I grumble. "Until the magic holding us together waned."

"Oh, don't be a grumpy, poo-poo bear." He follows me inside the tunnels. "You fought me on this, when clearly, the girl brought about the longest merge since the curse. It could save us. If we could only sustain the merge long enough to kill Morrigan—"

"A minute will not get us far. And it's not like we can have sex with Nell and kill Morrigan at the same time."

"We'll try again. Who knows where this might lead? Besides, I don't mind the practice one bit. We shared her, One. Didn't it feel amazing to fuck a woman again?"

It did, but I still have to correct him on the details. "Not any woman. *Nell*."

He huffs like I'm losing my mind. "You think she's different because you love her?"

From the corner of my eyes, I see Three rushing down the tunnels to meet us. "Yes!" There. I said it. "I love her! I know it's impossible, but I do."

Two's cocky smirk is simply wiped from his face, and Three waves his hands to get our attention.

He shows off four fingers. *We need Four.*

"Four?" I breathe, and he gives me a sharp nod.

Two giggles unkindly. "What's your plan? We tie him down, gag him, and hope she doesn't notice the raving mad man in the room?"

Three does his sign for Nell and makes a T-motion with his hand. *We take Nell to see Four. Now.*

My gaze flies to the other two broken pieces of Damian. The three of us are so different. I'm not even sure who I am anymore. "What— Have you gone mad?"

"He's right. We're already living on borrowed time. If we don't find a way to break the curse soon, we'll have to steal her powers, trudge through Morheim, and pray we survive until spring. I don't think any of us wants that," Two says, and I'm flabbergasted by his claim, to say the least.

He's not usually a helpful or rational Damian.

"But to take her to Four..." I trail off.

"We have to tell her about the curse, and who we really are," he adds.

My stomach flip flops at the mere thought of telling Nell the truth, and I shake like the ground below me is crumbling. "That's against the rules. You reminded me of them yourself!"

"Maybe if you'd followed them to begin with—"

Three slams a canvas to the wall to grab our attention, and the wooden frame splints into three parts. His chest rises and falls, his fury palpable. "Fuck the rules. Who is she going to tell? For Morpheus's sake, what are we so afraid of? We're dying! Little by little. Day by day. I don't want to go without a fight."

His gruff, hollow tone riddles me with fear...and hope.

Two's eyes bulge. "You're talking!"

Three's jaw hangs open for a second before he adds, "You two got to have sex. It's only fair."

"She won't love us as we truly are," I say quietly.

Two rolls his eyes at my pessimism. "Maybe she will. Three's talking. The curse is weakening."

"Or we'll lose the bet and take the kingdom down with us." I shake my head and twist open the door to Nell's bedroom.

We all come to an abrupt stop.

"Where is she?" Two asks.

A dark sense of acceptance settles in my chest as I take in the sight of her empty room. I close my eyes and hone in to her magical signature, but it's faint and fractured. "She's gone."

CHAPTER 38

TAKE ME

The fireplace burns bright, illuminating the bedroom I've been sleeping in since I was a child, and the pain in my calf that lured me back to Demeter finally relents.

Esme releases the head of the pin and tucks her socks back in place before she hurries over to me. "By the spindle! Where were you?"

Her hair, braided in two braids instead of one, wraps around her head like a crown. I'd compliment her if it wasn't for the terrified gleam in her eyes. "Faerie."

"Of course, Faerie. It didn't take me long to figure *that*. Your Father asked for you about twelve times. You were not supposed to leave for another couple of days. I didn't know what to tell him." Her hand shoots out to grab the emerald pendant hanging from my neck, and her throat bobs. "The Shadow King gave you that necklace... Why?"

A loud pounding on the door stops us cold. "The king wants to see you now, princess."

Judging by the last time my father summoned me to his office in the middle of the night, this is going to be far from pleasant. "Just a minute."

We exchange a quick glance, and Esme wrangles out a dress from the chest at the foot of my bed and starts unfastening the necklace. "You can't show this to your father. Might as well have come home with a promise ring."

The guard barrels through the door, and his eyes bulge as he takes in my appearance. "The king said that you should come immediately."

Esme slips the emerald in the fold of her skirts and glowers at the guard. Tipping her chin up, she slaps the man's arm, quick as a snake. "She needs a minute to change, you brute! Do you want me to tell the king you dragged his unmarried daughter out of her room in her undergarments?"

The guard shrinks at the reproach. "No, Ma'am."

I change and hurry downstairs, the flustered guard keeping a respectful distance on my heels.

"You asked for me, Father?"

His gaze darts over to me for the first time in what feels like months. "Where were you?"

I open my mouth to speak, but I'm missing some crucial information.

"You were in Faerie, weren't you? You sneaked out of your own free will. You've shamed yourself, and *me*," he adds with a defeated sigh.

I guess it doesn't matter what I did or didn't do because he doesn't control me anymore, and that's the real problem.

"He corrupted you, just like I knew he would." He clasps his goddess talisman. "May the Mother forgive her, she was such a lovely, innocent girl," he mutters to himself before facing me again. "You, young lady, need to reflect on your choices."

The anger inside me boils over. "*My choices*? You dare to call them mine when you were the one who sold me out. I never asked for this!"

He jumps to his feet, and I recoil out of instinct, his voice loud enough to pierce the confines of his study. "Your mother handled the specifics, not me. And what good did it do? She didn't have a boy, and now, I have to remarry."

My brows raise in understanding. *His visits to Danu...* If he's about to remarry, he can't keep me around, or my magic and its Faerie association will become too obvious.

I find solace in the knowledge that his outburst is totally unrelated to my growing feelings for the Shadow realm and its inhabitants. It has nothing to do with Isaac's engagement, after all.

"I am to marry Danu's princess. The entire royal family will be joining us for the weddings in less than a week, and you can't be here when they arrive," he explains.

Weddings...

Danu is known for its harsh winters and harsher treatment of women, and the royal family does not deal in half-measures when it comes to alliances.

My heart beats at my temples. "And Cece is now betrothed to their oldest son..." I reach for him and stop myself at the last second. "Father, no. *Please.* Danu priests twist our Mother's words to excuse their barbaric ways. You can't possibly—"

"Together, Demeter and Danu will thwart the assaults of the evil Faerie lands. I should have made this decision sooner. I shouldn't have banked on a weak, silly child to save my kingdom from demons."

Esme cracks open the servant door hidden in the tapestries, and our gazes meet, a flash of fear written across her severe features.

Father clears his throat at her arrival like he expected her to come. "Esmeralda, please join us."

Esme walks over to me, a fresh candle burning in her hand. "You sent for me, Your Highness?"

Father moves to grip her chin, and I jump at the sudden move. "You were my first mistake... I can't afford to let myself be distracted by your charms, anymore." He leers at her chest longingly and grazes her hair before spinning away with a hint of regret.

Wait. Esme...and my father?

If I can't be here when the Danu princess arrives, then his *lover* Esme can't, either.

He clears his throat again, and the dry noise scrapes my ears. "I saw you with your spellbooks, sorceress. I know what you were up to. You've been poisoning my daughters from the moment you set foot in this house, and you will be moved to the dungeons." He turns to me, hands tucked at his back. "And you... Are you still my daughter?"

"Yes!"

"I figured out a way to settle this once and for all. I asked the guards to move this in here." He unveils the huge golden-trimmed mirror that was in the basement and picks up a long-stemmed maillet.

My lids close, suddenly so heavy. *If he breaks that mirror...*

"It's a simple test. If you go through the mirror, I'll know for sure that you're no longer my daughter. If you don't, then you will stay away from your sister until this wretched Fae matter is resolved. Win the bet, and you'll be sent to the temple to become a priestess, and maybe then I'll allow you to see her again."

"Father. *Please*." My stomach clenches in a violent squeeze, and I hold an arm across my body.

The emerald and gold mask is heavy in my skirt's pocket. If I leave now, he'll never trust me again, but if I stay, there's no guarantee I can stop this wretched wedding from happening...

His eyes narrow, and he stalks forward. Under his cold, empty stare, I'm no longer his daughter, but something less-than. Something ruined. "But if you let the Shadow King defile my kingdom, your sister will never set eyes on you again. And I'll make sure she pays the price for your disgrace."

"How could you say that?" Cece squeaks from the dark corner of the room, standing behind a museum crate I hadn't looked twice at, and my eyes bulge.

By the Mother! Was she there all along? Did she sneak in behind me?

Father reels at her arrival, his cheeks flustered with a deep red hue, and his perfectly rehearsed manners are quickly replaced by the drunken mumblings of a confused man. "Cecelia, go back to your room at once! How dare you—"

He wraps a hand around her upper arm and attempts to push her out of the room, but she escapes his grip at the last second. He gives chase and ends up flat on his ass by the door. "Come back here!"

He struggles to stand, his movements heavily impaired by the booze.

Esme pulls on my elbow. "Now, Penelope. This is our chance."

I dig the balls of my feet into the carpet as Cece runs back over to us. She grabs my arm, her blue eyes full of unshed tears. "Nell, don't go."

Esme slips inside the glass and makes her escape, and I don't blame her, really, but I couldn't leave without saying goodbye.

My voice cracks in a million little shards as I squeeze Cece's hand. "I love you, Cece."

"Nell! Nell! Take me with you."

My heart practically booms out of my chest. Cece wrangles her hands in front of her as though she's about to kneel down to pray, her immense hope burning brighter than the sun.

Regrets drag down my chest, and if there's still blood in my veins, it's as cold and still as a dead horse in a frozen field.

"I can't."

There. The words that have been haunting me ever since I set foot in Faerie. Disappointment and betrayal twist Cece's lips, and guilt numbs my body.

Father grabs her by the arm and holds her away from me. "Go now, and never come back."

I concentrate on Cece. "I'll see you soon. I promise." I look down at my emerald mask, and my knuckles turn white.

There's no doubt, now. The princess mask is the one I need to break.

With a newfound resolve, I vanish through the mirror. The quill and ink in my skirts allow me to draw the correct runes on my arms, the process a little more complex in the midst of the sceawere, but not impossible. The bite of Faerie's maze of glass frosts my eyelashes as I draw "Fae" and "heart" and "flame" to reach One directly.

I've heard enough excuses. I need to know the stakes of the bet and figure out how to save Cece from a marriage she never wanted, hopefully without condemning my country to some wretched fate.

When I step out of the mirror, my dark Fae is alone in the gym, the string of his golden bow drawn.

"Good evening," I say quickly.

His shadow arrow runs straight through the closest mannequin, and a shiver quakes me from head to toe. Judging by the dark and desperate look on his face, he's not happy with me.

"You pleaded with me to help us, and then took off without a word…"

The icy pool of hurt brimming through his voice sparks a hot line of shame along my spine.

My throat bobs. I wish I could kiss him and cower inside his arms, but the time for hushed confessions and illicit affairs has passed. I need to petition the king for Cece's freedom so he gives me permission to bring her here. And I'll give him whatever he wants in return.

"I need to see him." One's eyes narrow, and I stand a little taller and tip my chin up to make him understand I won't take no for an answer. "Take me to the Shadow King."

He opens his mouth like he's about to argue or turn me down, but his shoulders hunch, and he finally nods. His regal-looking bow vanishes into thin air, and the shadows around him thicken. "You're right. It's time."

CHAPTER 39

FOUR OF A KIND

One laces our fingers as he pulls me inside the mirror, and my heart burns. He guides me through the sceawere and presses the runes on his lower arm. The foggy glass immediately clears, and I step out of the mirror with a snowflake stuck to my cheek.

"Here we are. The king's bedroom," One says, and the muted fear filling the cracks of his low voice spells trouble.

His resigned pout makes my pulse run wild, and I search the empty space for an explanation. A large bed is left unmade in the center of the room, the covers twisted in knots like the king's nightmares followed him home.

A pile of black clothes folded by the fire.

A feather laid over an unfinished letter.

A thick golden mask discarded on the bedside table...

I sense nothing out of the ordinary, and if it wasn't for the full-face mask, I'd think One was stalling.

The door leading to the balcony is left ajar. Cold night air billows inside the room, and I step outside to get a grip on my nerves. The third-floor balcony has always been a mystery—no stairs leading in or out of it. A forsaken place belonging to the monster responsible for my troubles and accessible only through the sceawere.

The cold breeze curls around my shoulders, and thick clouds obscure the moon. "Where is the Shadow King?" I whisper.

One fiddles with a crank at the bottom of a star-shaped music box and sets it down to the floor. "Dance with me." He offers me his hand, and I take it without hesitation.

His mask is gone. His gold irises are almost black in the night as he pulls me to the center of the balcony, and we start to waltz together. Music seeps through the air, and it's the same mournful melody I danced with the king. The same tune. The same pace. The same confident hand at my waist...

"Say my name, kitten."

"I—One."

"My real name." He twirls me around, our hands raised into the air, and I curtsy out of habit.

As we come to a halt, my heart hammers. "I don't know your name."

The corner of his mouth twitches. "I think you know. I think you've known for a while."

I close my lids for a moment. Is he saying—

When the truth hurts too much, or scares you senseless, you bury it. You dig a grave deep enough to conceal it with rubble of denial. I've shoveled quite a bit of monstrous truths over the years.

My father's a cruel drunk, and a cowardly king.

Back when my mother was alive, she let him beat her.

Demeter is a wretched place to live. The entire religious system that praises good over evil—all the while denying us the chance to look at ourselves in the mirror—is a lie.

In my defense, One's true name hadn't been obvious from the start. He's a master at deflection. The signs had been piling up—especially the last few days—but I'd buried them all.

"Say my name," he asks again, his lips inches from mine. "Say it with disgust if you have to, but I need to hear it from your lips."

Hot tears roll down my cheeks. "Damian."

He closes his eyes in a mix of awe and gratitude before opening them again. "I love you, kitten."

My clenched fists collide with his chest. "I didn't know—I *hoped* it wasn't true."

A destructive wave of anger topples me over, and the undertow of his revelation pulls me under. Drowning me.

It makes so much sense now. One was stronger than the absentee king. It didn't add up, but I couldn't bring myself—

A sob bubbles up my lungs. "I wanted to believe you wouldn't have lied to me for so long."

If One is the king, then everything he's ever said to me was tainted. Everything I feel for him is based on a lie. For the longest time, I thought he was holding me at arm's length to please the king. I worried about being forced into bed or into marriage...

"You tricked me!" I punch his chest, but he holds me closer to his torso to keep me from hitting him again.

"I'm sorry, kitten. I had to protect my secret."

"You pretended to be someone else to gain my trust. You and your *brothers*. You each take turns playing the role of king, but it's really you, isn't it? You're the one who made the deal with my father."

"Yes." He holds me tighter, my body trapped between the hard planes of his chest and his unforgiving grip.

How could I believe our love was real? He's the reason I'm here. The reason Cece and I are separated. The reason I can't bear the thought of going home—

"I'm dying, kitten. We all are."

The certainty in his tone steals my ire, and I shake my head. "No."

A soft breath ghosts over my lips. "Our magic is dwindling, and despite the hope I nurtured the last couple of days, the curse still holds strong. But the others are not *pretending* to be the king."

"How can you say they're not pretending? If *you* are the king," I breathe.

I'm so desperate to understand *why*.

His face darkens, and I know what comes next will change my life forever. "I set up this charade to protect myself and my kingdom from the vultures that circle us. When the other monarchs or the High Fae learn how broken I truly am, I will not last a day."

I tilt my head to the side, trying—and failing—to see the entire puzzle. "What do you mean? What charade?"

"I was so busy dealing with the other royals, the High Fae, the people. I had to hunt nightmares, protect the Dreaming, and keep fantasies from spiraling out of control... There weren't enough hours in a day to do it all perfectly. I didn't have time for lovers or friends— or even family." His chest deflates, and he turns away. "And so I fractured myself in different aspects of my personality—parts that would think independently and carry out the daily chores—while a fourth piece would be free to stay here and enjoy life." He rubs down his face with a dry snort. "It was selfish and stupid, of course."

"So, you're all—" My hand reaches out to brush his shoulder.

The golden chasm in his eyes burns with shame. "We're all a fraction of Damian, but Damian is dead."

He marches back inside, and I follow quickly on his heels. "No! I don't believe that."

"I need to show you something." He opens a hidden door in the tapestry.

The adjoining room is darker, and I tip-toe inside to see better. A handful of torches flicker to life along the walls. In the middle of a glass prison, a terrible version of Damian lies in tatters, and I cover my mouth with both hands.

"Nell. Meet Four."

Black hair grows over his skull in uneven patches like he tears a handful of roots from his scalp at random every once in a while. The untrimmed beard makes him look twenty years older, but I could probably pick him up without too much effort, his gangly, emaciated limbs almost childlike.

The absolutely heartbreaking shard of the man I love doesn't react as I walk closer, and his blank stare remains totally unfocussed. He appears to be somewhere else entirely, and his dark irises are the only clue that a soul still inhabits the confines of his...breathing corpse. His hands are busy playing with a ragged doll, the eyes of the toy half-torn from its head.

The familiar web of tattoos behind his ear turns my stomach.

"Four was the part of Damian that was more human. That could sing and laugh and love..."

I press my hands to the glass and fall to my knees, in absolute shock. Bloody scratches run along Four's arms and legs, and the betrayal and anger in my heart is replaced by a heavy sense of loss.

I try not to notice the blood under his fingernails or how he peeled the runes off his knuckles.

"What happened to him?" I croak.

"Morrigan was a talented Shadow huntress. The best seed the kingdom had ever seen before you, really. She rose through the ranks and made it all the way to immortality. But that wasn't enough for her. She figured out what we were doing, and how living as separate beings made us susceptible to spells and curses that would have otherwise been ineffective against a powerful Fae king."

One flattens his back to the glass and slides to the ground like he doesn't have it in him to stand anymore. "She stole a love arrow directly from Eros' quiver and shot Four with it. It affected all of us, and so we began this whirlwind romance... We had no idea what was going on."

I squeeze his hands and bring them to my lap as a gesture of encouragement.

"On the eve of our wedding, I found out about the missing arrow and confronted Morrigan about it. She denied everything, of course. And, however fake our love was, I still felt it... I wasn't sure. I took the Queen of Hearts aside to investigate while the rehearsal dinner was underway.

"Knowing her fate was sealed if she didn't act quickly, Morrigan coated her shadow needles with the venom of a dreamcatcher spider and pierced Four's heart with it. She stabbed him in the middle of dinner—just like that, and cursed him to never get better if the wedding didn't go through."

Flames fill my blood, and the rage in my body finds an entirely new target. "And she still expected you to marry her after that?"

"After Eros reversed the effects of the arrow, there was no way in the seven hells I would have gone through with the wedding, but Morrigan fled before we could kill her. The whole court was present —along with a handful of monarchs. Her escape was so formidable that it earned her the nickname of phantom queen."

Three tiptoes inside the room. "We tried everything to heal Four. We even tried to merge with him again, thinking we could reabsorb him...but it never worked."

His coarse explanation shivers through me. "You can talk!"

Two stands stock-still on the other side of the glass cube, his fists balled at his sides. "Worse than that, the three leftover pieces of Damian weren't able to merge anymore, and so we became different people. Identical to a point, with the same memories as the original Damian, but a quarter as powerful. Each of us broken in our own way."

"We casted a spell over the entire realm to alter the High Fae's memories of the Shadow King and enlisted the sprites to spread wild rumors about why he had to wear a full-face mask. All these years, we were forced to lie and scheme to keep anyone from finding out the truth." One tugs on my hands. "Until you."

"So when I first arrived..."

Three pretends to sting his thumb with his nail. "*I* pricked your finger."

"And *you* made me strip by the pool." I glare at Two, furious.

He presses his forehead to the glass, his chin tucked in. "Don't look at me like that. I'm the drunk, cruel Damian. If I hadn't been outvoted at every turn, we would have done a lot worse."

I turn to One, my heart in pieces at his feet. "What do you need from me?"

He grazes my bottom lip with his thumb like I'm a branch from his sacred tree. "I wanted to win the bet to strengthen our magic. To survive. I never expected to fall in love with you…"

I blink a few times, trying to put the last pieces of the puzzle together. "Tell me about the bet. What is it for, exactly? What do you plan to do to my people?"

"Your father made sure I couldn't tell you the details."

I've always believed Damian would enslave us all if I lost, but everything I've been taught about him, about Faerie, has been a lie. *Even Esme told me he was a monster…*

"I give up, then. You win."

His forehead wrinkles into a hopeless frown. "It doesn't work like that. The finality of the bet can only be decided through your actions, not your words."

"Then…I'll flee. After you win the bet, you can take my magic. It will save you, no?"

He recoils violently at the offer and grabs a fist of his hair. "Don't be ridiculous. If I take your magic, you'll forget ever meeting me."

"I know." My eyes dart to the ground. It hurts too much. "Lori told me about Mara."

He smears a fresh tear across my cheek with his thumb. "What's the point of fighting this curse, enduring all this pain, if you don't remember who I am?"

"But you'll *live*. Your kingdom will be saved." I try to sound confident, but the hushed words are sheer and brittle. "Your only sin is lacking the strength to do your duty."

"Winning the bet would help, but it would only buy me a few more months… That's not enough." He rests his forehead on mine and gives it a little push. "I *love* you, Nell."

"Then seek me out. Make me remember."

"Mortals can't live in Faerie. Not without magic." His tortured gaze hardens into something sharp. "I won't take it—it's out of the question."

My heart gives a painful squeeze. If mortals are not allowed to live here, it means that Cece can't, either. But I can't give up on her. If she has to stay in Demeter, then so should I. "It's the only way to save you, Damian."

He freezes for a moment, shock written on his face at hearing his name on my lips. "I don't believe that. Not anymore. All these years... I was merely *surviving* the curse. I want to *live* again."

I risk a glimpse at Four again, the ache in my bones almost intolerable. "Can I try to heal him?"

With a small nod, One cuts a window into the glass with his magic, large enough for me to reach the fourth, broken piece of them. Maybe my magic can heal him just as it healed One from the spider.

Four's breath hitches when I flatten my palm to his bony arm, and his lids droop like he's about to fall asleep. The same icy, destructive feeling I experienced when I failed to heal Firenze's dead leg grips my heart.

Shadows wisp out of his wound like a wraith's hand coming to greet me, and I draw back from the spooky apparition. "How is he still alive? He's so...cold." My voice cracks. "It's not going to work."

One squeezes my shoulder. "It's okay, kitten. The more powerful the curse, the thinner the thread... It won't be so easy."

The smoke clears when I let the magic go, and a pearly white shape in the middle of the wound becomes visible, smack-dab in the center of the festering black goo.

A nervous hiccup quakes my throat. "Wait... What is that?"

"Morrigan pushed her poisoned shadow needle directly through his heart. If we remove it, he'll die," One says.

The smaller but identical pin in my calf burns, and my belly cramps. "Do you have a painting of Morrigan? A picture?" I start unlacing my boots in a hurry.

Two walks around the corner of the glass prison and leans over my shoulder to see what I'm doing. "Why?"

I rip off my socks and pinch the head of the pin Esme gave me. The three Damians all clench their fists in perfect synchrony, and a terrible truth slowly sinks in.

One gasps, and our gazes meet. "You...You're the mole?"

I grip the pearly head of the sewing pin and tear it out of my calf, my heart beating faster and faster. "I didn't know—"

A thousand little moments of the last two years suddenly take on a totally different meaning. Esme kept so many secrets from me. She pretended that Damian was a monster and skewed my beliefs. And she was so eager to hear about the Shadow King...

Now, I know why she became my tutor in the first place.

"Hello, Damian." A sultry voice echoes in from the balcony behind us, and I whip my head around to the opened door.

Gone is the haughty governess. Everything about Esme—a-k-a Morrigan—is different, down to her perfectly round human ears. She leans in the doorway with a sly grace that leaves no doubt as to her cunning, her knee-high boots a vibrant shade of purple.

A secret smile tugs at her red-painted lips. "I've missed you, darling."

CHAPTER 40
WHAT'S LEFT OF ME

The phantom queen tilts her head to the side, and the motion sends her long black hair cascading down her shoulder. "Why are you sitting on the floor?"

The sight of her knocks the wind out of me. So familiar, like a sickness. I know every inch of this woman by heart. Every single inflection of her voice. *So many years without a viable lead... so many unfruitful hunts...*

I can't believe she's here. I've both dreaded and dreamed of this moment. A chance to kill her once and for all.

"It's not—" Nell says quickly.

Morrigan drowns out the rest of her sentence. "Nell here has only been spying on you, and reporting everything to me."

I summon every ounce of the old Damian I still possess to the surface and chuckle at the obvious lie, pushing my bluffing skills to their limits.

I can't fight a dozen more spiders. Despite the merge last night, I'm still at a tenth of my usual strength, and basically an ant compared to the king I was before the curse.

The arrogant curl of her mouth waivers. "Why are you laughing?"

Morrigan "Rye" Quinn loves to play games, but she would never have asked another woman to seduce me. No... Her plan sidetracked, and she's scrambling.

"If you need to scheme so hard, you must not be ready to fight me." I stretch my lips into a cruel smile.

She mirrors it right back. "Please. See for yourself." She backtracks and opens her arms to the scenery behind her. "They add a little something, don't you think?"

My pulse throbs. The gardens are crawling with spiders. A hundred of them at least.

"Damian, I swear I didn't know." Nell inches closer.

I raise my hand to warn her off. I need her to stay safe between Two and Three. "I know." I can't afford to look at her, but I hope she knows I still trust her. "Hiding within the Demeter court... It must have been *hell* for you, Rye. You went through all that trouble to spy on me?"

The familiarity in the nickname irks my tongue. It's a painful reminder of how I almost married this woman, and her presence brings out a side of me I thought I'd buried for good.

She crosses her arms over her chest. "When she returned to you early, I knew you were about to win your stupid bet. But you know me. I can pivot."

I'm too weak to summon nightmares to the fight. Too weak to win this outright. If the spiders attack, most of my hunters will die, and for what? For a dying king?

Exhaustion takes hold of my body. I've been working my fingers bloody for decades, barely holding on. "What do you want? My crown?"

With an exaggerated sigh, Rye walks away. The wind blows her hair forward as she reaches the railing and glances down to the interior courtyard with her arms braced on each side of her. "I've only ever wanted to marry you. I never asked for anything else. You've done all of this to yourself with your stubbornness."

The nerve... I rub down my face, feeling like I'm back at square one. "I told you before I'd never marry you."

"But your life is not the only one hanging in the balance anymore." Her tongue darts out to wet her red-painted lips. "You won't survive Morheim without Nell's magic, and you know it. So you either steal her essence right now, and we can fight like grown-ups, or admit that you're not willing to risk one hair on her head. Make one last deal with me, darling. You used to love our lovers' quarrels."

A dry chortle escapes me. "We were never in love, Rye."

Longing and desire flash in her eyes. "Mm. I remember it differently." She turns to Nell and winks. "He's a greedy lover, isn't he?"

"Don't"—my jaw clenches hard enough to hurt—"speak to her."

Rye used her to get to me, and I never saw it coming. I will *never* forgive myself.

"I should have known that you weren't telling me the whole truth, *Penny*. But you played the part of the demure, virginal princess so well."

Nell bares her teeth in warning. "You've been lying all this time. Don't pretend to care for me or Cece."

"I guess I don't." Rye's conspiratorial smile vanishes, replaced by pure disdain. "Given how highly you think of yourself, it must sting that you didn't figure it out sooner. I think it was pretty obvious that I wasn't in it for the joy of fucking a drunk brute and raising his spoiled magic brat. Your mother had more instinct. That's why I had to kill her."

"You monster!" Nell shrieks.

Three wraps an arm around her waist in time to stop her from running blindly at Morrigan, but Two marches out to the balcony with an equal spark of madness.

"Fuck it. Let's kill the bitch," he says.

Three licks his lips, his gaze riveted on our ex-fiancé. The third fraction of my shredded soul looks the phantom queen up and down like he wishes to kill and fuck her all at once. That traitor.

I raise a hand to calm them down. "Nobody moves."

A delighted giggle slips from Rye's throat. "Still fighting amongst yourselves, are you? Let me see if I remember..." She bites down on her bottom lip. "Ah... yes.

One dark shard to hunt nightmares.

A second, wicked piece for dreams.

Three for the fantasies we cannot speak.

Four for a man to simply *be*."

My teeth grit together. "I should never have breathed a word of that wretched spell."

In the gardens below, a cluster of spiders use their long, lethal legs to drag my hunters across the clearing one by one, each of them bound and bundled in webs. The creatures transport them to the foot of the Hawthorn and hang them from the branches like fucking Christmas ornaments.

Rye was just buying time with her speech, waiting for them to present me with a complete picture of my failure.

I'd rather die than marry her, but maybe it's all I deserve.

"It's time to choose, Damian. Marry me under the Morheim moon, and your little princess, hunters, and sprites will be saved. No one else has to die."

What's the alternative? Fight to the death and drag everyone with me? Even if I manage to kill Rye, I can't take on that many dreamcatcher spiders. Not before they kill the hunters. Not before they kill Nell.

A dry-heave rocks my sternum. "And you promise not to harm her in any way. You will let her live her life? No tricks?"

Rye's hazelnut eyes widen, and her demeanor loses its villainous quality, replaced by the poise of a woman who can taste her victory. And she knows enough not to squander it by gloating. "I swear it."

My arms fall at my sides. "You have a deal."

"No!" Nell screams. My kitten scratches her way out of Three's hold and lunges forward. Her arms fly around my neck, and she wraps herself around me with the strength and speed of an ensnarer vine. "Take my magic and kill her instead. *Please.*"

I nuzzle the side of her face and breathe in deep. I want to imprint her scent in my memory before I release her from the promise that brought her to my doorstep. I want to remember the feel of her skin. The beauty of her eyes. For a moment in her arms, I felt like a man again—foolish as it was.

I bury a hand in her white-blond hair, and the silky strands snake around my fingers. "Don't cry for me, kitten. I will visit you in your dreams until the day I die." I peck her lips, knowing I'm seeing her for the last time in this life. "Penelope Emanuelle Darcy, I release you from the deal."

CHAPTER 41

SWEET DREAMS

The last words I'd heard from his mouth had been sweet. His prison of dreams was sweeter still.

In it, there was no Morrigan. No curse. No bets to tear us apart or kingdoms hanging in the balance. In my dreams, there was only us.

Damian and Nell.

Visions of happiness and passion, twisted in bedsheets. Dreams of matching rings, and the cheer of friends bumping forks on crystal rims. A mirage of a family that existed only in this perfect, impossible place.

A loving hand on my round belly, and echoes of baby giggles that would never be.

Until the dreams faded, and the nightmares became real.

CHAPTER 42

MORHEIM

"Nell, wake up! Wake up—wake up—wake up." Hot sobs rumble over my stomach, wet and gooey. Each of them is punctuated by a hard blow to my breast bone, and my lids twitch.

The familiar voice drags me from the sweet, treacherous slumber the Shadow King imposed on me. Gone is my lover, the drugging scent of him replaced by the smell of heavy salt, vinegar, and bitter almonds.

Hurried footsteps echo up the hallway, and a gush of cold air reaches my cheeks. "Don't touch the body, princess. It's not safe."

"Stay back!" Cece's nails dig into my chest. "You've been keeping her from me, acting like she's already dead, but she still *breathes*."

"You shouldn't be in here, child. How did you sneak past the guards?" A patient voice asks, the gentle tone sweet and yet menacing. "Your sister's spirit is already with our beloved Mother."

The hard, more masculine voice draws closer. "There's nothing you can do for her now. The priest is here to end her misery."

"You take one more step toward my sister, and I will end you," Cece says.

318 ANYA J COSGROVE

My mouth is pasty and painful, but I finally manage to move my lips. "Cece?" I breathe.

"Nell? Nell, can you hear me?"

I fail to blink, my lids too heavy to obey, like a river of sand has been poured over my eyes to hold them closed. "Cece? Is that you?"

"Yes, Nell. I'm here." She presses her forehead to mine, and a wave of wet tears slides down the slope of my neck. "I'm here."

"We have to leave at once, princess. That creature is not your sister. Your sister is dead," the guard pleads with her, his voice thick with fear. "Let the priest deal with the demons that took over her body."

"Get out!" Cece shouts, inches from my ears.

Her small arms grip my shoulders, and I finally manage to open my eyes. Cece is curled like a wounded beast around my lifeless body. Her eyes are red, and her hair is sticking out in all directions, making her look like a very pissed off, very dangerous cat.

The guard reaches out for her. "You need to come with me at once."

The priest touches his forehead and chin in a silent plea. "She's been touched by the devil, too."

Cece squints at them, feral. "I said *get out!*" An inhuman shriek reverberates off the walls, and a forceful wind blasts them both out of the room. They pirouette and tumble to the hallway like paper dolls caught in the breeze, and the door slams shut behind them.

Magic ripples through the air, strong and wild, and I know none of it came from me.

I gawk at her. My Cece. "Did you just do that?"

"It's really you." She hits my chest again with her small fists. "They told me you were dead."

I wince at the pain, and a bit of life returns to my extremities. "I —I don't know what happened—" One minute, I was in the Shadow King's bedroom, and the next...

I sit up, gently pushing Cece off me. I remember everything.

Morrigan made a deal with Damian to spare my life. A deal to release me from the bet so she could marry him instead.

Adrenaline chases away the last remnants of the enchantment that was keeping me captive, and I jolt to my feet. "Where is my mask?"

Cece frowns at that, her gaze shiny and unfocused. "What?"

"My mask. Help me look for it."

"Nell, what the crops is going on? Why did Father send these men to—to—" her rushed voice dies down to a mere whisper. She's in shock.

I grip her hand and pull her to me. "Hey. I'm alright. I was under the effect of a Fae enchantment. A powerful one. You freed me."

"So you're not going to die?" she squeaks.

"No." I press her palm to my beating heart to comfort her. "I just —I need my mask to save someone I love. Do you understand?"

She gives me a sharp nod, looking a bit more like her usual self. The uneven bite of power rolling off her in waves warms my body from head to toe. My little sister has magic, too.

We search the room frantically, ruffling through all the dressers and chests. Cece crouches on her knees to look under the bed while I search the embers in the hearth for a sign of my emerald-plated mask.

"It's not here. Judging by the tantrum Father pulled when you returned, it must have already been destroyed," Cece finally says.

"It's not so easy to destroy. Where is Father? He must have it with him."

"He's out tonight. He said he had an important dinner with the ministers, but clearly, he only wanted to leave so he wouldn't be here when they *murdered* you."

I wrap her inside a tight embrace, and the powerful quakes of her body break my heart. "Hey, it's okay. I'm here."

A sob bubbles out of her mouth. "They boarded the windows from the outside after I tried to sneak along the ledge on the first night, but I finally managed to steal the keys to your room right before that awful priest came back from the kitchens."

The first night...

"How long have I been asleep?" The blood drains from my cheeks as I press my eyes closed.

"Three days."

I cover my mouth with one hand, about as shaky as Cece is. "What time is it?"

"Nine."

Only hours to go before Morheim starts.

A loud pounding on the door startles us both, and the thundering sound is followed by a loud *crack*. The door splinters. A guard's arm pokes through the hole, and I engulf me and Cece in shadows.

"Stay close to the wall. Quick." I tug on her hand and flatten myself to the wall as three guards blast into the room.

Their eyes search frantically for us. "They're gone."

The sleazy priest runs to the window to check on the latch, and a frown overpowers his wrinkled face. "Where did they go?"

Cece's mouth opens on a silent gasp. "They can't see us."

Sweat gathers on my forehead. The strain of keeping two people hidden instead of one encircles my ribs, and I don't know how long I can keep it up. "Let's go."

We run through the broken door to the hallway leading away from the women's quarters, down the grand staircase, and into Father's study. The door is locked, but I ram it with my foot. All the might of my magic gathers behind the kick, and the door gives in.

The groggy haze from the enchantment has almost completely lifted now, and I slip inside the king's private chambers with Cece on my heels.

No one has set foot in this room in days, but the mirror has been shattered, about thirty pieces of glass scattered across the carpet. Cece closes the door behind us, and we drag the heaviest armchair we can manage to hold it shut.

We search my father's writing desk and bedside tables, but find nothing aside from books, letters, papers and ink. Nothing under the pillows or mattress.

The mask isn't here. I feel it in my bones. I'll just have to do without. I grip an inked quill and draw the runes for "Fae" and "Faerie" over my lower arm before kneeling down to pick up a large piece of glass. "Here. Help me put it back together."

I don't know if it'll work, but I have to try. The only other mirror that I know of is miles and miles away. I can't wait that long.

Cece and I crawl on all fours across the thick carpet. We collect the broken pieces of glass and rotate them until we start to see a pattern.

In my haste, I cut myself on a sharp edge. "Ow. Be careful."

She gives me a grave nod and doubles her efforts, but a rattle at the door distracts us from our goal. A loud shout echoes in from the hallway, and I know it won't be long before the guards battle their way through.

The mirror is almost whole, and I flatten both of my palms to it. Desperate for it to work, I push every ounce of my magic forward, and the glass plies under my fingers. "Oh—thank the Mother," I cry out.

A faint voice reaches my ears. "I think they're in here!"

I turn to Cece, time ticking away too fast for a proper goodbye. "I need to go."

"I'm coming with you." She glares at me with her fists curled at her sides. She looks ten years older—and savage as a wounded hare. At that moment, I know no magic or monsters in all the worlds could keep her from me.

"We might get lost forever," I admit. "But there's no time to explain."

She rolls her shoulders back. "Better that than staying here."

"Close your eyes, and whatever you do, don't open them in there. Hold on to my hand, okay?" I entwine our fingers.

The both of us inch closer to the edge of the broken mirror. Its surface ripples in invitation, and a warm, intoxicating thrill shivers up my spine.

I'm going home.

Cece nods, the bob of her throat visible. "Okay."

I'm going home *and* I'm bringing Cece with me. Never mind the fact that we could be swallowed whole by nightmares and end up dead before midnight.

"On three." A loud screech comes from behind us, the guards slowly but surely breaking down the door. "One."

"Two." Cece screws her eyes shut with a slight bend in her knees.

The door booms open, and I pull her forward. "Three." Holding each other's hand tightly, we jump feet-first inside the depths of the sceawere.

I scramble to keep my balance. The conflicting gravity of both realms pulls me forward instead of down for a moment before it stabilizes.

I squeeze Cece's hand and check that her eyes are still closed. "I know it's cold and weird in here, but you're safe. I've got you, Cece."

"I trust you."

The sceawere is different without a mask. Blurry. I risk a glance behind us and see the priest kissing his goddess talisman, but I quickly turn my back on him—on my old life—forever.

I use my free hand to grab the pliable glass and move to touch the runes on my lower arm, but the various paths—the thousand glimpses of freedom—turn to black.

My stomach cramps.

Never remove the blindfold, or the nightmares that prowl the in-between will claim you, Damian said on our first meeting. I'm about to find out exactly what he meant.

A nightmare detaches from the mass and prowls forward. I put my body between it and Cece, ready to fight, but a shred of recognition tingles all over my body.

It's the one I made when I escaped Isaac's dream and lost my little bet with Two. The ragged runaway bride.

With a wink, she waves me along.

What the— I wrap an arm around Cece's shoulders to keep her close and follow the only nightmare I ever weaved through the labyrinths of the sceaware. If others follow in our wake, I don't catch a glimpse of them.

The runaway bride immobilizes in front of one of the blackened mirror shards. Before I can think of something to say, she plants both palms on my back and gives me a powerful push. I fall forward with Cece in tow.

The sceaware spits us out on the training balcony. The buffet table where I grabbed so many meals is still in its usual spot, full of rotten fruits. Flies and the smell of decay waft through the night air.

I don't want to draw attention to our arrival, but the balcony is empty, so I whisper to Cece, "You can open your eyes now."

She blinks and draws a sharp intake of breath. "Are we in Faerie?"

"Yes."

The full moon is slowly creeping towards the top of the sky, and I wipe the sweat from my brow. *What if it's already too late?* But, Morrigan wouldn't let it reach its peak before sealing Damian's fate.

"Stay right here." I leave Cece behind and crawl toward the railing to glance at the gardens below. Through the tiny slivers in the metallic patterns, I see the hunters and James are all lined up under the shadow of the Hawthorn, facing in my direction.

Lori is among them, standing in the first row without her mask. Her fists are bound behind her back with white, slightly transparent silk, and she's standing way too stiff—clearly under some kind of spell.

But the petrified audience isn't the most shocking sight about the gardens. I glance up and see a handful of dreamcatcher spiders have weaved a thick, giant web under the Hawthorn's canopy. The eight-legged monsters hang from transparent strings above the wedding party, and I flatten myself to the floor even more, remembering how they rely on movement to attack.

Garlands of white flowers and strings of lanterns hang alongside the spiders, the sight of the decorations filling me with pure hatred.

She was so confident in her victory that she decorated.

Damian and Morrigan stand on the big flat rock that serves as an altar in front of their witnesses, and the sight of them holding hands steals my breath. Somehow, I've managed to crash the ceremony *exactly* as it starts.

Cece crawls over to me on her hands and knees. "But—That's Esme!" she hiccups in surprise, and I cover her mouth with my palm to muffle the sound.

I lower my voice as much as I can, my hardened gaze fixed on Morrigan's wedding dress. "It's a long story."

CHAPTER 43

DARK VOWS

The devious woman who only pretended to care for Cece and me is wearing a short but gorgeous purple and black dress, looking nothing like the governess I've come to know. Intricate lace covers her arms and neck, the hem finishing right above her knees. The color contrasts nicely with her creamy thighs, and her hair falls around her face in glossy, youthful curls.

One is wearing a black evening coat, and the tailored ensemble fits him like a glove. I don't know why it bugs me so much, given the truth of the circumstances, but they look perfect together.

Cut from the same shadow cloth.

But it's the golden matching crowns laying on top of their heads that boil my blood.

The other three Damians are all there, too, standing to the side with their backs to me, the way groomsmen do at most weddings.

"Let's proceed with the vows," a sprite says. His loud, ceremonial pitch is easily recognizable. It belongs to the sprite who usually announces the king's arrival.

My pulse swirls at my temples. *Vows?* Mother help me, there's not much time left to stop this wedding.

"Nell! Something's coming!" Cece says on a rushed whisper.

I turn around in time to catch a glimpse of Baka hiding at the foot of the stairwell. The blue sprite clutches a crossbow with her tiny, wrinkled hands as she tip-toes up the first step.

"Don't worry. She's a friend."

I turn my attention back to the spiders, but none of them seems to have spotted Baka—or Cece and me. At least not yet. In fact, they look perfectly complacent. Almost...happy.

On the altar, Morrigan's red lips twist in a genuine smile. The smile of a woman who's about to marry the love of her life.

The lace of her long, triangular sleeve brushes One's neck as she cups his face. Anyone could believe they're actually in love if it wasn't for the petrified audience—and the nervous tick of One's jaw.

I force my eyes closed and draw in a few cleansing breaths. *In and out. In and out.*

Baka inches up the stairs until she's right beside me. "I knew ye'd come, deary. But by the spindle, ye kept me on me toes 'til the end." She hands over the weapon with a wink.

The crossbow is heavy in my hand. There's no bolt, which means I'm going to have to craft my own.

"One is enough." Her wrinkled hand squeezes my lower arm. "Don't miss."

She's right. I've only got one shot at this, but the weird angle makes it almost impossible to take proper aim at Morrigan, and the patchwork in the railing is too tight for a bolt to pass between the rectangular, interlocking pieces of metal.

The master of ceremonies below hasn't stopped the proceedings, his voice like sand slipping through an hourglass. "Mortal love wanes. Fae love cuts to the bone. Will you cut yourself to honor your commitment to each other, from this moment forth to eternity?"

"I will," Morrigan says. "Damian... I love you."

The shadow bolt that had just started to take form in my palm crumbles to dust, and I start all over again.

"I know," One sighs.

"All these people couldn't even recognize their own king. They don't see you like I do. Two will learn to accept it. We have enough in common. And Three's never been so discerning... It's up to you, One. Whether our lives become bliss or misery is entirely up to you." With that, she carves a line in her palm with the blade.

Cece draws in a sharp breath, and Lori angles her face to our hiding spot. A glint of recognition twinkles in her eyes, and she quickly glues her gaze to the altar.

"It's not right!" Lori screams loudly, buying me a bit of time.

A nearby spider scurries across the clearing and knocks the huntress down face-first into the earth.

She rolls over, but the spider takes a bite out of her chest. "Arrrrrgh." Her body arches from the ground, her hands still bound behind her back.

"If Lori dies—if you kill any of my people for nothing—our deal is off!" One shouts, and his voice reverberates across the gardens. "You can't rule alone, Rye. So if you don't want to be overthrown in a fortnight by any Shadow Fae with a title, you better think twice about your next move."

Thank the Mother! The spider stops abruptly, and I stifle a hot sob.

A fleeting frown ghosts over Morrigan's face, and I'm familiar enough with her facial expressions to know she's both worried and angry. "Obviously, I wasn't going to kill her. Now. What did we say about being rude to your new queen, Lorisha?"

The spider curves its belly forward to access its silk-spinning organ and sews Lori's mouth shut with its web. Tears flood my best friend's eyes. A grimace of pain and horror twists her face as the spider suspends her in the air like a perverse, bleeding ornament. Her legs dangle and sway from side to side.

The blazing disgust in my heart numbs me to the bone, and I shape my magic into a shadow bolt. The smokey projectile grows in my hands, and I fashion it between my palms until it's as sharp as my pain and as certain as my thirst for revenge. The lever shakes in my grip as I crank the string into place.

"Now, where were we?" Morrigan says.

"Let's get this over with." One steals the jeweled dagger from her grasp. The hunch of his back betrays how tired and defeated he feels, and—*No!*

He cuts his arm with the dagger and paints his palm with fresh blood. Morrigan entwines their fingers, their blood and magic mixing under the Morheim moon. The red liquid seeps inside their skin and disappears, and bile rises to my mouth.

The sprite clears his throat loudly, clearly shocked. "Um... Under the watchful eyes of the Seven, you may now claim your bride."

He's married. Married to the destructive traitor who used me to spy on him. The love we shared couldn't convince him that he was worth fighting for. And Morrigan used it to seal his fate.

One is enough...

My eyes narrow, and my heart wilts in my chest. One day, I'm going to kill that woman. I stand tall and aim directly for my mark, praying to the Mother and all the Faerie gods.

The magic bolt flies with a *zip*. Before I can even know if I succeeded, I'm stuck under the same immobilizing power as the others, unable to move my arms or my feet. A sluggish ache takes hold of my muscles, like I've been plunged into a tub of ice.

The projectile sinks inside its intended target, and the hunters' mouths open on a silent gasp. Four falls to his knees next to the scattered pieces of the Damian puzzle, my precious shadow bolt sticking out of his chest.

"Well...how about that for a woman scorned?" Morrigan chuckles, her brows pulled together. She waves me forward. "Come along, Penelope. Don't be shy, my little princess."

My spine hurts, but my body obeys. Using the staircase Baka climbed stealthily earlier to hand me the crossbow, I put one foot in front of the other until I'm standing in front of my conniving governess, more under her thumb than ever.

"How did you wake up so fast? You couldn't have traveled the in-between without your mask—" she rummages through her bag and clutches my emerald mask between her hands.

One looks shell-shocked. "You were safe, kitten. Why would you come back?"

Four coughs up a mouthful of blood, and Two and Three back away from him, eyes full of fright. Four's emaciated body curls into itself. I couldn't kill Morrigan with one bolt, but I could kill Four. I've finally figured out how the curse works.

"I came back to save you," I tell him.

Morrigan's face changes as she realizes my shot landed exactly where it was supposed to. "What did you do?" Her gaze bounces between us. "Come and heal him, quick. And I will let you live."

Still under her spell, I walk over to Four and put my hand over his heart. Black blood smears my fingers. Right next to the bolt is Morrigan's poisoned needle, and I pinch the area beneath the pearly tip. "I cannot heal what is already dead."

"Silly girl, you seem to want to make some kind of point, but Damian and I are married now. I don't know what you think you came here to accomplish—"

I turn to One, Two, and Three in turn. "You don't need Four."

"Shush," Morrigan orders.

The spiders glare at me, but Morrigan doesn't have enough magic to keep control of the entire congregation *and* steal my voice.

"Let her say her piece," One growls, raising his arm between us to warn her off.

Jo motions to his unbound hands behind Morrigan's back. Now, I just have to give the speech of my life.

I anchor my gaze to One. "You say you can't feel, can't love, can't reign as you are, but you're wrong. You've been doing it for decades. Maybe not the same way you used to, but you're doing it. You *do* feel and you *do* love. The day you used your magic to split into four parts, you might have been the dark and unfeeling nightmare hunter, and Two the cruel megalomaniac—"

"Hey!" Two protests.

"And Three the mute, sex-crazed animal."

Three grins from ear to ear.

"But that's not who you guys are anymore—or at least not *all* you are."

Jo moves with stealth and purpose, the spiders' complete attention fixed on me as he cuts Misha, Cary, and James' bindings.

"If you really couldn't love or feel true empathy without Four, you would have brought your kingdom into chaos, but you didn't. You all learned to be Damian in your own way, and I wasn't the one who allowed you to merge again. You did it all on your own." My breath catches in my throat when I slide the needle out of Four to bring an end to his suffering. "One of you is enough. It's always been enough."

Four's body flakes off into dark ashes under my palm, the dead piece finally put to rest. The ashes spiral in the wind and zoom toward the closest Damian, just as I've been praying they would.

I was right.

"Now that the dead limb has been cut off—now that her poison has nothing to feed on—you can finally *heal*, Damian. "

In the blink of an eye, only one of them stands in front of me, and my chest quakes with hot, blinding relief.

I can't begin to describe the sum of them together. The mask flaunted by the Shadow King is made of iridescent onyx and freckled with polished glass. The beauty of him makes it impossible for me to look away.

"But—we made a deal!" Morrigan motions to the bleeding cut on her arm. "We're married now. You can't deny me your magic."

Shadows swirl around him, drawn from the Hawthorn, the earth —the night sky itself.

A long sword stretches from his hand. "Come and take it then, *darling*," Damian snarls.

He strikes, but Morrigan blocks the blade with her own just in time not to be cut in two. The sound of the swords crashing together thunders across the clearing, and the leaves of the Hawthorn ripple at the force of the blow.

Chaos takes over. The spiders dart into the fray from above and below, Cary and Misha jumping into the fight, too. The renewed power of the Shadow King drums in the ground, instilling a new energy in all of us. I quickly jump over the edge of the altar to help James cut Lori down.

Jo holds the spiders at bay while we lay her down between us and tear the webs away. Despite the deep wounds between her ribs and the leftover spiderwebs filling her nose, Lori pulls herself up to her elbows next to me. The holes in her chest and side are full of venom, and my heart races at the extensive damage.

"Don't move." I push my powers forward desperately. I might not be a skilled hand-to-hand fighter, but I can save her. The steady current of shadow magic under my fingertips glitches near the end, unable to cure the venom-laced injury in its entirety.

"Are you okay?" I stand and help her to her feet.

"No, but it's a start," she croaks. A semblance of skin covers the infected lesion and relieves part of the pain, enough for my best friend to summon her shadow daggers to life.

Jo, Lori, and James form a protective bubble around me as more and more spiders hone in on our position. They're all looking at me and not them, which makes the creatures more reckless.

Because there's no question who Morrigan wants to kill most.

Damian and Morrigan both have access to the same well of magic, so their fight is evenly-matched. They parry and attack in turn until Morrigan manages to nick Damian's arm, right next to the cut he made during the ceremony.

The air pulses with darkness. With a powerful kick to the stomach, he sends the phantom queen flying to the ground.

"What now, Rye? No plan B?" Damian's voice slices through the gardens, as sharp and dangerous as the tip of his blade.

Blood drips down his arm and falls to the ground as he marches forward. Morrigan's heels dig into the earth between them in a frenzy. The woman struggles to find her footing, but her back collides with the roots of the Hawthorn. Just as she's about to open her mouth to speak, Damian impales her on his sword, sinking it right through her stomach.

The spiders screech in terror, the arachnids scurrying over to their mistress in a fury of arched legs and globulous eyes.

Morrigan scrambles to her feet, using the gnarly roots to hold herself up, and smiles from ear to ear. Blood rushes into her mouth, but she just spits it to the ground. "If I die, I'm bringing the kid along with me."

Damian finds my gaze and shrugs. "You can't touch her now."

But Esme has never once called me kid. My chest shrinks. Damian moves to finish her before a heart-wrenching scream rises from the balcony.

My head snaps back to the railing, and I run to the stairs, rushing up to my sister. "Cece!"

So much blood... Her wound is identical to Morrigan's. Without hesitation, I press my hands to the gaping hole in my sister's stomach.

I heal her, and for every ounce of magic that heals her, I figure the gash in Morrigan's stomach will close up, too. *No wonder she was so cocky.* Cece groans a series of unintelligible apologies, and after making sure she's alright, I peer over the banister. "What did you do to her, witch?"

"You know me, darling. I always have a plan B," Morrigan slurs, her mouth red with blood, but her body good as new. She tosses a glance in our direction. "As long as the kid lives, so do I."

The hunters form a circle to block her retreat. Her loyal spiders hiss in warning, swarming around the trunk to protect her. There's at least thirty of them left—enough to inflict real damage. Morrigan tilts her head back and laughs a horrible laugh. The edges of her body blur, and in the span of one breath, she turns into a spider under our frozen stares.

I quickly lose sight of her in the swarm, the creatures all identical as they skitter to escape. The hunters watch in shock, unable to capture them all, unwilling to risk Cece's life by killing the wrong one.

The heaviness in my belly throbs, scorching and cold.

We've lost her...

CHAPTER 44

ALL AT ONCE

Spiderwebs and blood pepper the gardens. I run to Damian, desperate to touch him. Desperate for the cut on his arm not to be real. My arms, my legs, my hopeless heart... I shake all over.

"You're married!" My fist collides with his chest. I want to scream and scold him for not believing in himself. In *us*. "How could you not believe in us?"

He captures both of my hands in his, steadying me. "Hold on. I'm technically married, but only until midnight. In Faerie, no consummation means no marriage. The ritual is incomplete, and the spell will wither as soon as the clock strikes twelve." He gives me a moment to digest the news before he grazes the angle of my jaw with his thumb.

No consummation... Of course!

It's new to see him like this. All of him. All at once. He's terribly beautiful.

A hint of tenderness pierces the hard king's exterior, and I let out a small cry when he crushes me to him for a very public, irrevocable kiss.

It's different from the sum of all the other kisses we've shared. More confident. Damian curls a hand around my neck and tilts my chin up, swallowing all my questions and grievances until the all-encompassing need to yell at him tapers down.

After a long, passionate kiss, he draws back and relaxes his grip on my waist with a nervous laugh. "Welcome to Faerie, Cecelia."

"Cece, this is Damian, my— The Shadow King."

A puddle of blood stains her dress, but my fearless little sister squints at my lover like he's not at all intimidating. "I know. We've already met."

My eyes bulge, and my gaze darts between them. "How—"

"Do you love her? Truly?" she asks with a solemn edge to her voice.

"I'd burn the world down for her," Damian responds with the same verve, raising goosebumps all over my body.

Air whistles out of Cece's mouth, and she looks down at her hands for a moment. "I believe you."

The scar in the middle of her palm shines under the Morheim moon, and I snatch her wrist to take a closer look. "What did that witch do to you?"

Cece breaks down in a quiet, regretful sob. "Esme said I had the genes to be like you, so she offered to do a little spell... She fed me her blood in my morning coffee, and I fed her mine. It made me feel stronger, somehow. She said that it would only strengthen my ties to Faerie. To you. She lied. I thought Fae couldn't lie!"

I wrap her in my arms, and her head weighs heavily on my shoulder. "Don't blame yourself, Cece. She wasn't Fae, after all."

Damian's breath catches in his throat. "And how long did it go on?"

"Months, really."

His lips press together. "You're bonded with her now, but don't worry. The next time we draw her out, she won't share my magic anymore." He squeezes my hand. "We'll figure this out, I promise."

Jo inches closer to us. "My king..." his voice waivers, and he averts his gaze. Considering his acrimonious relationship with One, the scene that played out on that altar must have shocked him quite a bit. He clears his throat. "Awaiting your orders, Your Highness."

Damian's gaze flicks over to his hunters. "I'll be back in a moment, kitten. Let me just make sure we're safe." He walks away to take stock of the damage.

Lori runs over to me. "You really know how to make an entrance, Old World. Well done." I move to squeeze her close, but she chokes on a pain-filled gurgle. "Careful." The frantic edge of her voice reeks of suffering.

My eyes dart down to the half-healed bite mark. "We have to take care of that wound."

"Baka flew to the infirmary to get supplies." Her attention falls on Cece, her clear eyes wrinkling at the corners. "Hey, Lil' Bit. Welcome to Faerie."

"This is Lori. She's my best friend." I clasp both of their hands.

Cece opens her mouth in mock outrage and brings her free hand to her chest. "I'm not your best friend?"

We all laugh. The three of us are together and safe...just the thought warms my body from head to toe.

"I was terrified for you both, earlier. Let's get you some water and a comfy seat before Baka works her magic on this venom," I say.

Lori's gaze falls to something behind me, and she hooks her arm around Cece's. "By the spindle, she's right. You're almost as pale as me, Lil' Bit. Let's get something to eat while your sister teaches her royal boyfriend a lesson." With a wink, Lori ushers Cece away.

Damian returns to my side. "A lesson, eh?"

I peel the mask from his face, and graze the faint scar splitting his right brow. "You look..."

He's the same man I've come to know, and yet—not. An iridescent silver ring frames his golden irises, and I bite back a nervous giggle.

He looks absolutely bewitching, but I'm not going to let him get away with his stupid decision to send me away. "I can't believe you agreed to marry that witch—even for a moment. And just so you know, if it weren't for Cece, I'd already be dead."

He shakes his head. "No. Morrigan promised not to touch one hair on your head."

"But my father made no such promise," I say with a hint of regret.

Something dark and dangerous clouds his features—the kind of look I'd expect to see on Two's face. He catches me in his arms, holding me close. "I was dumb, and you were right. Is that enough?"

"No, but it's a start. You can make it up to me, later."

He leans down, his breath hot on my ear. "Oh, I intend to grovel." His gruff tone reeks of sex, and the dark promise shivers through me. He runs his nose along the slope of my neck. "But Morheim is only just beginning. There's much to do if I want to keep my crown. Vicious royals to appease..."

Right. The first night of Morheim is the kick-off of a realm-wide hunt that lasts a little more than a week. The Shadow King is supposed to lead his hunters through the different Fae lands and slay the nightmares that escaped the sceaware, but all I want to do is crawl into bed with him, barricade the door, and never come out.

I pick the golden circlet from his head and hold it in front of his face. "This crown?"

"Burn that one. It's just metal. When I make you my queen, we'll use the real ones."

My stomach flip-flops at the certainty in his voice. "Real ones?"

His enigmatic smile quickens my pulse, and his brief mention of a proposal dispenses a fresh boost of adrenaline in my blood. I didn't have enough time to iron out all his revelations—not completely. I used to be so worried that the Shadow King would force my hand...

I could kick and scream and blame him for everything, but I love him without question. How I wish I'd been the one standing on that altar with him earlier, and spared us all this trauma.

I skim the lapels of his evening coat. "You lost the bet with my father."

"Yes, but I don't need Demeter's magic to survive anymore. Morrigan's curse is broken."

I search his gaze, trying to see past the Shadow King to the men I've come to love. "What was the deal exactly? Can you tell me now?"

Now that I know his secret, I have trouble believing he ever wanted to destroy my people. I graze his cheek, and he pecks my palm with his lips.

"In exchange for healing your mother, I asked your father to allow mirrors into your country, but he refused. By connecting your people to the sceawere, I hoped to recruit all the Shadow seeds from your world. It would have brought me so much magic... So instead, I proposed a gamble. You were to come and live with me and decide your own people's fate. I was supposed to convince you to stay here permanently to win."

"What— That's all?"

His lips quirk. "If I'd told you on your first day that I intended to pepper mirrors across your kingdom and keep you in Faerie with me for good, you wouldn't have found it so innocuous."

I force myself to consider the bet through the lens of my old beliefs. Mirrors would have been perceived as a threat for our entire way of life. A shortcut to ruin.

Damian holds me close to him, his hands hard at my waist. "If I'd been able to reach my seeds, so would the other Fae courts. It would have opened the doors to a different future for Demeter. A future your father didn't want. But I was running out of time and toyed with the idea of treating you so badly that you would flee. It would have triggered an early victory."

"I bet Two came up with that plan," I grumble.

"Well... Yes." His lips twitch, and he taps the space over his heart. "He's in here, you know. *We*'re all here... It's a complex feeling."

I kiss the back of his knuckles. "You're all exactly where you're supposed to be."

My eyes settle on Cece, Lori, and Baka near the entrance of the tunnels; the sprite is already tending to Lori's bite. While Baka works, my sister observes her wrinkled skin and flapping wings with her bottom lip tucked between her teeth. A bottomless curiosity burns in her gaze.

"We have to find a way to break the spell that links Morrigan to Cece."

Damian's throat bobs. "The only way to break a blood bond is for one half of the bounded duo to stab the other straight through the heart."

"But that means—" A quiet sob quakes my body.

"I'm sorry, kitten." He places a soothing kiss at the base of my ear. "But your sister will have to kill the phantom queen, or she'll live and die with her."

CHAPTER 45

AT THE BEGINNING

The lanterns cast a warm, colorful glow upon the reading nook I share with Cece. The closely-knit fabric of her jacket brushes my naked arm when she curls into me. "I can't believe that a few days ago, I was betrothed to a foreign prince, and now I'm living in Faerie with you... It's surreal."

I shift around to look at her eyes and tuck a strand of brown hair behind her ear. "I know the feeling."

The snug black fabric hugs her frame and makes her look smaller, somehow. This is going to take some getting used to.

Damian and the hunters have been gone for five days, but I stayed behind. Someone had to take care of Cece and teach her the basics of Faerie, and I couldn't abandon Lori to her fate, either. The venom from the bite she suffered during the aborted ceremony sank deep into the huntress' bones, and she needs Baka's constant care.

Thankfully, the magic that keeps us safe from outsiders is stronger than ever, and I spruced up the library in preparation for the big reopening.

The High Fae are all eager to return to the castle, and Damian needs to show off his renewed powers to snuff out the rumors of a formal challenge.

"When is he coming back?" Cece breathes.

"How did you know—"

She rubs the frown lines between my brows back and forth. "You look worried, sis. Worried and in love."

"I'm terrified." Even though his magic is stronger than ever, nightmare hunts across foreign lands aren't exactly safe. "I know his link to Morrigan fizzled out at midnight on the night of their horrific wedding, but she still might try to hurt him. Or you."

She squeezes my upper arm. "Believe me. She's still licking her wounds." Her cheeks all red, she looks down to her stomach. The blood bond between my sister and Morrigan is strong, and Cece is confident that the phantom queen will not bother us in the near future.

She peels herself from our comfy fort and jiggles her arms and legs. "I feel restless. I'm going to check on Lori and run a few laps around the garden."

I stand up to follow.

Cece smiles down at me with a bit of an eye roll. "I'm okay, Nell. You don't have to follow me around *all the time*. And Lori's out of the woods, too. We're at a point where the Fae salves are more efficient than your powers."

She's right, of course. I might have been coddling them both over the last few days...

She waves goodbye with a mysterious smile, like she knows something I don't, and for a moment, I envy her peace of mind. I'm not sure I'll sleep soundly until her link to Morrigan is broken for good.

The bond she shares with the evil witch cannot be short-circuited by Damian, or anyone. Cece will have to kill Morrigan herself, but I haven't told her, yet.

She's only fifteen. She needs to ease into this life, and I will make sure she doesn't have to grow up too fast.

After she's gone, the light dims. The entire library is suddenly shrouded in shadows, but I know better than to be afraid of the dark. He usually comes to me at night, stealing short, unforgettable pieces of time, but the last two nights were cold and lonely...

"You were gone for *three* days," I growl, my voice heavy with reproach.

Damian shimmers into view a few paces behind me as I turn around to face him. He unhooks the strap of his long bow and wrangles it past his head, discarding the weapon on the nearest table. "The Storm Court insisted I stay for a couple of nights. Their king is a bit of a diva."

"You're the Shadow King, are you not? Next time, tell him to fuck off."

He unzips his thick jacket and shrugs it off, dumping it over the bow before he saunters toward me, the playful glint in his eyes spelling trouble. "I couldn't agree more."

Without preamble, he takes hold of my waist and presses my back to the stack. Such a simple touch, and yet so efficient. My body arches into him, and my chest heaves as he teases my belly button and dips a hand down, below the lace, all the way to the space between my thighs.

I push him off half-heartedly. "Not here."

"I can't wait."

Damian's got One's intensity, and Two's fierceness, along with Three's raw charisma... I can't say no to him, not when he's so obviously hungry for me.

"I wish I was a patient man..." He works my belt open and slides it out of the way, his other hand quick to slither up my ribs and trace the underside of my breast. "But I've missed you terribly, kitten. I can't think of anything else."

Who am I kidding? I can't wait either.

He kneels in front of me to peel my pants and underwear off, and the seriousness on his face fills me with anticipation. The scrape of his nails down my legs scorches my skin.

Damian fucks like the entire world is on fire, and we're the only two people left in it. He loves me like he's doing it for the last time, every time, and I'm officially addicted to the rush.

A soft kiss at the junction between my hip and thigh coaxes a heavy sigh from my lungs. His eyes burn with greed, and the pride in them tingles through my entire body. He tugs on my shirt and peels the fabric over my head, his other hand claiming my breast before the thing is even completely off.

"You're cheating," I say.

With a chuckle, he picks me up and guides my thighs around his waist. I curl around him like a vine and rake my fingers along his skull, just the way he likes.

"Now, if you keep on like this, I might forget to be discreet." He deposits me on the librarian's desk and snaps off the rubber band holding my hair up.

Mortal love wanes, but Fae love cuts to the bone.

Damian might have lost the bet he made with my father, but in the end, he owns my soul. Flesh, blood, and bones—as they say here in Faerie. I struggle to breathe when he's not around, the magic inside me yearning for its king, and if it's a bit *too* much, I take solace in the knowledge that our love saved the entire kingdom from Morrigan.

I don't feel guilty for the depths of my obsession for him. I'm a mere mortal in love with the most beautiful and stubborn royal Fae in existence. I'm allowed to lose my head. He pulls his shirt over his head, the beauty of him laid bare for my pleasure.

Fresh scratches from his latest hunt decorate his ribs, and the sight fills me with fire.

"Are you ready for me, pet?" he asks, his thumb sliding over the roundness of my breast.

The *click* of his belt hitting the ground stokes the flames in my belly, and I let out a ragged whine, his impatience more than contagious. "Yes."

He enters me, and my heart beats in my throat, the tight fit made tighter by the tension in my belly, my legs hooked around him.

A groan escapes him as he starts to move, and I shift my ass on the desk, searching for the sweetest angle. The most delicious pressure. The naughtiest friction. Before long, I'm breathless and furious, the hollowness in my chest about to burst at the pressure of his slow, controlled thrusts.

"Harder," I cry out, ready to punish him for teasing me so.

His dark chuckle goes directly to that secret place inside me, pushing me closer to the brink. He tests my patience some more until I bite his shoulder.

The scorched and dark taste of him fills my senses, and he draws back, clearly surprised. "Playing rough, my kitten?"

I defy him with a long, baring stare. "Me—ow."

A laugh rumbles through us both, and I groan as he finally, *finally* gives me what I want. He grips the roots of my hair and tugs, the pressure of his cock threatening to erase what's left of my rational brain.

The more we have sex, the more I burn for him, becoming more demanding and possessive each time we do this.

An open-mouthed kiss on my temple sends me over the edge, and I come apart in his arms. The ecstasy erases the whole word and leaves me in pieces.

The sweet ache of desire gives way to a powerful, drugging sense of peace as he empties himself inside me, and we catch our breath together. My dark king shudders in my arms with nothing but words of love and worship on his breath, and it's ethereal to see him like this.

So undoubtedly mine.

He lays over me like a naughty, muscular blanket and runs a hand down my throat. "The Spring Court is expecting me in less than an hour... If I could, I'd spend all day inside you, kitten..."

"Ugh. I *hate* Morheim." I push his shoulder to move him off me and bend down to grab my discarded clothes, but Damian clasps my hand.

"Wait."

The soft tremble of his voice gives me pause.

"Next year, you'll come with me. As my queen." The Shadow King bends to one knee in front of me, his eyes full of devotion and hope...

A fierce blush colors my cheeks. "*Eek.* We're *naked.*"

"You saved me, kitten. You made mirrors of your eyes, and inside them I saw someone I didn't loathe. You're strong and kind and fearless, and I love you. Forever." He clicks open a velvet case, the onyx and gold ring within it burning like a flame in the darkness. "Marry me."

I bring a hand to my mouth to cover a hiccup. "Next year?"

Damian shakes his head like I've lost my mind. "I just meant that we'd never spend Morheim apart again. But I can't wait that long. Can you?"

"No!"

He grins from ear to ear at my outburst. "We'll get married in secret. The other monarchs might still move against me. I need you safe if that happens."

"And Morrigan will never be able to force your hand into marriage again."

A cloud passes over his face. "That's not why I proposed."

"I know." *Crops.* I didn't want to bring her up, though I'm relieved to know for sure.

"It'd be family only. When this is all over, we can have a real ceremony and flaunt our happiness in everyone's face, but Baka agreed to marry us as soon as I return. If you say yes."

By the spindle! I still haven't given him an answer. "Yes. I'll marry you."

He slips the ring on my finger and kisses the back of my hand with a smile that would bring any woman to her knees. "I love you, kitten. Now and forever."

"I love you more."

A secret wedding. I love the sound of that, not quite ready to share our love with the entire world—and all its vicious Faeries—just yet.

I escort him to the balcony to say goodbye. Wilted silver leaves pepper the gardens, the fifth Morheim moon high in the sky.

He licks his lips and holds me close. "There's something that's been bugging me."

"Mm?"

He buries a hand in my long hair and angles my gaze to his. "How did you manage to find your way back without your mask?"

"I just—came home to you."

"And nothing's happened since? You haven't had any unusual visions or fever dreams? No symptoms at all?"

I keep my voice steady and light. "None."

He wraps me up in a tight embrace and claims my lips, his goodbye kiss full of promise. "Be safe, kitten. I'll see you soon, and we can finally be together."

Days. We'll be married in mere *days*.

"Yes. Soon. Be careful out there."

Dark clouds billow across the mirror behind Damian's back. The storm of nightmares follows me from room to room, rolling in wherever I go. I should really mention it to him, but I can't bring myself to wipe the happiness from his handsome face. There'll be time to unpack more secrets later, when he's back for good.

Whatever comes next, we'll face it together. No nightmare, dream, or fantasy could ever keep us apart. He's the One.

Nell, Damian, Cece and Lori's story continues in A Bride for the Winter King.

AUTHOR'S NOTE

Thank you so much for reading. I fell in love with Damian's mesmerizing fantasy world, and there's a treasure-trove of stories left to be told. I look forward to bringing you Lori's story next, along with all the fun, heart-breaking tales of the Fae kingdoms. We'll explore each courts' customs and curses and circle back to Nell and Cece in time.

In the meantime, we'll give Cece a chance to grow up.

All the books will be interconnected, but each book will focus on a specific couple. Rest assured your favorite characters will cross paths a lot, and Lori will attend her best friend's wedding in A Bride for the Winter King.

See you there,

xoxo

Anya

Made in United States
Orlando, FL
02 October 2024

52284981R00214